# THE ONLY ONE LEFT

# THE
# ONLY
# ONE
# LEFT

A NOVEL

# RILEY SAGER

DUTTON

**DUTTON**

An imprint of Penguin Random House LLC
penguinrandomhouse.com

Copyright © 2023 by Todd Ritter

DUTTON and the D colophon are registered trademarks of
Penguin Random House LLC.

Interior images: Damask wallpaper © Graphic design; blood on wall © IS MODE /
shutterstock.com

LIBRARY OF CONGRESS CATALOGING-IN-PUBLICATION DATA
has been applied for.

ISBN 9780593183229 (hardcover)
ISBN 9780593474471 (export)
ISBN 9780593183236 (ebook)

Printed in the United States of America
1st Printing

BOOK DESIGN BY GEORGE TOWNE

*To my family*

# THE ONLY ONE LEFT

We're at the typewriter again, Lenora in her wheelchair and me standing beside her as I place her left hand atop the keys. A fresh page sits in the carriage, replacing the one from last night. Now faceup on the desk, it serves as a partial transcript of our conversation.

i want to tell you everything
things ive never told anyone else
yes about that night
because i trust you

But I don't trust Lenora.
Not entirely.
She's capable of so little yet accused of so much, and I remain torn between wanting to protect her and the urge to suspect her.
But if she wants to tell me what happened, I'm willing to listen.
Even though I suspect most of it will be lies.
Or, worse, the complete, terrifying truth.
The fingers of Lenora's left hand drum against the keys. She's eager to begin. I take a deep breath, nod, and help her type the first sentence.

The thing I remember most

The thing I remember most--the thing I still have nightmares about--is when it was all but over.

I remember the roar of the wind as I stepped onto the terrace. It blew off the ocean in howling gusts that scraped over the cliff before slamming directly into me. Rocked onto my heels, I felt like I was being shoved by an invisible, immovable crowd back toward the mansion.

The last place I wanted to be.

With a grunt, I regained my footing and started to make my way across the terrace, which was slick from rainfall. It was pouring, the raindrops so cold that each one felt like a needle prick. Very quickly I found myself snapped out of the daze I'd been in. Suddenly alert, I began to notice things.

My nightgown, stained red.

My hands, warm and sticky with blood.

The knife, still in my grip.

It, too, had been bloody but was now quickly being cleaned by the cold rain.

I kept pushing through the wind that pushed back, gasping at each sharp drop of rain. In front of me was the ocean, whipped into a frenzy by the storm, its waves smashing against the cliff base fifty feet below. Only the squat marble railing running the length of the terrace separated me from the dark chasm of the sea.

When I reached the railing, I made a crazed, strange, strangled sound. Half laugh, half sob.

The life I'd had mere hours ago was now gone forever.

As were my parents.

Yet at that moment, leaning against the terrace railing with the knife in my hand, the rough wind on my face, and the frigid rain pummeling my blood-soaked body, I only felt relief. I knew I would soon be free of everything.

I turned back toward the mansion. Every window in every room was lit. As ablaze as the candles that had graced my tiered birthday cake eight months earlier. It looked pretty lit up like that. Elegant. All that money glistening behind immaculate panes of glass.

But I knew that looks could be deceiving.

And that even prisons could appear lovely if lit the right way.

Inside, my sister screamed. Horrified cries that rose and fell like a siren. The kind of screams you hear when something absolutely terrible has happened.

Which it had.

I looked down at the knife, still clenched in my hand and now clean as a whistle. I knew I could use it again. One last slice. One final stab.

I couldn't bring myself to do it. Instead, I tossed the knife over the railing and watched it disappear into the crashing waves far below.

As my sister continued to scream, I left the terrace and went to the garage to fetch some rope.

That's my memory--and what I was dreaming about when I

woke you. I got so scared because it felt like it was happening all over again.

But that's not what you're most curious about, is it?

You want to know if I'm as evil as everyone says I am.

The answer is no.

And yes.

# ONE

The office is on Main Street, tucked between a beauty parlor and a storefront that, in hindsight, feels prophetic. When I was here for my initial job interview, it was a travel agency, with posters in the window suggesting freedom, escape, sunny skies. On my last visit, when I was told I was being suspended, it was vacant and dark. Now, six months later, it's an aerobics studio, and I have no idea what that might portend.

Inside the office, Mr. Gurlain waits for me behind a desk at the far end of a space clearly meant for retail. Free of shelves, cash registers, and product displays, the place is too vast and empty for an office staffed by only one person. The sound of the door closing behind me echoes through the empty space, unnaturally loud.

"Kit, hello," Mr. Gurlain says, sounding far friendlier than he did during my last visit. "So good to see you again."

"Likewise," I lie. I've never felt comfortable around Mr. Gurlain. Thin, tall, and just a bit hawkish, he could very well pass for a funeral home director. Fitting, seeing how that's usually the next stop for most of those in the agency's care.

Gurlain Home Health Aides specializes in long-term, live-in care—one of the only agencies in Maine to do so. The office walls bear posters of smiling nurses, even though, like me, most of the agency's staff can't legally claim the title of one.

"You're a caregiver now," Mr. Gurlain had told me during that fateful first visit. "You don't nurse. You *care*."

The current roster of caregivers is listed on a bulletin board behind Mr. Gurlain's desk, showing who's available and who's currently with a patient. My name was once among them, always unavailable, always taking care of someone. I'd been proud of that. Whenever I was asked what I did for a living, I summoned my best Mr. Gurlain impression and replied, "I'm a caregiver." It sounded noble. Worthy of admiration. People looked at me with more respect after I said it, making me think I'd at last found a purpose. Bright but no one's idea of a good student, I'd eked my way through high school and, after graduation, struggled with what to do with my life.

"You're good with people," my mother said after I'd been fired from an office typing pool. "Maybe nursing is something you could do."

But being a nurse required more schooling.

So I became the next best thing.

Until I did the wrong thing.

Now I'm here, feeling anxious, prickly, and tired. So very tired.

"How are you, Kit?" Mr. Gurlain says. "Relaxed and refreshed, I hope. There's nothing better for the spirit than enjoying some time off."

I honestly have no idea how to respond. Do I feel relaxed after being suspended without pay six months ago? Is it refreshing being forced to sleep in my childhood bedroom and tiptoe around my silent, seething father, whose disappointment colors our every interaction? Did I enjoy being investigated by the agency, the state's Department of Health and Human Services, the police? The answer to all of it is no.

Rather than admit any of that to Mr. Gurlain, I simply say, "Yes."

"Wonderful," he replies. "Now all that unpleasantness is behind us, and it's time for a fresh start."

I bristle. Unpleasantness. As if it was all just a slight misunderstanding. The truth is that I'd spent twelve years with the agency. I took pride in my work. I was good at what I did. I *cared*. Yet the moment something went wrong, Mr. Gurlain instantly treated me like a criminal. Even though I've been cleared of any wrongdoing and allowed to work again, the whole ordeal has left me furious and bitter. Especially toward Mr. Gurlain.

It wasn't my plan to return to the agency. But my search for new employment has been a total bust. I've filled out dozens of applications for jobs I didn't want but was crushed anyway when I never got called in for an interview. Stocking shelves at a supermarket. Manning the cash register at a drugstore. Flipping burgers at that new McDonald's with the playground out by the highway. Right now, Gurlain Home Health Aides is my only option. And even though I hate Mr. Gurlain, I hate being unemployed more.

"You have a new assignment for me?" I say, trying to make this as quick as possible.

"I do," Mr. Gurlain says. "The patient suffered a series of strokes many years ago and requires constant care. She had a full-time nurse— a private one—who departed quite suddenly."

"Constant care. That means—"

"That you would be required to live with her, yes."

I nod to hide my surprise. I thought Mr. Gurlain would keep me close for my first assignment back, giving me one of those nine-to-five, spend-a-day-with-an-old-person jobs the agency sometimes offers at a discount to locals. But this sounds like a real assignment.

"Room and board will be provided, of course," Mr. Gurlain continues. "But you'd be on call twenty-four hours a day. Any time off you need will have to be worked out between you and the patient. Are you interested?"

Of course I'm interested. But a hundred different questions keep me from instantly saying yes. I begin with a simple but important one.

"When would the job start?"

"Immediately. As for how long you'd be there, well, if your perfor-mance is satisfactory, I see no reason why you wouldn't be kept on until you're no longer needed."

Until the patient dies, in other words. The cruel reality about being an at-home caregiver is that the job is always temporary.

"Where is it located?" I ask, hoping it's in a far-flung area of the state. The further, the better.

"Outside of town," Mr. Gurlain says, dashing those hopes. They're revived a second later, when he adds, "On the Cliffs."

The Cliffs. Only ridiculously rich people live there, ensconced in massive houses atop rocky bluffs that overlook the ocean. I sit with my hands clenched in my lap, fingernails digging into my palms. This is unexpected. A chance to instantly trade the dingy ranch home where I grew up for a house on the Cliffs? It all seems too good to be true. Which must be the case. No one quits a job like that unless there's a problem.

"Why did the previous nurse leave?"

"I have no idea," Mr. Gurlain says. "All I was told is that finding a suitable replacement has been a problem."

"Is the patient . . ." I pause. I can't say *difficult*, even though it's the word I most want to use. "In need of specialized care?"

"I don't think the trouble is her condition, as delicate as it might be," Mr. Gurlain says. "The issue, quite frankly, is the patient's reputation."

I shift in my seat. "Who's the patient?"

"Lenora Hope."

I haven't heard that name in years. At least a decade. Maybe two. Hearing it now makes me look up from my lap, surprised. More than surprised, actually. I'm flabbergasted. An emotion I'm not certain I've experienced before. Yet there it is, a sort of anxious shock fluttering behind my ribs like a bird trapped in a cage.

"*The* Lenora Hope?"

"Yes," Mr. Gurlain says with a sniff, as if offended to be even slightly misunderstood.

"I had no idea she was still alive."

When I was younger, I hadn't even understood that Lenora Hope was real. I had assumed she was a myth created by kids to scare each other. The schoolyard rhyme, forgotten since childhood, worms its way back into my memory.

*At seventeen, Lenora Hope*
*Hung her sister with a rope*

Some of the older girls swore that if you turned out all the lights, stood in front of a mirror, and recited it, Lenora herself might appear in the glass. And if that happened, look out, because it meant your family was going to die next. I never believed it. I knew it was just a variation on Bloody Mary, which was completely made up, which meant Lenora Hope wasn't real, either.

It wasn't until I was in my teens that I learned the truth. Not only was Lenora Hope real, but she was local, living a privileged life in a mansion several miles outside of town.

Until one night, she snapped.

*Stabbed her father with a knife*
*Took her mother's happy life*

"She is very much alive," Mr. Gurlain says.

"God, she must be ancient."

"She's seventy-one."

That seems impossible. I'd always assumed the murders occurred in a different century. An era of hoop skirts, gas lamps, horse-drawn carriages. But if Mr. Gurlain is correct, that means the Hope family massacre took place not too long ago, all things considered.

I do the math in my head, concluding that the killings were in 1929. Only fifty-four years ago. As the date clicks into place, so do the final lines of the rhyme.

*"It wasn't me," Lenora said*

*But she's the only one not dead*

Which is apparently still the case. The infamous Lenora Hope is alive, not so well, and in need of care. *My* care, if I want the assignment. Which I don't.

"There's nothing else available? No other new patients?"

"I'm afraid not," Mr. Gurlain says.

"And none of the other caregivers are available?"

"They're all booked." Mr. Gurlain steeples his fingers. "Do you have a problem with the assignment?"

Yes, I have a problem. Several of them, starting with the fact that Mr. Gurlain obviously still thinks I'm guilty but, without further evidence, has no legal grounds to fire me. Since the suspension didn't drive me away, he's trying to do it by assigning me to care for the town's very own Lizzie Borden.

"It's just, I'm not—" I fumble for the right words. "Considering what she's done, I don't think I'd feel comfortable taking care of someone like Lenora Hope."

"She was never convicted of any crime," Mr. Gurlain says. "Since she was never proven guilty, then we have no choice but to believe she's innocent. I thought you of all people would appreciate that."

Music starts up in the aerobics studio next door, muffled behind the shared wall. "Physical" by Olivia Newton-John. Not about aerobics, although I bet those housewives working out in ripped sweatshirts and leg warmers don't care. They're simply content to be wasting money fighting off middle-age pudge. A luxury I can't afford.

"You know how this works, Kit," Mr. Gurlain says. "I make the assignments, the caregivers follow them. If you're uncomfortable with that, then I suggest we part ways permanently."

I would love to do just that. I also know I need a job. Any job.

I need to start building back my savings, which has dwindled to almost nothing.

Most of all, I need to get away from my father, who's barely spoken to me in six months. I remember with a clarity so sharp it could break skin the last full sentence he directed my way. He was at the kitchen table, reading the morning paper, his breakfast untouched. He slapped the newspaper down and pointed to the headline on the front page.

A floating feeling overcame me as I stared at it. Like this was happening not to me but to someone playing me in a bad TV movie. The article included my yearbook photo. It wasn't good, as photos go. Me trying to muster a smile in front of that blue backdrop set up in the high school gymnasium that appeared muddy and gray when rendered in dots of ink. In the picture, my feathered hair looked exactly the same as it did that morning. Numbed by shock, my first thought was that I needed to update my hairstyle.

"What they're saying's not true, Kit-Kat," my father said, as if trying to make me feel better.

But his words didn't match his devastated expression. I knew he'd said it not for my sake, but for his. He was trying to convince himself it wasn't true.

My father threw the newspaper into the trash and left the kitchen without another word. He hasn't said much to me since then. Now I think about that long, fraught, suffocating silence and say, "I'll do it. I'll take the assignment."

I tell myself it won't be that bad. The job is only temporary. A few months, tops. Just until I have enough money saved up to move somewhere new. Somewhere better. Somewhere far away from here.

"Wonderful," Mr. Gurlain says without a hint of enthusiasm. "You'll need to report for duty as soon as possible."

I'm given directions to Lenora Hope's house, a phone number to call if I have trouble finding it, and a nod from Mr. Gurlain, signaling the matter is settled. As I leave, I sneak a glance at the bulletin board behind his desk. Currently, three caregivers are without assignments. So there *are* others available. The reason Mr. Gurlain lied about that isn't lost on me.

I'm still being punished for breaking protocol and tarnishing the agency's sterling reputation.

But as I push out the door into the biting air of October in Maine, I think of another reason I was given this assignment. One more chilling than the weather.

Mr. Gurlain chose me because Lenora Hope is the one patient nobody—not even the police—will mind if I kill.

# TWO

It takes me less than an hour to gather my belongings. I learned early on that a caregiver should pack light. A medical bag, a suitcase, and a box. There's no need for more than that.

The medical bag is filled with the tools of my trade. Thermometer, blood pressure cuff, stethoscope. My parents gave me the black leather tote when I was first hired by Mr. Gurlain. Twelve years later, I'm still using it, even though the zipper sticks and the leather is cracked at the corners.

The suitcase is filled with a toiletry bag and my clothes. Bland, inoffensive slacks and cardigans ten years out of date. I've long ago given up trying to be stylish. Comfort and thrift matter more.

The box is filled with books. Paperbacks, mostly. They once belonged to my mother and bear the loving wear and tear of a voracious reader.

"You're never alone when there's a book nearby," she used to say. "Never ever."

While I appreciate the sentiment, I also know it's a lie. For six months, I've been surrounded by books, and I've never felt more alone.

All packed, I peek into the hallway to make sure there's a clear path to the back door off the kitchen. My father came home for lunch, which he sometimes does when a job site is nearby. He's now in the living room, watching TV and eating a sandwich while sunk deep into his La-Z-Boy.

In the past six months, the two of us have become experts at avoidance. Full weeks went by in which we never saw each other. I've mostly kept to my room, venturing to the kitchen only when I was certain my father was at work, asleep, or out with the girlfriend I'm not supposed to know about. We haven't been introduced. I'm only aware of her existence because I heard them talking in the living room last week, surprised by the sound of another woman's voice in the house. The next night, my father snuck out like a schoolboy, either too afraid to admit he's started dating again or too ashamed to risk my bumping into his new lady friend.

Now it's me sneaking out, moving on tiptoes as I make two trips to my car, one for the suitcase and medical bag, one for the box of books. On the second trip, I find Kenny leaning against my Ford Escort. Clearly, he saw me with the suitcase and came out of the house next door to investigate. Staring at the box in my hands, he says, "You moving out?"

"For now, yeah," I say. "Maybe for good. I got a new assignment."

"I thought you were fired."

"Suspended. It just ended."

"Oh." Kenny frowns. Rare for him. Normally he only sports a horny, hungry look. "Quickie before you go?"

Now *that's* the Kenny I've gotten used to seeing since we started sleeping together in May. Like me, he's currently out of work and living with his parents. Unlike me, Kenny is only twenty. He's my dirty little secret. Or, more likely, I'm his.

It started one afternoon when we were both lazing in our connecting yards at the same time, me with a Sidney Sheldon paperback, Kenny with a joint. We made eye contact across the lawn a few times before he said, "Not working today?"

"Nope," I replied. "You?"

"Nope."

Then, because I was bored and lonely, I said, "Want a beer?"

Kenny said sure. Which led to drinking. Which led to small talk. Which led to making out on the living room couch.

"You want to fuck or something?" Kenny eventually said.

A month into my suspension and full of self-pity, I sized him up. He wasn't bad-looking, despite the mustache that drooped like a dead caterpillar under his nose. The rest of him was much better. Especially his arms, which were wiry, strong, and tanned. I could do—and have done—much worse.

"Sure," I said with a shrug. "Why not?"

When it was over, I vowed never to do it again. I was eleven when Kenny was born, for God's sake. I remember his parents bringing him home from the hospital, my mother cooing at him, my father slipping an envelope of cash into his dad's sweaty palm. But when Kenny showed up at the back door two days later, looking like a stray dog seeking scraps, I let him in and guided him to my bedroom.

That's how it's been once, twice, sometimes three times a week. I know the score. This isn't romance. Half the time we don't even talk. And even though I feel guilty about it, I also know I needed something besides reading to get through the long, lonely days.

"My dad's inside," I tell Kenny. "And my new patient is expecting me."

I don't tell him just who that new patient is. I'm afraid of what he'll think of me if I do.

"Sure, I get it," Kenny says, doing little to mask his disappointment. "See you around, I guess."

I watch him walk the short distance back to his house. When he goes inside without a backward glance, a pang hits my heart. Not sadness, exactly, but something mighty close. It might have only been sex, and it might have only been Kenny, but at least it was something and he was someone.

Now there's nothing and no one.

I place the box and suitcase into the trunk before making one last trip into the house. In the living room, I find my father watching the noon news because that's what my mother used to do. It's a habit, and for Pat McDeere, old habits die hard. On the TV is a clip of President Reagan giving a speech about the economy while Just Say No Nancy stands primly beside him. My father, who hates all politicians regardless of party, lets out a derisive snort.

"Bullshit, Ronnie," he mutters, his mouth full of sandwich. "Try doing something that'll help guys like me for once."

Standing in the doorway, I clear my throat. "Dad, I'm leaving."

"Oh."

There's no surprise behind the word. If anything, my father sounds relieved.

"I'm back on the job," I add when he doesn't press for details. "My new patient's a stroke victim. Lives out on the Cliffs."

I say it hoping he'll be impressed—or, at the very least, intrigued—by the idea of rich people trusting me enough to take care of someone. If he is, he doesn't show it.

"Okay," he says.

I know the one sure way to get my father's full attention is to tell him the name of my new patient. Just like with Kenny, I don't even consider it. Knowing I'll be caring for Lenora Hope will only make my father think less of me. If such a thing is possible.

"Do you need anything before I go?" I say instead.

My father takes another bite of sandwich and shakes his head. The pang I'd felt outside returns with another kick. Harder this time. So hard I swear a chunk of my heart has broken off and is now dropping into the depths of my stomach.

"I'll try to check in every two weeks."

"No need," my father says.

And that's all he says.

I hover in the doorway a moment—waiting, hoping, silently pleading for more. Anything will do. Goodbye. Good riddance. Fuck off.

Anything but this hostile silence that makes me feel like nothing. Worse than nothing.

Invisible.

That's how I feel.

I leave after that, not bothering to say goodbye. I don't want to be met with silence when my father refuses to say it back to me.

# THREE

Duran Duran blasts from my car stereo as I follow a road that hugs the rocky coastline, climbing higher and higher until the Escort shimmies and the rough waters of the Atlantic become blurs of white crashing against strips of sand far below. In my rearview mirror is an area that is definitely the Cliffs. It practically screams old money, with massive houses clinging to the craggy bluffs like gannet nests, half hidden behind brick walls and swaths of ivy.

How the other half lives.

That's how my mother would have described those cliffside dwellings with turrets, widow's walks, and bay windows facing the sea.

I beg to differ. Not even the other half can afford to live at the Cliffs. The area has always been—and always will be—rarefied air. It's home to the cream of the crop, perched over everyone and everything, as if God himself had placed them there.

"Yet here you are, Kit-Kat," my mother would have said. "On your way to a job in one of these places."

Again, I would disagree. Where I'm heading isn't anyone's idea of a prime destination.

Hope's End.

Until today, I'd only heard it referred to simply as the Hope house, usually in that hushed tone reserved for tragic things. Now I know why. Hope's End strikes me as a startlingly apocalyptic name for an estate. Especially considering what happened there.

My knowledge doesn't extend far beyond the rhyme. I know that Winston Hope made a fortune in shipping and built his estate on the rocky coast of northern Maine and not in Bar Harbor or Newport because the land here was mostly undeveloped and he could have his pick of pristine ocean views. I also know that Winston had a wife, Evangeline, and two daughters, Lenora and Virginia.

And I know that one long-ago October night, three of them were murdered—with the fourth member of the clan accused of doing the killing. A seventeen-year-old girl, no less. No wonder I thought that morbid rhyme I first learned on the scrubby playground behind the elementary school was made up. It all seemed too Gothic to be real.

But it happened.

Now it's town legend.

The kind of thing kids whisper about at sleepovers and adults don't like to whisper about at all.

Lenora, the only one left, claimed to have had nothing to do with it. She told investigators that she was asleep during the murders and only knew about them after she woke up, went downstairs, and discovered the rest of her family dead.

What she couldn't tell the police was who else could have done it.

Or how.

Or why.

Nor could Lenora explain why she wasn't targeted by the killer, which led the police to suspect she was the one who did it, even though no one could prove it. All the servants had conveniently been given the night off, eliminating any possible witnesses. With no evidence physically linking her to the crimes, Lenora was never charged. But one need only look to that schoolyard chant to see what the public thought. The rhyme's first line—*At seventeen, Lenora Hope*—fully establishes that she's to blame for everything.

I'm not surprised. There's no such thing as presumed innocence.

I know that from experience.

When the town passed judgment on Lenora Hope, she hid away in her family's house, never to be seen again. But that didn't stop people from trying. When I was in high school, it was common for groups of boys to dare each other to sneak onto the property and peek into windows, angling for a glimpse of Lenora. As far as I know, none of them ever got one, which earns Miss Hope some grudging respect in my book. I would love to be able to disappear.

Up ahead, the land rises even higher, and the road inclines to meet it. The Escort does another shimmy as I spot a brick wall in the sun-streaked distance. It's tall enough to block out any hint of what's behind it and old enough that the road curves around it, as if in deference.

I follow the curve, driving slowly until I see spray-painted words on the wall. The graffiti, neon blue on stately red brick, tells me I'm in the right place.

# ROT IN HELL LENORA HOPE

I blink at the words, wondering if I should press ahead or drive away as fast as I can. I know the answer. It's the one I can't afford.

So I continue on, nudging the Escort closer to the ornate gate covering a gap in the vandalized wall. On the other side, the driveway slices across an emerald lawn toward the Hope house itself.

Looking at it now, I wonder why anyone ever called it that.

This is not a house.

It's a mansion.

Something I haven't seen in person since my parents took me on a day trip to Bar Harbor when I was fourteen. I remember how my father spent the whole day complaining about the rich bastards who'd built the palatial homes there. God knows what he'd say about Hope's End, which eclipses those stately mansions in that snooty town. It's bigger. Grander. This wouldn't be out of place on *Dallas* or *Dynasty* or any of those other silly primetime soaps my mother used to watch.

Three stories tall and seemingly as wide as a cruise ship, the mansion is a marvel of Gilded Age excess. The walls are redbrick. Around the front double doors and all the windows is marble detailing that serves no purpose except to show how much money the Hope family once had. A ton of it, to judge by the amount of sculpted curves and curlicues on display. The windows of the third floor retain the marble but jut from the pitched roof, which is topped by a dozen narrow chimneys that look like candles atop an ornate birthday cake.

At the gate is a small intercom system. I roll down my window and stretch to press it. Thirty seconds pass before it crackles to life in a burst of static, followed by a woman's voice.

"Yes."

It's not a question. In fact, the way she says it is packed with as much impatience as three letters can hold.

"Hi. I'm Kit McDeere." I pause to allow the source of the voice to also introduce herself. She doesn't, prompting me to add, "I'm with Gurlain Home Health Aides. I'm the new care—"

The woman interrupts me with a terse "Come up to the house" before the intercom goes silent.

In front of the car, the gate starts to open, giving off a nervous shimmy, as if spooked by my presence. It creaks as it slowly swings wider, making me wonder how often Hope's End welcomes guests. Not a lot, I assume, when the gate rattles to a stop even though it's only halfway open. I inch the car forward, trying to gauge if there's enough room to pass by. There isn't. Not if I want to keep both of my side mirrors, which I very much do. My budget, such as it is, doesn't include car repairs.

I'm about to get out of the car and push on the gate myself when a man's voice calls out in the distance.

"Is it stuck again?"

The source of the voice comes closer, pushing a wheelbarrow heaped with fallen leaves. He's handsome, I notice. Mid-thirties. In *very* good shape, as far as I can tell, under his flannel shirt and dirt-streaked jeans.

He has a full beard and hair grown a little too long so that it curls slightly at the back of his neck. I'd be interested under different circumstances. Completely different. Living-another-existence different. Just like car repairs, my life doesn't have room for romantic entanglements. And no, Kenny doesn't count.

"I don't know about the other time," I say through the open window, "but it's certainly stuck now."

"You should have said *times*," the man replies, flashing a smile that's endearingly crooked. "This is, like, the tenth. I keep forgetting to add it to the list of the hundred other things I need to do around here. Are you the new nurse?"

"Caregiver," I say. A necessary correction. Nurses go to school. Caregivers like me get specialized training—a state-mandated 180 hours in Maine—teaching us the basics. Checking vitals, dispensing medication, light physical therapy. But explaining all of that to a stranger takes more time than it's worth.

"Then let's get this gate open so you can start." The man pulls a pair of work gloves from the back pocket of his jeans. Making a show of putting them on, he says, "Safety first. I've learned the hard way—this place can bite."

He yanks on the gate, and it lets out a squeak so awful I would have described it as pained if it had come from someone in my care.

"Do you work here full-time?" I ask, raising my voice to be heard over the sound of the gate.

"I do," the man says. "There aren't too many of us here anymore, although once upon a time this place was overflowing with hired help. For instance, there used to be a gardener, a groundskeeper, and a handyman, along with a bunch of part-time helpers. Now I'm all of them rolled into one."

"Do you like it here?"

The man gives the gate one last shove, clearing it from the driveway. Turning to me, he says, "Am I scared, is what you mean."

Yes, that's what I mean. I'd intended it to be an innocent question. A natural one, considering what happened here. Yet in hindsight I realize how it also could be perceived as incredibly rude.

"I just—"

"It's okay," the man says. "You're only being curious. I know what people beyond these walls say about this place."

"I guess that means no."

"A correct assumption." The man removes one of his gloves and extends his hand. "I'm Carter, by the way."

I shake his hand. "Kit McDeere."

"Nice to meet you, Kit. I'm sure I'll see you around."

I pause before driving away. "Thanks for helping me with the gate. I'm not sure what I would have done if you hadn't come by."

"I think you would have managed somehow." Carter studies me, his head tilted in curious appraisal. "You strike me as being pretty resourceful."

I used to be. Not anymore. Resourceful people aren't suspended from their jobs, can find new ones if they are, and don't still live at home at age thirty-one. Still, I accept the compliment with a nod.

"One more thing," Carter says, coming to the open car window and bending down so we're eye-to-eye. "Forget what everyone says about Lenora Hope and what happened here. They don't know what they're talking about. Miss Hope is completely harmless."

Even though he intended them to be reassuring, Carter's words only underscore the surreal truth of the situation. Yes, I knew what the job entailed when I left Mr. Gurlain's office. But it was an abstract notion, pushed to the background by packing, dealing with my father's ambivalence, trying to find this place. But now that I'm here, it hits me like a sucker punch.

I'm about to meet a woman who slaughtered her family.

*Allegedly* slaughtered, I remind myself. Lenora was never convicted of any crime, as Mr. Gurlain so coyly reminded me. But who else could have done it other than Lenora? There was no one else at the house, no other suspects to consider, no one else left alive. The rhyme's final line clings to my thoughts.

*But she's the only one not dead*

A shudder runs up my spine as I pull away from Carter and head toward the main house. I drive slowly, my gaze fixed on the jaw-dropping structure looming up ahead. But as I get closer, the luxurious grandeur of the place fades like fog, revealing the neglect hiding in plain sight.

Up close, I realize, Hope's End is a mess.

One of the second-floor windows is missing panes and now has plywood covering the gaping hole. Chunks of marble have broken off the detailing around some of the doors and windows. The roof is missing a fifth of its slate shingles, giving it a battered, pockmarked look that's honestly a relief. At last, a place as broken as I feel.

The driveway ends in a roundabout in front of the house, with another spoke leading to a low-slung garage several yards from the main building. Turning through the roundabout, I count the garage doors.

Five.

How the other half lives indeed.

At the front of the house, I park, get out of the car, and hop up three steps to a massive set of double doors placed in the dead center of the mansion. Before I can even knock, the doors fly open, revealing a woman standing just inside. Her sudden presence startles me. Or maybe it's simply her monochrome appearance that's startling. White hair that brushes her shoulders. Black dress fitted tightly around a svelte frame. Lace collar that resembles the doilies my grandmother used to crochet. Pale skin. Blue eyes. Lipstick a bold cherry red. It's all so dramatic and severe that I can't quite pinpoint the woman's age. If I had to guess, I'd say seventy-five, knowing I could be off by at least ten years in either direction.

A pair of cat's-eye glasses hangs from a chain around the woman's neck. She brings them to her eyes and peers at me for a breath of a second—an instant appraisal.

"Miss McDeere," she finally says. "Welcome."

"Thank you," I say, even though there's literally nothing welcoming about the woman's tone. It's clear she's the same person I talked to over the intercom. The disinterested voice is unmistakable.

"I'm Mrs. Baker, the housekeeper." The woman pauses to take in what I'm wearing, seemingly finding my coat lacking. It's blue wool and pilled in too many places to count. I've had it for so long I can't remember when or where I bought it. Or maybe Mrs. Baker's apparent distaste is reserved for what's under the coat. White blouse. Gray skirt. Black flats last worn at my mother's funeral. If so, I can't help it. These are the nicest clothes I own.

After a moment of clear hesitation, Mrs. Baker adds, "Do come in."

I hesitate as well, hovering just outside. It's the doorway that gives me pause. Almost as wide as it is tall and surrounded by more of that ubiquitous marble detailing, it sort of resembles an open mouth. Looking at it reminds me of something Carter said.

*This place can bite.*

I suddenly long for home. A complete surprise, considering how that house hasn't felt like home since my mother died. But it had once been a happy place, full of equally happy memories. Snowy Christmases and birthday cakes and my mother in her silly floral apron making French toast on Sunday mornings. Does Hope's End have any happy memories? Or did they all vanish that one horrible night? Is sorrow the only thing that remains?

"Coming, dear?" Mrs. Baker says after an impatient clearing of her throat.

Part of me doesn't want to. The entire place—its size, its ostentatiousness, and especially its reputation—makes me want to turn around and head right back home.

But then I think about my father, my bedroom, the dregs of cash in my savings account. None of that will change if I don't do something about it. If I leave—which I desperately want to do—I'll be stuck in the same limbo I've inhabited for the past six months. But working here, even for just a few weeks, could change everything.

With that in mind, I take a deep breath, pass through the door, and allow Hope's End to swallow me whole.

# FOUR

The inside of Hope's End is nicer than the outside, but only slightly. Just beyond the door is a grand foyer with marble tile, velvet drapes at the windows, and tapestries on the walls. The furnishings range from potted palms to fancy wooden chairs with dusty cushions under brocade pillows. Overhead, an oil-painted sky full of puffy-pink clouds adorns the arched ceiling. It all looks simultaneously fancy and shabby and stopped in time. Like the lobby of a four-star hotel that had been suddenly abandoned decades ago.

To the left, a long hallway runs past tall windows and a single open doorway, on its way to a set of wide double doors that are currently closed. It then takes a sharp right, disappearing around a corner. On the right is another hallway, offering a straight shot to a sun-drenched room.

My attention, though, is mostly focused on what's in front of me. A red-carpeted staircase directly across from the front door that rises a dozen steps before splitting in two like a pair of wings. Each symmetrical half then curves upward to the second floor. A stained-glass window looms over the center landing, through which slant streaks of sunlight in rainbowed hues that color the carpet.

"The Grand Stairs," Mrs. Baker says. "Built with the house in 1913.

Very little about the place has changed since then. Mr. Hope made sure to choose a design that was timeless."

She keeps moving, her heels clicking like a metronome on the marble tile. I trail after her, tripped up slightly by the floor. It's uneven in spots, swelling and ebbing like the ocean outside.

"You can collect your belongings later," Mrs. Baker says. "I thought it would be nice to chat in the sunroom first. It's a cheerful little room."

I'll believe it when I see it. So far, nothing about Hope's End suggests cheerfulness, even the few pretty bits. Gloom and doom seem to have taken up residence in the corners, gathered there like cobwebs. There's also a chill to the air—a salt-tinged, intangible *something* that makes me shiver.

I know it's just my imagination. Three people died here. Horrifically, if legend is to be believed. Knowledge like that can mess with your brain.

As if to illustrate that point, we pass a framed oil painting that depicts a teenage girl in a pink satin gown.

"Miss Hope," Mrs. Baker says, not bothering to glance at the portrait as she trots by. "Commissioned by her father to mark her birthday."

Unlike Mrs. Baker, I'm stopped cold by the portrait. In it, Lenora is seated on a white divan, with pink-striped wallpaper behind her and, just over her shoulder, a sliver of mirror in a gilt frame. Lenora leans somewhat awkwardly against the armrest of the divan. Her hands rest on her lap, fingers intertwined, suggesting a tension the painter tried hard to disguise with a too-casual pose.

Her pale skin and delicate features make me think of a flower just before it blooms. Young Lenora had a pert nose, ripe lips, and green eyes almost as bright as the stained glass over the Grand Stairs. She stares directly at the painter, a spark of mischief in her gaze, almost as if she knows what people will be saying about her decades in the future.

Mrs. Baker, five paces ahead of me, turns to give me an impatient look. "The sunroom is this way, Miss McDeere."

I move on, although not before taking one last look at Lenora's portrait. Three others, identical in shape and size, hang in a row next to it, all hidden behind black silk crepe. Rather than draped over the paintings, the fabric is stretched taut and held in place by nails driven directly into the frames. All that effort, though, doesn't entirely hide the portraits. I can faintly see them behind the sheer crepe, hazy and featureless. Like ghosts.

Winston, Evangeline, and Virginia Hope.

And Lenora's the only one still on display because she's the only one left.

I catch up to Mrs. Baker, following her quickly down the rest of the hall, passing rooms with their doors firmly shut, suggesting places that are forbidden. At each one, I feel another brief chill. Drafts, I tell myself. Happens all the time in big, old mansions like this.

The sunroom is at least brighter than the rest of the house, if not exactly cheerful. The furniture is the same kind of musty antiques spotted elsewhere around Hope's End. So much velvet and embroidery and tassels. A grand piano anchors the far end of the room, its lid lowered and shut tighter than a casket.

The room's stuffiness is leavened by the rows of floor-to-ceiling windows along two walls. One row of windows faces the lawn, through which I can see Carter in the distance, back to raking leaves. The other set of windows looks out onto an empty terrace. A short marble railing, not even waist high, runs the length of the terrace. I can't see anything past the railing because there's literally nothing else to see. Just an endless expanse of cerulean sky that makes it seem like the mansion is literally floating in midair.

Mrs. Baker grants me a few more seconds of gawking before gesturing to a red velvet love seat. "Please, sit."

I lower myself onto the edge of the love seat, as if I'm afraid of breaking it. Which I am. Everything at Hope's End seems so old and so expensive that I assume nothing here can be replaced. Mrs. Baker shows no such hesitation as she drops onto the love seat across from me. The motion produces a small plume of dust that rises from the fabric in a miniature mushroom cloud.

"Now, Miss McDeere," she says, "tell me a little about yourself."

Before I can speak, someone else bursts into the room with a clomp and a rattle. A young woman carrying a metal pail in one hand and using the other to drag a vacuum cleaner behind her. She freezes when she sees us, giving me a few seconds to take in the sheer spectacle of her appearance. About twenty, if that, she wears a formal maid's uniform that wouldn't have been out of place in a black-and-white movie. Black, knee-length dress. Starched white collar with pinpoint tips. White apron bearing a smeared print where she presumably wiped her hands.

The rest of her, though, is pure Technicolor. Her hair, dyed a garish shade of red, also contains two streaks of neon blue that trail down both sides of her face, dangling like octopus tentacles. A similar shade of blue streaks across her eyelids before fading at her temples. Her lipstick is bubblegum pink. Rouge colored a darker shade of pink cuts over her cheekbones.

"Oops, sorry!" she says, doing a double take when she sees me, clearly surprised by the presence of a stranger at Hope's End. I suspect it doesn't happen often. "I thought the room was empty."

She turns to leave, producing another rattle that I realize is coming from the half-dozen plastic bracelets in rainbow hues that ride up each of her wrists.

"It's my fault, Jessica," Mrs. Baker says. "I should have informed you I'd be needing the room this afternoon. This is Miss McDeere, Miss Hope's new caregiver."

"Hi," I say with a little wave.

The girl waves back, her bracelets clattering. "Hey. Welcome aboard."

"The two of us were about to get better acquainted," Mrs. Baker says. "Perhaps you can continue cleaning in the foyer. It's looking a little neglected."

"But I cleaned there yesterday."

"Are you suggesting my eyes have deceived me?" Mrs. Baker says, displaying a smile so clenched it borders on the vicious.

The girl shakes her head, setting her hoop earrings in motion. "No, Mrs. Baker."

The young maid curtsies, an act of sarcasm Mrs. Baker seems to mistake for sincerity. Then she leaves, giving me another curious glance before hauling her pail, vacuum, and rattling jewelry out of the sunroom.

"Please forgive Jessica," Mrs. Baker says. "It's so hard to find good help these days."

"Oh" is all I can say in return. Aren't I also considered the help? Isn't Mrs. Baker?

She puts on her glasses, adjusting them atop the bridge of her nose before peering at me through the thick lenses. "Now, Miss McDeere—"

"You can call me Kit."

"*Kit*," Mrs. Baker says, flinging my name off her tongue like it's a bad taste. "I assume that's short for something."

"Yes. Kittredge."

"A bit fancy for a first name."

I understand her meaning. Fancy for someone like me.

"It was my maternal grandmother's maiden name."

Mrs. Baker makes a noise. Not quite a *hmmm*, but close. "And your people? Where are they from?"

"Here," I say.

"You'll have to be more specific than that."

Again, I understand. There's more than one *here*. There are the mansions clinging to the Cliffs, home to the moneyed ranks the Hope family used to tower over. Then there's everyone else.

"Town," I say.

Mrs. Baker nods. "I thought so."

"My father is a handyman, and my mother was a librarian," I volunteer, trying to impress upon Mrs. Baker that my family is just as worthy of respect as the Hopes and their ilk.

"Interesting," Mrs. Baker says, in a way that makes it clear she finds it anything but. "Do you have much experience as a caregiver?"

"Yes." I tense, unsure how much she already knows. "What did Mr. Gurlain tell you?"

"Very little. I wish I could say you came highly recommended, but that would be a lie. I was told next to nothing about you."

I take a deep breath. This could be a good thing. Then again, maybe not. Because it means I'll have to explain everything myself if asked.

*Please don't ask*, I think.

"I've been with Gurlain Home Health Aides for twelve years," I say.

"That's quite a long time." Mrs. Baker holds my gaze, her face unreadable. "I assume you learned a lot in those twelve years."

"I did, yes."

I start listing all the things I know how to do, ranging from the pedestrian—light cooking, light cleaning, changing sheets with a person still in the bed—to the professional. Giving sponge baths and inserting catheters, drawing blood and injecting insulin, checking shoulder blades and buttocks for bedsores.

"Why, you're practically a nurse," Mrs. Baker interrupts when I've droned on too long. "Do you have much experience caring for stroke victims?"

"Some," I say, thinking of Mrs. Plankers and how I cared for her less than two months before her poor husband ran out of money to pay for the agency's services. Mrs. Plankers was moved to a state-funded nursing home, and I was assigned to another patient.

"Miss Hope's condition might require more attention than you're accustomed to," Mrs. Baker says. "She's been plagued by bad health most of her life. A bout of polio in her twenties weakened her legs so much that she's been unable to walk since. Over the past twenty years, she's suffered a series of strokes. They left her unable to speak and the right side of her body paralyzed. She can move her head and neck, but it's sometimes difficult for her to control them. All she has, really, is limited use of her left arm."

I flex my own left arm, unable to imagine only having control of that single, small part of my body. At least now I know why Lenora never left Hope's End. She couldn't.

"Is that why the previous nurse left?"

"Mary?" Mrs. Baker says, seemingly flustered. The first genuine emotion I've seen from her. "No, she was quite good at her job. She'd been with us for more than a year. Miss Hope adored her."

"Then why did she leave so suddenly?"

"I wish I knew. She didn't tell anyone why she was leaving, where she was going, or even that she was leaving at all. She simply left. In the middle of the night, no less. Poor Miss Hope was left unattended all night, during which time something terrible could have occurred. As you well know, considering what happened to the last person in your care."

My breath hitches in my chest.

She knows.

Of course she does.

Squirming beneath Mrs. Baker's withering gaze, all I'm able to say is, "I can explain."

"Please do."

I break eye contact, ashamed. I feel exposed. So completely naked that I start to smooth my skirt over my legs, trying to cover as much of myself as the fabric will allow.

"I had a—" My voice breaks, even though I've told this story a dozen times to just as many skeptical people. Cops. State workers. Mr. Gurlain. "I had a patient. She was sick. Stomach cancer. By the time she found out, it was far too late. It had spread . . . everywhere. Surgery wasn't possible. Chemo only went so far. There was nothing to do but keep her comfortable and wait until the end arrived. But the pain, well, it was excruciating."

I continue staring at my lap, at my hands, at the way they keep smoothing over my skirt. My words, though, aren't as cautious. They get faster, freer—something that never happened in that gray box of an interrogation room at the police station. I chalk it up to being inside Hope's End. This place is familiar with death.

"Her doctor gave her a prescription for fentanyl," I say. "To be taken only sporadically and only when necessary. One night, it was necessary. I'd never seen someone hurt so much. That kind of pain? It's not fleeting. It lingers. It consumes. And when I looked into her eyes, I saw sheer agony. So I gave her a single dose of fentanyl and monitored the pain. It seemed to help, so I went to bed."

I pause, just like every time I reach this point in the story. I always need a moment before diving into the details of my failure.

"I woke up earlier than normal the next morning," I say, remembering the dark gray sky outside my window, still streaked with remnants of night. The gloom had felt like a bad omen. One look at it and I knew something was wrong. "I went to check on the patient and found her to be nonresponsive. Immediately, I called 911, which is standard protocol."

I leave out the part about already knowing it was a waste of time. I recognize death when I see it.

"I was waiting for the EMTs when I saw the bottle of fentanyl. It was company policy to keep all medications in a locked box beneath our beds. That way only the caregiver has access to them. Maybe I had been tired. Or shaken by how much pain she was in. Whatever the reason, I'd forgotten to take the bottle with me."

I squeeze my eyes shut, trying not to picture the bottle lying on its side against the bedside lamp. I do anyway. I see it all. The bottle. The cap sitting a few inches away. The lone pill that remained. A small circle colored a light shade of blue that I always thought was too pretty for something so dangerous.

"During the night, she had swallowed all but one of them," I say. "She died while I was sleeping. She was pronounced dead at the scene and taken away. The coroner later said she died of cardiac arrest brought on by an overdose of fentanyl."

"Do you think it was intentional?" Mrs. Baker says.

I open my eyes and see that her expression has softened a bit. Not enough to be mistaken for sympathy. That's not Mrs. Baker's style. Instead, what I see in the old woman's eyes is something more complex: understanding.

"Yes. I think she knew exactly what she was doing."

"Yet people blamed you."

"They did," I say. "Leaving the bottle within reach was negligent. I won't disagree about that. I never have. But everyone thought the worst. I was suspended without pay. There was an official investigation. The police were involved. There was enough fuss that it made the local paper."

I pause and picture my father with the newspaper, his eyes big and watery.

*What they're saying's not true, Kit-Kat.*

"I was never charged with any crime," I continue. "It was ruled an accident, my suspension eventually ended, and now I'm back on the job. But I know most people think the worst. They suspect I left those pills out on purpose. Or that I even helped her take them."

"Did you?"

I stare at Mrs. Baker, both startled and offended. "What kind of question is that?"

"An honest one," she says. "Which deserves an honest answer, don't you think?"

Mrs. Baker sits calmly, the epitome of patience. Her posture, I notice, is perfect. Her plank-straight spine doesn't come close to touching the back of the dusty love seat. I'm the opposite—slumped in mine, arms crossed, pinned under the weight of her question.

"Would you believe me if I said no?"

"Yes," Mrs. Baker says.

"Most people don't."

"Those of us at Hope's End aren't like most people." Mrs. Baker turns toward the row of windows and the terrace railing just beyond them. Beyond that is . . . nothing. A chasm made up of sky above and, presumably, water below. "Here, we give young women accused of terrible deeds the benefit of the doubt."

I sit up, surprised. From Mrs. Baker's no-nonsense demeanor, I'd assumed it was forbidden to talk about the tragic past of Hope's End.

"Let's not pretend you don't know what happened here, dear," she says. "You do. Just like you know that everyone thinks Miss Hope is the person responsible."

"Is she?"

This time, I surprise even myself. Normally, I'm not so bold. Once again, I suspect the house is to blame. It invites bold questions.

Mrs. Baker smirks, maybe pleased, maybe not. "Would you believe me if I said no?"

I look around the room, taking in the fussy furniture, the rows of windows, the lawn and the terrace and the endless sky. "Since I'm here, I'll need to give her the benefit of the doubt."

It's apparently the right answer. Or, at the very least, an acceptable one. For Mrs. Baker stands and says, "I'll show you the rest of the house now. After that, I'll introduce you to Miss Hope."

That makes it official. I'm Lenora Hope's new caregiver.

It doesn't matter that I lied to Mrs. Baker.

Not just about my previous patient.

But about Lenora Hope, my opinion of whom hasn't changed. I still think she's a killer. I also know it doesn't matter what I think. She's my patient. My job is to take care of her. If I don't do my job, I won't get paid. It's that simple.

We leave the sunroom and head back down the hallway, toward the heart of the house. When we reach the portraits, I sneak another glance at the only one on display.

Lenora's oil-painted eyes seem to follow us as we pass.

# FIVE

Budgetary restrictions force us to keep only a small household staff," Mrs. Baker says as we return to the foyer. "Outside work is done by Carter, whom I believe you've already met."

I stiffen, slightly unnerved. How did she know that?

"I have, yes," I say.

Mrs. Baker guides me past the Grand Stairs and into the hall leading to the other end of the house. "Inside the house is Jessica, who cleans, and Archibald, who cooks."

"And what do you do?"

Another bold question. Accidentally so. This time, there's no mistaking Mrs. Baker's reaction. Definitely displeased.

"I am the housekeeper," she says with a sniff so disgruntled it lifts her bosom. "I keep the house in the best condition possible under severely limited circumstances. All decisions are made by me. All decisions I make are final. With Miss Hope unable to serve as caretaker of this estate, I have assumed the burden. *That* is my job."

"How long have you been with Miss Hope?"

"Decades. I arrived in 1928, hired to tutor Miss Hope and her sister in the ways a young woman should behave. Only nineteen myself, I'd intended to stay a year or two. That plan changed, of course. When the household staff was reduced following the . . . incident, I left and went to Europe for a time. When my fiancé died, I chose to return to Hope's End and devote my life to Miss Hope's care."

Not the choice I would have made. Then again, I've never had a fiancé. Or even a boyfriend for any significant length of time. The job doesn't allow it. "Get out while you've still got your looks," a fellow Gurlain Home Health Aide once told me. "Otherwise you'll never snag a man."

Now I wonder if it's already too late. Maybe I'm already fated to become like Mrs. Baker—a woman in black with white hair and pale skin, drained of all color.

"If you never got married, why are you called Mrs. Baker?"

"Because that's the title given to the head housekeeper, dear, whether she's married or not. It commands respect."

Continuing down the hallway, I survey my surroundings. Double doors closed tight straight ahead, open doorway to my right. I peek through it to see a formal dining room, unlit but brightened by two sets of French doors that lead to the terrace. Between them is an ornate fireplace so big I could park my car inside it. A pair of chandeliers hang over each end of a table long enough to seat two dozen people.

"Hope's End has thirty-six rooms," Mrs. Baker says as we reach the closed double doors at the end of the corridor. "You need only concern yourself with three. Miss Hope's quarters, your own quarters, and here."

I follow Mrs. Baker as she cuts right, around the corner and into a kitchen large enough for a restaurant. There are multiple ovens and burners and a brick-lined fireplace, inside of which a small blaze crackles. Shelves full of porcelain containers line the walls, and dozens of copper pots hang from the ceiling on wrought iron racks. A massive wooden counter sits in the center of the room, running from almost one wall to another.

Decades ago, an army of cooks and servers likely scurried over the black-and-white-tiled floor on their way to the adjoining dining room. Now there's only one—a man with a thick chest and even thicker stomach wearing checkered pants and a white chef's coat. In his seventies, he has a shaved head and a slightly bent nose, but his smile is wide.

"Archibald, this is Miss Hope's new caregiver," Mrs. Baker says. "Kit, this is Archibald."

He looks up from the counter, where he's kneading dough for home-made bread. "Welcome, Kit. And call me Archie."

"All of Miss Hope's meals are prepared by Archibald, so you won't be needed in that capacity," Mrs. Baker tells me. "He also cooks for the rest of the staff. You're free to prepare your own meals, of course, but I'd advise against it. Archibald is the best cook on the Maine coast."

It dawns on me how quickly my life has changed. This morning, I woke up in the same bed I've had since I was ten. Tonight, I'll be fall-ing asleep in a mansion that has a professional cook. And a maid. And a terrace with a bird's-eye view of the sea.

As if to silently bring me back to earth, Mrs. Baker moves on, guid-ing me to a set of steps tucked into a corner of the kitchen. The oppo-site of the Grand Stairs, these are steep, narrow, and dark. Clearly meant for servants. Of which I am one. I can't forget about that.

"Archibald and Jessica have rooms on the third floor," Mrs. Baker says, her voice echoing down the narrow stairwell as she climbs. "Your quarters are on the second floor, next to Miss Hope's room."

"She's upstairs?" I say, surprised. "If she's immobile, shouldn't she be on the ground floor for easier access?"

"Miss Hope doesn't mind, I assure you."

"The house has an elevator?"

"Of course not."

"Then how do I take her outside?"

Mrs. Baker comes to a dead stop halfway up the stairs. So quickly that I almost bump into her. To avoid a collision, I drop down a step, which allows Mrs. Baker to tower over me as she says, "Miss Hope doesn't go outside."

"Ever?"

"Ever." Mrs. Baker's on the move again, quickly climbing the rest of the rickety staircase. "Miss Hope hasn't been outside of this house in decades."

"What if she needs to see a doctor?"

"Then the doctor comes to her," Mrs. Baker says.

"But what if she needs to be taken to the hospital?"

"That will never happen."

"But what if—"

There's an emergency. That's what I try to say. I can't get the words out because Mrs. Baker stops once more, this time at the landing.

"Miss Hope was born in this house, and this is where she will die," she says. "Until then, she is to always remain indoors. Those are her wishes, and my job is to enact them. If you take issue with that, then you may leave right now. Am I understood?"

I lower my eyes, fully aware that after less than five minutes on the job I'm *this* close to being fired. The only thing keeping me from being forced to return to my old bedroom and my father's silence is what I say next.

"Yes," I reply. "I apologize for questioning Miss Hope's wishes."

"Good." Mrs. Baker gives me a red-lipped smile that's as brief and cutting as a razor slash. "Let's continue."

We start off down a long corridor. Like the downstairs hallways, it runs from one side of the mansion to the other, with the top of the Grand Stairs positioned in the middle. Unlike those wider, better-lit corridors, this one is as narrow as a tunnel and just as dim. The carpet is red. The wallpaper is peacock blue damask. A dozen doors line each side, all of them shut.

Moving through the corridor, I feel a strange sensation. Not dizziness. Nothing as strong as that.

Instability.

That's what I feel.

Like I've just had a few very strong drinks.

I touch the wall for support, my palm skimming across the blue wallpaper. It's overwhelming. The color is too dark and the print too florid for such a confined space. All those ornate petals bursting open and intertwining give the impression of a garden that's grown wild and vicious and is now overtaking the house. My hand recoils from the wall at the thought, which sends me listing ever so slightly in the other direction.

"What you're feeling is the house," Mrs. Baker says without looking back. "It tilts slightly toward the ocean. It's not very noticeable on the first floor. You can only feel it on the upper levels."

"Why is it tilted?"

"The cliff, dear. The ground here at the top has shifted over time as the cliff has eroded."

What Mrs. Baker doesn't say, but what's abundantly clear from the slanted floor, is that Hope's End has been eroding with it. Someday—maybe soon, maybe a century from now—both cliff and mansion will break apart and slide into the ocean.

"Doesn't that worry you?"

"Oh, we've all become quite accustomed to it," Mrs. Baker says. "It just takes some time. Like getting your sea legs."

I wouldn't know. My sailing experience is limited to a whale-watching field trip I took in the sixth grade. But I can't imagine ever getting used to this. When Mrs. Baker stops at one of the tightly closed doors on the left, I lean against the wall, relieved.

"These are your quarters," she says, turning the knob but not opening the door. It does that on its own, creaking ajar thanks to the mansion's pernicious tilt. "After you're done changing, I'll introduce you to Miss Hope."

"Change?" I push off the wall into a standing position. "Into what?"

"Your uniform, of course."

Mrs. Baker steps away from the door, allowing me to peek inside. The room is small but tidy. Butter yellow walls, a dresser, a reading chair, a large bookshelf blessedly filled with books. There's even a view of the ocean, which under different circumstances would make my heart sing. But I'm too focused on the bed and the white nurse's uniform sitting on top of it, folded as neatly as a napkin in a fancy restaurant.

"If it doesn't fit properly, I can find a seamstress who'll be able to do some alterations," Mrs. Baker says.

I eye the uniform like it's a ticking time bomb. "You seriously want me to wear this?"

"No, dear," Mrs. Baker says. "I *require* that you wear it."

"But I'm not a nurse."

"You are here."

I should have known this was coming. I'd seen Jessica in her ridiculous maid's outfit and Archie in his chef's gear.

"I know you think it's silly," Mrs. Baker says. "The nurses before you did as well. Even Mary. But we abide by the old ways here. And those ways involve a strict dress code. Besides, it's what Miss Hope is accustomed to. To deviate now would likely confuse and upset her."

It's that last bit that makes me concede defeat. While I don't give a damn about abiding by the old ways—why follow them if no one is ever here to notice?—I can't argue with not wanting to upset a patient. I have no choice but to suck it up and wear the uniform.

Mrs. Baker waits in the hall as I close the door and strip out of my coat, skirt, and blouse. On goes the uniform, which doesn't quite fit. It's loose at the hips, just right at the bust, and tight at the shoulders, making it simultaneously too snug and not snug enough. By the time the winged cap is pinned to my head, I feel positively ridiculous.

In the adjoining bathroom, I check to see how I look.

It's . . . not bad, actually.

While undeniably formal, the tightness in the uniform's shoulders makes me stand a little taller. Forced out of my perpetual slump, I appear less like a caregiver and more like a legitimate nurse. For the first time in months, I feel resourceful again. A refreshing change of pace.

Mrs. Baker certainly approves. When I emerge from the bedroom, she lifts her glasses to her eyes and says, "Yes, that's much better."

Then she's off again, to the next door down the hallway.

Lenora Hope's room.

I suck in a breath when Mrs. Baker opens the door, feeling the need to brace myself. For what, I don't know. It's not as if Lenora Hope will be standing just inside, a knife in one hand and a noose in the other.

Yet that's the only thing I can picture as Mrs. Baker gestures for me to step inside.

After another deep breath, I do.

The first thing I notice about the room is the wallpaper. Pink stripes. Exactly like in the portrait downstairs. The white divan is there as well, its fabric darkened by time but clearly the same one Lenora posed on. On the wall behind it is the gilt-edged mirror glimpsed in the portrait. Staring at the entire mirror—and my uniformed reflection in it—makes me feel a bit like Alice going through the looking glass. Instead of Wonderland, though, I've ended up inside the portrait of Lenora Hope and now stare at myself from outside the frame.

The next thing to catch my eye are the tall windows that face the Atlantic. The view beyond them is even more stunning than the one in the sunroom. The ocean is visible from here—a vast canvas of churning water that looks like a fun house–mirror version of the sky. Two blues, one scudded with clouds, the other whitecaps. The second floor's higher vantage point gives me a better idea of how close the house is to the cliff's edge. Right against it, in fact. There's no land beyond the terrace railing. Just a straight drop directly into the sea.

Because of the slight tilt of the house, the view seems extra vertiginous. Even though I'm in the middle of the room, I feel like I have my forehead pressed against one of the windows, looking down. Another twinge of instability hits me, and I spend a fraught moment worrying I'm about to tip right over.

But then I finally notice the wheelchair parked in a corner of the room, facing the windows. It's old-fashioned, constructed of wicker and wood, with two large wheels in front and a small one in the back, like a tricycle. The kind of wheelchair that hasn't been used in decades.

In it is a woman, silent and still, her head lolled forward, as if she's asleep.

Lenora Hope.

My vertigo fades in an instant. I'm too spellbound by Lenora's presence to notice the tilted floor anymore. Or the view out the windows.

Or even the presence of Mrs. Baker behind me. All I can focus on is Lenora, seated in that old-timey wheelchair, bathed in sunlight so bright it makes her look pale, almost translucent.

The infamous Lenora Hope, reduced to a ghost.

Everything about her, really, seems sapped of color. Her robe is threadbare and gray, as are the slippers on her feet. Gray socks run to just below her knees, where they bunch and sag. The nightgown under the robe was likely white once upon a time, but too many washings have left it the same ashen shade as her skin. The grayness extends to her hair, which is kept long and straight and cascades down her shoulders.

It isn't until Lenora lifts her head that I see a single bit of color.

Her eyes.

Their green is almost as bright as her eyes in the portrait down-stairs. But what's fascinating in the painting is downright startling in person, especially when surrounded by all that gray. They remind me of lasers. They *burn*.

That blazing green draws me in. I find myself wanting to stare into those startlingly bright eyes and see if I can recognize a piece of my-self in them. If I can't, then perhaps it means I'm not as bad as peo-ple think.

Even my father.

I take a wobbling step toward Lenora and the tilt returns, more pronounced this time. Then again, maybe it's not the slanted floor that's causing it. Maybe it's simply because I'm in a room with Lenora Hope—a realization as surreal as it is surprising. The chant snakes back into my thoughts.

*At seventeen, Lenora Hope*

I wonder if I should be scared.

*Hung her sister with a rope*

Because I am.

*Stabbed her father with a knife*

Even though there's no reason to be scared.

*Took her mother's happy life*

This isn't the Lenora Hope of that awful rhyme. It's not even the Lenora of the portrait downstairs—young and ripe and possibly that very moment plotting the murders of her family. This Lenora is old, withered, a wisp. I think of reading *The Picture of Dorian Gray* in high school. This is like the opposite of the book—the painting in the hall getting fresher by the day as Lenora's crippled body atones for her sins.

I take a few more steps, no longer bothered by the tilting house. Maybe Mrs. Baker is right. Maybe I *am* getting used to the place.

"Hello, Lenora," I say.

"Miss Hope," Mrs. Baker says from the doorway, correcting me. "The help must never refer to the lady of the house by her Christian name."

"Sorry," I say. "Hello, Miss Hope."

Lenora doesn't move, let alone acknowledge my presence. I kneel directly in front of the wheelchair, hoping to get a better look at her startling green eyes. My body tenses, bracing for whatever insights might be gleaming within them. About Lenora. About myself.

But Lenora isn't cooperating. She stares past me, out the window, gaze fixed on the churning sea below.

"I'm Kit," I say. "Kit McDeere."

Lenora's eyes suddenly lock onto my own.

I stare right back.

What I see is unexpected.

Curiosity, of all things, shimmers inside Lenora's gaze. As if she already knows me. As if she knows everything about me. That I've been trapped. And accused. And judged and ostracized and ignored. Gazing into Lenora Hope's eyes feels like looking into that gilt-framed mirror and seeing my reflection staring back at me.

"It's very nice to meet you," I say. "I'm going to take care of you from now on. Would you like that?"

Lenora Hope nods.

Then she begins to smile.

Before we continue, I need to make one thing clear. Don't try to help me write this. I know what I want to say. You're simply here to replace the hand I can't use. Just do what I need you to do, when I need you to do it.

Understand?

Good.

Second, I'm not writing this so you'll feel sorry for me. I neither want nor need your pity. I'm also not doing it to prove my innocence. That's for others to decide, if and when I ever finish this.

I'm writing it because when I die, which could be any day now, I want there to be a record of the facts. This is the truth--good and bad.

And the truth is that it all started the day of the portrait. The beginning of the end, although I had no idea then that would be the case. It was eight months before the murders. A lifetime when you're as young as I was then.

It was also my birthday. The last birthday ever celebrated in this house.

That year, my father decided to have everyone sit for a portrait on their birthday. It was his idea of a gift, which might have been

fine for him and my mother, but not so much for my sister and me.
No girl our age wanted a portrait as a present, especially when it
meant getting dolled up and sitting for hours on end, not being
allowed to move. The best thing about it was the artist, who was
quite handsome.

Peter was his name.

Peter Ward.

Since my father had commissioned him to paint portraits of
every member of the family, it was his fourth time at Hope's End.
By then, I was quite enamored of him. I put on my best dress--a
pink satin gown--and made sure I looked as pretty as possible.
I very much wanted to catch his eye.

Unfortunately, so did my sister, who hovered over him the
whole time, even though Miss Baker was already keeping a close
watch on the artist. Because the portrait was being painted in my
bedroom, she was worried something inappropriate might happen
if Peter and I were left alone. Such behavior was typical for Miss
Baker, who had been hired a year earlier to teach us etiquette and
elocution. I knew what she really was, though. A governess for
girls who didn't need a governess.

I sat on the divan, trying not to move. Miss Baker stood rigidly
in the corner, a disapproving look on her face. My sister, though,
mooned about the room behind Peter, checking his canvas and
saying things like, "Oh, that's wonderful. It's her very likeness."

Every time she did it, I couldn't help but laugh, which caused
Peter to reprimand me several times.

"Keep still, please," he'd say in a tone so deathly serious it
made me laugh even more. I spent most of the sitting trying not
to crack a smile, although it came through anyway in the finished
portrait. My sister had been right about that. Peter captured me
perfectly.

"But I'm so bored," I said as the sitting dragged on well into the
afternoon. "Can I at least read a book while you paint?"

"You could, but then I wouldn't be able to see your eyes," Peter said. "And you have such lovely eyes."

Now that was a birthday gift any girl my age would want. No one had ever called any part of me lovely before, and hearing it from Peter made my whole body quiver.

Out of the blue, I began to wonder if Peter had ever painted someone nude. Someone more mature and developed than me, someone who was unashamed of her body. I wondered what it would feel like to slide out of my pink dress, lean back on the divan, and have Peter gaze at my naked form. Would he still think I was lovely? Would he feel compelled to leave his easel, join me on the divan, touch my skin, caress my hair?

I began to blush, shocked by the wildness of my thoughts. I looked to Miss Baker, who contemplated me with dark eyes, as if she knew exactly what I was thinking.

Apparently, my sister did as well. She approached Peter, coming up behind him until she was pressed against his back. She placed a hand on his shoulder, where it remained as she cooed, "Peter, you really are the most talented man I've ever met."

The room suddenly felt hot, and in that moment, all I wanted was to be away from all of them. I longed to be outside, perched at the cliff's edge with the cool wind in my hair.

"Are we almost finished?" I asked.

"Another hour or two," Peter said.

"Be patient," Miss Baker added.

But I no longer had any patience left. I hated her. I hated my sister. I hated my father for bringing Peter into this house. At that moment, the only member of my family I didn't despise was my mother.

Her I pitied.

Unable to sit still a moment longer, I leapt off the divan and headed for the door.

"I'm not finished yet," Peter called after me.

"I most certainly am," I called back.

I hurried down the back steps and into the kitchen, which was a riot of activity as the cooks and maids readied my birthday dinner. My anger surprised me. I knew my sister had no real interest in Peter, and that Peter had no interest in me. Honestly, I had no interest in him, either. But I did so desperately want someone to notice me, to see me, to understand me.

Also, I was sick and tired of being at Hope's End. The name fit, for it felt like we were at the end of the world, cut off from any hope of being anywhere but here.

My father built Hope's End as a tribute to himself. He claimed otherwise, of course. A peculiar trait among most self-important men is the need to try to hide their self-importance. My father did this by claiming Hope's End was constructed for his beloved wife and the baby girl she had just given birth to.

Not true.

He built it because he wanted to show everyone just how rich he was.

It worked. For one cannot get a glimpse of Hope's End without thinking, "This is the home of a very wealthy man."

Wealthy we were. Happy? Not so much. And the house, though opulent, reflected that. It's a cold place. An unwelcoming place. I know you can feel it. There's little comfort to be found here.

And all I wanted to do was meet people, go places, experience the things I'd only read about in books. It was 1929, and the world was alive with fast cars and jazz and dancing all night while drinking bathtub gin. I had experienced none of it. And how was I to become a great writer without having any experiences to write about?

Some days, Hope's End felt so much like a prison that I thought I'd scream if I had to spend one more minute inside its walls. Whenever I got that way, the only cure was to be outside.

I loved the grounds and the sea and the sky. They always managed to soothe me, which is exactly what they did that day.

Standing on the terrace, I inhaled the salty air and felt the cool wind on my face. I leaned against the railing and stared up at the tall windows that ran around the southeastern corner of the house. My mother's bedroom, which was separate from my father's. The two of them had long stopped sharing a bed.

The drapes were drawn, which meant she was suffering another one of her "nervous episodes." By then, she rarely left her bedroom.

I shuddered at the sight of those tightly closed curtains. I couldn't imagine being trapped in my room all day, every day, never leaving. To me, that seemed like a fate worse than death.

Yet here I am, living that exact scenario.

It turns out I was right.

Because here's an intriguing fact about Hope's End: The doors to all the bedrooms can only be locked from the outside, with individual keys required to open them. When my sister and I were young, one of my father's favorite games was to lock us in our bedrooms. Whoever went the longest without begging to be let out received a prize. Usually a bit of money or a fancy dessert and, once, a gold bracelet. The winner also got to decide how much longer the loser had to stay in her room.

My sister won every single time.

She never minded the game, but, oh, how it drove me crazy. I could never last more than a few hours before the walls felt like they were closing in and would trap me forever if I didn't get out.

Because I was always the first to beg my father to open the door, I then had to stay in my room for as long as my sister decided. Once, she chose to keep me locked in for an additional twelve hours. I spent that entire night screaming and pounding on the door, demanding to be let out. When that didn't work, I tried breaking down the door by throwing myself against it. The door never budged. Even though I had lost, my father and sister never relented. I remained locked inside until midmorning.

That's how it feels to be in this house, this room, this body. Like I've been locked inside during one of my father's games and there's no one on the other side of the door holding the key that can set me free.

# SIX

Lenora and I have adjoining rooms, a fact I discover after bringing my belongings upstairs. The first thing I unpack is the metal lockbox I use to store medication. The same one that got me suspended and investigated by the police after I failed to use it. Now empty, I slide it under the bed and drop the key in a nightstand drawer.

Next are my clothes. After opening the suitcase, I try the door to what I think is a closet. Instead, I find myself looking straight into Lenora's room. Mrs. Baker is still there, putting a slim pair of headphones over Lenora's ears. They're attached to a brick-like Walkman resting in Lenora's lap.

"Ah, Kit," Mrs. Baker says as she presses the Walkman's play button. "Let's go over Miss Hope's routine."

I drift into Lenora's room, curious. She's a strange sight—a woman in her seventies, slumped in a wheelchair that likely hasn't been made since the forties, enjoying the latest technology of the eighties.

"What is she listening to?"

"A book on cassette tape," Mrs. Baker says, as if offended by the very concept. "Jessica records herself reading aloud and then gives the tapes to Miss Hope to listen to."

"That's very nice of her."

"If you say so."

Mrs. Baker goes to a sideboard beneath the window. Inside are dozens of cassette tapes in plastic cases. Scrawled on the labels in red Magic Marker are many titles I recognize. *The Thorn Birds. Clan of the Cave Bear.* More than a few books by Jackie Collins.

Nearby, Lenora listens to one of the tapes with a look of contentment on her face. Like a child just handed their favorite toy. She remains that way as Mrs. Baker gives me a crash course on how to take care of her. We first go over Lenora's medications, of which there are many. Aspirin, a water pill, an anticoagulant, a statin, a pill to control muscle spasms, another to prevent osteoporosis. All of them sit on Lenora's nightstand. Six little orange bottles arranged in a row atop a silver serving tray.

I open each bottle, familiarizing myself with the pills' shapes, sizes, and colors. Also on the tray are a mortar and pestle. Their presence tells me I'm to crush the pills.

"I mix them in with Miss Hope's food, right?"

"Three with breakfast, three with dinner," Mrs. Baker says. "The bottles are marked."

I note the stickers on the bottles as she continues, telling me how I'm to spend two hours each day—one in the morning, one in the evening—gently moving Lenora's arms and legs to improve her circulation. Each morning and evening I'm also supposed to brush her teeth, brush her hair, and change her out of her sleeping clothes and into her daytime clothes and back again. I need to feed her. And bathe her. And help her onto the toilet when she can manage to go or change her adult diaper when she can't.

We talk as if Lenora isn't in the room with us, silent and still in her wheelchair. Occasionally, I glance her way, trying to get a read on how much she's aware of what's going on around her. Half the time, she seems oblivious to our presence, content to stare out the window and listen to her book on tape. The other half, though, I sense acute concentration. As if she's keeping track of my every move. At one point, Lenora's gaze leaves the window and drifts my way. A sidelong glance she doesn't want me to notice. When I do, her eyes snap back toward the window.

"What does Miss Hope do for fun?"

"Fun?" Mrs. Baker says, as if she's never heard the word. "Miss Hope doesn't have fun. She rests."

"All day?"

I scan the room, which is larger than mine but also stuffy, in both air flow and furnishings. The windows are firmly shut, making me question when they were last opened. A crisp ocean breeze would do wonders. But it doesn't smell like a sickroom, either. A relief. I've spent far too much time moving around sticky rooms that smell of sweat, body odor, and decay.

As for the furniture, well, not much can be done about that. In addition to the sideboard and faded divan, there's an armoire against the opposite wall, a desk in the corner, an armchair that matches the divan, and several side tables with Tiffany lamps. It's frilly and slightly girlish and makes me conclude that this was Lenora's childhood bedroom and has remained unchanged for decades. The idea of a woman sleeping in the same room she had as a child would be weird if not for the fact that I have just been doing the same thing.

The only nod to modernity is a Hoyer lift next to the bed, which allows for easier transfer to and from a wheelchair. I've used them plenty of times, although this looks to be an early model. Its U-shaped base, angled support pole, and hydraulic pump aren't as sleek as other versions. At the top, dangling from what looks like an oversize coat hanger, is a nylon sling.

The bed itself is crowded with pillows, which bear a human-shaped indentation. I shudder at the thought of being forced to lie there all day with nothing to do.

"Surely there's something she likes to do," I say, searching for a television somewhere in the room. Most of my other patients loved having the TV on, even if they didn't really watch. Just the sound of it kept them company.

Instead of a television, I spot a typewriter atop the desk. It's old—mint green, off-white keys, clearly a relic of the sixties—but in working condition, as evidenced by a sheet of paper slid into the carriage.

"Is that for Miss Hope?"

Mrs. Baker gives the typewriter a passing glance. "In her youth, she wanted to be a writer. When Mary discovered this fact, she bought a typewriter with the intent of teaching Miss Hope how to use it."

"Did she?"

"No," Mrs. Baker says. "But over the years, we've devised a way for her to communicate her needs. She can answer yes or no questions by tapping her left hand. Once for no, twice for yes. It's not perfect, but it's worked well so far."

I again flex my left hand, unnerved by the idea of having only that with which to communicate.

I shoot another quick glance at Lenora, who's resumed watching me. This time, she doesn't try to hide it. Lenora simply stares.

"As for Miss Hope's *care*," Mrs. Baker says, stressing the word to make it clear she thinks all other topics are frivolous, "dinner is served at seven. While you're certainly welcome to join us in the kitchen after feeding Miss Hope, most of the nurses have found it easier to eat here with her. After dinner, it's time for a second hour of circulatory therapy, followed by Miss Hope's bath."

She opens a door on one side of the armoire. Inside is a bathroom with gleaming white tile, a radiator hissing beneath the towel rack, another Hoyer lift beside the clawfoot bathtub, and a sink high enough to accommodate Lenora's wheelchair.

"Miss Hope is put to bed promptly at nine. If she requires assistance during the night, Miss Hope will use this call button to summon you."

Mrs. Baker goes to the nightstand on the left side of Lenora's bed and picks up a thick plastic square that resembles an Atari controller missing its joystick. The button is the same, though. A fat red circle Mrs. Baker presses with her thumb. A loud buzz erupts from my room.

Accompanying it is a red light I can see through the open adjoining door, flaring from a plastic stand on my night table.

"Are there any questions?" she says.

"If I think of any, I'll be sure to ask."

"I don't doubt that in the least," Mrs. Baker says, her voice dry as tumbleweed. "I now officially entrust Miss Hope to your care. May you serve her well."

The words are uttered with zero enthusiasm, as if Mrs. Baker doubts this will come to pass. Then she turns and leaves the room, her black skirt swishing. I remain by the door a moment, swaying slightly. While I'd like to think it's the fault of the mansion's tilt, I know the real cause.

I'm now alone with Lenora Hope.

My pulse quickens unexpectedly. After seeing that bit of myself in Lenora's eyes, I didn't think I'd be so nervous. But the room feels different now that it's just the two of us. There's a charge in the air, likely muffled by Mrs. Baker's presence. With her gone, I can feel the full weight of it, electric and vaguely foreboding.

And scary. Surprisingly so.

Years ago, when I was young and my father still spoke to me, we were in the backyard when a bee landed on my arm. Before I could shriek or run away, my father gripped me by the shoulders and held me in place.

"Never show fear, Kit-Kat," he whispered. "They can tell if you're scared—and that's when they sting."

I remained still, pretending to be brave as the bee crawled up my arm, across my neck, onto my cheek. Then it flew away, leaving me unscathed.

I try to summon that same illusion of fearlessness now as I approach Lenora, leaning slightly to counterbalance the tilted floor. I check the Walkman in her lap. The cassette inside no longer turns, having come to the end an unknown number of minutes ago. I gingerly remove the headphones from her ears and set them on the sideboard with the Walkman. It prompts an annoyed look from Lenora.

"Sorry," I say. "Now that it's just us, I thought we should—*I* should—talk. Let you get to know me better."

I take a seat on the divan and face Lenora, whose gaze drifts a bit before those green eyes zero in on me once again. In addition to being unnervingly bright, her eyes are subtly expressive. A byproduct of not being able to speak. Lenora's eyes must do all the work. Right now, they flicker with wariness and a wee bit of indecision. As if she doesn't quite know what to make of me.

Likewise, Lenora. Likewise.

"So, Miss Hope—"

I stop, hating the way it sounds. It's too formal, no matter what Mrs. Baker says. Besides, I've always found that addressing a person by their first name makes them seem less intimidating. Which is likely why Mrs. Baker never shared hers. It was a power move. Since Miss Hope is intimidating enough without the formality, I make the split-second decision to use her first name when Mrs. Baker isn't around.

"So, Lenora," I begin again. "As I said earlier, my name is Kit. And I'm here to help you with anything you need."

Which is everything.

Another daunting realization.

All my previous patients could feed themselves or walk with assistance. And all of them could speak, letting me know what they needed and when. All Lenora can do is use her left arm, and I have no idea if that goes beyond her being able to press a red button.

"Let's start by testing that communication system Mrs. Baker told me about," I say. "You can do it, right?"

Lenora curls the fingers of her left hand inward, forming a loose fist. She then drops her knuckles against the armrest of her wheelchair once, twice. That's a yes.

"Awesome," I say. "Now let's see what kind of shape you're in."

I fetch my medical bag and do a routine check of Lenora's vitals. Her blood pressure is a little high, but not worrisomely so, and her pulse is normal for a woman her age and in her condition. When I test her reflexes, all of Lenora's limbs react in some capacity. Normal for both her right arm—paralysis doesn't mean the body can't react—and her legs, which are too weakened by polio to use. As for her left arm, it responds exactly the way the working arm of someone in their seventies should.

The only cause for minor concern is a faded bruise on the inside of Lenora's forearm. It's small—just a smudge of purple surrounded by yellow—and seems to be healing correctly.

"What happened here?" I say. "Did you bump into something?"

Lenora taps twice. Another yes.

"Does it hurt?"

A single tap this time. No.

"Let me know if it does. Now, let's see what else this arm can do." I clasp Lenora's left hand. It's cold and pale. Practically translucent. A road map of veins runs just beneath the papery skin. "Move it for me, please."

Lenora's fingers wiggle in my hands.

"Good. Now make a fist. As tight as you can."

Her nails scritch against my palm as her hand curls into a fist tighter than the one she made to tap on the armrest.

"Not bad," I say. "Let's see how much that hand can hold."

I grab a pill bottle from the tray on the nightstand and place it in Lenora's open palm. She wraps her fingers around the bottle, keeping her grasp steady.

"Very good," I say as I return the pill bottle to the tray.

Searching the room for another object to use, I spot a snow globe atop the sideboard. Roughly the size of a tennis ball, it's clearly old. The globe is glass, not plastic, and inside is a hand-painted scene of Paris, including a tiny Eiffel Tower rising to the top of the dome. I give the snow globe a shake. Any liquid that had once been there is long gone, leaving the gold flakes inside to dryly tumble like reused confetti.

I put the snow globe in Lenora's left hand. Though small, it's heavy, and her hand trembles under its weight. A noise leaves her throat. A tiny, tortured croak that makes me immediately take the snow globe as Lenora's hand drops back onto the armrest. She frowns, looking disappointed that she failed.

"It's okay. You tried your best." I put the snow globe back on the sideboard, the motion setting off another glittery plume. Back at Lenora's side, I take her hand. Under her skin, the veins pulse slightly. "Have you ever been to Paris?"

Lenora curls her hand into a loose fist and gives my palm a single, sad tap.

"Same here," I say. "Was the snow globe a gift from someone who was?"

Two taps this time.

"Your parents?"

Another two taps.

"Do you miss them?"

Lenora thinks about it. Not for very long. Just enough for me to notice the pause. Then she taps twice against my palm.

"And your sister?" I say. "Do you miss her, too?"

I get a single tap this time. One so adamant it stings my hand.

No.

A troubling answer, accompanied by a more troubling thought— Lenora used this hand when she killed her sister.

*With a rope.*

And her father

*With a knife.*

And her mother.

*That happy life.*

Knowing that the hand I'm holding did all those horrible things makes me let go of it with a gasp. Lenora's hand plops into her lap, prompting a sharp look, part surprised and part hurt. But soon her expression changes into something more aware, almost amused.

She *knows* what I was thinking.

Because I'm not the first caregiver to think such things.

Others have, too. Some might have also dropped her hand like a hot potato immediately after. Even Mary. Like me, they probably also wondered not just how Lenora killed her family, but why. That's the big mystery, after all. There must be a reason. No one slaughters their entire family without motive.

No one sane, that is.

I look at Lenora, wondering if beneath her silence and stillness madness churns. It doesn't seem that way, especially when Lenora stares back. I sense a keen intelligence at work behind those green eyes as she moves them from me to the typewriter at the desk. The look is urgent. Almost as if she's trying to tell me something.

"You want to use that?" I ask.

Lenora taps twice.

"Mary showed you how?"

Another two taps. Emphatic ones that echo through the room. Even so, I have my doubts. It seems impossible that someone in Lenora's condition could use it, even with assistance. I was fired from a typing pool. I know how hard those machines can be for someone who has the use of *both* hands.

Still, I wheel Lenora to the desk and place her left hand on the keyboard. She's changed subtly now that we're alone at the typewriter. Brighter and more alert, her fingers slide over the keys, as if she's carefully deciding which to press first. Settling on one, she uses her index finger to push down with all her might. A typebar springs from the machine and strikes the paper with a loud *thwack*.

Lenora beams. She's enjoying this.

After pressing eight more keys, including the space bar, she exhales, satisfied.

Because she can't do it herself, it's up to me to tap the return bar, bringing the carriage back to its starting position. The motion inches the page up a line, letting me see what she just typed.

hello kit

I smile despite my nervousness. "Hello."

Lenora bobs her head toward the typewriter. A sign she wants to keep going.

"Isn't this hard for you?" I say.

Once again, her left hand roams the keys before pressing a letter. Her typing isn't fast. I suspect she averages about a word per minute, which isn't much worse than me in the typing pool. Unlike me, she's persistent, working with intense concentration. As she hunts and pecks, her brow furrows and her tongue pokes from a corner of her mouth. Soon she's typed nine more words, each one broken by a thwack of the space bar.

**my body is dead but my mind is alive**

Lenora stares up at me expectantly, nervously biting her lower lip, trying to gauge my reaction. It's such a pure expression. Her feelings are so evident that she reminds me of a teenager. Someone who can't help but wear her heart on her sleeve.

It occurs to me that Lenora could still be like a teenager in so many ways. For decades, she's been living in this house, in this very room, surrounded by objects of her youth. Nothing about her life has changed since she was seventeen. Without family or friends or even a change of scenery to push her into maturity, Lenora might still mentally be a teenager.

Which means there's a chance her emotional state now is exactly how it was the night her family was murdered. The rhyme again skips through my memory, taunting.

*At seventeen, Lenora Hope*

Unnerved, I pull my hand away from the typewriter, as if Lenora's about to reach out and grab me. She notices, of course, and nods for me to hit the typewriter's return bar. I do, quickly and abruptly, making sure there's no contact between us.

In response, Lenora types out three small but meaningful words.

**dont be scared**

Another nod from her. Another swift swipe of the return bar from me, allowing Lenora to type another line.

i cant hurt you

If the goal was to put me at ease, then Lenora has failed miserably.

*I won't hurt you.*

Now *that* would have calmed my nerves.

What Lenora ended up typing does the opposite. That insidious, apostrophe-less *can't* suggests a lack of capability, not willingness.

And that Lenora would hurt me if she could.

# SEVEN

We eat dinner in silence, something I've become quite used to in the past six months. I sit facing Lenora, making sure our knees don't touch. Since we left the typewriter, I've kept physical contact to a minimum.

Our plates sit on the wooden tray I attached to Lenora's wheelchair. Roasted chicken and glazed carrots for me, mashed acorn squash seasoned with crushed pills for Lenora. Since I don't know who to feed first, me or her, I decide to alternate bites. One mouthful for Lenora and one for me until both plates are cleaned.

After dinner is dessert. I get chocolate cake. Lenora gets pudding.

After dessert, it's time for Lenora's evening circulation exercises. Something I'm not looking forward to because it means our limited contact must come to an end. For the rest of the evening, Lenora and I are going to be uncomfortably close.

I use the Hoyer lift to get her out of the wheelchair and onto the bed. It requires sliding the sling under her, raising her out of the wheelchair, moving the whole contraption while she dangles like a kid on a swing, lowering her onto the bed, then pulling the sling out from under her. It's easier in theory than in practice, especially because Lenora is heavier than she looks. A surprising sturdiness hides inside her bird-like frame.

On the bed, I lift Lenora's right leg before bending it, pushing the knee toward her chest. Lenora stares at the ceiling while I do it, seemingly bored. I think about how many times—with how many different nurses—she's had to do this. Thousands, most likely. Morning and evening, day after day after day. When I move on to her left leg, Lenora lolls her head to the side, as if trying to see past me to the window.

Even though it's dark now and there's not much to see, I understand why. It's better than looking at the ceiling. At least there's variety out there, even in the darkness. The full moon sits so low on the horizon it looks like it's bobbing on the ocean's surface. Clouds as thin as fingers drift in front of it. In the distance, a ship cruises through the night, its lights as bright as stars.

I glance down at Lenora and notice longing in her eyes. I can relate. All my life, I've felt like the world is passing me by. I was born in 1952, and my late teens coincided with the end of the sixties. I spent my high school years working in a diner, watching as my few friends decamped to San Francisco, skipped north into Canada to avoid the draft, went to Woodstock and came back tuned in, turned on, dropped out. I watched the moon landing on the evening shift, catching glimpses of history while carrying trays of blue plate specials.

My mother assured me not to worry. That by reading, whole worlds could be explored without ever leaving home. My father, on the other hand, warned me to get used to it.

"It's our lot in life, Kit-Kat," he told me. "People like us toil. The rich bastards running everything make sure of that."

I believed him. I think that's partly how I ended up a caregiver, so willing to put others' needs before mine, not even daydreaming about a bigger life.

"I don't get out much, either," I tell Lenora. "I've basically been stuck inside for the past twelve years."

Phrasing it that way startles me. Twelve long years. Not as long as Lenora, but stuck all the same. Only the rooms and patients have changed. I try to remember them all and am surprised when I can't.

How strange it is to have spent so much time in a single place with someone and forget everything about it. About *them*. I chalk that up to monotony. The people and places were different, but the job was the same. Day after week after year until it all became a blur. It dawns on me that, probably like Lenora, I completely missed the seventies. All those touchstones everyone else got to experience passed me by like a speeding car. I never went to a disco. I didn't see *Jaws* until it was shown on TV. I breezed through both gas crises without ever waiting in line to fill my tank. Watergate and all the political upheaval that came afterward was mere background noise as I spoon-fed patients and gave them their pills and sponged their withered bodies.

A brief pain pierces my side. Like a knife poking into my ribs. Longing, I realize. For a life I've never had—and likely never will.

"You ever feel that way, Lenora?" I say. "That there's a whole life out there you could have lived but didn't?"

Lenora taps twice against the mattress.

"I thought so."

Soon we're done with the exercises and on to the next task—bath time. In the bathroom, I start filling the tub before wheeling Lenora in next to it. When it's full, I reach for Lenora's left hand but can't bring myself to grasp it. Just like that, I'm back to being nervous touching her.

Mentally cursing Mr. Gurlain, I force my hand around Lenora's and dip it into the water. "Too hot?"

Lenora raps once against the tub. No.

"Are you sure?" I say, stalling, not wanting to face what's next—slipping Lenora out of her clothes.

After two taps signaling the affirmative, there's no more avoiding it. Lenora Hope and I are about to get intimately acquainted.

At the start of my career, I used to avert my eyes when undressing a patient. Out of respect for them, yes, but also because I didn't want to see what the future had in store for me. All those wrinkles and blotches and saggy breasts. Now I've come to terms with it. This is what I'll eventually look like. What *everyone* will look like. If they're lucky, that is. Or maybe if they're unlucky. I'm still on the fence about that.

Seeing a patient naked is simply part of the job. It's the same with bodily fluids. In the past twelve years, I've encountered most of them. Blood and urine. Puke and snot. And shit. Way too much of that.

I use the Hoyer lift to get Lenora into the tub. A task made more difficult by the cramped bathroom, my ill-fitting uniform, and that lingering urge to have as little physical contact between us as possible. It all leaves me awkward and fumbling, to the point where I accidentally knock Lenora's elbow against the tub's edge. She flashes a narrow-eyed look of annoyance.

"Sorry," I say.

Lenora sighs, and for the first time I sense frustration that she's not able to speak. The feeling is mutual. There's so much I want to ask her. So much I need to know. Because I don't think I can continue like this. Nervous in her presence. Afraid to even touch her, which is pretty much the reason I'm here—to do all the things Lenora's right arm and legs can't.

"We need to talk," I say. "I mean, *I* need to talk."

I pause, as if Lenora can respond. Instead, her silence fills the bathroom like steam, making it feel small, almost oppressive.

"You're right. I'm scared. I'll try not to be. But it's hard. Maybe it would be easier if I knew why—"

I catch myself before I can finish the sentence. *Why you killed the rest of your family.* Lenora knows what I mean anyway. I can sense it as I squeeze shampoo into my hands and start to lather her hair.

"Because I might understand."

I cup water into my hands and pour it over Lenora's head, taking care to keep soapy water from getting into her eyes. My mother did the same thing when I was young. I returned the favor when, years later, I had to bathe her. The act has always struck me as something sacred. Like a baptism. Doing it now, in this stuffy, silent bathroom, puts me in a confessional mood.

That's something my father suggested, right before he all but stopped talking to me. Go to the priest. Confess my sins.

I didn't then. But I attempt it now.

"It turns out, we're a lot alike, Lenora." I cup more water, splash it onto her head, let it trickle down her hair as if the act will absolve us both. "We both like books. We haven't been anywhere for years and years. And I know what you're going through."

I pause, unsure if I should continue. Or if I even want to. But then Lenora gives me a sidelong glance, looking as curious about me as I am about her.

"That's the biggest thing we have in common," I finally say. "That everyone thinks I also killed *my* mother."

# EIGHT

Even though I would have cared for my mother for free, my parents insisted on hiring me through Gurlain Home Health Aides. My mother's idea. Such a proud woman. There was no way Kathleen Mc-Deere would accept charity. Even though stomach cancer was eating away at her—and even though everyone knew it was far too late to do anything about it—she insisted on paying.

So I left the patient I had been caring for, a rather boring octogenarian with chronic arthritis, and moved back into my childhood bedroom. At first, it was weird treating my own mother like one of my patients. They all seemed so old. She didn't.

Not that she was young. My mother was thirty-four when she had me and my father thirty-nine. I always assumed that one day I'd be expected to care for them. I just didn't think it would be this soon.

Or this brutal.

That was something I wasn't prepared for, no matter how many other patients I'd cared for. It's different when it's your own mother. It matters more. It hurts more, too. But none of the hurt I felt could compare to what my mother was going through. She spent the first few weeks of her illness in a daze, gobsmacked by all the ways in which her body had betrayed her. Then came the pain, so sharp it sometimes left her doubled over and weeping. I urged her doctor to prescribe fentanyl, even though he wanted to wait.

"Just a few more weeks," he said.

"But she's in agony *now*," I said.

He wrote out the prescription.

Two weeks later my mother was dead of a fentanyl overdose.

To an untrained eye, it might have looked like a tragic accident. A sick woman rendered mad by pain taking more pills than she should have. To a trained eye, however, it was worse than that. Because of her condition, it could be argued that my mother was not in a sound state of mind. Which meant that I, as her caregiver, was responsible for making decisions on her behalf and in her best interests. Since I'd left a drug known for its overdose potential within her reach, one could also argue that I was negligent in her care and therefore responsible for her death.

That's what Mr. Gurlain thought, once I admitted I forgot to put the pill bottle in the lockbox under my bed. He didn't tell me this, of course. He simply contacted the state's Department of Health and Human Services, who then contacted the local police.

A day after my mother's funeral, a detective came to the house. Richard Vick. Because he and my father had been friends back in the day, I knew him slightly. He had the look of a sitcom grandfather. Full head of white hair. Friendly smile. Kind eyes.

"Hello there, Kit," he said. "My deepest condolences on your recent loss."

I looked at him with confusion, even though by then I should have known why he was there. "Can I help you with something, Mr. Vick?"

"Detective Vick, if you don't mind." He gave a half smile, as if apologizing for the formality. "Is your dad around?"

He wasn't. My father, stoic in his grief, went to work as usual that day, off to fix the clanging pipes in old Mrs. Mayweather's house. I told this to Detective Vick, adding a polite "I'll tell him you stopped by."

"I'm actually here to see you."

"Oh." I opened the door wider and told him to come in.

Detective Vick straightened his tie, cleared his throat, and said, "It might be better if we did this down at the station."

"Do I need a lawyer?"

I was told no, of course not, it was just an informal chat about what happened. I wasn't a suspect because there was nothing to suspect. All lies, as I learned when I followed Detective Vick to the station and was escorted into an interrogation room with a tape recorder he turned on the moment we sat down.

"Please state your name," he said.

"You know my name."

"It's for the record."

I stared at the tape recorder, watching the reels turn and turn. That was when I knew I was in trouble.

"Kit McDeere."

"And what is it you do, Kit?"

"I'm an in-home caregiver with Gurlain Home Health Aides."

"How long have you been doing this?"

"Twelve years."

"That's a long time," Detective Vick said. "I assume you're probably an expert at it by now."

I shrugged. "I guess."

Detective Vick opened a folder in front of him, inside of which was the coroner's report on my mother's death. "It says here your mother died of an overdose of prescription painkillers and that you, acting as her caregiver, had been the one to find her body."

"That's correct."

"How did you feel when you realized your mother was dead?"

I thought back to that morning. How I woke early, took one look at the gray-streaked sky, and just knew my mother was gone. Before crossing the hall to her room, I could have woken my father, who had taken to sleeping on the couch to give my mother more space in bed. We could have checked on her together, sparing me the burden of being the one to find her dead. Instead, I peeked into her bedroom and found my mother with her head on her pillow, her eyes closed, her hands folded over her chest. Finally, she was at peace.

"Sad," I said. "And relieved."

Detective Vick arched a brow. His eyes were no longer kind. Instead, they radiated suspicion. "Relieved?"

"That she was no longer suffering."

"I suppose it's natural to think that."

"It is," I replied, with more bite than was appropriate under the circumstances. I couldn't help it.

"Your employer, Mr. Gurlain, told me it was standard procedure to lock away all pills while you're asleep to prevent patients from having access to them. Is that true?"

I nodded.

"I'll need you to answer that, Kit," Detective Vick said with a nod toward the tape recorder.

"Yes," I said.

"But Mr. Gurlain also told me you confessed to not doing that with the pills your mother overdosed on."

"I didn't confess," I said, thrown off by the word.

"So you *did* put the pills away?"

"No," I said. "I left them out. But I didn't confess. That makes me sound guilty of something. I simply *told* Mr. Gurlain I left them out."

"Have you ever left medication out like that before?"

"No."

"Never?"

"Ever."

"So this was the first time you forgot to lock away the pills like you're supposed to?"

"Yes," I said, sighing the word as my frustration increased. I looked again to the tape recorder and wondered how the sigh would sound when played back. Impatient? Guilty?

"Did you intentionally leave them out?" Detective Vick asked.

"No. It was an accident."

"I find that hard to believe, Kit."

"That doesn't mean it's not true."

"For the twelve years you've been a caregiver, you've never once left medication within a patient's reach. The one time you do, the patient just happens to overdose. But not just any patient. Your very own mother, who was in so much pain that you begged her doctor to prescribe the very drugs that killed her. And when she died, you admit to feeling relieved. That doesn't sound like an accident to me, Kit."

I continued to eye the tape recorder, the reels turning and turning and turning.

"I'd like a lawyer," I said.

After that, everything fell like dominoes. A formal police investigation began, Mr. Gurlain suspended me, and I was assigned a public defender who told me I'd likely be charged with involuntary manslaughter at best and homicide at worst if the police thought I forced those pills on my mother. He recommended I take whatever plea deal they offered. The last domino—the final straw for my father—was when the investigation made the front page of the local newspaper.

*Police Suspect Daughter Caused Mother's Fatal Overdose*

In the end, though, there was no way to prove I left those pills out on purpose or that I made my mother take them. I have no doubt that lack of proof is the sole reason I'm walking free today. I know Detective Vick thinks I'm responsible. Everyone does.

"Including my father," I tell Lenora after giving her my sad story as I lifted her from the tub, toweled her off, put her in a clean nightgown and fresh adult diaper, and tucked her into bed. "He might never speak to me again. That's why I'm here instead of there."

I collect her medication from the nightstand and drop the bottles into the lockbox, which then goes back under my bed. Even though there's no way Lenora could reach them on the nightstand, I can't be too cautious. Not after what happened with my mother.

Back in Lenora's room, I place the red call button next to her left hand so she can easily use it.

"I'll be right next door if you need me," I say, which is what I also told my mother every night I was caring for her.

Lenora looks up at me, apprehension dulling her green eyes. My stomach clenches as I realize what it means.

Even she thinks I'm guilty.

I guess that makes us even.

My birthday dinner was unbearable. Such an unhappy affair, despite all the effort put into it. There was spring lamb, leek soup, and potatoes roasted in rosemary.

The dinner was attended by only me, Miss Baker, my father, my sister, and a special guest at her request--Peter. Although there was a place setting for my mother, she sent her maid to inform us that she felt too weak to come down to dinner.

For dessert, the kitchen staff wheeled in a massive three-tiered cake with pink frosting and birthday candles ablaze. I tried to appear enthusiastic as I blew them out. I truly did. But since everything felt so awful, I couldn't quite manage it.

Not that anyone noticed. My sister was preoccupied by flirting with Peter and my father was too busy ogling the newest maid, Sally. I could have grabbed a handful of cake and shoved it into my mouth and only stern Miss Baker would have batted an eye.

After dinner, I went upstairs to see my mother. She was in bed, of course, the duvet pulled to her chest. She looked so small and pitiful that it was hard to believe she had once been a great beauty.

"The most beautiful girl in Boston," my father liked to boast back when my sister and I were younger and my parents had at least pretended to love each other.

I know he was telling the truth. In her youth, my mother had been astoundingly beautiful. It didn't hurt that she also hailed from one of the wealthiest families in New England. That fact, combined with her good looks, made her irresistible to my father, who was New Money through and through. A striver of unchecked ambition, he set his sights on Evangeline Staunton.

It didn't matter that all of Boston whispered about how she had taken up with one of the servants, scandalizing her family and edging herself to the brink of being disowned. My father still pursued her with vigor.

My mother, of course, enjoyed the attention. More than once, I'd heard her described as a rose blossoming in sunlight. My father's sun must have shone bright, because in a matter of weeks they wed. My mother got pregnant immediately after and my father built Hope's End.

Years later, when his attention began to wane, my mother--like any flower removed from the light--withered. There was nothing roselike about her the night of my birthday. Pale, shriveled, and thin to the point of gauntness, she was all thorns.

"Hello, my darling," she said, using the term of endearment meant only for me. My sister and I each had one, chosen by our parents the day we were born. My sister was dear. I was darling.

Although that night, my mother murmured it in a way that made me unsure if she was addressing me or the brown bottle of liquid resting on the pillow next to her.

Laudanum.

Her cure-all, although as far as I could tell, it cured nothing.

"Did you have a happy birthday?"

Certain it was indeed me she was talking to, I lied and told her that I did.

"I do wish we could have celebrated it in Boston," my mother said.

As did I. To me, Boston was another universe I was only allowed to enjoy once a year before being whisked back to the banality of Hope's End. It had everything this place didn't. Restaurants and shops, theaters and cinemas. The last time we visited was right after Christmas. I tasted champagne for the first time, rode a swan boat in Boston Common, went to the movies, and saw Mickey Mouse in "Steamboat Willie." I couldn't wait to return.

"Perhaps my next birthday," I said hopefully.

My mother gave a sleepy nod and said, "There's a gift for you over there. Just a little token from your father and I."

On the dresser was a small box in pink paper and blue ribbon. Inside was a small snow globe with a miniature Eiffel Tower rising above a row of tiny mansard roofs.

"Shake it," my mother said, and I did, sending tiny gold flakes spinning around inside the globe.

"I so wanted to take you girls to Paris," my mother said, as if such a journey were no longer possible. "Promise me you'll go one day."

I gripped the snow globe tight and nodded.

"Go to Paris and fall in love, then write all about it. I know how much you love to write. Write down all your thoughts and hopes and dreams as you go on grand adventures. Promise me you'll do that, my darling. Promise me you won't remain here."

"I promise," I said.

My mother began to cry then. Openly weeping, she reached for the laudanum and lifted the bottle to her lips.

I left just before she began to gulp it down.

# NINE

I'm not surprised to discover that there's no TV in my room, either. I've seen enough of Hope's End to know it exists mostly in the past, from the antique box of a phone I spotted in the kitchen to the old-timey toilet in my bathroom, which can only be flushed by yanking a pull cord. While I don't mind not having a TV—I never watched much anyway—I am glad I brought plenty of books.

I set the box of them on the floor and open it up, wondering if I have the energy to try to cram them onto the already-full bookshelf. Spending the day caring for Lenora while subconsciously overcompensating for the leaning house has left me feeling sore and exhausted. Being a caregiver is hard work. It uses muscles you never know you have until that first day spent with your first patient.

Or maybe it was talking about my mother that's left me exhausted. It usually does. Speaking about what happened gives weight to the bad memories, making them feel raw and recent. Right now, I'm so burdened by them that instead of unpacking the box and my suitcase, I'm tempted to collapse into bed and not wake until the sunrise peeks over the horizon. But then I hear a sharp rap on my bedroom door. Mrs. Baker, I assume, ready to either criticize, chastise, or inform me of something else I need to do.

Instead, it's Jessica I find standing in the hall. Gone is her uniform, which has been replaced by stirrup pants and an oversize Madonna T-shirt. The jewelry remains, however, jangling as she offers a happy wave.

"Hi," she says. "It's Kit, right?"

"Right. And you're Jessica."

"Jessie. Only Mrs. Baker calls me Jessica." She starts fiddling with one of her bracelets. "Anyhoo, I just wanted to officially welcome you to Hope's End. The name fits, by the way. Abandon all hope, ye who enter here."

I force a smile, even though her joke is more alarming than amusing. For the umpteenth time that day, I wonder what, exactly, I've gotten myself into.

"You settling in okay?" Jessie asks.

"Trying to." I gesture to the suitcase on my bed and the box of books on the floor. "I haven't had a chance to unpack yet. Lenora—Miss Hope—kept me very busy today."

"You can drop the whole Miss Hope act around me. It's only Mrs. Baker who cares about that." Jessie puts her hands behind her back and stands on her tiptoes. "But since you've been busy, I guess you don't feel like getting a tour of the house now."

"Mrs. Baker already showed me around."

"This is an unofficial tour," Jessie says. "The murder tour. Mary did it for me when I first got here. She said it was good to know where everything went down that night. Who died where. That kind of thing."

"That's very nice of you, but I think I'm okay," I say, repelled by the idea. It's bad enough knowing what happened here. I don't need details. "I was hoping to avoid those places."

Jessie shrugs. "Fair enough. But how do you plan to avoid them when you don't know where they are?"

A very good point. For all I know, a member of the Hope family could have been murdered in this very room. But that's not the only reason I decide to take Jessie up on her offer. Between my father and Lenora, I've spent so much time with people who can't—or won't—talk back that I've forgotten how nice it feels to converse. Especially with someone under the age of sixty.

"Fine," I say. "You can show me. And then I'll know to never enter those rooms again."

"Impossible," Jessie says with an impish grin. "One of them isn't a room."

She sets off down the hall, going in the direction of the Grand Stairs. I follow, trying to keep quiet, even though Jessie's rattling jewelry makes her sound like a one-woman wind chime as we pass Lenora's room. Music drifts from behind the closed door of the room next to it. Something jazzy and old that takes me a moment to recognize: "Let's Misbehave."

Jessie lifts a finger to her lips and mouths, *Mrs. Baker.*

I slow my steps, moving on tiptoes. Even Jessie quiets down, walking with her arms outstretched to keep her bracelets from clattering. She stays that way until we reach the top of the Grand Stairs. I head down one side; Jessie uses the other.

"How do you like it here?" she says when we meet again on the landing.

"It's a lot to take in."

"Totally," Jessie says. "But it's not so bad. Have you met Carter yet?"

"Yeah. On my way in."

"He's, like, totally dreamy, right?"

"I guess," I say, even though I'm in agreement there.

We stand in the shadow of the stained-glass window, its colors muted by the darkness outside. Directly beneath our feet, an unruly red splotch two shades darker than the surrounding carpet takes up most of the landing. Earlier today, I thought it was caused by light streaming through the stained glass. Standing on it now, though, I see it for what it is.

A bloodstain.

A big one.

I leap away from it, onto one of the lower steps, where I find another, smaller stain. And another on the step below that. Hopping to the foyer floor, I stare up at Jessie and say, "You could have warned me."

"And miss that reaction? I don't think so."

She descends the rest of the stairs, stepping on several more blood-stains in the red carpet and making me notice a pattern to the splotches. It looks like someone bleeding profusely had tried coming up the Grand Stairs before being stopped at the landing.

"Evangeline Hope," Jessie says, knowing exactly what I'm thinking. "It's assumed she was stabbed in the foyer, tried to escape up the steps, and was stabbed again on the landing, where she bled out."

I shudder and turn away, looking instead to the large front door leading to outside. "Why didn't she try to leave?"

"No one knows," Jessie says. "There's a lot about that night that remains unknown."

She starts moving down the hall on the right, the one that ends at the sunroom. We don't make it that far. At the halfway point, just past Lenora's portrait, Jessie stops at one of the hallway's many closed doors. She pushes it open and flicks a switch just inside. Light floods the room, coming from both a green-glass fixture on the ceiling and matching sconces on the walls.

"The billiard room," she announces with an enthusiasm usually reserved for tour guides who really, really love their job. "Where Winston Hope met his end."

My first thought is that yes, this feels very much like a room where a man of Mr. Hope's stature would die. The décor is brutish. Various antique firearms hang on the walls, along with the heads of animals that were probably killed by them. A lion. A bear. Several deer. A pair of matching leather armchairs sits atop a zebra pelt in front of a fire-place. On one wall is a rack of pool cues, although there's no pool table to be seen. The only sign it was ever here is a rectangular path in the middle of the room where the floor has been worn down by well-heeled soles.

"What happened to the pool table?"

"Winston Hope died slumped over it," Jessie says. "Since his throat was slit, I guess it was too bloody to salvage."

I turn her way, startled. "The rhyme says he was stabbed."

"Oh, he was," Jessie says. "Once in the side, before his throat was slit. I guess that was too complicated to make rhyme."

"How do you know so much about all of this?"

"Mostly Mary," Jessie says. "She knows a lot about what happened that night. She's, like, totally obsessed with the murders. I think it's why she took the job, you know?"

I don't. Other than my father's house, this is the last place I want to be.

"Why did *you* take a job here?" I say.

Jessie gives a jewelry-rattling shrug. "This place seemed as good as any. I needed to do something, right? Work is work and money is money."

Now that's a sentiment I can get behind. I never thought I'd be a caregiver, just like I'm sure Jessie never thought she'd be cleaning a murder mansion. But it's better than nothing, which is what I had before today.

With nothing more to be explored in the billiard room, we leave. Jessie cuts the lights and closes the door before taking me to the one across the hall from it.

"What's in here?"

"A surprise," Jessie says as she flicks on the lights, revealing a library. I take in the floor-to-ceiling shelves, a leather sofa, and two matching armchairs scooted next to a marble fireplace. On the mantel are three cloisonné vases in a matching pattern of ivory flowers and twisting blue vines. Behind them looms a large rectangle of wallpaper darker than the surrounding area.

"Did there used to be a painting there?"

"Yep," Jessie says. "An original Winslow Homer, according to Archie. Mrs. Baker had to sell it years ago."

I move to the mantel to get a better look at the vases. Hidden among the vines are tiny hummingbirds with little ruby dots for eyes. In the center of each ivory blossom is a circle of gold.

"Why didn't she sell these, too?"

"Those are probably the last thing she'd sell," Jessie says. "It might even be illegal. I think there are laws about selling dead people."

I take a step away from the mantel, understanding my mistake. These aren't vases. They're urns. And inside are what remains of Winston, Evangeline, and Virginia Hope.

"Want to take a peek?" Jessie says.

"Definitely not. Have you?"

Jessie makes a face. "No way. It's bad enough I have to dust them once a week."

"I'm surprised they weren't buried."

"I guess it was easier to cremate them," Jessie says. "It was more private. Kept the looky-loos away, at least. By then, Lenora probably knew everyone thought she did it."

We're near the door now, having both unconsciously drifted away from the urns. Being near them unsettles me. The problem isn't what's inside the urns. That's just the dust and ash of three people. What bothers me is how those people died.

Tragically.

Violently.

On the landing of an opulent staircase, sprawled across a pool table, and in a place I haven't seen yet but am sure Jessie will reveal next. To get it over with, I leave the library, with Jessie close behind. Back in the hallway, we pause at the portraits, three covered, one exposed. Although the hallway is dim, Lenora's green eyes still gleam from the canvas, as if it's been lit from the inside.

"Why do you think she did it?" I say.

"Maybe she didn't," Jessie says with a shrug. "I have a hunch it was Winston Hope himself. The murders took place the night of October 29, 1929. Black Tuesday. The stock market crashed, a bunch of rich guys lost millions, and the Great Depression began. That's why not many people outside of Maine even know what happened here. Black Tuesday hijacked all the headlines. People were too worried about being poor to pay attention to Winston Hope and his dead family."

I can't blame them. As someone who *is* poor, I understand how it can eclipse all other concerns.

"I think Winston Hope knew he was about to lose everything," Jessie continues. "Rather than live like the rest of us—which, let's face it, totally sucks—he decided to end things. He offed his wife, then Virginia, then—" She mimes dragging a knife across her throat. "A good, old-fashioned murder-suicide."

"But what about the stab wound in his side?" I say, before an even more logical question appears. "And why would he let Lenora live? And why wouldn't she tell the police the truth?"

"*And* what happened to the knife?" Jessie adds. "Winston's throat was slashed and Evangeline was stabbed multiple times, yet no murder weapon was ever found."

"Which means it had to be Lenora. She killed them and tossed the knife."

"That's what most people seem to think." Jessie tilts her head, studying the portrait as if she's an art scholar. "And this painting does make her look capable of murder, doesn't it?"

"So why wasn't she arrested and put on trial?"

"There wasn't enough evidence," Jessie says. "They dusted for fingerprints, but there were so many from every family member and servant that it was impossible to tell who was responsible. With the murder weapon missing, there was no way to prove Lenora was guilty."

"Or that she was innocent," I say, fully understanding the hypocrisy of my counterargument. Lack of evidence is the only reason *I* wasn't arrested and put on trial.

"True. Then there's the idea that maybe she lied to cover for someone else. Like him."

Jessie points to a signature in the bottom righthand corner of the portrait. I lean in and read the name scrawled in white paint.

"Peter Ward?"

"The artist. That's Mary's wild guess. She's full of theories. Another one is that Hope's End is haunted. She claims to have seen the ghost of Virginia Hope roaming the second floor."

The chill I'd felt the first time I was in this hallway returns. Definitely not a draft. It's too cold, too unnatural. Even though I don't believe in ghosts, I can understand why Mary thought one haunted Hope's End.

"Is that why she left?"

"Yes," Jessie says, her voice going quiet. "I think she was scared. Hope's End isn't a normal house. There's a darkness here. I can feel it. Mary did. And I think she couldn't take it anymore."

We head back down the hall, Jessie checking over her shoulder, as if something is lurking just behind us. At the Grand Stairs, I can't help but take another morbid peek at the bloodstains in the carpet. From there, we move through the other side of the house, stopping at the set of double doors before the hall makes a right toward the kitchen.

"The ballroom," Jessie says solemnly before pushing open the doors. "Where Virginia Hope died."

She turns on the lights, which include sconces set between large mirrors on the walls and three chandeliers that droop from the ceiling. They're enormous, with more than three dozen bulbs each. Half have burned out. Others buzz and flicker, giving the room a jittery feel.

While Jessie roams freely, I remain on the edge of the parquet dance floor, knowing that wherever I step might be the spot where Virginia Hope's body once lay.

"Don't worry," Jessie says. "Virginia died up there."

She points to the chandelier in the center of the ballroom. It hangs lower than the others and at a slight angle, like the weight of Virginia's body partially tugged it from the ceiling.

"So the rhyme was right about that."

"Yup," Jessie says. "Hung her sister with a rope."

I take a few cautious steps toward the center of the room to get a closer look at the chandelier. While it's low enough to possibly reach with a rope while standing on a chair, I can't picture a girl of seventeen doing it and then hoisting her sister high enough to hang her. It seems unlikely, if not impossible.

Then again, none of these murders makes sense, including where they occurred. Three deaths in three different spots throughout the first floor. If it was Winston Hope, did he hang Virginia first, get caught in the act by his wife, and stab her at the Grand Stairs before going to the billiard room to kill himself? Or was he killed first—by Lenora or someone else—and did Evangeline find his body, run to the stairs covered in his blood, and bump into the killer on the landing? Without knowing who died first, it's impossible to tell. And none of it explains poor Virginia's fate or the missing knife.

"I wonder why Virginia was hanged when the others were killed with a knife," I say.

"You and everyone else," Jessie says. "I guess we could always ask."

"We could. But Lenora can't answer. Even when she could, she didn't say much."

"I meant Virginia." Jessie nervously twists one of her bracelets around her wrist. "What if Mary is right and Virginia really is haunting this place? If so, we could contact her spirit and ask what happened."

"If only we had a Ouija board."

I mean it as a joke. For one, I don't think Hope's End is haunted. Nor do I believe Ouija boards can contact the dead. But as soon as I say it, Jessie's eyes light up.

"I'll go get mine," she says. "Wait here. I'll be right back."

Jessie scurries off, leaving me alone in the ballroom, my reflection caught in the many mirrors on the walls. It's dizzying seeing so many different versions of myself. Everywhere I turn, there I am. It makes me think of Virginia Hope swinging from the chandelier. A horrible way to go. Made worse by the fact that, if her eyes were open, she would have seen a dozen reflections of the life being strangled out of her.

I pray she kept them shut.

Above me, one of the bulbs in the chandelier Virginia hung from buzzes and brightens before going dark with an eerie, electric pop. While I'm certain the cause is ancient wiring and a bulb that likely hasn't been replaced since 1929, I take it as a sign to leave the ballroom.

But as soon as I'm about to exit, Jessie enters, carrying a battered Ouija board. Atop it sits a wood planchette that slides around the board as Jessie moves, as if it's being moved by invisible hands.

"Aren't we a little old for this?" I say.

"Speak for yourself." Jessie places the Ouija board in the center of the ballroom. "I'm young and stupid. At least, that's what Mrs. Baker says. Now join me or I'll tell everyone you're a scaredy-cat."

I do, more for Jessie's benefit than mine. It must be hard being so young yet living and working in this big, old house. I suspect this whole tour was the result of her feeling lonely and wanting to make a new friend. I want that, too. My circle of friends had shrunk to the size of a dot before my mother died. After her funeral, I found myself with none at all.

We place our fingers on the planchette, and Jessie says, "Is there a spirit present?"

"This is silly," I say.

"Shush." Jessie stares at the planchette. "I feel something."

"No, you don't."

"I said shush. Don't you feel it?"

At first, I don't. But soon the planchette begins to slide toward the word printed in the upper-left-hand corner of the board.

YES

Jessie gasps with delight. I roll my eyes. She's obviously guided us to the word.

"Spirit, is there something you want to communicate to us?" Jessie says.

Once again, the planchette moves, slowly circling the same word.

YES

It continues to circle, even though the pads of my fingers are barely touching the planchette. Which means it's still Jessie's doing.

"Spirit," she says, "please identify yourself."

The planchette slowly slides to the center of the board and the two arched rows of letters printed across it. Unsurprisingly, it comes to a stop near the end of the second row.

V

Next, it slides to the letter directly above it.

I

The planchette then glides back down to the second row and the inevitable next letter.

R

"Quit pretending you're not moving it," I whisper.

"I'm not," Jessie whispers back. To the empty room, she says, "Spirit, are you Virginia Hope?"

The planchette again moves to the upper-left corner of the board. Faster, this time. A sudden, startling jerk.

YES

Jessie looks at me from across the board. There's surprise in her eyes—and just a touch of fear.

"That wasn't me," she says.

It had to be. I certainly didn't do it. My touch on the planchette is so light it barely exists. But when I look down, I see that Jessie's fingertips are also barely touching it. Yet the planchette still moves, sliding back and forth beneath the word YES as if trying to underline it.

Jessie gulps and looks to the chandelier directly above us, as if Virginia Hope is still hanging there. "Virginia, did your sister murder you?"

The planchette rockets to the other side of the board, zooming directly onto the word in the upper-right-hand corner.

NO

The planchette keeps jerking forward, its tapered point stabbing at the word. Then it flies off the board entirely before skittering across the floor.

I jerk my hand away from the Ouija board as Jessie lets out a shocked cry. "What the hell just happened?" she says.

"That's not funny."

"But I didn't do it! I was barely touching it! It had to—"

Jessie's mouth drops open and her eyes go wide, startled by something behind me. I whirl around to face the mirrored wall at my back, expecting to see—well, I don't know. What I do see is my alarmed reflection and, just over my shoulder, Jessie breaking into a wide grin she tries to hide by slapping a hand over her mouth.

"Not cool," I say.

"I'm sorry," Jessie says, laughing openly now. "But you should have seen the look on your face. I, like, totally got you."

I stand and brush dust from the skirt of my uniform. "So what you said about Mary thinking this place is haunted is—"

"Totally made-up," Jessie admits as she picks up the Ouija board and retrieves the planchette. "I was just messing with you."

"Then why did Mary really leave?"

"I don't know." Jessie turns off the lights and leaves the ballroom. I follow, closing the doors behind me. "One day, she was just . . . gone."

"Weren't the two of you close?"

"*I* thought we were," Jessie says. "Close enough for her to tell me she was leaving, at least."

"And no one else knows why she left?"

"Nope."

We're in the kitchen now, Jessie heading to the service stairs and me leaning against the center counter. "Aren't you worried about her?"

"A little," Jessie says. "But Mary's smart. And normally super responsible. I know she wouldn't leave like that without a good reason."

"Do you think Lenora had something to do with it?"

"Like Mary was scared of her?" Jessie shakes her head. "No way. She adored Lenora. I think she left because of a family emergency or something. Her parents live in the next county. One of them probably got sick and she had to leave, like, immediately. I'm sure she'll reach out and tell me what happened when she gets the chance."

I hope that's true, for Jessie's sake. But I know from personal experience it doesn't work that way. When I left a patient to care for my mother, a replacement for me needed to be arranged. I didn't just leave in the middle of the night like Mary did.

"I should get back to my room," Jessie says with a tiny yawn. "I'm about to start recording a new book for Lenora. *Lace* by Shirley Conran."

"I read it," I say. "It's good. Racy."

"Awesome. Lenora loves racy."

I wish her goodnight and stand for a moment in the vast, empty kitchen. I run my gaze along the walls, trying to estimate its size, which might be larger than my father's entire house. This fact would have impressed the hell out of my mother. Not so much my father, who hates the rich almost as much as he hates politicians.

I touch the telephone, which is so old it could be in a museum. But it still works. Lifting the receiver from its cradle, I hear the steady buzz of a dial tone. Quickly, I dial my father's number, rationalizing it by telling myself he'll at least want to know where I am. According to the kitchen's equally ancient clock, it's just past ten o'clock, so I assume he's still awake. Sure enough, he answers after three rings.

"Hello?"

I say nothing, the urge to speak fleeing at the sound of his voice. In the background, I hear a woman talking. It might be the TV. Or it could be his new girlfriend, allowed to stay the night now that I'm not there.

"Hello?" he says again. "Who is this?"

I hang up and back away from the phone, worried he's certain it was me and will now try calling back. An impossibility. He doesn't know where I am or the phone number for Hope's End. And since he didn't want to talk to me while I lived with him, I see no reason why he would now that I'm gone.

The only thing I'm certain about as I head upstairs is that at least now my father knows how it feels to be met with silence.

# TEN

Just like when Mrs. Baker first led me to it, my bedroom door seemingly moves on its own. One touch of the handle is all it takes to send it swinging open with a pronounced creak.

Inside, the room glows red. An uneven, pulsing light coats the walls and makes the bedroom look nightmarish. With each flash of red comes an insistent buzzing sound.

Lenora's call button.

She needs me.

I push into the room, my eyes stinging from the pulsing red light on the nightstand. I trip over the box of books sitting in the middle of the floor, sending it toppling. Paperbacks spill around my ankles as I keep moving.

To the adjoining door.

Into Lenora's room.

To her bed, where she lies with her left hand clenched around the call button. Her eyes are open wide and wild.

"What's wrong?" I say, too worried to think about the fact that she can't answer me. Anything could be wrong. Another stroke. A heart attack. Seizure or sickness or impending death.

When she sees me, Lenora's grip on the call button loosens. She sighs, looking childlike and embarrassed, and I think I understand what happened.

"Did you have a nightmare?"

Lenora, still holding the call button, uses it to tap twice against the bedspread.

"Must have been a real humdinger," I say, which is what my mother called especially nasty nightmares. The kind that linger after you wake. The kind that make you afraid to close your eyes again. "Do you want me to stay here until you fall back asleep?"

Two more taps.

When I was little and had a real humdinger of a nightmare, my mother would crawl into my bed and wrap her arms around me, which is what I do now with Lenora. She looks so rattled—still so utterly scared—that it feels wrong not to.

"Nightmares are just your brain thinking it's Halloween," I tell her. Something else my mother said. "All trick, no treat."

Lenora's left hand finds my right one and clasps my fingers. The gesture, despite being tender, almost desperate, leaves me reeling. Lenora Hope, my town's version of the bogeyman and the woman whose guilt kids to this very day chant about, is holding my hand.

Part of me wants to recoil from her touch. Another part of me feels terrible about that. No matter what she did in the past—which, let's be clear, was very, *very* bad—Lenora's still a human being who deserves to be treated like one.

If she even did all the things she's accused of. The same thought I had in the ballroom occurs to me now: Would a seventeen-year-old girl even be capable of killing three people like that? These were physical crimes. Slitting her father's throat. Stabbing her mother. Tying a noose around her sister's neck and hoisting her to her death. I wouldn't be able to do it, which makes it hard for me to believe someone half my age could.

Maybe Jessie's theory is right and it was Winston Hope or someone else. If so, Lenora has paid a terrible price. No, she never went to jail. But she's been imprisoned for decades.

In her own home.

In her childhood bedroom.

In a body that refuses to function.

Then again, if what everyone has said is true, then it means I'm embracing a murderer. One whose care and well-being I'm responsible for. I'm not sure which scenario is worse. I'm also not sure I can continue to work here without knowing the truth. Maybe that's what made Mary leave without warning. She could no longer take the not-knowing.

"Lenora," I whisper. "Did you really do it?"

She releases my hand, and I hold my breath, preparing for the answer about to be tapped against the bedspread. To my surprise, Lenora doesn't tap. Instead, I get a nod toward the typewriter on the other side of the room.

"You want to *type*?"

Lenora taps twice against my hand.

"Right now?"

Two more taps. More urgent this time.

Because it seems easier to bring the typewriter to Lenora instead of the other way around, I carry it across the room in an awkward waddle and plop it down on the edge of the mattress. Then I climb back into bed and prop up Lenora against me so she can easily access the keyboard. All that effort leaves me perspiring. This better be worth it.

"Go ahead," I say as I place her left hand on the keys.

Lenora knits her brows, thinking. Then she types four words before nodding, signaling for me to hit the return bar.

**i wont hurt you**

My pulse quickens as I read the sentence.

"I appreciate that," I say, not sure how else to reply. How did Lenora know I wanted to hear this? Are my emotions as easily read as hers?

Lenora resumes typing.

**i suppose youve heard the song about me**

"The rhyme?" I say, surprised she knows of its existence. It must be horrible having her life—and her family's deaths—reduced to a child-ish chant. "I have. It's . . . cruel."

**i find it amusing**

Another surprise. "You do?"

**all that effort for little old me**

"Is it true?"

**you can find out**

Curiosity tugs at me. As does fear and a healthy dose of uncer-tainty. "How?"

**i want to tell you everything**

"Everything? What does that mean?"

**things ive never told anyone else**

"About the murders?" I say, surprised I can hear myself over the sound of my heartbeat pounding like a drum in my ears.

**yes about that night**

I look at Lenora. The dim light of the room somehow makes her green eyes brighter. They glint fiercely now. Emeralds lit from within, holding me hostage in their gaze.

My God, she's serious.

"Why me? Why now?"

**because i trust you**

"Are you sure?"

Lenora's hand slides from the typewriter and drops to the mattress. Her body language is crystal clear. She's sure.

"I'll think about it," I say as I carry the typewriter back to the desk. By the time I return to the bed, Lenora is asleep. I can tell by her breathing—a deep, steady rhythm. I switch off the lamp and place the call button next to her left hand before tiptoeing away.

Back in my room, I finally ditch the nurse's uniform. Taking it off feels like removing armor. I feel freer, yes, but also oddly vulnerable. Gone is the sense of purpose I'd felt when I first put it on. Now I'm back to being aimless, slump-shouldered me.

After putting on a nightgown and fuzzy socks, I press a hand to my heart. It's still galloping. This time, I know exactly why.

After decades of silence, Lenora Hope wants to tell all.

And I need to decide if I want to hear it.

Part of me thinks, obviously, yes. This place, with its murderous past, mind-messing tilt, and general dourness, is already a lot to deal with. I suspect it would be easier if I knew what happened that night—and Lenora's role in it. Especially because I'm the one who'll be spending the most time with her. The one tasked with feeding her, bathing her, dressing her, keeping her alive. At the very least there'd be no more wondering, no more suspicion.

Then again, not knowing provides at least a sliver of optimism. If Lenora confesses to killing her family, that will be gone.

I'm still weighing my options as I start to unpack, beginning with the books I'd abandoned when Jessie showed up at my door. I grab a handful and take them to the bookshelf, which is already filled with paperbacks, leaving no room for my own. I grab one—*Eye of the Needle* by Ken Follett—and open it. Inside the front cover, written in ballpoint pen, is a message.

*This book is the property of Mary Milton*

Those same words are in the next book I pick up, a battered copy of John Irving's *The Hotel New Hampshire*. While it seems odd that Mary left so many books behind, I also understand. Books aren't easy to move—and maybe Mary thought whoever replaced her would enjoy them.

Things start to make less sense when I abandon the books and try to unpack my clothes. The dresser's top drawer is filled with pristine nurse's uniforms exactly like my own. While I totally get why Mary left those behind—I would have done the same thing—more of her clothes fill the other drawers. Not just uniforms, but slacks, blouses, and underwear. I assume they belong to Mary because some of the tags bear initials written in Magic Marker.

*MM*

Sorting through the clothes, I see a pair of Jordache jeans, a pink Lacoste polo shirt, a striped blouse with the price tag still attached. Sears. Twelve dollars. All of it looks to be new and in good condition—far nicer than my own clothes.

In the closet, I find a wool coat drooping from a hanger. And boots on the floor below it. And an empty cardboard box bearing a word again written in Magic Marker: *Books*.

Beside it, surrounded by a thin coating of dust, is a narrow rectangle of clean floor where something else used to sit. What it was, I have no idea. Another box, presumably. Now gone.

On the closet shelf is a medical bag similar in shape and size to the one my parents gave me. I pull it down and peek inside, seeing most of the same items I keep in mine, arranged in an orderly manner. Its presence makes no sense. If there had been a family emergency, as Jessie suspects, Mary surely would have spent a minute grabbing her medical bag and at least some of her clothes.

Instead, she left almost everything behind.

I give up trying to unpack. It's late, I'm tired, and there's no place to put any of *my* belongings. As I turn out the lights and climb into bed, two thoughts hit me in quick succession—a fact and a question.

The fact: Mary left in a hurry.

The question: What drove her away?

After putting the snow globe in my room, I crept downstairs, hoping to gorge myself on leftover birthday cake. But there was no cake to be found. Only Berniece Mayhew, who looked none too pleased to be washing dishes at that late hour.

"Happy birthday, Miss Hope," she muttered when she saw me, not a drop of happiness in her tone.

On my way down the hall, I noticed that the door to the billiard room was ajar. Maybe some of the servants were playing, which they sometimes did behind my father's back. Usually, they let me join in, much to Miss Baker's alarm.

"Ladies shouldn't play pool," she once told me.

"Lucky for me I'm not a lady," I replied.

I paused at the door and peeked into the room. Indeed, there was a servant inside. I couldn't see who it was because she was spread facedown against the billiard table, her skirt pushed up to her waist.

Behind her was my father, his trousers around his ankles and his face turning crimson as he thrust into her.

I gasped. Loud enough for them to hear. My father looked to the door as I scrambled away. But it was too late. I'd been caught. I ran anyway, down the hall, past the portraits of my family that Peter had painted earlier. Their faces stared at me, as if I was the one who'd done something wrong.

I ran to the other side of the house and slipped into the ballroom. There, I collapsed onto the floor, my mind a jumble of thoughts, many of them wicked. I wondered how many other servants my father had screwed, in how many different rooms. I wondered who this one was, and if she was taking pleasure in it or if my father had forced himself on her. I wondered if Peter at that very moment wanted to be doing the same thing to my sister. Mostly, I wondered if anyone would ever want me in that way.

My father soon appeared in the doorway, casting a long shadow across the ballroom floor. For a moment, I thought he was about to confess his misdeeds, apologize, promise to do whatever he could to atone for them. If he did that, maybe my mother would feel fit enough to leave her bedroom. Maybe my sister and I wouldn't be treated like prisoners. Maybe there could be some happiness again in this godforsaken house.

Instead, my father joined me on the floor and wiped away the tears that had started falling down my cheeks. It was, I realized, the first time he had touched me in months.

"Hush, my darling," he said. "This isn't worth getting upset about."

"Who was that?" I asked.

"It doesn't matter."

It did to me. By then, I'd known about the rumors that my father liked to seduce the servants. Berniece whispered about it so much I couldn't help but hear. But I wanted to know who it was and why my father did it.

"Don't you love Mother?" I said, trying hard to halt my tears.

"I do," my father said. "In a very complicated way. Do you love her?"

"Of course."

"Then it's best not to tell her about this. It would kill her. And you wouldn't want that, would you?"

"No, sir," I replied, my eyes downcast because I couldn't stand to look at him.

He chucked my chin like I was a baby. Or, worse, a dog. "That's my good girl."

As my father turned and left the ballroom, I almost called out that he was the parent I wanted dead. After all, he deserved it. I didn't because I felt the need to behave like the good girl he expected me to be.

But here's the thing--I wasn't a good girl.

Not in the least.

You'll see for yourself very soon.

# ELEVEN

Sleep doesn't come easy.

Granted, I never sleep well the first few nights with a new patient. Different room. Different bed, some more comfortable than others. Different house, with all its unique nocturnal sounds. At Hope's End, the dominant night noises are the ocean and the wind—a discordant duet that keeps me awake. The waves are low and steady, crashing into the cliff below with a rhythm that would be soothing if not for the wind, which hits the house in irregular gusts. Each blow rattles the windows and shimmies the walls, which in turn creak and groan, reminding me where I am.

A mansion teetering on the edge of the ocean.

Inside of which is a woman most people assume murdered her family.

A woman who has now offered to tell me everything.

The pattern repeats itself. Thinking about Lenora, being lulled to sleep by the waves, then startled awake by the wind. Every time it hits, I grip the edge of the mattress, certain I can feel the house leaning toward the sea. But then the wind calms, my thoughts roll, the waves continue, and the whole process starts anew.

This goes on until I hear another noise.

Not the wind.

Not the waves.

It sounds like a floorboard, emitting the faintest of creaks.

I sit up and scan the room, looking for—well, I don't know what to expect. An intruder? A burglar? The mansion beginning its inevitable slide into the Atlantic? But there's nothing to see. I'm the only person in the room, making me conclude it was just the wind causing Hope's End to creak in a way I hadn't yet heard.

I crawl out of bed, crack open the door to my room, and peer into the hallway. Right now, it's empty. Knowing I could have just missed someone passing by, I step into the hall and listen for the sound of departing footsteps or a door closing.

"Hello?" I say, my voice hushed. "Is someone out here?"

No one answers.

Not another sound is heard.

Until I return to my bedroom.

When the creaking resumes, I realize exactly where it's coming from.

Lenora's room.

I press my ear to the door between our rooms, listening for signs of movement. Again, there's nothing. Just nocturnal silence and a sliver of moonlight from Lenora's room slipping through the crack between the door and the floor.

The noise sounds again.

This time, I open the door and peek inside.

There's no one else there. Just Lenora, exactly how I left her—in bed, flat on her back, hands at her sides, the left one beside the call button. The low, slow sound of her breathing tells me she's still asleep.

As for what caused those creaks, I have no idea. It certainly wasn't Lenora.

I close the adjoining door and crawl back into bed, where the waves and the wind resume vying for my attention. When I finally fall asleep, I have a nightmare.

A real humdinger.

I'm a girl again, on the metal slide at my elementary school playground. The one I never liked because it got too cold in the winter and scalding hot in the summer. Around me, a group of kids—unseen but unnervingly heard—chant in unison.

*At seventeen, Lenora Hope*

I remain on the slide, not stuck exactly, but not going fast, either. Instead, I inch down it as the chanting continues.

*Hung her sister with a rope*

At the bottom of the slide stands my mother, looking the way she did not when I was young but in the final days of her life. A teetering pile of skin and bones in a powder-blue nightgown.

*Stabbed her father with a knife*

My mother pleads with me, only I can't hear what she's saying. Whenever she opens her mouth, instead of words, all I hear is the clack of typewriter keys.

*Took her mother's happy life*

Still, I know what she's saying, almost as if the words are being typed across a blank page.

*Please, Kit-Kat.*

*Please.*

*I'll only take one.*

*I promise.*

# TWELVE

I was wrong about the sunrise.

It doesn't peek over the horizon.

It stares.

I sit up, squinting at the yellow-orange light blasting through the window. As I do, I notice something strange. Everything on the bed—mattress, blankets, me—is slightly bunched at the bottom of it. Because of the house's tilt, we've all slid a few inches lower during the night. That at least explains the inching-down-a-slide feeling from my nightmare.

I sway when I get out of bed, as if the floor has sloped a few degrees more overnight. Which, for all I know, it could have. In the shower, I notice the water is slightly higher on one side of the tub than the other as it rushes toward the drain. The same happens in the sink as I brush my teeth. Watching the pooled water gurgle down the drain, I wonder if this is why Mary left. She couldn't spend another minute inside this crooked house.

After dressing in one of Mary's abandoned uniforms, I go to the adjoining door to check on Lenora. I pause before opening it, remembering the creaks I'd heard during the night. I can't think of anything that would have caused them except a person walking around inside that room.

But no one else had been there.

Just Lenora.

I crack open the door and peek in, finding her still asleep and in the same position as when I last saw her. Which of course she'd be. Lenora can't move anything but her left arm without assistance. To think otherwise is ridiculous—and paranoid.

Careful not to wake her, I quietly close the adjoining door before slipping out of my room and going downstairs. Halfway down the service stairs, I notice a crack in the wall that I'm almost certain wasn't there last night. About four feet long and as jagged as a lightning bolt, it's impossible to miss. Either I did just that all day yesterday—or it appeared overnight.

I think of last night's wind and how it seemed to jostle the entire house. My mind turns, wondering if that's what caused the crack. And if there are more just like it now scattered about Hope's End. And, if a few wind gusts can do all that, how much damage an actual storm would cause. The thought sends me rushing down the remaining steps, eager to be on solid ground. Well, as solid as ground can be atop a cliff that's being eaten away by the ocean.

In the kitchen, I find Archie at the stove, looking like he's been cooking for hours, even though it's barely past seven. A stack of pancakes sits atop a platter on the counter, along with a plate full of bacon and a basket of fresh-baked blueberry muffins.

"Nice to see a fellow early riser," I say.

"It's Tuesday," Archie says. "Delivery day. All the groceries for the week arrive bright and early every Tuesday." He gestures to the food on the counter. "Help yourself, by the way. There's fresh coffee, too."

I make a beeline toward the coffee and pour myself a mug. The scent alone perks me up.

I take the mug to the counter and down half the coffee in three huge gulps.

Archie notices and says, "Rough night?"

"I had trouble sleeping."

"Doesn't surprise me. New place and all that. Probably didn't help that the wind was wicked last night." At the stove, Archie measures out some Quaker Oats from a cardboard cylinder and dumps them into a pot of boiling water. "We always get a few gusts, being up here on the bluff with nothing to protect us. But last night was something else."

That doesn't explain what else I heard during the night. I know what wind sounds like. And it doesn't sound like footsteps. I think again of Mary. Had she heard them, too? Could *that* be the reason she left so suddenly?

"Did Miss Hope's previous nurse ever mention hearing things or having trouble sleeping?"

"Mary? Not that I can recall."

I reach for a muffin on the counter and start peeling away the liner. "How well did you know her?"

"Well enough, I guess. Nice girl. Seemed to be great with Miss Hope," Archie says, proving Jessie wrong about only Mrs. Baker not calling Lenora by her first name. "Can't say I'm a fan of the way Mary left, though. I understand this place isn't for everyone. But you don't just leave in the middle of the night."

"There were no signs anything was wrong?"

"Not that I saw."

"So she had no problems with Miss Hope?"

"I don't think so."

"And Mary never mentioned being nervous around her?"

Archie, stirring the oatmeal now bubbling on the stove, turns my way. "Are *you* nervous around Miss Hope?"

"No," I say, aware the reply is too fast, too emphatic. To cover, I take a bite of muffin. It's so delicious that I already know I'm going to be eating a second one, with maybe a third to snack on later.

"It's good, right?" Archie says. "I coat the blueberries in flour. Keeps them from sinking to the bottom."

"Where'd you learn to cook like this?"

"Here," he says, turning back to the pot. "I pretty much grew up in this kitchen. Started as a dishwasher when I was fourteen. By eighteen, I was the sous chef."

"How long have you worked here?"

"Almost sixty years."

I pause, the muffin top in my hand lifted halfway to my mouth. "So you were here in 1929?"

"I was. Me and Mrs. Baker are the only two left from the good old days."

"Were you here the night of—"

"No," Archie says, also too fast and emphatic. "None of the help was here that night. Including Mrs. Baker. She'd left Mr. Hope's employ earlier that day."

An interesting tidbit. Especially since Mrs. Baker mentioned yesterday how she'd left Hope's End *after* the murders. I take another bite of muffin, mostly to cover the fact that my head is spinning with more questions.

"You must like it here," I say after swallowing. "Or Miss Hope likes you. I heard most of the staff was let go."

"A lot, yeah. The rest quit immediately after . . ."

Archie lets the rest of the sentence remain unspoken. Not that it needs to be said. I get the gist. Most of the staff would rather quit than continue working for a murderer.

"I'm sorry to have brought it up," I say. "I was just surprised you've known Miss Hope all this time."

"Since we were kids." Archie's voice has returned to its usual warmth. A relief. The man preparing my meals is the last person I want to piss off. "Growing up, Miss Hope and I were quite close."

"Are the two of you still close?"

"Not like we used to be," Archie says as his broad back stiffens and the hand stirring the pot goes still. "Things changed."

What he doesn't say—but what I infer—is that one thing changed. Namely, the murders of the rest of the Hope family.

"You're welcome to come up and see her," I say. "I think she's lonely."

"That's why you're here," Archie says, once again all coldness as he ladles oatmeal into a bowl placed atop a wooden serving tray. He sets the tray in front of me and says, "Miss Hope's breakfast. You should bring it up to her before it gets cold."

I get the hint, even before Archie turns back to the stove. There'll be no more talk about Lenora today. Or maybe ever.

"Thanks for breakfast," I say before placing my coffee and another muffin atop the tray and carrying it up the service stairs.

At the halfway point, I'm met by Mrs. Baker on her way down. She's dressed the same as yesterday: black dress, pale skin, red lips, glasses she lifts to her face to inspect my appearance.

"Good morning, Kit. I hope your first night here was pleasant."

"It was," I lie. "Thank you for asking."

My gaze flicks to the jagged crack in the wall, wondering if Mrs. Baker's noticed it yet. Surely she has. It's *very* noticeable. Yet she acts as if nothing is wrong.

"And you're finding your new quarters satisfactory?"

"Very. Although I do have a question about Mary's things."

"Things?" Mrs. Baker says with a schoolmarmish head cock. "You'll need to be more specific, dear."

"Her belongings. Everything's still in my room."

"Everything?"

"Her books, her clothes, even her medical bag," I say. As I'm talking, a thought pops into my head. "Is it possible she plans on coming back?"

The notion should have occurred to me sooner. It makes more sense than anything else about why she left everything behind. It could be that Mary really was called away—by her family or some other pressing matter—and has every intention of returning.

"If Mary were to return, she wouldn't be welcomed back," Mrs. Baker says. "Not after leaving Miss Hope all alone like that."

I let out a little huff of relief. At least I still have a job. "But she could come back for her stuff, right?"

"It's been a week," Mrs. Baker says. "If she wanted any of it, she would have done that by now."

"So what should *I* do with it?"

"Just hold on to everything, if you don't mind," Mrs. Baker says, though in fact I do mind. This is literally a mansion, with dozens of empty rooms. Surely there's somewhere else to store it all. "I'll decide what to do with it all later."

She acts as if that settles the matter, when in fact it doesn't. She resumes her descent, forcing me to call after her.

"I have another question, actually." I pause, waiting for her to stop, which she does with obvious reluctance after taking three more steps. "Were you in Miss Hope's room last night?"

"Now that you're here, I have no cause to enter Miss Hope's quarters."

"So that's a no," I say.

"Yes, dear. A definite no."

"But I thought—" I look down at the tray, stalling. "I thought I heard someone walking around in there last night."

"Walking?" Mrs. Baker couldn't look more incredulous if I had mentioned aliens or Santa Claus. "That's ridiculous."

"But I heard the floorboards creaking."

"Did you investigate?"

"Yes. I didn't see anyone."

"Then perhaps it was your imagination," Mrs. Baker says. "Or the wind. Sometimes, when it hits the house just so, it makes all sorts of noise."

"Does anyone else go into Miss Hope's room on a regular basis? Like Archie? Or Jessie?"

"The only person who's supposed to frequent Miss Hope's quarters is you," Mrs. Baker says. "So I suggest you get back there before she wakes."

"Yes, Mrs. Baker," I say, feeling the urge to curtsy the same way Jessie did yesterday. I'd probably do it, too, if not for the tray in my hands. "Sorry to have bothered you."

I head into Lenora's room, finding her awake in a triangle of morning sun that gives her a disconcertingly angelic glow. Rather than squint like I did, Lenora appears to luxuriate in the light. She has her head tilted back, mouth slightly open, from which escapes a contented sigh.

The patch of sunlight slowly moves across Lenora's bed as I prop her into a sitting position and feed her oatmeal with her morning pills crushed in. By the time I get her cleaned, changed, and through her circulation exercises, the sunlight's slid off the mattress and onto the floor in a tidy rectangle. Lenora eyes it from her wheelchair as I check her vitals and make sure the bruise on her forearm continues to heal. When that's over, her gaze slips to the typewriter.

She remembers last night.

Part of me thought she'd forgotten.

A bigger part of me wishes she had.

Because whatever she intends to type, I still haven't decided if I want to see it.

Lenora's mind, though, is made up. She moves her gaze from the typewriter to me, giving me a look that's half anxious, half hopeful. One without the other probably wouldn't have been able to sway me. But the combination of the two makes me realize this has nothing to do with what I want.

It's what Lenora wants.

And right now, she wants to type.

I still have no idea why. I can't think of any reason she'd wait so long to talk about that night. If she was innocent, she would have told her story decades ago.

Unless she thought no one would believe her.

Yesterday, Mrs. Baker told me Hope's End was a place where young women are given the benefit of the doubt. That's not true everywhere. It's true hardly anywhere. Perhaps Lenora tried to tell her story all those years ago and no one believed her. Or, worse, no one even listened.

Maybe she thinks I will.

And that I'll believe she's innocent.

Because she thinks the same of me.

That idea—that Lenora's urge to talk stems not from shared guilt but possibly shared innocence—is ultimately why I wheel her to the desk, where the page from last night sits next to the typewriter. Even though I don't remember removing it, I must have. I wrack my brain, trying to recall the events of last night.

Lenora offering to tell me everything.

Finding Mary's belongings.

The wind and the waves and the creaking floorboards.

The more I think about it, the more convinced I am that I left that page in the typewriter.

"Lenora, was someone in here last night?"

She responds with a single-tap no against the wheelchair armrest.

"Are you sure?"

Two taps.

I stare at Lenora. She stares back, looking utterly guileless. If she's lying—and I see no reason why she would be—she hides it well. And even though I'm close to certain I didn't move that page, I'm also aware someone else could have done it while Lenora was asleep. Mrs. Baker slipping in to do some snooping, for instance. Or Jessie coming in bright and early to tidy up.

"It doesn't matter," I say, because it truly doesn't. What matters is that Lenora is about to reveal all. And my job is to help her do it.

In a desk drawer, I find a partial ream of paper and insert a new page into the carriage. I then place Lenora's left hand on the typewriter, wondering if this is the start of something wonderful or something I'll regret.

Or if it will end up being anything at all.

Lenora's fingers twitch atop the keys, almost as if she's unable to keep them still any longer.

I inhale, exhale, nod.

Then we begin.

# THIRTEEN

The thing I remember most--the thing I still have nightmares
about--is when it was all but over.

That's what Lenora typed first, hours ago, when the sun was still
rising over the Atlantic. The full sentence took me by surprise. Until
then, she'd only typed fragments, ignoring rules of capitalization and
punctuation. It took a few confused seconds from me and a few exas-
perated taps from her before I realized she wanted me to press the shift
key while she typed that first capital T. It took even longer for us to
settle into some semblance of a rhythm. We got there eventually,
though.

And that's where we remain, even though the sun has left the sky
and the murky light of dusk now settles over the ocean outside. Lenora
uses her good hand to brush against mine, a signal she needs me to
press the shift key. When the typewriter dings, I hit the return bar,
bringing the carriage back to a new line. She types some more and
nods, the sign I'm to nudge it again and start a new paragraph.

We keep the door closed so no one will bother us. Lenora insisted,
although I don't know why. Other than Archie, who delivered lunch
with a terse rap on the door, I haven't heard anyone moving about the
second floor. And while it feels as if Lenora is an afterthought in her

own estate, it might be because I'm now here. Her caregiver. A role I try to continue while doubling as a secretary.

After each page, I massage Lenora's left hand, make her take a sip of water through a straw, and ask if she wants to continue. The answer is always two eager taps against the typewriter. There's an unmistakable zeal to her typing. She rarely pauses to think about what she's going to write. The story simply crashes onto the page, as if Lenora had written it all in her head years ago and is just now setting it free.

What that story is, I still don't know. Between responding to Lenora's signals, constantly tapping the return bar, and removing and inserting pages into the typewriter, I haven't had much opportunity to see what she's writing.

Lenora brushes my hand, and I press the shift key. Two more presses and two nods later, she finally lays her hand flat against the keys—her signal that another chapter is finished.

I pluck the page from the typewriter and place it facedown atop the sixteen others we've typed today. A staggering amount. Yet if Lenora's tired, she shows no sign of it. She gives me an expectant look, as if waiting for me to insert a fresh page into the carriage.

"We've done enough for today," I say. At least I have. Unlike Lenora, I'm exhausted. Being hunched next to her all day has left me stiff and aching. When I stand up straight, half my joints let out a relieved crackle. "It's almost dinnertime."

The rest of the evening proceeds on schedule. Dinner and pills. Dessert. Circulation exercises, then bath, then bed. Lenora spends all of it lost in thought. Presumably composing what she plans to type tomorrow.

I know the feeling well. When that article about me ran in the newspaper, I called the reporter and demanded he hear my side of the story. The reporter listened with disinterest while I told him my mother's death was suicide, that leaving those pills within her reach was simply an accident, that I would never do anything to hurt her.

"Detective Vick says otherwise," the reporter said, as if the police's word was gospel and I was merely a liar trying to cover my tracks.

That was six months ago, and I still sometimes get the pent-up urge to shout my innocence from every rooftop in town. I can only imagine how Lenora feels. It's been fifty-four years for her. No wonder she doesn't want to stop typing.

After putting her to bed and placing the call button next to her hand, I say, "Do you want me to stay until you fall asleep?"

Lenora taps twice on the bedspread.

I nod. "Then I'll stay."

She closes her eyes and I gather the typed pages and take them to the divan. As Lenora's breathing deepens with sleep, I begin to read what she typed. Despite seeing snippets all day, I'm surprised by the quality of her writing. I assumed the prose would be choppy and weak—a string of half sentences not unlike the typed responses she's given me. Instead, Lenora is a natural storyteller. Her writing is clear and unfussy, while retaining a distinctive voice. From the very first line, I'm hooked.

By the time I'm near the end, though, my surprise has curved into shock.

Now I know what happened to the knife used to kill Winston and Evangeline Hope.

Lenora tossed it into the ocean.

That act—plus the fact that her nightgown was covered in blood—makes her look more guilty than ever.

It doesn't help that she declares herself both good and evil. Now, some of that could be attributed to her home life, which was anything but happy. An addict mother. A philandering father. A sister she seemed to have nothing in common with. No wonder Lenora longed for escape and the attention of someone of the opposite sex. I know that feeling all too well, even now in my thirties. It's why I started sleeping with Kenny, after all. But Lenora was so young, so inexperienced. When you're that age, full of raging emotions and, yes, desire, it's very possible Lenora saw those natural feelings as wicked—or worse.

Yet that doesn't explain the bloody nightgown.

Or getting rid of the weapon that killed her parents.

Or why she fetched a rope as her sister's screams rang through the house.

I can't stop thinking about all of that as I read the last three sentences Lenora typed today.

> But here's the thing--I wasn't a good girl.
> Not in the least.
> You'll see for yourself very soon.

I lower the pages and look to the bed, where Lenora lies fast asleep. As I watch her, a sense of unease creeps over me.

I'd assumed she wanted to tell her story in an attempt to finally clear her name. And that she chose me to help because she saw us as kindred spirits. One falsely accused woman telling her story to another, working together to declare her innocence.

Now I fear it's the opposite.

Lenora didn't pick me because she thinks I'm innocent.

She did it because she thinks I'm guilty.

And what we've been typing today isn't an attempt to clear her name.

It's a confession.

# FOURTEEN

I put the pages in the lockbox under my bed, pretending I'm not hiding them, when that's exactly what I'm doing. Secreting them away beneath Lenora's rolling, rattling pill bottles because I don't want anyone else to find them. But it's not Lenora I'm worried about as I lock the box and slide it back under the bed. My concern is that having Lenora Hope's partial confession in my possession will somehow make me look equally bad.

Guilt by association.

I'm dropping the lockbox key into the nightstand drawer when I hear a series of noises from above and outside.

A crack, a scrape, a clatter on the terrace.

I rush to the window, struggling to see what it was. It's dark outside, and the lights inside the bedroom merely reflect my worried, tired face onto the window's glass.

Thinking whatever I just heard could be related to the noises coming from Lenora's room last night, I decide to investigate. I whisk out of my room and take the service stairs to the kitchen. From there, I move through the dining room on my way to the terrace. As soon as I step outside, something crunches beneath my feet.

A slate shingle recently fallen from the roof.

That's at least one mystery noise explained.

A dozen more shingles litter the terrace, many broken into a hundred pieces, a few still miraculously intact. I step over and around them on my way to the terrace railing. A frigid breeze comes off the ocean in steady, brine-scented puffs. I close my eyes and lean into it, enjoying the chill. It feels good after spending so much time inside the stuffy confines of Hope's End. Lenora doesn't know what she's missing.

The terrace runs the length of the entire mansion, ending on both sides with four short steps. The ones on the left descend to a flagstone patio surrounding an empty swimming pool. On the right, the steps lead to a swath of lawn. On the other side of it sits a one-story stone cottage so quaint and tidy it could have been plucked from a storybook. Warm light glows from a window beside the arched door.

Light from another window flicks on above and behind me, in the mansion itself. It casts a slanted rectangle of brightness across the terrace. In that patch of light, a curl of metal glints among the shards of broken tile.

I pick it up and hold it to the light. At first, I think it could be a paper clip bent into an oblong ring. But it's much thicker than a paper clip. Sturdier, too. It takes some force to bend it further. Both ends are curved toward each other, one more so than the other, making me deduce it was a hook of some kind that either broke or fell off. Maybe it's what caused the shingles to drop from the roof.

I turn back to the lit window to scan the roof one story above it. Craning my neck, I try to see where it is in relation to my room. Two doors down, it looks like. On the other side of Lenora's room.

Mrs. Baker.

I take a few backward steps, angling for a better glimpse inside the room. I can make out frilly curtains, a hint of purple floral wallpaper, a shadow stretching across the ceiling.

Something else then catches my eye.

To the right of the lit window, in Lenora's room.

There, framed in the darkened window, is a gray blur.

I gasp, watching as the blur passes the window and disappears. I can't make out what it is. The room is dark and the movement too brief. All I know is that I'm certain someone is walking around Lenora's bedroom.

I keep moving backward, eyes fixed on the window, hoping for another glimpse of whoever it is. I'm so focused on Lenora's room that I stop paying attention to the slate shingles on the terrace. I trip on one and stumble backward into the railing, which hits the small of my back and throws me off-balance.

The twist of metal flies from my fingers as I reel wildly.

Arms flailing.

Heart jittering.

My shoulders and head lean beyond the railing, out over the waves crashing far below. For a second, the chasm at my back feels like it's reaching up, as if trying to yank me over the edge and into its depths.

I manage to lunge to the side, flipping over until my stomach is pressed against the railing and I'm staring straight down the cliffside. Fifty feet below is the Atlantic, its waves collapsing onto the shore at the base of the cliff. A narrow strip of rock-studded sand sits between the cliff and the water, glowing white in the moonlight. I'd find it lovely if not for the fact that one wrong move would have sent me crashing into it.

On my right, I hear the swish of footsteps across the dew-dusted lawn. Carter's voice cuts through the night. "Mary?"

I turn to see him already halfway across the lawn and coming closer. He halts when he realizes it's me.

"Sorry." He pauses, befuddled, like he's literally just seen a ghost. "Are you okay?"

"I think so," I huff, still breathless from my near miss.

Carter resumes his approach, reaching the end of the lawn and hopping up the steps onto the terrace. "For a second there, I thought you were going to topple over the railing."

"So did I."

I step away from the railing on rubbery legs. It's the same feeling I had when I was first hit with the tilt on the second floor of Hope's End. Which makes sense, seeing how the terrace is likely also slanted toward the sea. The thought makes me take another wobbling backward step.

Carter rushes to my side to prop me up. "Let's sit you down for a few minutes."

"I'm fine," I say. "Really."

"You don't look fine."

Instead of leading me back into the mansion, Carter guides me down the steps and across the lawn to the stone cottage. Its open door spills golden light across the grass.

"Do you live here?" I say.

"I do indeed. It's not much, but it's home."

"Why don't you stay in the main house?"

"Because I'm the groundskeeper and this is the groundskeeper's cottage," Carter says. "Besides, it's nicer than that crooked old mansion. Cozy."

When he ushers me inside, I see what he means. The cottage, while not large, has an undeniable charm. A single room divided into two areas—kitchen and bedroom, with a small closed-off bathroom in the corner—there's a rustic feel to the place. Exposed beams run across the ceiling, and diamond-pane windows face the ocean. Throw pillows on the couch and neatly made bed add splashes of color, while Audubon prints of native seabirds brighten the walls.

Carter sits me down at a woodblock dining table big enough for only two people. My chair faces a boxy black-and-white TV on the kitchen counter, which broadcasts Game One of the World Series. Orioles versus the Phillies. Carter lowers the volume before opening a nearby cupboard.

"I have it on for background noise," he says. "I'll care about the World Series when the Red Sox are in it. Which will be never."

From the cupboard, he produces two rocks glasses, into which he pours an inch of whiskey. One glass is placed on the table in front of me. He holds the other as he leans against the counter.

"Drink up," he says. "It'll calm your nerves."

"I don't think Mrs. Baker would approve."

"Mrs. Baker probably has three glasses of Chardonnay under her belt and is now working on number four."

"Oh." I stare into my glass, surprised. I never would have pegged Mrs. Baker as someone with a drinking problem. She seems so . . . serious. It makes me wonder if she was that way before arriving at Hope's End or if the place slowly drove her to drink. "I didn't know."

"Of course you didn't. You just got here. But give it enough time and you'll know all our secrets."

I allow myself a tiny sip of whiskey. Carter is right. Its amber warmth instantly calms me. "Anything else I should know about Mrs. Baker?"

Carter leaves the counter and approaches the table, turning the remaining chair around so he can straddle it, his arms folded across the backrest. Inside and in the light, I notice things about him that I missed earlier. Like the small cleft in his chin barely visible beneath his beard. Or the way he smells freshly showered. The scents of soap and shampoo rise off his skin.

"Such as?" he says.

"Her first name, for starters."

"Beats me. I have no clue. What's your guess?"

"Morticia," I say. "Or Cruella."

Carter, caught mid-sip, snort laughs. "Maybe Archie knows, since he's been here as long as she has."

"Do you think they're a couple?" I say.

"I doubt it. From what I can tell, they barely speak to each other."

"Then why do you think they've stayed here this long? Archie told me he's been here almost sixty years, and Mrs. Baker left but eventually came back. I assume both of them could have gotten jobs anywhere."

"I think the situation is more complicated than that," Carter says. "They knew Lenora before the murders. And the truth is, she'd be helpless without them. I think they know that, which might explain why they've been here so long."

"And how long have you been here?"

"Ah, now you're interested in *my* secrets," Carter says with a smile that could be considered flirtatious but is more likely out of politeness. No one has flirted with me for a very long time. Kenny certainly didn't. He skipped the flirting and got straight to the point. Sadly, it worked.

"You said I'll find out eventually," I say, trying a little weak flirting myself. I blame the attempt on the whiskey. "You might as well tell me now."

"*My* secret is that I'm not a groundskeeper. At least I wasn't until I took this job."

"What were you?"

"A bartender." Carter raises his glass, takes a sip. "That feels like a lifetime ago, even though it's only been a year. One of my regulars was the former groundskeeper here. When he retired, he suggested I be his replacement. Even put in a good word for me."

"That seems like quite a leap, from bartender to groundskeeper."

"Oh, it was. My guess is he thought I was trustworthy, which is necessary for a place like Hope's End. Mrs. Baker agreed, and now here I am."

A muffled roar drifts from the TV. On the tiny screen, someone from the Phillies circles the bases after hitting a home run. Carter reaches for the television and switches it off.

"And you really do like it here?" I say.

Carter spreads his arms wide. "I've got my own place, and it comes with a view of the ocean. Not many people can say that. Sure, the job's a bit much for just me, but then again, Hope's End doesn't get too many visitors, so there's no need to impress anyone. What's not to like?"

"Um, the fact that three people were murdered here. And that there are still bloodstains in the carpet."

"I see you've taken the murder tour."

"Jessie showed me around last night," I say with a nod.

"Please don't tell me you're now thinking of running away like Mary did."

"How well do you know her?"

"Enough to think you were her," Carter says.

I look down at my uniform, which had once been worn by Mary. The fact that I can fit into it means we're about the same size and height. No wonder Carter mistook me for her in the dark.

"It must have been strange thinking she'd suddenly come back."

"Not as strange as the way she left," Carter says. "No notice or warning. One day, Mary was simply gone. It was a surprise. I'd assumed she was happy here."

"Jessie also said she was surprised."

"She and Mary were pretty close. I, on the other hand, mostly keep to myself. Don't get me wrong. Mary and I were friends. The truth is, I didn't see much of her. I live here. She stayed in the mansion, spending most of her time with Lenora. So we didn't exactly hang out. Most of the time, we'd chat on the terrace in the evenings. Every time I spotted her uniform, I'd come out and say hi."

"Do you think Lenora had something to do with why she left?" I say. "That Mary was, I don't know, frightened of her somehow?"

"It sounds like you think Lenora's guilty," Carter says.

I stare into my drink, contemplating my reflection wobbling atop the amber liquid. Fitting, for I feel wobbly myself. My opinion of Lenora has shifted so much in the past two days that I no longer know how I feel.

"It sounds like you think she isn't. So who do you think did it? Winston Hope or the painter?"

"Neither," Carter says. "I think it was Ricardo Mayhew."

I look up from the whiskey, confused. "Who?"

"The groundskeeper at the time. He and his wife were living in this cottage when the murders occurred. She wasn't here. She worked as a kitchen maid and was given the night off with the rest of the servants. She went into town and saw a movie. Ricardo, though, stayed behind."

"Did the police know this?"

"They did," Carter says. "Back in 1929 it was widely suspected that not every member of the household staff left for the night."

"How do *you* know this?"

"From my predecessor. I poured the drinks, and he told me stories about this place. Another reason I took the job. After hearing so much about Hope's End, I wanted to experience it for myself."

"So this groundskeeper—"

"Ricardo," Carter interjects.

I nod. "Right. Ricardo. He stayed behind and did . . . what?"

"No one knows."

"The police didn't question him after the murders?"

"They couldn't. Ricardo Mayhew was gone. After that night, he was never seen again."

Carter eyes me over his glass, waiting for my reaction. I respond appropriately, my jaw dropping in surprise.

"And his wife—"

"Berniece."

The name jars my memory. Lenora mentioned her in passing. Berniece was the kitchen maid who wished her a half-hearted happy birthday.

"She never saw him again, either?"

"Nope."

"And she had no idea where he went or what happened to him?"

"None," Carter says. "She's still around, though. Most folks say she never left town because she's waiting for her husband to return. It's more likely the poor woman has nowhere else to go."

"So you think Ricardo Mayhew murdered the rest of the Hope family and then ran?"

"That's my guess. Short of Lenora killing them, it's the only thing that makes sense."

"But why would the groundskeeper want to kill Winston Hope and his family?"

"I don't know," Carter says. "Why would Lenora?"

A fair point. One I'm still trying to understand myself. But Carter didn't just spend the entire day helping her type. He didn't read about the bloody nightgown. Or Lenora tossing a knife into the ocean. Or leaving the terrace to get rope that, I assume, was later tightened around her sister's neck.

And even though I want to tell him all those things, I don't. It seems wrong to mention anything until I learn the whole story. Only then will I spill any details. I think that's what Lenora ultimately wants—for me to be the voice she doesn't have. Even if what I'm saying is her long-delayed confession.

"If you're right—and that's a very big if—it still doesn't make sense. Why wouldn't Lenora say anything? If Ricardo killed her parents and her sister, why wouldn't she tell that to the police?"

Or to me, for that matter. So far, she hasn't once typed the name Ricardo Mayhew. If she thought he did it, why wasn't that the first thing she wrote? Instead, she began when, to use her phrasing, it was all but over.

"Maybe she didn't know," Carter suggests.

But Lenora *did* know her parents were dead. She told me so. They were dead and her nightgown was bloody and she threw the knife over the terrace railing despite knowing it was evidence of two brutal crimes. Why would she do that if she wasn't the one who had used it?

I finish my drink, my thoughts rattling like the ice in my now-empty glass. In that tumbling mental chaos, a new theory takes shape. One I can't share with Carter.

Not just yet.

"I need to go," I say, standing suddenly. "Thanks for the drink."

Carter watches in confusion as I give a quick wave goodbye, leave the cottage, and cross the damp lawn. On the terrace, I watch for shingles underfoot and steer clear of the railing. Only when I'm under Lenora's window do I risk an upward glance. Although her room is still dark and nothing appears at the window, I can't stop thinking of Lenora lying within, wide awake and mentally repeating a single line from the rhyme I've known since grade school.

*"It wasn't me," Lenora said*

Maybe that part of the rhyme is true.

But I suspect there's more to the story than Lenora is letting on—then or now.

Inside the house, I quickly climb the service stairs. On the second floor, I begin to sway, the mansion's tilt made worse by the whiskey. Instead of just one drink, it feels like I've had four, which explains why I brazenly lurch into Lenora's room.

I switch on the bedside lamp, startling her awake.

Or maybe Lenora's only pretending to be startled. I can't shake the sense that she was already awake—and that she knew I'd be coming. Before she saw it was me storming into the room, her left hand made no move to press the call button. Then there's the intrigued look in her eyes. While the rest of her face retains a shocked, questioning scrunch, they glisten with satisfaction.

"I want you to tell me about Ricardo Mayhew," I say.

I spent ten minutes weeping in the ballroom before running through the house, looking for Archie. He'd know what to say to make me feel better. He always did. But Archie had made himself scarce recently. My only glimpse of him today was as I passed through the kitchen before dinner, and even then I didn't dare say anything to him. My sister and I were forbidden from socializing with the staff and vice versa, but that had done nothing to stop me and Archie from becoming best friends.

Unable to locate Archie, I found myself outside on the terrace. Even though it was technically spring, winter's grip remained tight, making the night air bracingly cold. I didn't mind, though. I was just happy to be anywhere but inside that awful, awful house.

I climbed atop the railing. Another thing I was told not to do but did anyway, mostly because the railing was so low. If my father hadn't wanted me to climb on it, then he should have made it higher. Sitting there, balanced precariously, I stared down at the water below. Moonlight sparkled on the ocean swells and the whitecaps glowed in the night. It was so beautiful that, just for a moment, I considered leaping off the railing to join them.

It seemed a better alternative than life at Hope's End.

I was young and bursting with yearning. For love. For adventure. For life. Yet none of that awaited me here, in a place where my mother medicated herself into a stupor, my father openly cheated with the maids, and my sister pretended nothing was wrong. Was this how I was going to spend the rest of my life?

If that was the case, I'd rather end it now. And what a fitting end it would be, making the day of my birth also the day of my death.

Before I could entertain the notion further, a voice spoke up from behind me.

"Careful. If you fell to your death, this place would have nothing worth looking at."

I whirled around, almost losing my balance in the process. I teetered on the railing a moment, suddenly terrified I was about to fall. A second earlier, I'd been thinking of ending it all. Now I wanted nothing more than to live--if only to chastise my unknown companion for spying on me.

After righting myself, I hopped off the railing. At the same time, the source of the voice crept from the shadows along the side of the mansion. I knew who he was because I'd heard Berniece mention him in the kitchen and eavesdropped on the maids talking about how handsome he was.

And indeed he was handsome. Wearing just work pants and a cotton undershirt, he had a primal look to him. Strong and slightly brutish. Rather than slick his hair back with pomade like most men did at the time, he let it grow wild and unruly. He swiped a lock of hair from his eyes and stared at me in a way that can only be described as wolfish. A smile played across his lips, as if he knew every wicked thought I'd had earlier that day.

"You weren't really going to jump, were you?" he said.

I looked his way, even though I'd been trying not to. I didn't want to stare, for I knew it would make him think I considered him worthy of staring at, which he very much was. But his remark forced me to face him head-on. While completely true, it also smacked of impropriety.

"I don't need to explain myself. Especially to someone like you."

"You're right," he said. "You don't. But I am curious why someone with your life would even risk death by climbing up on that railing."

I turned back to the ocean, refusing to look at him a moment longer. "You know nothing about my life."

"I'm all ears." He joined me at the railing, focusing his attention solely on me, as if he couldn't wait to hear what I had to say. "Tell me what's wrong."

"Everything."

He let out a low whistle. "That sounds quite serious."

"Do my problems amuse you?" I asked.

"Not at all, Miss Hope. But surely not everything is terrible."

"This house is," I said. "It's downright awful."

He turned around and gazed up at the glittering mansion behind us. "It looks quite nice to me."

"It's not, I can assure you," I replied. "Honestly, I would kill to leave this place."

He moved closer until we were mere inches apart. So close I felt the heat coming off his skin, which in turn gave me delicious chills.

"We haven't been properly introduced," he said, holding out a hand. "I'm Ricky."

# FIFTEEN

**Ricky**

Lenora types the name with such force that the letters scar the page as if they've been applied with a branding iron. Now she stares up at me, defiant and irritated. Her eyes, narrowed like a cartoon villain's, seem to ask if I'm satisfied.

I'm not, despite the chapter she just banged out in the middle of the night and the questions she tapped answers to before the typing began. The first one, posed immediately after I burst into her room, was "Did you know him, Lenora?"

She replied with taps in the affirmative against the bedspread.

"Do you know what happened to him?"

A single tap that time. No.

"Did Ricardo do it?"

Carter was right. Short of her being the culprit, it was the only explanation that made sense. Ricardo was here that night. Then he vanished—most likely after killing Winston and Evangeline Hope. And I think Lenora either knew this or suspected it.

Lenora turned away from me and gazed across the room at the typewriter. I knew that look well enough by then to march to the desk, put a fresh sheet of paper in the typewriter, and carry it to the bed.

Lenora then began to type, the thwack of the keystrokes loud enough to echo through the nighttime quiet of her bedroom.

i cant tell you yet

"Why not?"

because i need to do it in order

I repeated my question: "Why?"

She nodded, signaling me to hit the typewriter's return bar.

so youll understand what happened

Another nod.

and how

A third nod.

and why

"Or you could just type who did it now," I said hopefully. "And help me understand later."

A hint of a smile played across Lenora's lips. She was, I realized, enjoying this. Teasing out her story bit by tantalizing bit. Keeping me on edge.

She placed her hand flat atop the keys. Usually a sign that a chapter was over. In this case, it meant she wanted a fresh page. I obliged, fetching a few sheets of paper from the desk and rolling one into the typewriter.

A new chapter was about to start.

Lenora and I spent the next two hours typing. As time passed—and midnight came and went—the mood of the room subtly began to change. It got colder. Not all at once. Slowly. The chill crept in the same way winter does after a glorious fall. By the time Lenora started typing the third page, I was shivering from cold.

Worse was the sense halfway through her writing that we weren't alone, even though no one else was in the room with us. I know because I began to check, my gaze darting to the closed door and the dim corners where light from the bedside lamp couldn't reach.

No one else was there.

Just us.

Yet I couldn't shake the sense that someone else was nearby, watching us. Even as Lenora typed about meeting a handsome stranger on the terrace, my thoughts drifted to what Jessie had told me on the murder tour.

That Mary claimed to have seen the ghost of Virginia Hope roaming the second floor.

That she was scared of this place.

That it was why she fled.

*Hope's End isn't a normal house. There's a darkness here. I can feel it. Mary did.*

Even though Jessie had said it to set up her prank in the ballroom, I wondered if maybe there was some truth behind it. In my experience, most lies contain at least some kernel of truth.

Because I felt the darkness, too.

And I didn't like it one bit.

Lenora slapped my hand then, yanking me from my thoughts while also indicating that I needed to press the shift key. I did and said, "Do you feel that? Like someone else is here?"

She tapped no and resumed typing as I continued to feel the gaze of unseen eyes watching us and the creeping chill that got stronger and stronger until that final word was embedded onto the page.

Ricky.

The room gets warmer the moment Lenora types it. The chill I'd felt vanishes in an instant, as does the feeling that someone else is here, hiding and watching. Now the only person watching is Lenora, who continues to stare at me, asking without words if what she's just typed is enough.

"For now, yes," I say as I return the typewriter to the desk, the page in the carriage flapping as I go.

I still don't know half of what happened before, during, or after her parents' murders, but Lenora doesn't need to type it all out tonight. What she did write was breathless enough for me to infer several key facts.

For instance, I now think I know why Lenora got rid of the murder weapon. It's the same reason she told the police so little about that night.

She was trying to protect someone.

Why she did it also seems clear.

Eight months before the murders, Lenora had fallen in love with Ricardo Mayhew.

# SIXTEEN

I wake with a scream caught in my throat. Swallowing hard, I gulp it down before it can be released into the darkened bedroom. Then I sit up and do a little shimmy, trying to shake off another humdinger of a nightmare that prompted the near scream.

My mother again.

Standing over my sleeping form.

Stuffing pills into my mouth until I begin to choke.

The nightmare was so vivid that I shove an index finger into my mouth, feeling for pills that couldn't possibly be there.

That's when I hear it.

A creak.

The same kind I heard last night, coming from the same location.

Lenora's room.

The sound of a second creak pulls me out of bed. All thoughts of the nightmare I'd just had evaporate as I tiptoe to the door between our rooms. Now I'm only concerned about one thing: discovering what the hell is making those noises.

Standing at the door, I look down at my feet. The thin strip of moonlight coming from under the door runs across the floor, an inch from my toes.

A shadow joins it.

Eclipsing the moonlight as it passes the other side of the door.

I gasp, twist the doorknob, and throw open the door.

There's no one else in Lenora's room. Just her, flat-backed and fast asleep in her bed.

I think of the gray blur I saw at her window earlier, momentarily forgotten in the events that followed. Me almost tumbling over the terrace railing. The long talk with Carter. An even longer typing session with Lenora. But I'm certain someone was moving around inside this room, then and now.

I approach the bed and kneel by Lenora's side, checking to see if she really is asleep and not just pretending like I suspect she was when I burst into the room hours earlier. I wave my hand in front of her face, eliciting no reaction. Definitely no flinch signaling she's aware I'm doing it. I then touch her left wrist to check her pulse. It's slow, steady.

"Lenora?" I whisper anyway. "Was that you?"

She doesn't answer me, of course. She can't. Just like she can't walk. Even if she could, Lenora is seventy-one. There's no way she'd be fast enough to hop into bed as soon as I opened the door. A person half her age wouldn't be able to do that.

Since it wasn't Lenora and there's no one else in the room, I know I should blame my imagination. It's late, I'm exhausted, and it's possible the house is messing with my mind. But those noises were real. So were the shadow at the door and the blur at the window.

I didn't imagine them.

I heard them and saw them and know there must be a logical reason for them.

*It will all make sense in the morning.*

That's something else my mother used to tell me, back when I was struggling to deal with all the pain and pressure of adolescence. Go to bed. Get a good night's sleep. It will all make sense in the morning. Usually, she was right. Even when things still didn't completely make sense, I often felt better in the morning.

This time, though, the advice is dead wrong.

Nothing makes sense when I wake a few hours later with the rising sun poking my retinas and the mattress slid a few inches lower than when I went to sleep. Exhaustion grips me as I get out of bed and start my morning routine.

Showering in a tilted tub.

Brushing my teeth over a tilted sink.

Putting on a uniform that belonged to someone who fled this place.

Before going downstairs, I look in on Lenora, pausing at the door before throwing it open. Like a suspicious lover. Or a distrustful father. Trying to catch her in the act. Of what, I have no idea. Other than typing, she mostly just observes, which is what she does now, giving me a quizzical look from the bed.

The first thing I do is check the desk.

The typewriter is exactly where I placed it during the night.

The page in the carriage, however, sits next to it, typed side up, as if someone had been reading it.

But unlike yesterday, I'm certain I left that paper in the typewriter. I remember seeing the page flutter as I carried the typewriter back to the desk.

I turn to Lenora. "Someone was in here during the night. I'm right, aren't I?"

She gives me another one of those vague nods that I'm still learning to interpret. This time, I again know it's to bring the typewriter to the bed. After I do, I place her hand on the keys and let her answer.

**you didnt sleep well**

I have trouble discerning her tone. Without punctuation, it looks like a statement, meaning Lenora knows I didn't sleep well. With a question mark—missing because it requires me to press the shift key—it becomes more innocent. A query, likely prompted by the dark circles under my eyes.

Lenora gazes at me, waiting for an answer. Her expression—expectant and confused—tells me it's the latter.

"I didn't," I say.

She starts moving her hand across the keyboard again, eventually typing out a familiar word.

**a humdinger**

This time, I can tell it's a question by Lenora's brows, which arch inquisitively. I nod my head and smile.

"Yes. But even before that, I couldn't sleep."

More typing.

**the wind**

Still more typing.

**makes strange noises**

I take a step back and give Lenora a look. "How do you know I heard noises?"

*Because she caused them.*

The thought pushes into my brain like a drill bit. Sudden, unnerving, and unwanted.

Also, ridiculous.

No, it was someone else.

And Lenora's lying to me.

Probably not for the first time.

It occurs to me that much of what she's typed so far could be, if not a lie, then at least a bending of the truth. Shaping the story in a way that suits her best. I did it myself when talking to Mrs. Baker upon my arrival. I could have said it was my mother who overdosed on pills. Instead, I told her it was merely a patient. Not a lie, exactly, but also not the full truth. Not by a long shot. I suspect Lenora's been doing the same.

And I'm getting tired of it.

"I know someone was in here last night," I say. "Now tell me who it was or no more typing. And certainly no more telling your story."

Lenora studies me, trying to decide if I'm bluffing. Good luck with that. *I* don't even know how serious I am. While I suspect I'm as eager to hear the full story as she is to write it, I'm also hesitant. Again, it might not be the whole truth. And if it is, I might not want to know it.

Apparently, I look more decisive than I feel, because Lenora starts typing again.

**someones been here**

I enjoy a moment of vindication. I knew it wasn't my imagination! "But not just last night, right? The night before as well."

**many nights**

Jolted with alarm, I say, "Then who is it? Who's been in your room?"

Still hesitant, Lenora sizes me up again. Then she resumes typing with pronounced reluctance. It takes her a full minute to press eight keys. When she's done, I rip the page from the typewriter. Marking the white paper in ink as black as night is a single name.

**virginia**

# SEVENTEEN

Muzak squawks from the kitchen telephone as I wait for Mr. Gurlain to pick up. It's been five minutes since he put me on hold. Long enough for a queasy rendition of a Captain & Tennille song to be replaced by an even worse cover of "You Don't Bring Me Flowers." I wait, receiver at my ear, as I look around the empty kitchen, hoping no one enters while I'm here. I don't want to explain why I've left Lenora alone in her wheelchair while I make a phone call. I especially don't want to talk about the reason for the call. Telling it to Mr. Gurlain is going to be hard enough.

When he gets on the line, blessedly cutting off the Muzak, he sounds nervous. I assume he's thinking about the morning I found my mother dead, which was the last time he got an urgent phone call from me.

"Is something wrong?" he says.

"No. Well, yes." I inhale, hold the breath in my chest, exhale. "I'm calling to ask for a new assignment."

"I just gave you a new assignment," Mr. Gurlain says.

"I'd like a different one," I say, tacking on a polite "please."

"It's only been a few days, Kit."

"I know. I just—"

My voice seizes up. I have no idea what to say. That I'm afraid? I'm not. Fear involves certainty. You know what you're afraid of. I'm the opposite. Uncertain and unnerved. And who can blame me? I'm in a slanted mansion where three people were murdered. There are blood-stains on the Grand Stairs and a ballroom where a dead girl swung from the chandelier. A dead girl who, apparently, roams my patient's bedroom at night.

I don't believe in ghosts.

I absolutely do not think that what I heard was the spirit of Virginia Hope.

But something's not right at Hope's End. Obviously. And it might have frightened Mary enough to make her leave in the middle of the night without taking anything with her. I don't want to stick around and wait to see if I'll eventually get that desperate. I'd rather leave now, in broad daylight, taking all my belongings with me.

"I don't like it here," I finally say. "I told you I wasn't comfortable working in this house."

"And I told you there wasn't a choice," Mr. Gurlain says.

"But there are other caregivers available. I saw their names on the assignment board. Can't you send one of them here and put me some-where else? It doesn't have to be immediately. I can wait a week or two until another assignment becomes available."

That last bit is a stretch. I might not have enough money to last me a few weeks. But Mr. Gurlain doesn't need to know that. He just needs to put me somewhere else—something he doesn't seem too in-clined to do.

"We went over this, Kit," Mr. Gurlain says with a sigh. "I make—"

"The assignments and the caregivers follow them. Yes, I know. I was just hoping you would consider making a onetime exception."

"I can't," Mr. Gurlain says without giving it a moment of thought. "Again, you're welcome to leave your assignment. But if you do, it means you're leaving my employ for good. I've already given you a onetime exception. Most other agencies would have fired you six months ago. Take it or leave it."

I have no choice but to take it. Yes, I could quit on the spot or, like Mary, leave in the middle of the night, but the only person I'd be hurting is myself. I have next to no money and no job prospects. I'm not even sure I have a house to return to. Quitting would make those problems worse.

In short, I'm stuck at Hope's End.

"I understand," I say, talking quickly so Mr. Gurlain can't tell I'm on the verge of tears. "Sorry to have bothered you."

Resigned to my fate, I hang up and look around the massive, empty kitchen inside this massive, empty house.

How the hell did I get here?

I think about all the ways my life could have been different—and when everything went wrong. Was it when my mother got sick? Or was it before that? When I got fired from the typing pool and decided to become a caregiver, for instance? Or when, bored by school, I realized I'd never amount to very much and decided not to try? Maybe I was set on this path the first time I heard the chant about Lenora.

*At seventeen, Lenora Hope . . .*

There's one blueberry muffin left over from breakfast, sitting in a basket on the counter. I grab it, taking a bite as I move through the dining room and out onto the terrace. Outside is brisk but bright—the perfect weather for clearing my mind. A necessity after my call with Mr. Gurlain. The sun, wind, and salty air combine to calm me down, make me start thinking rationally again.

Now that it's clear I'm stuck here, I need to focus on how to get myself unstuck.

The answer is obvious: do my job.

Collect a paycheck, save enough to get as far away from here as possible, start over.

It also means I need to follow through on my threat to Lenora if she didn't tell me who was in her room.

No more typing.

No more story.

I tell myself it's probably all lies anyway. If Lenora can't be honest with me about who's been creeping around her room, then she's certainly not going to tell me the truth about the night her family was murdered. It all leaves me feeling duped, not to mention stupid, for ever trusting her to be honest.

I decide the next thing to do is figure out what's been causing the noises in Lenora's room. There has to be a logical explanation for them. Same with the shadow that slid past the door and the blur I saw at the window.

Since Archie, Mrs. Baker, and even Lenora suggested the wind, that makes it the likeliest culprit. They know Hope's End better than I do. Similarly, the blur at the window could have been a trick of the moonlight on the glass. As for the shadow at the door, it might have been caused by clouds scudding in front of the moon, momentarily blocking its light. A plane or large bird could have done the same thing. Considering the sad state of the house, it's even more likely that a loose shutter or a broken drainpipe was the cause.

I turn around and face the back of the mansion, its three formidable stories looming over me. Taking care not to lose my balance, I lean against the railing and scan the exterior. Nothing appears to be out of place around Lenora's windows. There's certainly no shutter swinging in the breeze or slanted drainpipe bobbing from the roofline.

But there are plenty of birds. Seagulls whirl overhead before diving to the water, lured by sand crabs left exposed by low tide. I rotate and look down at the strip of sand between the water and base of the cliff. Smooth waves calmly collapse against the shore, pushing foamy water around the rocks jutting from the sand.

I lean forward and look closer, realizing I'm mistaken.

Those aren't rocks rising out of the wet sand.

They're something else.

A hand.

A foot.

A head.

Humped beneath the sand is the corpse they're attached to.

And even before I begin to scream, I know with dreadful certainty that I'm looking at the body of Mary Milton.

# EIGHTEEN

I'm in the sunroom, although there's no sun to be found. Outside, the sky is streaked with dark clouds that rolled in not long after I found Mary's body. It makes everything gray and oppressive, as if the gathering storm is pressing against the house, trying to force its way in. Joining me in this gloom is the last person I want to see.

Detective Vick.

He sits in the same dusty love seat Mrs. Baker occupied the day I arrived, looking rumpled and not pleased to be here. Or with me. The feeling is mutual. I tense up in his presence. An ingrained reaction. The result is a clash of emotions—disbelief, sorrow, and bone-deep unease that Detective Vick has come not to ask about Mary but to finally arrest me.

"Well, Kit," he says, "I sure am surprised to see you."

I yank the hem of my uniform, trying to tug it an inch or so closer to my knees. I'm cold, thanks to a chill that's clung to me since the moment I realized I was looking at Mary Milton's corpse. It's shock, I know, exacerbated by the fact that I'm talking to the man who wanted to throw me in jail.

"Surprised I'm at Hope's End?" I say. "Or surprised I'm still allowed to work after you accused me of murder?"

The detective sighs. "This doesn't need to be contentious, Kit. I'm just trying to figure out what happened."

"You didn't seem too interested in that the last time we talked."

"I'll let that slide," Detective Vick says. "You're understandably distressed."

I am. I'm afraid to even blink out of fear the image of Mary's corpse poking from the sand will be projected onto the backs of my eyelids. Making it worse is the realization that I spotted her body last night, after I almost tumbled over the terrace railing.

I looked down and saw dark objects in the sand that I thought were rocks but now know was Mary. And I can't stop thinking about how long she'd been there—and how, had I understood what I was looking at, I could have at least spared her a few more hours of indignity. Knowing that I didn't leaves me so sad and guilty I can barely catch my breath.

But I refuse to let Detective Vick see any of that. I'll sprint from this room and never come back before that happens.

"Just ask me your questions," I say.

"What's your job here at Hope's End?"

Even though my uniform and history should give it away, I provide an answer. "I'm a caregiver."

"And who is it you care for?"

I hesitate, not wanting to tell him because I know the kind of reaction it'll bring. An ironic smirk, probably. Detective Vick might even make a crack about the appropriateness of a killer caring for a killer.

"Lenora Hope," I finally say.

To the detective's credit, there's no smirk. But I do notice the slight lift of his brows, indicating surprise.

"How long have you been caring for her?"

"This is my third day."

The detective's brows rise again, higher this time, as he says, "Quite an eventful first week on the job."

The understatement of the year, considering everything else I've experienced since arriving at Hope's End.

"You're the one who first saw the body, correct?"

I give a quick nod, again trying not to picture Mary mostly covered by sand that had been packed over her for more than a week. She might have been completely buried in a few more days. Maybe less. I know it's a good thing she was found before it was too late, even though I deeply wish it wasn't me who did it.

"Walk me through it," Detective Vick says.

I do, quickly recounting being on the terrace, noticing the seagulls, looking over the edge of the cliff, and seeing Mary.

"Why were you out there in the first place?"

It feels like a trick question, even though I know it's not. But to answer it honestly would mean talking about strange noises and shadows moving around Lenora's room. There's no way I'm going to go there. Instead, I give a not entirely dishonest reply.

"Just getting some fresh air."

I look out the row of windows that face the ocean. Outside, a pair of cops mill about the terrace. One of them paces back and forth, eyes aimed at the ground. The other keeps peering over the railing at the water below, even though Mary's corpse was recovered more than two hours ago. Because of the steepness of the cliff, the police needed a boat to reach it. A small army of officers then stormed the narrow beach and dug Mary out before the tide rolled in again.

"What are they looking for?"

"Anything that might give us an idea of what happened," Detective Vick says.

"But Mary fell, right?"

I continue to eye the terrace railing, thinking about how I almost tumbled over it last night. The raw panic of that moment remains fresh in my memory. First surprise, then fumbling, then pure fear. I imagine the same thing happening to Mary. A trip. A slip. A long, terrifying fall. It makes me wince. That poor, poor girl.

"It's one of several possibilities," Detective Vick says in a noncommittal way that makes it sound like he's considered only one possibility.

I study his face, so expressionless it could be a mask. I've seen that look from him before. I know it means he's already made up his mind.

"You think she jumped," I say.

It makes more sense than falling, despite my recent near miss. The terrace, with its low railing and cliff's edge access, seems tailor-made for suicide. It would be so easy for someone to climb over the railing and make that final leap.

Under normal circumstances, I'd spare another thought for poor Mary Milton, feeling sad and sorry for a woman whose personal demons drove her to take her own life. But right now I can only focus on my mother, another woman driven to suicide, and how Detective Vick refused to believe she acted alone.

"I don't want to make any assumptions at this time," he replies in that same maddening tone.

"Yet you were fine making them about me."

Those assumptions eventually found their way into the local newspaper, caused me to be suspended for six months, and almost landed me in jail. They made my few friends vanish and my own father suspect the worst about me. Anger rises inside me, so fast and volcanic I think it's about to propel me off the love seat and across the room to attack Detective Vick. Only sheer force of will keeps me in place. I sit with my arms tightly crossed, unable to make eye contact. I fear just looking at him will set me off again—and that I'll no longer be able to control it.

Sensing my anger, Detective Vick tries to calm me by saying, "This is more than just an assumption, okay? A note was found in a pocket of Miss Milton's uniform, indicating that she intended to kill herself."

I don't ask what it says. One, it's none of my business and, two, I'm too busy wondering how different my life would be right now if my mother had left behind a suicide note. I suspect it would be very different, seeing how a note seems to be all Detective Vick needs.

"Are you aware of any reason why Mary Milton would want to take her own life?" he says.

"I don't know. I never met her. She was gone before I got here."

I cringe as I say it. *Gone* has multiple meanings. Dead is one. Missing is another. So, too, is left, although it turns out Mary never did. She was here the whole time.

Detective Vick tries a different tactic. "Do you think she liked working at Hope's End?"

"From what others have told me, I guess she did," I say.

"Do you like working here?"

Caught off guard by the question, I shift on the love seat. "I just got here."

"That doesn't answer the question. Which is a simple one. You either like it here or you don't."

"I like it here," I say, flashing a tight smile so it doesn't seem like the lie it is. Completely unnecessary, it turns out.

"That's not what you told your employer," Detective Vick says.

"When did you talk to Mr. Gurlain?"

"About fifteen minutes ago. Before you and I talked, I wanted to confirm you were indeed the same Kit McDeere I thought you were. When I spoke to Mr. Gurlain, he told me that *you* also called him not long ago."

My anger returns. Before he even set foot in this room, Detective Vick knew I worked at Hope's End, how long I've been here, and what my job entails. He also knows I asked Mr. Gurlain for a new assignment mere minutes before finding the body of Mary Milton. This whole interrogation feels like a trap to prove I'm untrustworthy. One I walked right into.

I'd walk right out of it, too, if I could. But there's Mary to consider. While I didn't know her, everyone else at Hope's End seemed to like her. That alone is enough to make me continue to face Detective Vick. Then there's the fact that Mary was a fellow caregiver. She *cared*. I owe it to her to try to help make sense of her untimely end. Yet none of that means I need to go easy on Detective Vick.

"Are you going to ask me something you don't already know?" I say.

"I don't know why you just lied to me about liking it here."

"Because I want to keep my job."

"Even though, according to Mr. Gurlain, you asked for a new one?"

"I *need* to keep my job," I say through teeth gritted so hard it makes my jaw ache. "Thanks to you, this is my only option."

Detective Vick's mouth drops open, as if he wants to say something but feels he can't. In that absence of words, I can only wonder what it is. An apology seems unlikely.

"You told Mr. Gurlain you weren't comfortable here," he eventually says. "Why is that?"

"Three people were murdered in this house, Detective. Are you comfortable being here?"

"Yes. Then again, I'm used to crime scenes. Do you think Mary was uncomfortable here?"

"I honestly don't know."

"You have the same job she did. Surely you can provide some insight into what it's like caring for Lenora Hope. How is she as a patient?"

"Fine," I say.

"Any problems?" Detective Vick says, pressing.

"Just the usual growing pains that happen with every patient."

Along with Lenora's sordid reputation, noises in the night, and the still-eerie fact that she claimed her dead sister was roaming her bedroom. But those are best left unmentioned. Detective Vick has always looked for a reason to not believe me. It's not a good idea to toss him a few more, even if it leaves him looking disappointed. I think my answer is exactly what he expected to hear.

"You're not concerned that Lenora Hope might be the person who committed those three murders you just mentioned?" Detective Vick says.

"I'm not worried she's going to kill me, if that's what you're asking."

The detective purses his lips. A surprisingly dainty gesture on a face that's grown rugged with age. "It wasn't," he says. "But since you brought it up, do you think Mary was worried about that?"

"Maybe, but I doubt it. Lenora's harmless," I say, echoing what Carter told me when I first arrived.

"Do you think Mary had any problems with Lenora? Or, for that matter, any other aspect of living and working here?"

I've wondered that myself, especially when I thought Mary had abruptly left in the middle of the night. Even though I now know better, it still tugs at me. Did something about Hope's End—its history, its quirks, its unidentifiable noises—drive Mary to jump from the terrace? Or could it have been the history and quirks of the person she was caring for? I can think of only one person who might be able to provide some insight.

"I'm not sure," I say. "But I know someone who does."

"Who?"

At last, I'm able to give Detective Vick an answer I know he isn't expecting.

"Lenora Hope."

# NINETEEN

I lead the way, guiding Detective Vick up the Grand Stairs.

"Watch the bloodstains," I say dryly as we climb. I swerve around them. Detective Vick walks right over them, not breaking stride. A disappointment. I was hoping he'd react the same way I did the first time I noticed them.

I do get a reaction at the top of the stairs, though. Stepping onto the landing, the detective immediately reaches for the wall and says, "Whoa."

"The mansion's tilted," I tell him, as if I've been here years and not mere days.

"Is that safe?" Detective Vick says.

"Probably not."

"Man, it wasn't like this last time I was here."

I stop in the middle of the hallway. "What do you mean?"

"I used to work here." Detective Vick removes his hand from the wall, thinks better of it, slaps it back onto the blue damask. "Just for one summer, plus some weekends that spring and fall. Mr. Hope used to hire boys from town when things got busy."

"When was this?"

"It was 1929," the detective says. "I remember because of the murders."

"So you know Lenora?"

"Only from a distance."

I start off down the hall again, talking over my shoulder to a still-wobbly Detective Vick. "Is that why you became a detective?"

"Because I spent a summer working in a place where there was a triple homicide?" Detective Vick chuckles, as if he finds the idea preposterous. "It was more than that, I can assure you. Detective work's a calling. It's in our blood to find the people who do bad things and make them pay."

Even though I walk ahead of him, I know the detective is shooting daggers at me. I can feel his stare burning the back of my neck. No doubt he thinks I'm someone who did a bad thing and managed to get away.

For now.

I turn left into Lenora's room, where she sits in her wheelchair, the Walkman in her lap and earphones on her head. My sudden arrival with a stranger startles her. Her left hand flutters against the blanket laid over her lap and her green eyes go wide.

She'd spent most of the day with Archie or Mrs. Baker as I waited downstairs in the sunroom. And while I'm not sure which one of them told Lenora what happened to Mary, it's clear she knows. Once the surprise fades, her eyes shimmer with grief.

Outside, the storm clouds have gotten darker and more menacing, plunging the bedroom into a gloom that feels both suffocating and appropriate.

"Lenora," I say as I go to her side. "This is Detective Vick. He'd like to ask you some questions about Mary. Is that okay?"

Lenora stares at him, uncertain. She looks so hesitant that I expect her response to be no. I'm surprised when, after a few more seconds of contemplation, she taps twice against her lap.

"Two taps mean yes," I explain to Detective Vick. "One means no."

The detective nods and approaches Lenora the way I first did—with awestruck trepidation. From the way he talked in the sunroom, I suspect the detective thinks Lenora is guilty as sin. Still, he kneels beside her wheelchair on legs made unsteady from the slanted floor and says, "Hi, Lenora. I'm sorry about Mary. I heard the two of you were close?"

Rather than tap out an answer, she gives a slow, sad nod.

"So you liked her?"

Lenora returns to tapping, giving two quick raps.

"And Mary liked you?"

Another two taps.

"How was she as a nurse?" Detective Vick shakes his head. "Sorry. There's no way for you to answer that."

"There is." To Lenora, I say, "You feel like typing your answers?"

Before she can tap a response, I wheel Lenora to the desk and insert a fresh sheet of paper into the typewriter. I place her left hand on the keys and turn to Detective Vick.

"She can't type very fast, so try to ask her things that only require short answers."

"Uh, sure." The detective rubs his hands together, uncertain. I can only assume this is the first time he's questioned someone via typewriter. "Lenora, when was the last time you saw Mary?"

Lenora blinks, confused.

"He wants you to type your answer," I say, gently prodding her.

Instead of typing, Lenora stares at the typewriter as if she's never seen one before. She lifts her hand, hovering it uncertainly over the keys before dropping it back down. The force of the landing hits a key hard enough to slap a single, faint letter onto the blank page.

h

"Do you need my help?" I ask her.

Simmering with impatience, Detective Vick says, "Is something wrong?"

"I don't know."

I look to Lenora. Normally so expressive, her face has taken on a frustrating blankness. It dawns on me that this could be too much for her. Mary's death. The detective's presence. All his questions. I kneel next to her, put my hand over hers, and say, "Are you too upset about Mary to type?"

Beneath my palm, Lenora curls her hand into a fist and raps the keyboard once.

"Then why aren't you doing it?"

"Do you even know how to type?" Detective Vick asks her.

Again, Lenora gives another single rap.

Outside, a gust of wind slams against the mansion, making the whole room—including those of us in it—shudder. Drops of rain smack the windows as the wind howls.

The storm has arrived.

With it comes another shudder. One only I can feel. An internal shimmy brought on by a single realization.

Lenora is pretending.

Detective Vick kneels on the other side of her wheelchair. He shoots me an annoyed look and asks Lenora, "Just to be clear, Miss McDeere is lying about you being able to type?"

This time, Lenora raises her hand and taps the typewriter twice.

My stomach drops. "She can," I say. "I swear."

I give Lenora a desperate stare, as if she can confirm what I just said any other way besides actually pressing one of the typewriter keys. But she can't. And she won't. For reasons I don't understand.

The storm's at full force now. Water pours down the windowpanes, casting undulating patterns on the bedroom floor. I watch them, furious at Lenora for making me look like a liar, wondering why she's doing it, and trying to think of some way to prove I'm right. That's when it hits me.

"We typed this morning," I say. "Before I found Mary. The page is right here on the desk."

I search the desk for the page I know was still in the typewriter when I went downstairs to call Mr. Gurlain. I even remember the words that had been typed on it—Lenora telling me her dead sister was in this room.

But the page isn't on the desk.

It doesn't seem to be anywhere.

"It was just here," I say, scanning a desktop that contains nothing but a typewriter and a lamp.

"There wasn't a page in the typewriter," Detective Vick says, maybe trying to be helpful but coming off smug instead. "Are you sure you didn't imagine it?"

"I'm sure." I start opening desk drawers, searching for the page that bore Virginia's name. It's not in any of them. Nor is it on the floor. I look to Lenora and say, "You know it was here."

Her left hand remains atop the typewriter keys, motionless and seemingly useless.

"Tell him I'm not lying, Lenora," I say, my voice sliding perilously close to outright begging. *"Please."*

Detective Vick stands, grabs me by the wrist, and drags me into the hallway, seething.

"Is this some kind of game to you, Kit? Because I didn't believe a word of what you said about your mother, you've decided to toy with me?"

"I'm not toying with you," I say. "Lenora does know how to type. We spent all of yesterday doing it. She's been telling me what happened the night her family was murdered. I think she plans on either confessing or telling me who really did it."

"That's insane, Kit. The woman can barely sit up. Do you seriously expect me to believe that Lenora Hope is typing her goddamn life story?"

"But it's the truth!"

"Sure," Detective Vick says, dripping sarcasm. "Let's go with that. But why now? After so many years, why has she decided to tell you, of all people, what happened that night?"

"I don't know. But she *has* told me things." The words tumble out in a mad rush, so desperate am I to have Detective Vick believe me about *something*. "About the months leading up to the murders. About her family. And her sister. She said the ghost of her sister has been in her room."

"You don't believe that, do you?"

"No," I say, because I don't. Not really. Not yet, anyway. "But I do think something is wrong with this place. It's . . . not right."

Detective Vick takes a step back and stares at me, his anger dissolving into something else. It looks like pity.

"We're done talking, Kit," he says as he pulls a business card from his pocket and presses it into my hand. "Call me if you ever feel like telling the truth."

He stalks off down the hall toward the Grand Stairs. I march back into Lenora's room. Seeing her at the desk, now in full typewriting mode, makes me break one of the cardinal rules of a Gurlain Home Health Aides employee—no swearing at patients.

"What the fuck was that about?"

Lenora, exuding the patience of a saint, nods for me to join her. She then types two words.

im sorry

"You should be. You made me look like a complete liar in front of the detective."

i had to

"Why?"

it must be a secret

"You knowing how to type needs to be a secret?" I say. "From whom?"

everyone

It would have been nice to know that before I invited Detective Vick up to her room. Now that I do know—and now that I've completely blown my chance of him ever believing me about anything—I feel compelled to ask the same questions I think he would have posed.

"Did Mary tell you she was leaving?"

Lenora taps once on the keyboard.

"The last time you saw her, how did she act?"

Lenora starts typing, stops to give it some thought, starts over. The result is a strange beast of a word.

**weirnervous**

I study the word, which is a pretty accurate summation of my own current state. "Which is it? Weird or nervous?"

**both**, Lenora types.

"Had she been acting this way for a while?"

Lenora taps the keyboard twice. Yes.

"Did Mary ever mention hearing strange noises at night?"

She gives the keyboard two more taps. Another yes.

I'm hit with a memory of what Jessie told me my first night here.

*I think she was scared. Hope's End isn't a normal house. There's a darkness here. I can feel it. Mary did.*

Even though Jessie assured me it was a joke, I'm now starting to think it wasn't. Not entirely.

"Do you know if she ever found out what they were?" I say.

Rather than tap, Lenora types out her answer.

**no**

"And that's what made her weird and nervous?"

Lenora bangs out two more words.

**and scared**

My heart hiccups in my chest. So it is true. Maybe Jessie knew because Mary told her or maybe she just subconsciously suspected something was amiss. Either way, it doesn't change the fact that something at Hope's End frightened Mary Milton.

"What was she scared of, Lenora?"

I watch Lenora's hand slide over the keyboard in a way similar to the planchette on Jessie's Ouija board. Eight keys and one press of the space bar later, I see the answer I'd been expecting all along.

**my sister**

My sister knew I was in love. Sisters can tell such things. Even ones who never get along, which certainly was the case for the two of us.

"Who is it?" she asked on one of those rare occasions we found ourselves in the same room at the same time. Usually we managed to steer clear of each other. But that night we both chose to occupy ourselves in the library.

"I have no idea who you're referring to," I replied as I sat by the fireplace, reading one of my mother's romance novels that I ordinarily would have found beneath me. I wanted to write serious literature and normally read only that. I started to feel differently once I fell in love with Ricky.

And it was love.

Love at first sight, to use the cliche. In my case, though, it was true. The moment I saw Ricky, I knew I was in love with him. It was impossible not to feel that way. Not only was he the most handsome man I'd ever seen, but he understood me in a way no one else did. I could tell from the way he looked at me. He didn't see a wealthy man's spoiled daughter, content with flirting and flouncing about in pretty dresses. He saw a young, intelligent woman with hopes, dreams, ambition.

He saw the person I wanted myself to be.

"You're so different from the rest of your family," he told me that first night, after we'd spent an hour talking on the terrace.

"In a good way, I hope," I said.

"In a wonderful way."

I let him kiss me then. My first kiss. It was greater than I ever dreamed it could be. When his lips touched mine, it felt as if my entire existence was exploding like a firework. Bright and sparkling and white hot.

I pulled away, short of breath and blushing. For a moment, I thought I was going to faint. I swooned against the terrace railing, dizzy. I likely would have fallen over if Ricky hadn't caught me in his arms and whispered, "When can I see you again?"

"Tomorrow night," I whispered back, as if I were Juliet and he my Romeo, meeting at my balcony. "Right here."

Two weeks had passed since then, and the two of us saw each other every night. We'd meet on the terrace and rush off somewhere we couldn't be found. When we were together, the world melted away, turning everything to sheer bliss. When we were apart, he was all I thought about, dreamed about, cared about.

We kissed again the second night we met, this time without restraint. We were by the cottage, half hidden in shadow, telling each other our dreams and our disappointments. I told Ricky about wanting to flee to Paris, living like a bohemian, experiencing everything and then writing it down.

Ricky told me how, through tough times and hard luck, he came to work here. "My family is piss-poor," he said, using a term that both shocked and thrilled me with its crudeness. "My mother died when she had me. My father's a mean drunk who'd rather beat me than work. I learned right fast that school was useless. Money beats knowledge every single time. Since I'm good with my hands, I came here."

He sighed and looked up at the sky. "I want more than this, I can tell you that. It's crushing, not having the life you're meant to live. It weighs a man down."

I tried to alleviate that weight the only way I knew how, by letting Ricky wrap his thick arms around my waist, pull me close, and kiss me as passionately as he wanted.

We were still kissing when I heard the whisper of footfalls in the grass. It was Berniece, returning home from her duties in the kitchen. I broke away and fled before we could be caught. But that close call didn't change anything. I knew that what Ricky and I were doing was wrong, but I didn't care. I longed for the fireworks his kiss created. I needed them.

We grew more daring with each meeting. Kissing, touching, exploring. On the third night, when Ricky's hand moved to my breast, I let it remain there. On the fourth night, I slipped my hand into his trousers and grasped his manhood. I'll spare you the sordid details, but it progressed like that until, exactly one week after the night we met, I allowed Ricky to take my virginity.

When it was over, I laid in his arms and whispered, "I love you."

Ricky grinned and said, "I love you, too."

In that moment, I became a woman. I suspect that was the change my sister saw in me that night in the library.

"You're clearly mad about someone," she said. "And I know who it is."

I looked up from my book, numb with worry. Had Berniece seen us? Did she know? Was she now telling others?

"What have you heard?"

"Nothing," my sister said. "But it's obvious you're in love with Archibald."

I struggled not to laugh as relief poured over me. So many things prevented Archie and me from being together, starting with the fact that he felt more like a sibling to me than my own sister did.

"It's not Archie," I said.

"Don't tell me you still carry a torch for Peter. It's hopeless. He has no interest in you."

"Or you."

"He'll come around," my sister said. "I'm certain of it. Then we'll marry and spend the rest of our days here."

"At Hope's End?"

My sister spread her arms wide, as if trying to embrace the house itself. "Of course. I'm never going to leave this place."

"But there's a whole world out there you haven't yet seen," I said. "I, for one, intend to explore as much of it as I can."

"With your secret boyfriend?" My sister smiled at me, a look I'd seen so many times that it rarely registered how vicious it could be. Her smile contained neither humor nor warmth. It was as cold and calculating as the girl it belonged to. "You should just go ahead and tell me who he is now. You know I'm going to find out at some point."

In the end, she was right.

She eventually did find out, and disaster soon followed.

At least she also got her wish. All these years later, she's still here, roaming the halls. And she's never going to leave.

As long as Hope's End still stands, my sister will remain.

# TWENTY

The third floor of Hope's End surprises me. Although everything looks the same, save for the top of the Grand Stairs in the center, it feels completely different. Up here, the mansion's tilt is more pronounced. Something seen and not merely felt. Staring down the hallway from the top of the service stairs is akin to being in the hold of a listing ship.

No wonder Carter chooses to stay in the cottage. I have no idea how Jessie and Archie can live up here. I start off down the hall, slightly woozy. The floorboards rasp beneath my feet while from above comes the sound of driving rain hitting the roof. Up ahead, an open door spills out light and music.

Jessie's room, I presume.

I doubt Archie listens to the Talking Heads.

I'm proven correct when I peek inside and see her sitting cross-legged on the floor, sorting through a stack of Polaroids.

"Hey," I say. "How are you holding up?"

A pointless question. It's obvious to anyone with a set of eyes that Jessie's not doing well at all. She looks up from the photos, revealing streaks in her makeup left by recent tears.

"Shitty," she says.

I step into the room, struck by how different it is from mine. While almost identical in shape and size. Jessie has truly made it her own. The walls are covered with posters of bands, some I'm familiar with, most I've never heard of. A silk scarf has been thrown over one of the lamp-shades, giving the room a muted red glow that reminds me of Lenora's call button. Near the door, the ceiling is standard height. On the other side of the room, it slants dramatically to the dormer windows, one of which is open, letting in the sound of pouring rain—a fitting compan-ion to Jessie's tears.

"I can't believe Mary's gone," she says, holding up one of the Polaroids.

I join her on the floor and take the photo from her hand. It shows her and Mary on the terrace, with puffy clouds hanging in the sky be-hind them and the wind tossing their hair. It's the first time I've seen Mary—what was mostly buried under sand at the base of the cliff doesn't count—and I'm struck by how young she was. Still in her twen-ties, from the looks of it. And so familiar to me it squeezes my heart. Bright smile, sensible haircut, gold studs in her ears because anything more elaborate would get in the way of the job. A caregiver through and through. I can see why everyone seemed to like her. I think I would have liked her, too.

"I knew she couldn't have left like that," Jessie says. "Not without saying goodbye or telling me where she was going."

"Why did you think she left in the first place?"

"Because that's what Mrs. Baker told us."

"Why did *she* think that?"

"I guess because that's what it looked like," Jessie says. "I should have known not to believe it. Leaving like that wasn't Mary's style. Neither is suicide. I don't care what that detective says. Mary didn't kill herself."

"Sometimes people do things you don't expect," I say, thinking about my mother and the way she ended things. No goodbye. No note. No closure. I miss her, but I'm also furious at her for leaving me and my father alone to pick up the pieces. Something, it turns out, we couldn't do. "Maybe there was something wrong that no one knew about."

"Like what?"

Like being tormented by the ghost of Virginia Hope, for starters. But I don't want to go there just yet. It's best to ease into the topic. If such a thing is possible.

"How did Mary act the last time you saw her?"

Jessie sniffs and wipes her cheek with the back of her hand, turning the mascara streaking her face into a sideways smear. "You sound just like that detective."

"What did you tell him?"

"That Mary seemed fine." Jessie picks up another Polaroid and stares at it while adding a small, quiet, "Even though it wasn't entirely true."

"Something seemed wrong?"

She nods, drops the Polaroid onto the floor, picks up another one, and shows it to me. It's Mary in the second-floor hallway, the white of her uniform—possibly the same one I'm now wearing—a stark contrast to her dark surroundings.

"Why didn't you tell the detective?"

"I don't know," Jessie says with a shrug. "I guess I was trying to protect Mary."

An urge I understand well. Even after her death, I felt the need to protect my mother. It's why, in the beginning, I floated the idea that she had no idea how many pills she was taking. That her overdose was accidental, even though everyone knew it wasn't. I eventually came to realize that instead of protecting her, I was clinging to the idea that she wouldn't leave my father and me the way she did. Not by choice.

"Right now, the best way to help Mary is to find out exactly what happened."

"She fell," Jessie says. "That's the only explanation."

I've heard that tone before from my father. Uncertain confidence.

*What they're saying's not true, Kit-Kat.*

"Maybe not. Especially if Mary was acting weird or nervous," I say, purposefully using the two words Lenora had crammed into one.

Jessie stares past me to the wall, where a poster of the Eurythmics gazes back at her. "Why are you so interested in what happened? You didn't even know Mary."

No, I didn't. But I am the one who found her. I'm the one who looked down, saw her dead body, and screamed so loud the sound echoed off the back of the house. I'm the one who now fears I'll be seeing her sand-covered body in my nightmares later tonight.

But that's not my only worry. The main one—the concern that might keep me from sleeping at all—is that what happened to Mary could happen to me, a notion that's both utterly paranoid and completely rational. We have the same job, the same bedroom, even the same uniform. If something about this job led to Mary's death, I'd really like to avoid a similar fate.

"Did Mary ever mention hearing strange noises at night? Coming from Lenora's room? Or seeing things?"

"No," Jessie says. "Have you?"

I don't answer, which is an answer in itself. Sometimes not saying no means yes.

"The other night, you told me Mary was scared of this place."

"I was joking," Jessie says.

"So you said." I pause again. "But I think there might have been some truth to it."

Although Jessie begins to respond with a shake of her head, it soon changes direction, swerving upward into a tentative nod. She muddies things further by saying, "Maybe. I don't know anymore."

"Did Mary ever say outright she was scared?"

"Yeah, but it was, like, obviously as a joke. Both of us joked about it all the time. Stupid shit like, 'I just saw Virginia in the hallway. She says hello.' Dumb things like that to lighten the mood. God knows, this place needs it. But then Mary stopped playing along."

I lean in, curious. "When was this?"

"A few weeks ago. I'd make a joke about Virginia or Winston Hope and Mary would shake her head and be like, 'Don't say stuff like that.' She became real serious about everything. Like she was actually scared."

"Of Virginia?" I say, thinking of the things Lenora had typed. That Virginia was in her room. That Mary was afraid of her.

"Maybe?" Jessie returns her attention to the Polaroids on the floor. They're all faceup, a dozen images of Mary that Jessie slides around like a tarot card reader. "I know I'm making it sound like Mary was some kind of weirdo scaredy-cat. She wasn't. I don't think she believed in ghosts. But . . ."

"But what?" I say, pressing.

"Something seemed to spook her," Jessie says. "I don't know what. Maybe she really did see the ghost of Virginia Hope. Or maybe she just didn't want to joke about it anymore. Probably because she'd been spending a lot of time with Lenora."

"That's part of the job," I say. "Constant care."

"But I'm talking, like, *a lot* of time. Maybe she thought it was disrespectful or something."

"Did Mary ever mention a guy named Ricardo Mayhew?"

Jessie scrunches her face. "Who?"

"He used to work here," I say. "Carter told me about him."

"Never heard of the guy," Jessie says. "If Mary knew who he was, she never told me. And I don't know why she wouldn't. She told me everything else about this place. She probably knew more about the Hope family murders than anyone except Lenora."

One particular Polaroid in the pile catches my attention. Taken in Lenora's room, it shows Lenora and Mary at the desk. Lenora's in her wheelchair, hunched over the typewriter. Mary's behind her, leaning in close. A sight so familiar it stings.

I pick it up and show it to Jessie. "When was this taken?"

"A couple weeks ago." Jessie plucks the photo from my fingers and arranges it in a pile with the others. "They were always typing."

"Do you know what?"

"Mary never told me," Jessie says as she stands and crosses the room to her dresser, where she drops the Polaroids into the top drawer. "At first, I thought it was some kind of physical therapy. You know, working on Lenora's motor skills. But they were there all the time. Sometimes even after Lenora was supposed to have been put to bed."

She moves to a tape recorder sitting atop the dresser next to a hardcover copy of *Lace* with a library sticker on its spine. She pops a cassette from the recorder and hands it to me. "This is for Lenora. Part one of the new book. Maybe it'll take her mind off everything."

"Thanks." I pocket the cassette and head to the door. Before leaving, I turn back to Jessie and say, "Did anyone else know about the typing?"

"I don't think so," Jessie says. "I only knew because I walked in on them one night. I thought it would be a cool picture, so I stood in the doorway and took it before they realized I was there. Mary kind of freaked out about it. She made me swear not to tell anyone. I probably shouldn't have even told you."

But I'm glad she did.

Because now I know why Mary knew so much about the Hope family and what happened that night.

Lenora told her.

I see that look you're giving me. I'm more observant than people give me credit for. And right now I can tell that you think you won't like where all this is going.

You won't.

But I promised to tell you everything, so that's what I'm giving you. My deepest, darkest secrets. Things I've never told anyone before.

Only you, Mary.

Only you.

# TWENTY-ONE

The fingers of Lenora's left hand sit atop the typewriter, atypically still. Under normal circumstances, they'd be sliding from key to key, slowly but surely adding words to the blank page I've wound into the carriage.

But these circumstances are anything but normal.

A pall has settled over the house now that the police have left. The place is quiet and the mood somber. A resident of Hope's End is gone, and while I never knew Mary Milton, I feel her loss all the same. We were alike in so many ways. More than I ever imagined.

That's why I brought Lenora to the typewriter after dinner instead of guiding her through her circulation exercises. An infraction I know Mrs. Baker wouldn't approve of. I stand next to Lenora, hugging myself despite the gray cardigan thrown over my uniform. Although the storm has passed, it's left behind a damp chill that seeps through the windows, giving her room the shivery air of a ghost ship.

Fitting, seeing how on the desk next to the typewriter is the page Lenora had typed on earlier. Two words catch my eye.

my sister

"Why did you lie to me about Mary being scared of your sister?"

Lenora looks up at me, apprehension flashing in her green eyes. Then she types.

it wasnt a lie

"Your sister is dead, Lenora," I say, tightening my cardigan around me. "And ghosts don't exist. So you'll have to do better than that to hide the fact that you and Mary spent a lot of time typing."

Lenora can't hide her surprise. She tries, but her expressive face betrays her. There's a slant to her lips and a twitch at her right eye, like she's working hard to keep it from widening.

"You were telling her your story, weren't you?"

Lenora taps twice against the typewriter. With it comes a twinge of disappointment that I wasn't the only person she trusted enough to tell. I'd thought I was special and that there was a specific reason Lenora chose me. Now I have no idea why she's doing it.

"Why didn't you tell me? Or Detective Vick?"

Lenora slowly pecks the keys.

**it had to be a secret**

"Who decided that? You or Mary?"

**mary**

"And whose idea was it to start typing your story?"

Rather than signal for me to hit the return bar, Lenora types Mary's name a second time, running it together with the first.

**marymary**

I'm not surprised, given that Jessie told me Mary had been obsessed with the Hope family massacre. She said it might have even been the reason Mary took the job caring for Lenora. If that's true, then it makes sense she would want to hear Lenora's version of things.

"That's why she bought the typewriter, isn't it?" I say. "She wanted you to write it all down for her."

This brings another two taps from Lenora.

"Did you want to?"

Lenora thinks about it a moment, her face falling into that pensive expression I've come to know so well. When she types, her response is as rambling as I imagine her thoughts to be. Further evidence that what she'd typed with me had all been written before. The second draft, so to speak.

**not at first i didnt want to talk about what happened because
the memories make me sad but i loved the idea of writing again
so i told her yes**

"How long had you been working on it?"

**weeks**

Even though I'm pretty sure I already know the answer, I say, "So what you typed with me, you also typed with her?"

Lenora taps twice before typing additional information.

**and more**

"How much more? About you and Ricky?"

Lenora keeps typing. Ten keys she presses slowly and deliberately, making the importance of her response clear.

**everything**

"When did you finish telling her?"

Lenora doesn't need to think about it.

**the night she left**

My stomach suddenly drops. Mary knew everything about the night of the murders—including who did it, how they did it, why they did it. And the day she learned all that, she—

Jumped.

That's what I should be thinking, since it's what Detective Vick said happened. Yet it feels wrong. Like a lie. Instead, a different word ricochets through my brain.

Died.

That's the brutal truth.

And it can't be a coincidence.

"Did Mary ever tell you why it needed to be a secret?"

Lenora types instead of taps.

**yes**

She then adds three more words to the line.

**she was scared**

I glance again to the page beside the typewriter, onto which Lenora had typed the same answer to a different question. As I do, a thought occurs to me. Something I should have considered sooner but was likely too scared myself to contemplate. But now there's no avoiding it.

"Lenora, did you really think Mary left?"

I study her face—the key to all her emotions. Even the ones she's trying to hide. This time, though, she doesn't even attempt to disguise the way she feels. Sadness clouds her features as she taps once against the typewriter.

No.

"You thought she jumped?"

Another single tap. One that kicks my pulse up a notch.

"Do—" I swallow. My mouth, suddenly dry from fear, can barely get the word out. "Do you think what happened to Mary is because of what you told her?"

Two taps from Lenora confirm my worst fear.

She thinks Mary was murdered.

Swirling within that dreadful realization is another, smaller thought. One brought about by another quick glimpse of the page next to the typewriter.

"What did Mary do with the pages the two of you typed?"

Lenora responds with a confused look.

"She helped you write the whole story." I think about the pages the two of us have typed, now sitting with Lenora's pill bottles in the lockbox under my bed. If Mary and Lenora had typed for weeks, why haven't I seen any evidence of it? Every piece of paper inside the desk is blank, and I saw no sign of typed pages anywhere else in Lenora's room or mine. "That must have been a thick stack. What did Mary do with them?"

Lenora's reply—**she hid them**—doesn't help me.

"Do you know where?"

This time, her response provides a bit more clarity.

**in her room**

A bad feeling skitters down my back. What had once been Mary's room is now my room—and the truth about the murders has been hidden there all this time.

A truth that might have gotten Mary killed.

The rest of the evening passes with agonizing slowness. I bathe, dress, and lift Lenora into bed, the whole time telling myself that we could be mistaken. Maybe Mary really did jump. Maybe she had deep wells of despair within her that she could no longer control. Maybe this is just another sad chapter in the overall tragic story of Hope's End.

Or maybe she was murdered because she knew that story.

After leaving Lenora with the call button, I go to my room and conduct a thorough search. Since all of Mary's belongings are here, it stands to reason that whatever she and Lenora typed is still in here as well. Where, I have no clue. But I'm determined to find out.

I begin with the dresser, removing Mary's clothes until every drawer is empty. I even check behind the dresser and beneath it. There's nothing.

Next is the bed, both under it and between the mattress and the box spring. The only item of interest is my lockbox. I open it with the key from the nightstand and check its contents. A stack of typewritten pages and six bottles of pills.

After that, I do a scan of the bookshelf, thinking the pages could be tucked among all the books Mary had left behind, and check the bathroom for potential hiding spots. Both yield no results.

The last place I look is the closet, since I did a thorough inspection of it the night I arrived. Nevertheless, I check Mary's medical bag, root through her coat pockets, and check the box on the floor that had once held books but now holds nothing.

I stand, wiping the front of my uniform, and stare at the patch of clean floor next to the box. Unlike my uniform, it's free of dust, as if something had sat there until very recently. I noticed it my first night here but gave it little thought. Now, though, I can't help but wonder what used to be there—and when it was removed.

I take a closer look. The dust-free area is rectangular, which would suggest a second box if not for the rounded corners.

That means it was something else.

Like a suitcase.

Mary was a caregiver. She knew the score. A box and suitcase are all we need.

With adrenaline buzzing through me, I grab my suitcase and bring it to the closet. With a nervous breath, I place it over the clean patch. It's like the uniform—not an exact fit, but close enough.

As I lift the suitcase from the closet, I notice something that amps up my adrenaline level from a buzz to a roar.

On each end of the handle is a metal ring attaching it to the suitcase itself.

Each ring is about the same shape and size of the bent piece of metal I found on the terrace.

Everything goes sideways, as if Hope's End is finally, inexorably tipping into the ocean. But it's only me, shell-shocked by the realization that Mary took a suitcase with her when she left.

Inside that suitcase might have been the typewritten truth about Lenora and the night her family died.

Now, like Mary, it's gone.

I stagger into the hallway and down the service stairs. The crack in the stairwell, I notice, has gotten larger. It now runs the entire height of the wall, with a second, smaller crack branching out of it. Another crack has formed on the opposite wall. At this rate, the whole stairwell will soon be webbed with them. I shudder, thinking of spiders and flies and sticky strands of cobwebs clinging to my skin.

In the kitchen, I head straight to the phone and dial the number printed on the card Detective Vick gave me. The phone rings six times before he answers with a groggy "Hello?"

"It's Kit McDeere."

"Kit." There's a rustle as the detective no doubt checks the clock on his nightstand. I do the same with the kitchen clock. Just before midnight. "Do you know what time it is?"

"Yes," I say, my bluntness making it clear I don't care. "But I thought you'd like to know that Mary Milton didn't jump."

"What do you think happened to her?" Detective Vick says after a disconcerted pause.

I pause myself, trying to collect my thoughts. I can't believe I'm thinking it, let alone about to say it. Yet I do, the words tumbling out with unforced urgency.

"She was pushed."

# TWENTY-TWO

"Here's a question I'm sure I'll regret," Detective Vick says. "But why do you think Mary Milton was pushed?"

"There was a suitcase in her room."

"And?"

"Now it's gone."

"*And?*"

"Mary took it with her."

Detective Vick sighs. "You have exactly one minute to explain."

I waste not a second trying to get him to believe the unbelievable. A tall order for someone so skeptical. Yet I do my best, telling him about the bare patch in the closet, how I think it was created by a suitcase recently removed from the bedroom, and why I suspect Mary left the house with it the night she died.

"If she intended to kill herself, why would she take a suitcase with her?"

"I have no idea," Detective Vick says.

"Because she wasn't planning to leave," I say. "That's why everything else she owned is still here. Mary intended to come back."

"I suppose you also have a theory about what was inside this alleged suitcase."

"The truth about the Hope family murders."

The sudden squeak of bedsprings tells me the detective just sat up. I finally have his undivided attention.

"I think Mary came here with the intention of finding out what really happened that night," I say. "And she did. Because Lenora told her."

"Let me guess," Detective Vick wearily says. "She typed it."

"Yes."

"Kit, we already—"

I cut him off, unwilling to give him yet another chance to call me a liar. "I know you think I'm making this up, but Lenora *can* type. I have an entire stack of pages I can show you. All typed by Lenora. And if you still don't believe me, there's photographic proof. Jessie has a picture of Mary and Lenora typing together. They were doing it in secret. With Mary's help, Lenora wrote about everything that happened the night her family was killed. When they finished, I think Mary planned to go public with it. She took what Lenora typed, put it in her suitcase, and left. But someone at Hope's End knew what she had planned and stopped her before she could do it."

"By pushing her to her death?"

"Yes."

"Why would someone do that?"

"Because they didn't want the truth to get out."

There's silence on Detective Vick's end. Either he's thinking over what I've said or is on the verge of hanging up. It turns out to be the former, although from his tone, the latter still feels like an option.

"This all sounds pretty outlandish, Kit."

"I'm not lying," I say.

"I didn't say you were. I think you sincerely believe it's what happened."

"But you don't." Pain throbs at my temples. A headache's brewing, no doubt caused by lack of sleep and an abundance of frustration. "What part don't you believe?"

"All of it," Detective Vick replies. "First of all, do you know how hard it is to shove someone over a railing?"

"Not this railing," I say, remembering the way it hit the small of my back, sending me off-balance enough to make me fear I was about to flip over it. "It's short."

"Duly noted. But you also said Mary put everything she and Lenora typed into this suitcase. Where do you think she was taking it?"

"You, most likely." A wild guess based on my own instincts. Lenora had just told her everything about the town's most infamous crime. I haven't given any thought about what I'll do when Lenora finishes telling me what happened. But my gut tells me I'd take it to the police. "Mary had the truth about that night."

"And that's the first of many holes in this theory of yours," Detective Vick says. "Mary's time of death was around two a.m. Do you really think she'd be going to the police at that hour?"

I look to the kitchen window. Outside, there's just enough moonlight to make out the railing running the length of the terrace. I imagine Mary there, bathed in a similar glow, flipping over the railing and vanishing out of sight.

"How do you know when she died?"

"Because it was low tide," Vick says. "Mary disappeared on Monday night. Low tide that day was shortly after two a.m. If there had been any water there, her body would have been swept out to sea. Instead, Mary hit the exposed beach and died upon impact. When the tide came in, she got buried in sand."

I get another image of Mary. One I don't need to imagine because I saw it. Her corpse mostly covered by sand and seafoam. I close my eyes and turn away from the kitchen window.

"But there's a suitcase missing from her belongings," I say.

"There very well could be," Detective Vick says. "But a week passed between Mary's death and your arrival. During that time, anyone could have taken it from the room. Why are you so certain Mary had it with her?"

"I found a piece of it on the terrace."

"You did?"

Detective Vick's tone changes from dismissive to interested in a snap. I allow myself a smile, even though he can't see it. It feels warranted. A small moment of triumph.

"A metal hook that attaches the handle to the suitcase. It was bent and lying on the ground, making me think the handle broke when someone snatched the suitcase from Mary."

"Now we're getting somewhere," Detective Vick says. "Do you still have it?"

My smile falls away. "I lost it."

Detective Vick doesn't ask how, and I don't volunteer that information. Telling him I dropped it when I almost fell off the terrace will only make him more convinced that what happened to Mary wasn't murder. Not that he doubts himself in any way.

"I knew it," he says. "I wanted to give you the benefit of the doubt. I really did. But please, enough of this bullshit."

"It's not bullshit."

"I know what you're trying to do, Kit. It's the exact same thing you attempted this afternoon. You're taking what happened to Mary—a very serious, very tragic event—and twisting it into a way to ease your guilt."

"*My* guilt? You still think I'm making all of this up?"

"I'm not blaming you," Detective Vick continues, as if I've said nothing at all. "I don't even think you're aware you're doing it. But it's obvious what's happening. Your mother took her own life. How big of a role you played in that is still up for debate."

"It's *not* up for debate. It was an accident."

"So you keep trying to convince me," Detective Vick says.

I want to scream.

And cry.

And rip the phone off the wall and smash it against the kitchen floor. Considering its age and my rage, I suspect I'm capable of it. But common sense grips me harder than frustration. If I sound hysterical, Detective Vick will be convinced that I am. Which is clearly the only thing I can convince him of.

"I am telling you I think a woman was murdered," I say. "Shouldn't you take that seriously? Shouldn't you at least investigate it?"

Detective Vick sighs. "I have investigated it. After talking to you and everyone else at that house, my conclusion is that Mary Milton took her own life."

"How can you be so certain?"

"The coroner's preliminary findings show that her injuries are consistent with a fall from that height. There were no defensive wounds, which there would likely have been if she had been attacked in the manner you suggest. I had officers search the grounds, the beach, even the terrace. They found nothing to indicate there was a suitcase or a struggle or a murder. In fact, they found nothing at all."

"That doesn't mean it didn't happen."

"I'm sorry," Detective Vick says. "I'm not the person you thought I was."

I grip the receiver tight, flummoxed. "What?"

"Mary's suicide note. That's what it said. 'I'm sorry. I'm not the person you thought I was.' Found neatly folded in the pocket of her uniform. The paper sustained heavy water damage, but it was still readable. Now, give me one reason not to hang up right now."

"Lenora didn't kill her family," I say, more out of desperation than anything else. I certainly have no plan. But I hope dropping a bombshell like that will keep Detective Vick listening. "At least, I don't think she did. We haven't gotten that far yet."

"We?"

"Me and Lenora. I told you, we're typing her story, just like she did with Mary. But there was a worker here. Ricardo Mayhew."

"I know," Detective Vick says. "I used to work there, remember?"

"Did you also know Lenora was in love with him? And that it's possible he's the one who killed her parents and sister? I'm pretty sure

Lenora knew he did it and covered for him. Now I think she wants to come clean, maybe in the hopes that he'll be caught, even though he vanished the night of the murders."

When I finally give Detective Vick a chance to speak, his voice wavers between intrigue and wariness. "Are you sure about this?"

"You have access to the police report from that night," I say. "Look at it and see. You'll also see that there's a whole lot of unanswered questions from that night. Mary had those answers. Now she's dead. That's not a coincidence. And it's sure as hell not suicide."

I hang up before Detective Vick can poke another hole in my theory, tell me I'm wrong, and then smugly trot out some other bit of evidence to prove it. I know I'm on to something here.

And it terrifies me.

Because Lenora's also telling me her story, I could be next.

Yet that's not the scariest part of all this. The truly chilling, scarier-than-Stephen-King part is that Mary wasn't killed by some random stranger. In a twisted way, that would put me more at ease. But whoever pushed her off the terrace knew what she was up to.

They knew *her*.

Which means it was likely someone at Hope's End.

Other than me and Lenora, only four people fit that description—Mrs. Baker, Archie, Carter, and Jessie.

Why one of them would feel the need to kill Mary over something Lenora typed is beyond me. I reach for the phone again, itching to call Detective Vick back. He needs to hear this, even if it's doubtful he'll believe me.

He hasn't yet.

About anything.

I'm about to dial when I hear a noise behind me. Footsteps. Moving from the darkened dining room into the kitchen. I whirl around to see Carter halt in the doorway. Hands raised in innocence, he says, "I didn't mean to startle you."

Yet he did. My heart pounds so loud I suspect he can hear it. Adding to the pounding is this: Carter is one of the four people who could have shoved Mary off the terrace.

He sways slightly as he steps fully into the kitchen. He's been drinking. A truth he acknowledges with an unapologetic "It's been a shitty day."

I remain with my hand on the phone, frozen. "It has."

"I was out on the terrace and heard someone on the phone. Thought I'd come in and investigate."

"How much did you hear?"

"Some of it."

"Some of it or all of it?"

"Most of it," Carter says. "And I get why you're nervous right now. You should be. But not around me. I knew what Mary was doing."

"Then tell me."

"She was trying to help me." Carter crosses the kitchen, drawing closer. Close enough for me to smell the whiskey on his breath. "And I think it's my fault she died."

"You have exactly one minute to tell me what you mean by that," I say, fully aware that I sound exactly like Detective Vick.

"Not here," Carter says.

I stay where I am. "Yes, here."

I'm not about to walk off alone with a killer. If that's what Carter is. While his words make it sound like he's about to confess, his body language says otherwise. Hunched and shambling, he appears incapable of harm. But appearances can be deceiving.

"There's something you need to see," he says, adding, "And I can't show you here. So you're just going to have to trust me for five minutes."

"You said Mary was helping you?"

"She was, yeah," Carter says. "And now I want to help her by finding out what really happened. Because she didn't jump. I know that, and judging by that phone call you just made, you know it, too."

The fact that he believes me is the only reason I follow Carter to his cottage. Even then, I make him walk several paces ahead of me, hands where I can see them. Once inside the cottage, I stay by the door in case I need to make a run for it. But Carter's movements are anything but threatening. After clearing the almost-empty whiskey bottle from the table, he pours himself a cup of black coffee to sober up.

"Want some?" he says.

"Coffee or whiskey?"

"Take your pick."

"I'd rather see what it is you needed to show me so bad," I say.

"In a minute." Carter sits at his table for two and takes a sip of coffee. "First, I need to admit something. I lied about why I took a job here."

I edge a half step toward the door. "If you want me to trust you, that's the wrong way of doing it."

"It is indeed," Carter says. "But it's important you know that. Now, remember that regular customer I told you about? The one who used to work here and suggested I take his place?"

"I do," I say. "And I'm assuming he had a name."

"Anthony," Carter replies. "Although everyone called him Tony. Well, Tony did more than suggest I work here. He insisted on it."

"Why?"

"He worked here for decades. Knew all the nooks and crannies. One day, he was poking around in the rooms above the garage. Some of the servants used to live there."

"I thought they lived in the house or this cottage," I say.

"In its heyday, Hope's End was overrun with servants. There was a mechanic whose sole job was to look after Winston Hope's collection of Packards. He had five of them. Archie told me that Mrs. Baker had to sell them over the years to help pay for this place's upkeep."

It's strange to consider how populated Hope's End once was. Every room filled, including ones over the garage. A small village atop a windswept cliff, all here to serve one outlandishly wealthy family.

"After the murders, the rooms above the garage were used for storage," Carter says after another sip of coffee. "Boxes of stuff from the twenties, even earlier. It was winter and there wasn't much to do around the grounds, so Tony decided to make himself useful and get rid of whatever was in those boxes. Most of it was junk. Moth-eaten clothes, cracked plates, stuff from people who worked here way back when. Basically, all the stuff they left behind when this place cleared out."

Carter retreats to the sleeping area of the cottage and pulls an envelope from its hiding place under his mattress. When he brings it to the table, I join him there, my caution overruled by curiosity.

"In one of those boxes, Tony found this."

He removes something flat from the envelope and slides it toward me, facedown. From its shape and sepia color, I can tell it's a photograph. An old one, as evidenced by the date scribbled on the back.

*September 1929*

I pick it up, turn it over, and see it's a picture of Lenora in her youth. By now, I have no problem recognizing her. Even if I did, the divan Lenora sits on and the wallpaper behind her give it away. It's her bedroom through and through. A photographic re-creation of the portrait in the hallway.

The only differences between the two are the dress—the one Lenora wears in the photo is flowing cotton instead of satin—and her position. Gone is the studied pose from the painting. Instead, Lenora leans against the back of the divan in a fashion that's anything but ladylike, her hands resting over her rounded stomach.

I go numb with shock.

"No," I say. "That can't be."

But the photograph doesn't lie.

A month before her family was slaughtered, Lenora Hope had been pregnant.

It was an accident, Mary.

Or foolishness.

Or likely a bit of both.

Ricky and I were too besotted with each other--and, yes, brimming with lust--to think about the consequences. Not that I knew what they were. No one had thought to teach me about the birds and the bees. What little I knew of sex had been gleaned from the records my sister loved to listen to. Songs of mischief and romance that made it all seem like harmless fun.

And it was incredibly fun. Ricky brought me pleasure in ways I didn't think possible. When someone makes you feel that good, it's hard to pay attention to the fact it could all go bad.

In hindsight, I suppose it was inevitable that I would get pregnant. I could tell immediately, by the way, despite my limited knowledge. Between the morning sickness, my insatiable appetite, and my missed period, I knew without a doubt I was pregnant. What I didn't know was what to do about it.

I waited weeks before telling Ricky, fearing he'd react badly to the news. I'd read many books in which women in my position were treated poorly by the men who put them there. I feared I'd be

just like those doomed characters. That Ricky wouldn't believe
me or, worse, run away, leaving me all alone in my very dire
predicament. To my relief and surprise, he was elated.

"So you're happy about this?" I asked after I told him.

"I'm going to be a father," he said. "I'm overjoyed!"

But both of us knew we were in a tricky situation, for so many
reasons. Ricky told me he needed time to plan, and I did, too.

Our unexpected joy thus became our biggest secret. One that was
surprisingly easy for me to keep. No one paid me much mind to
begin with, so it went mostly unnoticed when I started gaining
weight. Yes, I heard tut-tutting from my mother's maid when
I asked her to let out my clothes an inch or two. And of course I
noticed the servant girls stifle their judgmental giggles when I
requested a second helping at dinner. I didn't mind that everyone
thought I was simply getting fat. It meant that no one suspected
the truth.

Those five months or so were the happiest I'd ever been. For the
first time in my life, I didn't feel alone. I always had someone with
me--a constant companion right there in my belly.

I took great--albeit secret--pride in knowing I was about to
bring another life into this world. Gone was the girl who'd
considered jumping from the terrace on her birthday. I was now
a woman with a purpose. The thought of bearing a child and
raising it with Ricky made me hopeful about the future.

One evening in early September, I snuck Ricky up to my room
to discuss that future. It was a Tuesday, and the house was mostly
empty. Miss Baker had been given the night off with the rest of the
servants, which was customary every other Tuesday, and my
sister had gone off with friends. My father was gone as well,
heading to Boston on some emergency business. The London stock
exchange had just crashed, and there were growing fears the
same thing would happen here.

Since I knew my mother wasn't about to leave her room--or her laudanum--I felt confident I could bring Ricky upstairs and we could share a bed like a proper couple.

We made love that night. Tenderly at first, mindful of the child growing in my womb. But lust soon took over, as it always did, and Ricky ravaged me in a way I never knew I wanted or needed.

Afterward, as we contently laid together, I pictured our lives being exactly like that night. Just me, Ricky, and the baby, together in a small cottage somewhere far away from Hope's End.

"I wish things were different and we didn't have to sneak around like this," Ricky said as he held me in his arms. "I wish I was a better man."

I looked at him, concerned. "What do you mean? You're wonderful."

"Hardly," Ricky said with a dismissive sniff. "You deserve better than what I have to offer. You--and our child--deserve a man who can take care of you properly. I've been saving for months and yet I still barely have two nickels to scrape together."

He tried to slide out of bed, but I clung to him, keeping him from leaving. "If it's money you're worrying about, don't. My family has plenty."

"I refuse to take a penny from your father," Ricky said.

I wasn't talking about my father, whom I'd started to suspect didn't have as much money as he claimed. Recently, when passing his office, I'd heard a heated phone call between him and the man who managed his company's finances.

"What do you mean the money's no longer there?" he shouted into the phone. "What happened to it?"

I was referring to me and my sister, who were set to inherit the sizable fortune left behind by my grandparents. They had neither liked nor trusted my father, and when they died, they left nothing to their only daughter out of fear it would be squandered. Instead, their money was split between me and my sister and placed in a trust that neither of us could access until we turned eighteen.

"I'm talking about my money," I said. "Well, what will soon be mine."

Even about that, I wasn't certain. The main reason I hadn't yet told my family I was pregnant was out of fear they'd disown me once they found out. That seemed the likeliest course of action, considering Ricky's situation and status. Add in the fact that we had conceived out of wedlock and it was a recipe for disappointment, anger, and punishment. If it weren't for the money, I wouldn't have minded being disowned. I hated Hope's End and wanted nothing more to do with it. That humble cottage with Ricky and our child was all I needed.

Ricky seemed shocked by the prospect of possessing money he hadn't earned. "What kind of man would I be if I let you pay our way?"

"The man I love," I said.

He finally freed himself from my grasp and reached for his trousers. "Can you love a man with zero pride? Because that's what I'd become. I'm not some charity case."

I watched, hurt, as Ricky slid on his pants and began pacing the room, his hands shoved into his empty pockets.

"I didn't mean to upset you," I said.

"Well, you did."

"Then forget my money. We'll figure something out, even if it'll be hard at times."

Ricky stopped pacing long enough to glare at me. "Hard? You don't know the meaning of the word. Have you ever worked a day in your life?"

"I never needed to," I admitted.

"And that's your problem," Ricky said. "You and your family sit around all day letting the rest of us do the real work. If the shoe was on the other foot, I bet none of you would last a day."

I'd never seen him angry before, and the only reaction I had was to start crying. I tried to hold the tears back, but they fell anyway, streaming down my cheeks.

Ricky's tone softened as soon as he saw them. Pulling me close, he said, "Hey now. No need for that. I'll think of something. It'll just take a little more time. Don't you worry about a thing."

Because Ricky told me not to, I didn't.

A mistake, Mary.

For there was much to worry about.

But don't think for a second that this is simply a tale of a young girl used and discarded by a callous man. There's more to it than that. Nearly everyone at Hope's End played a role in what happened--and most paid dearly for it.

Including me.

Especially me.

# TWENTY-THREE

The photograph remains on the table, Lenora staring out from it in shades of sepia. Minutes have passed since I first saw it, yet I remain flabbergasted.

Lenora was pregnant.

And even though she hasn't revealed it yet, I'm pretty sure Ricardo Mayhew was the father. What I can't begin to understand is what this has to do with Mary. Or, for that matter, Carter.

"Why did your friend Tony insist you work here?" I say. "Because of this picture?"

Carter nods. He's sobered up in the past few minutes, likely from a combination of coffee and confession. Although what he's confessing is far from what I expected.

"I started working here because I needed to know."

"Know what?"

"If I'm Lenora Hope's grandson."

"I still don't understand," I say.

"On Christmas morning in 1929, a baby was left at the front door of the Episcopal church in town," Carter says. "The baby was freezing, barely alive. Because it was Christmas, the priest who found him got to the church earlier than normal. If he'd arrived even a few minutes later, the baby would have died. That's why the church called it a Christmas miracle."

"That baby," I say. "He was—"

Carter, like me, can't stop looking at the picture of Lenora. "My father, yeah. He was adopted by a young couple at the church who couldn't have children. My grandparents. My father never tried to find out who his birth parents were, mostly because he had no idea where to start looking. Besides, he was literally abandoned. Why bother trying to find someone who didn't want you? So my birth grandparents remained a mystery. Until Tony found this photo."

"Why did he think your grandmother is Lenora?"

"Because of the date," Carter says, tapping the photo. "How many months pregnant does she look to you?"

I peer again at the picture. "Six?"

"That's what I thought, too. Which means her ninth month would have been—"

"Around Christmas," I say.

"Exactly."

Carter doesn't elaborate, nor does he need to. Since there's no child of Lenora's living at Hope's End—nor even a mention of one—I assume the baby either died during childbirth or was given up for adoption.

"And you think Ricardo Mayhew's the father," I say.

"That's what Mary thought," Carter says, confirming what I already knew—that Lenora told Mary everything.

And that Mary shared at least some of it with Carter.

He tips back his coffee cup and empties it. "It makes sense, too. In fact, it's the only reason I could see for Ricardo killing the rest of Lenora's family. He was a married man caught in an affair with Winston Hope's older daughter. Either they didn't approve and he killed them out of spite, or they demanded he make an honest woman out of Lenora and he killed them to get away."

"And it's why he spared Lenora," I add. "She was pregnant with his child."

And, I suspect, it's why Lenora's been covering for him all this time.

"Anyway, that's why I started working here," Carter says. "It's stupid, but I thought that if I saw Lenora—if we came face-to-face—I'd know."

"That's not stupid at all," I say, thinking about my mad urge to stare into Lenora's eyes, hoping that doing so would give me some small insight into my own life. "I guess it didn't help once you did see her."

"Not really. There's no resemblance that I saw. But it also doesn't mean we're not related."

I finally take a seat at the other side of the table. Either I trust Carter enough to remain within arm's reach of him or the news of Lenora's pregnancy has made me toss all caution to the wind. I'm not sure which one it is.

"Have you considered asking Mrs. Baker?"

"For about two seconds, yeah," Carter says. "But she's not exactly happy to talk about the past. Neither is Archie."

He's right about that. Despite both having been here in 1929, neither seems like the type to willingly discuss anything about that time.

"So you went to Mary instead."

"Not until I learned what she and Lenora were up to. The typing and all that." Carter pauses. Long enough to make me think he's waiting for me to admit I've been doing the same thing with Lenora. I let him keep waiting. I might trust him, but only so much. "When I realized we were both working toward the same goal, I got her involved."

Now I understand why Carter assumes it's his fault Mary is dead. He thinks she knew too much. As does Lenora. I can still hear her response when I asked her if she thought Mary died because of what she'd been told. Those two dreadful taps.

"There are ways to tell if you're related to someone," Carter says. "Blood tests. They're using them all the time now to settle paternity cases. I thought, well, if they can do that, then there's no reason to think they can't tell if someone's my grandparent."

"That's where Mary came in," I say.

Carter nods before filling me in on the rest. He contacted a lab that could conduct the tests. All he needed were two blood samples—one from him, one from Lenora. Two weeks ago, he went to the lab and got his own blood drawn to be analyzed.

"I convinced Mary to help me with the rest. She agreed to draw a sample of Lenora's blood for me to take to the lab. After that, all we had to do was wait to see if it was a match. It was supposed to happen the night Mary—"

Carter can't bring himself to say the rest.

The night Mary died.

"She told me she'd get Lenora's sample just before putting her to bed," he says. "I planned to store it in the fridge here and take it to the lab first thing in the morning. When Mary didn't show, I thought she'd changed her mind or wasn't able to do it. Then when it looked like she had left Hope's End entirely, I started to worry my request is what made her leave. Like I'd asked too much of her or put her in an awkward position."

I'm certain he did. That's a big request of a caregiver—even a registered nurse like Mary. But she had followed through on it. The bruise I found on Lenora's forearm is exactly the kind that would appear after having blood drawn, especially from an elderly patient taking the kind of anticoagulant she's on.

It also means there might have been more than Lenora's writing inside Mary's suitcase. A sample of her blood could have been there as well, a theory that only makes Carter feel worse after I share it.

"So it *was* my fault."

"You're not the one who pushed Mary," I say, as clear a sign as any that Carter fully has my trust.

"No, but I put her in a dangerous situation."

"That you didn't know was dangerous."

Carter looks into his empty coffee cup, as if he longs to refill it with more whiskey. "But I should have. I asked Mary to help me prove that I'm related to Lenora Hope. Some people would kill to keep that from happening."

"Why?"

"Because if I'm really Lenora's grandson, I might inherit everything when she dies," Carter says. "Hope's End. The house and the land and whatever money she has left."

"Who gets it now?" I say. "Do you know if Lenora has a will drawn up?"

"No. But if she did, I guess everything would be divided up between the two people who've known her the longest."

Mrs. Baker and Archie. The last time Carter and I sat in this exact spot, I wondered aloud why the two of them stayed. Now I think I know why—they'll get Hope's End when she dies.

"So one of them killed Mary," I say. "Or maybe they both did it."

A corner of Carter's mouth twitches, as if he wants to say something but knows he shouldn't.

"What aren't you telling me?" I say.

"There's another reason I think it's my fault." Carter pauses, still hesitant. "I left the gate open."

"When?"

"That Monday. I found it open that morning. I guess it got stuck and didn't close after the guy who delivers the groceries left. Since I assumed I'd be leaving first thing the next day to head to the lab, I didn't bother to push it shut."

"So on the night Mary died, the front gate was open the entire time?"

"Yeah," Carter says with a sigh. "Anyone could have gotten in."

I become unsteady. A moment of dizziness as I realize the list of suspects, recently narrowed down to only two, has now grown to, well, everyone. Only when it passes can I say, "Who else knew what you and Mary were doing?"

"Tony," Carter says. "I asked him not to tell anyone, but that's no guarantee he didn't."

"Do you know if Mary told someone?" I say, thinking specifically of Jessie, who, despite being the closest with Mary, seems to be in the dark about everything. Unless it's all an act. The fact that I'm even considering it makes me feel both guilty and paranoid.

"Not sure," Carter says.

"What about Detective Vick? Did you tell him any of this?"

"Almost," Carter says before finally reaching for the whiskey bottle he's been wanting to grab for the past five minutes. He empties what's left into his mug and holds it out to me, offering a first sip of the coffee-tinged whiskey inside. "I didn't want to sound crazy."

"That was my job, apparently." I take the mug, have a sip, grimace. It tastes awful but gets the job done. "Which is why, for now, I think it's a good idea to stay quiet. Even if we told him, I doubt he'd believe us. Especially me."

"So what should we do?"

A very good question. One I'm at a loss to answer. The likeliest way to get Detective Vick to believe us is to present him with proof that we're right. Then it will be impossible for him to ignore us. Right now, the only thing I can think of is to go straight to the source.

"We ask Lenora," I tell Carter. "And get her to—"

I'm interrupted by a noise from outside.

A great deafening, tearing sound that shakes the cottage and everything in it, including me and Carter. We clutch the rattling table as it continues for one, two, three seconds. By the time it's over, Carter's coffee cup is shattered on the floor and I mentally feel the same way.

"Was that an earthquake?" I say.

Carter lets go of the table. "I . . . think so?"

The two of us rise on unsteady legs and make our way outside to investigate. On the terrace, Mrs. Baker, Jessie, and Archie have done the same. All five of us realize at once what just happened—a section of cliff between the terrace and the cottage broke off, leaving a jagged semicircle that looks as if something has taken a bite out of the lawn.

Carter and I take a few cautious steps toward it, both of us testing the ground, fearful the entire lawn might fall away beneath our feet. Which it very well could. We stop when we can just see over the edge. Far below, chunks of fallen earth sit surrounded by foamy waves.

"Welp," Carter says. "That's not good."

# TWENTY-FOUR

For the second day in a row, I skip Lenora's exercises and take her straight to the typewriter. Even though I know it's bordering on dereliction of duty, I'm too impatient.

On a normal night—not that any night at Hope's End can be described as normal—I would have shaken Lenora awake after leaving Carter's cottage, carried the typewriter to the bed, and demanded the truth about the baby. But the night before was particularly abnormal.

After the partial collapse of the cliff outside the cottage, Carter wisely decided to move into the main house until the damage could be assessed. Not that it's any safer in here. While helping Carter carry some of his belongings to an empty bedroom on the third floor, I spotted a new crack at the service stairs and a broken tile on the kitchen floor. Bad omens all.

Jessie sidled up to me while I examined the stairwell walls and whispered, "What were you and Carter up to?"

"Just talking," I said.

She winked. "Sure. Right. Totally."

"We *were*."

"Did you find out anything else about Mary?"

I stopped on the landing and studied her. Dressed in a pink sleepshirt and missing her makeup and jewelry, she looked like a complete stranger. Which she technically was.

"No," I said before continuing on.

I wanted to trust Jessie. I really did. Of everyone at Hope's End, she seemed the least likely to have a reason for wanting Mary dead and the most likely to be an ally to me. But since I'd already ruled out Carter as a suspect, I couldn't risk doing it for anyone else. Even Jessie. While I'm not usually a suspicious person, in this case I needed to be. I doubted Mary was suspicious, either, and look at what happened to her.

Carter must have been thinking the same thing when he came to my door while on his way to his temporary room on the third floor. "Are you going to be okay?" he said in a half whisper.

"Yeah," I replied, even though I knew what he was really asking. Barring the possible but unlikely scenario that someone from town had snuck through the open gate and killed Mary, someone under this roof was a murderer. "I'll be fine."

I wasn't fine.

I ended up spending most of the night wide awake, thinking about Lenora and Carter and the idea that Mary was dead because she knew too much about them both. That led to wondering if I now knew too much. The answer I came up with—a resounding yes—prompted more questions. How much danger was I in? Should I just up and leave in the middle of night like everyone thought Mary had?

With ideas like that clanging through my skull, the fact I managed to fall asleep at all is a minor miracle. When I woke to sunrise piercing my eyes and the mattress slid lower on the bed frame, I realized that I hadn't heard any mysterious noises coming from Lenora's room. Either I slept right through them or whoever—whatever?—is causing them decided to take the night off.

Now I stifle a yawn while getting Lenora into typing position. When she's ready, I kneel beside her and say, "Lenora, I think we should talk about the baby."

She pretends not to be surprised I know.

But she is.

Her face, as expressive as a silent film star's, can't hide such shock. This is especially true of her eyes, which widen at the same time they go slightly dim. An unspoken answer to the biggest question I had: Could Carter have been wrong about Lenora's pregnancy? Yes, that photograph of her in 1929 is very persuasive, but it doesn't confirm anything.

"I know you were pregnant," I say. "And Mary knew, too, didn't she?"

Lenora's left hand rises and falls twice against the typewriter. That's a yes.

"What happened to the baby?"

Lenora lets out a long, sad sigh. Then she types a single word—gone—before letting her hand slide off the typewriter.

"Gone?"

It's strange how a word so short can contain so many possibilities. Lenora could have had a miscarriage. Or the baby was stillborn. Or left this world shortly after entering it. Or was bundled up and left on the front steps of a church on Christmas morning. That single word—gone—could also mean something happier. The child was born, grew up, left Hope's End, and now has a family of their own. Although, going by Lenora's reaction, I don't think that's what happened.

"Did the baby die?" I say.

Lenora makes no indication she wants to type more. Her hands sit in her lap, the useful left one atop the useless right, and she stares at them as if she didn't hear me.

"Who was the father?" I say, pressing. "Was it Ricky?"

Still nothing from Lenora. No acknowledging the question. No acknowledging me. Without saying a word, she's made her message clear—she doesn't want to talk about it.

I can't blame her. She was pregnant. The baby's now gone. She probably thinks there's nothing else to be said.

Only there is.

And Lenora told it to at least one other person—Mary.

Considering what happened to her, I should be grateful Lenora now refuses to tell me. Maybe that's another reason for her silence. She doesn't want to put me in more danger than I might already be.

Once again, I think about leaving. It would take only minutes to pack my suitcase and box, grab my medical bag, and walk away from Hope's End without looking back. But I can't bring myself to do it. Even though I haven't been told everything, what I do know is enough to keep me here. I need to learn the rest.

The Hope family murders. Lenora's pregnancy. Mary's death. They're all tied together in a complex knot of secrets, lies, and misdeeds both past and present. I'm certain that if I can unravel it, the truth will be revealed. About Carter and Mary, yes, but most of all about Lenora. She's the person I need to understand the most.

So I stay, letting the morning pass slowly and silently. With any other patient, I would have busied myself with light housework or cooking lunch or even just watching TV with them. None of those options are available to me at Hope's End. So I pass the time reading a Danielle Steel novel on the divan while Lenora sits in her wheelchair and stares out the window.

It reminds me of my mother's final days, when she was too fragile and pain-wracked to be moved to the couch in the living room. Stuck in a room without a television and its comforting background noise, the silence became so thick it was almost unbearable.

Today isn't quite that bad, but it's enough to make me appreciate the few moments of sound and activity. Fetching lunch. Feeding Lenora. Even assisting her in the bathroom because it's something to do besides sitting here and thinking. While I tackle the tasks with endless chatter, Lenora does nothing in response.

No taps.

Certainly no typing.

She's become the person I thought she was when I first arrived. Silent, still, almost a nonentity. It makes me wonder if this is what she was like with all the nurses before Mary breezed in with a typewriter. If so, does Lenora regret indulging her? Does she feel the same about me and has decided this will be the way things are now?

And it *is* her decision. An afternoon at the typewriter could end all this. Yet we spend this long, dreary day in more insufferable silence. I finish my book. Lenora stares out the window. The day fades into dusk, which darkens into night.

Eventually Archie arrives, carrying dinner on a tray. Salmon and sweet potatoes that are roasted for me, mashed for Lenora. On the side are piping-hot rolls for me and a chocolate milkshake for Lenora.

"I thought Miss Hope could use a pick-me-up," Archie explains. "She loved them when she was a girl."

The gesture is so thoughtful it takes me a second to remember that he could have killed Mary. It doesn't matter that Archie looks about as threatening as a teddy bear. He was here when Lenora's family was murdered in 1929, and he was here when Mary plummeted off the cliff.

Yet that also makes him a perfect source of information about both of those nights. The challenge is figuring out if Archie's a friend or a foe, a suspect or a potentially trusted resource. For now, I decide it's best to treat him as all of the above.

"You didn't need to go to all the trouble," I say, taking the food from his hands. Because I haven't yet attached Lenora's meal tray to her wheelchair, I set it on the sideboard next to her snow globe and the cassette Jessie gave me yesterday.

"It's no trouble," Archie says. "Besides, I wanted to see how Miss Hope is doing."

I glance at Lenora, who acts like neither of us is in the room with her. "Not too well."

"I think that goes for all of us," Archie says. "Poor Mary. Had I known she was hurting so much, I would have tried to help her somehow. And then the cliff giving way like that. These are not happy times at Hope's End."

I wonder if there's ever been a time here that was happy. From what Lenora has written, I've gathered the place was doomed from the start.

"The other day, you told me that you and Lenora used to be close."

"I did," Archie says. "And we were."

"How close?"

"Best friends, I guess. Although that was more from proximity than anything else. We were roughly the same age in a place where that wasn't common."

"What about Virginia? Were the two of you also close?"

"No. Can't say we were."

His answer, refreshing in its swift honesty, makes me decide to continue the conversation. It might be risky—and I might eventually come to regret it—but if Archie's currently in a talkative mood, I'm not going to stop him.

And Lenora, I know, is listening, even though she pretends she isn't. I retrieve the Walkman, pop in the latest book-on-cassette from Jessie, and put the headphones over Lenora's ears. I lodge the Walkman itself between her motionless right hand and the side of the wheelchair so it won't slide off.

"A new book from Jessie," I explain to Lenora. "Would you like to listen to it while I talk to Archie? After that we'll have dinner."

Knowing she's not going to respond, I press play and turn back to Archie, who says, "What else do we need to talk about?"

I hesitate, trying to think of the best way to phrase my question. After concluding that there's no good way to pose it, I blurt out, "Did Lenora have a baby?"

"A baby?" Archie stares at me, perplexed, like I've just asked if she had two heads or a pet rhinoceros. "Where'd you get that idea?"

"Lenora made a passing reference," I say, nodding toward the typewriter on the desk. I figure it's fine to give Archie an indication that Lenora can use it. He might already know.

"What have the two of you been doing on that thing?"

"Just getting to know each other better," I say, presenting the truth in its simplest form. "I like to learn about the people I'm caring for."

Archie eyes me with skepticism. "And she told you she had a baby?"

"She hinted at it."

"You must have misunderstood her."

"So Lenora was never pregnant?" I say.

"Never."

Apparently done talking, Archie turns to leave. I pose one last question to his retreating form, hoping to get if not an honest answer, then at least an unconscious reaction.

"When you were close, did she ever mention the name Ricardo Mayhew?"

Archie's formidable frame comes to a stop in the doorway. "No," he says.

"He used to work here."

"I know," Archie says. "But Miss Hope never mentioned him. There's your answer."

He starts moving again, walking stiffly into the hall. Only then does he face me again, his hard stare a silent warning.

"If I were you, I wouldn't spend too much time typing with Miss Hope," he says. "The past is in the past. It does no one any good to start digging it up."

"The baby just kicked."

"No, it didn't."

"It did, I swear," Archie said, his hand still pressed to my swollen belly.

I pushed it away. "I think I'd know."

It was another Tuesday night with the rest of the household staff gone and my family scattered. Archie often spent those nights off in my room, where we'd laugh and talk and dream about the future. It was a ritual we had performed almost since he first started working at Hope's End.

By that September, though, the ritual had become a rarity. In the past few months, Archie and I had spent little time together. He'd grown distant, and I worried it was all my doing rather than his. I'd neglected him terribly since meeting Ricky, so my decision to tell him of my pregnancy was an attempt to involve him once again in my life.

He was happy for me, but also concerned. As I told him my plans for the future, he pretended to be pleased, but worry lines kept rippling over his brow.

"Are you sure you want to do this?" he said. "With someone like him?"

"Why wouldn't I be sure?"

Archie leaned against me on the divan, our shoulders touching. "You know exactly why."

"It's a tricky situation," I said. "But we have a plan."

We didn't yet, but I couldn't tell that to Archie. I knew it would only make him more concerned. He had always seen himself as my protector. Even when we were younger and he was just a runaway given a job in the kitchen out of pity. I think that's what drew us to each other. We were two lonely souls in need of someone to care for.

"I wish you had told me you were sweet on him," Archie said.

"Why?"

"Because I would have tried to stop you."

"Stop pretending like I'm the only one in a tricky situation," I said. "I know what you've been up to."

"It's not the same," Archie said, and indeed it wasn't. The only situation more scandalous than mine was Archie's.

"I knew what I was getting myself into when I met him," I said, when in truth I had no idea how deeply I'd fall in love with Ricky and how quickly it would happen.

"That's one thing. Having a baby is another." Archie reached for the camera he'd just purchased. An extravagance I knew he couldn't easily afford. Buying it required months of saving. "I know of someone who can help, if you decide you don't want to have it. A doctor."

"Who told you this?"

"One of the maids. She went to him when she got pregnant. She couldn't keep it because the father--"

Archie stopped himself, too kind to speak aloud the truth we both knew.

"Was my father," I said. "I know."

I'd heard Berniece talking about it in the kitchen one morning when she thought none of the High and Mighty Hopes was around.

That's what she called us. The High and Mighty Hopes, always spoken with a derisive snort. She mentioned that one of the new maids had been ruined by my father, forced to get rid of the baby and then kicked out of Hope's End.

That was the previous year, and based on the compromising position I'd caught him in on my birthday, my father hadn't learned his lesson. Although no one said as much, I knew it was one of the reasons my mother kept to her own bed. She and my father barely spoke, let alone saw each other.

It made me sad to see them so miserable with each other. My sister, however, merely pretended nothing was wrong. I knew it was pretend because it was impossible to miss the tension strung like trip wire throughout the entire mansion.

"I won't end up like my parents," I said. "I'll make sure of it. I love him, Arch. I really do."

"Well, I wish you didn't."

I wasn't hurt by Archie's words. I knew he didn't say them to be cruel. It was simply his way. He had a gentle soul and told things the way he saw them, unlike most everyone else at Hope's End.

"If things were different, you know I'd have chosen you," I said.

"I know," he replied. "But they are different. With me and with him. People like us and people like you and your sister--we're not meant to mingle. Society won't allow it. The longer you let this thing go on, the worse it'll be when it inevitably ends."

I sat up, adamant. "It won't end."

Archie raised his hands in surrender. "I believe you. But whatever happens, good or bad, know that I'll be with you the entire time."

"Thank you," I said.

He raised the camera, prompting a sigh from me. The last thing I wanted at that moment was to have my picture taken. Even though Ricky told me I was beautiful every time he saw me, I didn't feel beautiful. Into the sixth month of my pregnancy, I felt bloated and restless. I couldn't even muster a proper pose for Archie, although he didn't seem to mind.

"Perfect," he said as I cradled my swollen stomach.

The shutter clicked, and Archie joined me on the divan. I leaned my head against his shoulder, as I had done a hundred times in the past few years. He was so big, so solid. I knew he would always be there for me, no matter what.

"Just to make it clear," Archie added out of the blue. "If he--or anyone--ever hurts you or makes you unhappy, I won't hesitate to kill them."

# TWENTY-FIVE

A minute after Archie leaves, Carter pops into Lenora's room to check on us. He looks, for lack of a better word, haggard from lack of sleep.

"Guess the third floor didn't treat you well," I say.

He answers with a yawn. "How can any of you stand it in here? All night I felt like I was sleeping in a bed with two of its legs sawed off."

"Right now, it's safer than the cottage. How does the lawn look?"

"Like there's a big hole in it," Carter says.

"Has something like this ever happened before?"

He shakes his head. "Not while I've been here."

"So why is it happening now?" I probe.

"That's a very good question. One I can't answer. Besides, I'm more worried about if it's going to happen again."

I look toward the night-shrouded window, grateful I can't see the edge of the terrace and the ocean waves careening toward the base of the cliff far below it. Still, I wonder if after last night the mansion has shifted even more—and how much more it can go before toppling over entirely.

While I glance at the window, Carter sets his gaze on Lenora. "Learn anything new?"

I check to make sure she's still listening to her Walkman before pulling him into my room. "She confirmed she was pregnant," I say.

"What happened to the baby?"

"I don't know. She stopped typing after that. She made it very clear she doesn't want to talk about it."

"Do you think the baby was born?" Carter says, avoiding what he really wants to ask: Do I think the baby was his father?

I study his features, trying to detect even the slightest resemblance to Lenora. There's nothing. Especially in the eyes. Carter's are a warm hazel. A far cry from Lenora's startling green. Yet I can't rule out the possibility, either. We have no idea what Ricardo Mayhew looked like, other than Lenora's description of him as incredibly good-looking. Carter's definitely got that part covered.

"I don't know. All she told me is that the baby is gone, which could mean anything. I even asked Archie—"

"Do you trust him?"

"No," I say. "Because he lied. He told me Lenora was never pregnant."

"Maybe he didn't know."

"It's more likely he doesn't want anyone else to know. Including Mary."

Carter flinches, and I can tell he's picturing the same thing I am. Mary on the terrace, suitcase in hand, Archie barreling toward her, twice her size.

"You shouldn't have asked him about it," he says, his voice going quiet. "Now I'm worried he thinks you know too much."

I am, too. But for a reason different than Carter's. Mine is an abstract fear that none of what we're doing will change things. *The past is in the past*, Archie said. *It does no one any good to start digging it up.* Am I doing more harm than good by forcing Lenora to talk about the child who's no longer with her and the night her family was slaughtered? Will Mary's family and friends be better off knowing her cause of death was murder instead of suicide? Maybe Detective Vick was right about my having an ulterior motive for doing all this. That it's not Lenora or Mary or even Carter I'm concerned about.

It's me.

And what will happen if I can't prove anything?

"He doesn't," I say. "Because I don't. We only have theories, not facts."

"So what now?"

"I don't know. Maybe Lenora will soon want to start typing again."

I move through the adjoining door back into Lenora's room, knowing it's not a good idea for someone else to see me and Carter conferring in mine. I still remember the way Jessie sounded last night. Full of innuendo. Like she was suspicious—or jealous. Who knows how Archie or, God forbid, Mrs. Baker would react if they saw us together like this.

"Let me know if she does." Carter heads to the hall, pausing in the doorway to take one more look at Lenora, checking for a resemblance that isn't there. "And be careful. Right now, I don't trust anyone but you."

By the time he's gone, it's fifteen minutes past dinnertime. Which will make us equally as late for Lenora's evening exercises, bath, and bedtime. I go back to my room and the lockbox under the bed, shaking out the proper amount of pills I need to mix with her dinner. The pages Lenora and I have typed remain under the rolling bottles. I wonder if more will eventually be added to the stack—and if that would make things better or worse.

Back with Lenora, I start to get ready for dinner. She's exactly as I left her. Wheelchair. Window. Headphones over her ears. The only thing that's changed is the Walkman.

The cassette inside no longer turns.

When I lift the headphones from Lenora's ears, no words come out.

"It turned off?" I ask Lenora.

She taps her left hand twice against the wheelchair armrest, where it's been since before I turned the Walkman on. The Walkman, meanwhile, sits exactly where I left it between her right hand and the side of the wheelchair. Even if Lenora had moved her left hand at some point, there's no way she could have reached across her lap and turned off the Walkman without disturbing its position.

"How did it stop?"

Lenora gives me a blank look that's her substitute for a shrug.

I pick up the Walkman and examine it. My initial thought is that it automatically shut off when the first side of the cassette ran out of tape. Thinking the cassette needs to be flipped, I eject it from the Walkman. There's plenty of tape around both reels, suggesting only half of it has been played.

Since the only other thing that could have caused it to stop working is a dead battery, I slide the cassette back into the Walkman and press the play button. Jessie's voice, muffled but unmistakable, pops from the headphones in my hands.

I hit the stop button, my mind turning faster than the reels inside the Walkman a mere moment earlier. Since the cassette didn't run out of tape, the batteries still work, and Lenora didn't use her left hand, I can think of only one other way for the Walkman to have stopped playing.

Lenora turned it off herself.

With a hand she can't use.

# TWENTY-SIX

It's ten p.m., Lenora's in bed, and I'm in my room next door staring at a Walkman she may or may not have turned off using a hand she may or may not be able to use. After an hour of obsessing over it, I'm still not sure.

One thing I'm certain of is that it's nearly impossible for the Walkman to have accidentally shut off without Lenora using her right hand. I know because I've tried. Jostling it. Smacking it. I even knocked it against the side of a chair multiple times, testing to see if it was enough to bump the stop button. It wasn't. Nothing Lenora could have done with her left hand would have somehow made the Walkman turn off if it bumped her right one.

Now I watch the reels inside the Walkman spin, waiting to see if they stop on their own for any reason other than the one I'm thinking of. A warp of the cassette tape. Faulty wiring in the Walkman itself. Just random occurrence that has never happened before and never will again. But everything works exactly the way it should, even as I keep pressing buttons.

Stop, rewind, play, stop, rewind, play.

My thoughts do a similar herky-jerky dance.

Stop.

Lenora turned off the Walkman. I'm convinced of that now. But how?

Rewind.

Because it's possible she's capable of more than she's letting on. I've thought this before, when I realized the page in the typewriter had been moved.

Play.

If that's true, then it means Lenora has been pretending all this time.

Stop.

But I can't think of a single reason why she'd do that. Lenora's day is filled with indignities. Having someone feed her, bathe her, remove her soiled adult diaper, and wipe her clean before putting on a fresh one. No one would willingly subject themselves to that.

Rewind.

Yet what about that page taken from the typewriter? And the footfalls I keep hearing inside her room? And the blur at the window and the shadow at the door? Someone is causing them—and I don't believe it's the ghost of Virginia Hope.

Play.

Which means the only logical source is Lenora, who's been lying to me. Possibly about everything.

Stop.

Not necessarily. Maybe Lenora has no control over what her body can and cannot do. It sometimes happens in patients with paralysis. Sudden muscle spasms can occur like an electric shock to their system, moving muscles against their will, just like what happened when I checked her reflexes my first night here. Now *that's* something that could have caused her to shut off the Walkman.

My finger's still on the stop button when I hear a noise.

A heavy thud.

*Lenora*, I think when I hear it a second time. *She's moving around. Again.*

I hurry through the adjoining door into Lenora's room. Inside, it's as still and silent as a tomb. Outside, waves gently lap at the base of the cliff. Lenora appears to be asleep. Eyes closed, flat on her back, blanket to her chin. I tiptoe to her bedside and listen to the steady sound of her breathing.

All is well.

Except for more noise. Footsteps this time, shushing over the carpet in the hallway. I go to Lenora's bedroom door, open it a crack, and see Mrs. Baker passing by. A white-robed blur holding a—

*Is that a shotgun?*

My unspoken question gets an immediate answer when Mrs. Baker halts and does a half-turn in my direction. Clutched in her arms *is* a shotgun, its double barrel propped against her right shoulder.

"They're outside," she says.

"Who?"

"Reporters. They've been loitering at the gate all day. It's either them or boys from town who've hopped the wall and now they're prowling the grounds."

When Mrs. Baker hurries off toward the service stairs, I follow, unsure who's in bigger danger, us or the trespassers. If they're teenage boys and anything like the ones I went to school with, then they're mostly harmless. Mrs. Baker, on the other hand, is armed.

From the kitchen, we move into the hallway, where I glimpse movement through the front-facing windows.

A dark figure, streaking by.

Then another.

And another.

In the foyer, Mrs. Baker throws open the front door and marches outside, shotgun barrel leading the charge. The night is foggy, with mist languidly curling over the lawn. In the haze, two more dark figures zip by, bringing the number of known trespassers to five. They all carry flashlights, the beams cutting through the dense fog like lasers.

"You'll leave right now if you know what's good for you!" Mrs. Baker shouts at them.

The trespassers scatter in all directions, footsteps squishing on the damp lawn and flashlights bobbing in panic. Once a safe distance from the house, one of them stops and turns, backlit by the moon-drenched fog.

"It's Lenora!" he yells. Then he calls out, "Killer!"

That settles it. They definitely aren't reporters.

Another one joins him, shouting, "Killer!" before the others also start chiming in. Their voices ring out in the night, echoing through the fog.

"Killer! *Killer!*"

The trespasser who'd started the chant—the ringleader, apparently—keeps shouting it after the others have stopped, adding one more word to the insult.

"Killer bitch!"

I flinch when I hear it.

Like he had yelled it at *me*.

*About* me.

I bolt past Mrs. Baker and hurtle into the frigid night, not thinking about what I'm doing or why I'm doing it. All I can focus on is catching the punk who said it, shaking him by the shoulders, and making sure he knows I'm innocent.

The dark figure starts running when he sees me coming, his sneakers slipping on the dew-slicked grass. It gives me the extra second I need to catch up just before he can get away. I lunge forward, grab him by the shirt collar, and yank. His feet slide out from under him, and he drops to the ground like a sack of wheat. The flashlight flies from his hand and rolls across the grass, its light flickering. In that stuttering glow, I leap on top of him, surprising him and surprising myself even more.

Yet there's another surprise in store for both of us.

Writhing in the grass beneath me, the trespasser looks up at me and says, "Kit?"

No matter how shocked he is, I'm doubly surprised.

It's Kenny.

"What are you doing here?" he says.

Winded, I slide off him and plop onto the grass. "I work here. What are *you* doing here?"

"Just having a little fun with the boys," Kenny says as he sits up.

"Aren't you a little old for this shit, Kenny?"

"Yeah," he says, now grinning the same way he did whenever I met him at the back door. "But it's not like it's hurting anyone."

He'd be singing a different tune if Mrs. Baker had shot one of them, which I wouldn't put past her. A woman like her surely has an itchy trigger finger.

"You really work here?" Kenny says. "At Hopeless End?"

I sigh. So that's what they're calling it now. "I do."

"Who's your patient?"

"Who do you think?"

Kenny blinks. "No way! What's she like?"

"Not a killer bitch," I say.

"Yeah, sorry about that," Kenny says, eyes to the ground. "I didn't mean anything by it. That's just what everyone says about her."

"They're wrong."

"Then what's she really like?"

"Quiet," I reply, which says everything while also revealing nothing.

I look down the long driveway to the front gate, where the rest of Kenny's friends have gathered. At least it's fully closed tonight. Not that it matters. One of Kenny's "boys" is boosting the others over the brick wall. At the top, another reaches down to help him up. Gate or no gate, it proves that literally anyone could have come onto the property and killed Mary.

One of Kenny's friends shouts at him from atop the wall. "Hey! You coming?"

"In a minute!" Kenny calls back.

"Do you guys do this often?" I say as his friends vanish over the wall.

"Not since high school," Kenny says, which in his case was only two years ago. "A few of us were drinking and decided to come see if what everyone's saying is true. You know, about her dead nurse."

"What about her?" I sit up straighter, genuinely curious about what people in town think about Mary's death. So far, the only outside opinion I've been privy to is Detective Vick's. "What are they saying?"

"That Lenora Hope killed her."

Of course they do. I should have known not to put any stock in what my fellow townies are saying. "That's impossible."

"Why?"

"There's a reason Lenora hasn't been seen in decades." I stand and brush the skirt of my uniform, now wet from the grass. I then reach down and help Kenny to his feet. "She can't walk. Or talk. Or even move anything but her left hand. She's harmless."

"How do you know?"

"Because I'm her caregiver," I say. "I've spent more time with her than you."

"I know you think I'm stupid." Kenny says it without a hint of anger. Instead, there's a gentle resignation in his voice that makes me reconsider our relationship, such as it was. I honestly didn't think he cared what I thought. Now I'm not so sure.

"I don't," I say.

He gives me a sad smile. "It's okay. I am stupid. About a lot of things. But I think that sometimes helps me see things that smarter people like you overthink."

"Like *me*?" I say, both flattered he considers me smart and insulted that he believes I overthink things.

"What I mean is that sometimes facts just get in the way. Sure, you're Lenora Hope's caregiver and you think she can't hurt anyone."

"Because she can't."

"You're still overthinking," Kenny says. "There's more to everyone than meets the eye. You, me, even Lenora Hope. Look at us. Back when we first decided to . . ."

"Fuck," I say, because that's all it was.

"Right. Back then, I knew what happened to your mom and what everyone was saying about you. But I didn't spend any time thinking about it. I just knew in my gut that you were a good person."

A lump forms in my throat. No one has said that about me for a very long time. That it comes from Kenny, of all people, makes me understand just how much my father's silence has hurt me. He's the one who should be telling me this. Not the guy I started sleeping with just because I was starved for human contact.

"Thank you," I say.

"No problem," Kenny replies with a shrug. "But on the flip side, sometimes your gut tells you something else. So while Lenora looks like she can't do much, maybe, like you, there's more than meets the eye."

There's certainly more to Kenny than I expected. Back when we were having no-strings afternoon sex, I had no idea there was this kind of wisdom inside him. But before I can give him too much credit, he grabs my waist, pulls me close, and sloppily kisses me.

I push him away, worried that Mrs. Baker is still watching from the front door.

"It's not going to happen, Kenny."

"Thought I'd give it a shot," he says, flashing that horny grin I've seen dozens of times since May. "I should go anyway. Take care of yourself, Kit. If you ever change your mind, you know where to find me."

Kenny gives me a playful wink before sprinting to the wall at the end of the lawn and scaling it with zero effort. Then, with a corny salute, he turns and hops off the wall, vanishing from view.

Turning around, I take in the entirety of Hope's End. From the vantage point of the lawn, it looks enormous, forbidding. It's easy to forget that when you're on the inside, navigating its bloodstained stairs and tilted halls. Lenora's the same way. I remember the fear I felt when stepping into her room for the first time. Her reputation preceded her. Now that I've gotten to know her, that reputation has, if not faded, at least been made more benign by familiarity.

Not anymore, thanks to Kenny.

Now my gut tells me I was wrong about initially thinking there are only four people at Hope's End who could have shoved Mary off the terrace. There's someone else.

A fifth, highly unlikely suspect.

But now a suspect all the same.

Lenora.

# TWENTY-SEVEN

Back in the house, I find Mrs. Baker still in the foyer and Jessie on the Grand Stairs, obliviously standing on the bloodstains in the carpet. Her eyes widen at the sight of the shotgun in Mrs. Baker's hands. "What's going on?" she says.

"Trespassers," Mrs. Baker replies before moving down the hall toward the kitchen.

"I took care of them," I say.

Jessie lets out a relieved huff. "What did they want?"

"Nothing. Just some kids messing around."

Although, in Kenny's case, no longer a kid. And his warning still reverberates through my thoughts. Yes, Lenora's the one who typed her story, but maybe she regretted telling Mary so much. Or had second thoughts. Or didn't think Mary would tell anyone else and felt the need to act when she realized that was the plan. I even consider the bruise on Lenora's arm, now all but healed. Could Mary have drawn blood against her will? Is that why she took it from Lenora's working left arm instead of her nonworking right? So Lenora had no way to fight the needle's approach?

That idea runs counter to the theory that Lenora, of all people, killed Mary. Could she push someone if she only has the use of one arm? If so, how could she do it when she can't even walk?

The answer, of course, is that she's just pretending she can't.

I've experienced too much to keep me from outright dismissing the idea that Lenora is faking it. First, there's the Walkman and the unlikelihood that it turned off by itself. Then there are the noises coming from Lenora's room almost nightly. Creaks and footsteps and rustling. Connected to them are the shadow passing the adjoining door and the gray blur I saw at the window. Until I learn what caused some, if not all, of those things, Lenora must remain a suspect.

Upstairs, I peek into her room. Despite the ruckus outside, Lenora's still asleep. Or at least pretending to be.

Just like she might be pretending that she's incapable of doing more than just move her left hand.

Much more.

Like talking.

And walking.

And shoving.

The only way to find out is to catch her in the act. If it even is an act. Someone else could be causing the noise and movement in her room each night. If so, I want to know who it is—and why.

I cross Lenora's room and enter mine through the adjoining door. Instead of closing it, I prop the door open with a stack of paperbacks from the bookshelf. I change out of my uniform, crawl into bed, and pick up a book I'd pulled at random from the shelf. *Scruples* by Judith Krantz. Next to it is a thermos I filled with leftover coffee from this morning. It's cold and bitter, which is exactly what I need. If someone walks around Lenora's room tonight, I plan on being awake to notice them.

I position myself at a slight angle on the bed, making sure the open doorway remains in my line of sight at all times. Then I settle in for a night of no sleep. Fueled by bad coffee and an okay book, I remain awake for hours.

Long enough to finish a hundred pages of the Judith Krantz.

Long enough to then count the waves as they crash against the base of the cliff.

Long enough to give up after tallying two hundred of them.

And long enough to see my mother creep into the room through the adjoining door.

In silence, she crosses to the foot of my bed, swaying on legs whittled thin by disease. Her teeth clatter, sounding again like the struck keys of a typewriter. She raises a bony arm and points at me as her lower jaw drops open.

Then she screams.

I bolt upright in bed, my eyes still closed and my ears still ringing with the noise my mother made in the nightmare. Not a scream, but a buzz. A loud, steady one that I continue to hear even though I'm now awake.

I open my eyes to a bedroom glowing red and Lenora's alarm buzzing on the nightstand. I look to the adjoining door.

It's closed.

I jump out of bed, fling it open, rush into Lenora's room. She's awake in bed with the call button smashed under the palm of her left hand. Her mouth droops open, releasing a gurgling moan of pure terror. Her eyes are saucer-wide as she stares at something on the other side of the room.

The typewriter.

A fresh page sits in the carriage, filled with a single sentence typed over and over and over.

**It's all your fault**
**It's all your fault**
**It's all your fault**
**It's all your fault**
**It's all your fault**
**It's all your fault**

I rip the page from the typewriter and turn to Lenora. "Let me guess. Your sister?"

Lenora taps twice.

# TWENTY-EIGHT

"Which one of you did this?" I hold up the sheet of paper so everyone can see what's been typed on it. "I know it was someone in this house."

All of us are crammed into Lenora's bedroom. Every single person living and working at Hope's End. Carter and Jessie share the divan. Archie sits on the edge of Lenora's bed. And Mrs. Baker stands in the doorway, arms crossed and eyeglasses on so she can get a better view of what she probably thinks is a mental breakdown.

I deserve more credit than that. If I was truly hysterical, I wouldn't have waited until after breakfast to demand everyone gather in Lenora's room. I would have done it at four in the morning, right after I spotted the page.

"Who does Miss Hope say did it?" Mrs. Baker says.

"Her sister."

Mrs. Baker's eyes grow large behind her cat's-eye frames. Archie coughs, probably trying to suppress a laugh. Carter and Jessie look worried.

Or weirded out.

Or both.

As for Lenora, she simply sits by the window in her wheelchair, observing the proceedings with keen fascination. From the Mona Lisa smile on her face, I assume she's enjoying it. She likely hasn't had this many visitors in decades.

"That's impossible," Mrs. Baker says.

"I know it is," I say. "Which means one of you snuck into this room and did it."

"Why would one of us do that?" This comes from Jessie, who asks while twisting one of the many bracelets around her wrist.

"I don't know," I say, when in truth I think I do. Whoever did it is likely trying to scare Lenora to keep her from telling me as much as she told Mary.

Because the mystery typist is also the person who killed her.

The very idea makes me short of breath.

I am in a room with a killer.

It doesn't matter that the gate was open the night Mary was killed or that, as Kenny and his friends proved, it's so easy to hop the wall. The typed page in my hand leaves me convinced this was an inside job.

I look from person to person, studying their facial expressions and body language, searching for signs of a tell. Jessie's bracelet twirling, for instance, could be a nervous tic. The same with Mrs. Baker's eyeglasses, which she's lowered but I'm sure will raise to her face again before speaking. As for Archie, he's harder to read. So quiet and still. Other than that single cough, he's done nothing to bring attention to himself. Maybe that's his tell.

"I have a question," Mrs. Baker says as she puts on her glasses just like I predicted she would. "How was Miss Hope able to tell you she thought her sister did it?"

"She tapped yes."

"So you specifically asked if it was her sister?"

"That's a weird thing to do," Archie says, finally piping up.

"Indeed," Mrs. Baker says. "I can only assume you did it because you went through all of our names with Miss Hope and was told no."

"That part doesn't matter," I say. "What's important is that she said it was Virginia. Which we all know isn't the case."

"Why does she think that?" Jessie says.

Honestly, I don't know. My best guess is that talking about the past has Lenora dreaming about it. Those humdinger nightmares that linger. When she wakes, she thinks they're real. Just for a moment. And that her sister is with her still.

But saying that would reveal all. A tempting idea. Tell them everything and see what happens. Admit that I've been helping Lenora type her story, that Mary did the same thing, and that it's why I think someone shoved her off the terrace. I don't because it would also give away Carter's secrets. Something the nervous ping-ponging of his eyes tells me he wouldn't like.

"It's the power of influence," Mrs. Baker says, answering in my place. "Something in Kit's body language or the way she spoke our names indicated to Miss Hope it wasn't the answer she wanted. But the way she mentioned Miss Hope's sister did. Miss Hope was merely trying to please her."

Not knowing how to respond, I begin to smooth the skirt of my uniform. *My* tell. "What are you suggesting?"

"That the culprit is you, dear," Mrs. Baker says.

"Why would I type this?"

"Attention?" Jessie suggests while shooting a quick glance at Carter she probably doesn't want me to notice.

I glare at her. "I don't need anyone's attention."

"Then why are we all here?" Mrs. Baker tilts her head, staring directly at me, her blue eyes boring into me like the sunrise. "You're the one who demanded we all come here so you could show us the words on that page and tell us Miss Hope claims it was her sister. Why go to all that trouble?"

"Because I want whoever did it to stop," I say. "Please. And stop sneaking into Miss Hope's room at night."

Mrs. Baker's body goes rigid. "Someone's been doing that?"

"Yes."

"Why didn't you tell me?"

"I did," I say. "The morning after my first night here. I told you I heard footsteps in Miss Hope's bedroom and you said it was just the wind. But I heard it again the next night. And saw someone at that window. And watched a shadow pass the door between our rooms. That wasn't the wind. So it was either one of you or it was Lenora."

I stare at Mrs. Baker, silently daring her to chastise me for not saying "Miss Hope." She doesn't. Instead, she says, "Tell me immediately if it ever happens again."

Then she leaves, thereby bringing an end to this melodramatic—and ultimately fruitless—household meeting.

Archie is the first to follow her out. Then Carter, who gives me a we-need-to-talk-later look before slipping out the door. Jessie, however, lingers. Remaining on the divan, she says, "Sorry about that. I don't really think you did it for attention."

"Gee, thanks."

Jessie stands, steps closer, touches my arm. "What I mean is that I don't think you did it at all."

Out of the corner of my eye, I see Lenora pretending she isn't paying attention to every single word. Before Jessie can say anything else, I pull her into my room and shut the adjoining door behind us.

"Did you do it?" I ask her. "Did you type it and get Lenora to tell me it was her sister?"

Jessie drifts away from me, toward the bookshelf. "No way. How could you, like, even think that?"

Because she's done this kind of thing before. In the ballroom. With a Ouija board. Like we're in a goddamn game of Clue.

"If it was some kind of prank, I'd—"

"I told you it wasn't me," Jessie snaps. "How do you know it wasn't Lenora? She can type, right?"

"Not like this." I glance at the page in my hand, filled with proper capitalization and punctuation. "And not without help."

"Maybe she can do more than you think."

Kenny said the same thing last night. And I thought it myself before that, as I fiddled with the Walkman to see if it could shut itself off.

"Did Mary—" I have no idea how to phrase this without sounding insane. *Did she ever say Lenora is stronger than she looks? Did she ever think Lenora's faking this whole thing?* "Did Mary ever say she thought it was possible for Lenora to recover?"

"In what way?"

*Walk*, I think. *Shove. Kill.*

"Any way," I say. "Mentally. Physically."

"Like, learning to walk again?" Jessie says. "No. She never did."

"But it's possible, right?"

Jessie leans against the bookshelf, her hands behind her back. "I was just talking about typing. I didn't mean for you to think Lenora is running around without telling anyone. Sure, we've all heard stories about people suddenly snapping out of a coma or paralyzed people miraculously being able to walk again. So I guess it can happen. But probably not to someone Lenora's age. You can't teach an old dog new tricks. That kind of thing."

"But what if this isn't a case of an old dog learning a new trick?" I say. "What if they've known this particular trick since they were young?"

"You think Lenora's faking this?" Jessie says. "Why would she do that?"

I don't have an answer other than that Lenora seems to enjoy keeping secrets. She's been doing it for decades, never telling a soul what she knew about the Hope family massacre until Mary came along. And now, despite all common sense and reason, I can't shake the feeling that once she revealed her biggest secret to Mary, Lenora decided to take it back.

If such a thing is possible.

"I'm kind of worried about you, Kit," Jessie says. "You're acting like Mary."

"In what way?"

"Um, every way."

I'd be worried about me, too, if I didn't know what I do. That someone's been walking around Lenora's room. That she's lied to me repeatedly about who it is. That she turned off a Walkman using a hand everyone thinks she can't use.

"I'm fine," I say, even though I'm not.

When Jessie departs, claiming she needs to dust the urns in the downstairs library—a sure sign she wants to get far, far away from me—someone who's fine wouldn't transfer Lenora from her wheelchair to the bed.

Someone who's fine wouldn't then examine Lenora's legs and right arm, searching for signs of untapped strength, feeling for muscles tense from disuse.

Someone who's fine wouldn't also tickle Lenora's palm, looking for a twitch, a twinge, a flicker of movement.

I do all those things as Lenora watches me from the bed, more wary than suspicious. I think she knows what I'm up to. If she's capable of resisting, she shows no sign of it. Her limp right arm is easy to stretch across the mattress, palm up, fingers spread. When she sighs, as if she's been through this before, I wonder if Mary also tried it.

I wonder if it worked.

I wonder if Lenora then felt the need to make her disappear.

With that in mind, the next logical step would be to try the opposite of tickling—inflict pain, which is more likely to induce a reaction. It would be so easy, too. Grab a syringe and needle from Mary's medical bag. Jab it into Lenora's right hand. Watch for the wince.

I shove the thought out of my mind. It goes against everything I've been trained to do. I might not trust Lenora right now—and I might be far from fine—but I'm still a caregiver.

So I cross to the desk, grab the sheet of paper I'd found in the typewriter, and read the accusation running from the top of the page to the bottom. I'm so tired that the words begin to blur, the letters rearranging themselves before my very eyes.

**It's all your fault**
**It's all Kit's fault**
**What they're saying's not true, Kit-Kat**

I crumple the paper into a ball, take it to the bed, and drop it into Lenora's open right hand. My hope is her reflexes take over when it hits her palm, the same way we catch something without thinking about it. It just happens. At some point, instinct takes over.

Not in this case. The balled-up paper bounces off Lenora's palm and onto the floor.

I pick it up and try again.

Then again.

Then I throw it across the room, where it ricochets off the window before rolling into a corner.

I need something heavier. Something Lenora will really feel when it lands in her hand.

I eye the open door between our rooms and the paperbacks that once propped it open but were pushed out of the way when some-one (Virginia? Lenora?) pulled it shut. I grab one—*Ordinary People* by Judith Guest—and hold it spine down a few inches from Lenora's hand.

I let it drop.

The book stands upright a second before flipping onto its side over Lenora's thumb and forefinger.

Still nothing.

Because, I realize, it doesn't matter if she catches it. The book, like the ball of paper, is expendable. Both mean nothing to her. If Lenora's faking all of this, she's not going to reveal it without a good reason. To get her to move her right hand—if she *can* move it—I need to provide a bigger incentive than a wad of paper and a dog-eared book.

I scan the room, considering and dismissing its contents. A hair-brush? Too worthless. A handheld mirror? Too unwieldy. The Walk-man? A strong candidate. But it, too, could be replaced.

My gaze lands on the Eiffel Tower snow globe on the sideboard. Stereotypical Paris under glass.

Now we're talking.

A gift to Lenora from her long-dead parents, it has sentimental value. It's likely also worth a lot of money. It's an antique, for one thing, and I doubt people like Winston and Evangeline Hope went for a cheap snow globe when choosing one for their daughter.

I pick it up, convinced Lenora would never, ever, not in a million years let it fall from her grip. The journey from the sideboard to the bed kicks up some of the gold flakes resting at the bottom of the waterless globe. They sparkle and swirl as I hold it upside down over Lenora's hand.

Flat on her back, Lenora strains to see what I'm doing. When she spots the gold flakes inside the snow globe, she takes on a panicked look. Her eyes burn bright, and a grunt rises from the back of her throat.

I ignore it, holding the snow globe steady, waiting for the right moment to drop it. I tell myself I'm doing nothing wrong. That Lenora can catch it if she really wants to. That the reason she's so stressed is because she knows I'm on to her.

Both of us stare at the snow globe, watching the gold flakes settle into the curve of the overturned dome. When the last one falls, I let go.

The snow globe smacks against Lenora's palm.

I hold my breath, watching and waiting.

For her fingers to curl around it.

For her to prove that she can use her right hand.

For the moment when at least one of my suspicions is confirmed.

Instead, the snow globe topples from her hand and rolls across the mattress.

Then it hits the floor and shatters.

The sound coming from behind the closed door of my mother's room was unmistakable.

Breaking glass.

Upon hearing it, my sister gasped. I merely flinched, as if whatever my mother had just thrown across the room was flying directly at me and not at my father.

"For Christ's sake, Evie," I heard him grumble. "Haven't you destroyed enough?"

"I could ask the same of you."

My mother's voice was loud and clear behind the door. A sign that she was well and truly furious. Normally, the laudanum kept her sounding meek and muddled. It pleased me to hear her sounding like her old self again, even though I knew it was prompted by the worst fight my parents had had in years.

"Nothing is destroyed," my father said. "Everything is fine. The firm is just going through a rough patch. Which is why it's so important right now that we have the money to keep it going."

My mother let out a derisive snort. "Our daughters' money, you mean."

"It should be our money."

"Over my dead body," my mother said.

This prompted my father to reply, "Don't tempt me."

"My parents had good reason for creating that trust," my mother said. "If you could get at that money, you'd spend it all in a year and Lenora and Virginia would have nothing."

"Nothing is exactly what they'll have if the business goes under and this place is foreclosed on."

My sister and I exchanged worried glances. We had no idea things were that bad, even though we should have suspected it. My parents barely spoke, let alone fought, which is why when their argument echoed down the hall, we both ran for the door to listen in. We knew something big had to have caused it.

"They'll be just fine if it does," my mother said.

"And what about me? You won't care if I lose everything?"

"I've already lost everything," my mother said. "Why shouldn't you? Or are you more worried about your little whore? I suppose I should say whores, since there have been many over the years."

"Don't act so innocent with me, darling," my father shot back, spitting the term of endearment he used on me with undisguised venom. "We both know the truth."

My mother's reply was so quiet that my sister and I had to press our ears against the door to hear it. Even then, we could barely make out the half-whispered "I don't know what you're talking about."

"Yes, you do," my father said. "I know why you married me. Just like I know that Lenora isn't my daughter."

I gasped. So loudly I was certain my parents heard it through the door. My sister was certain, too, for she clapped a hand over my mouth and whisked me down the hallway to the first open room. She yanked me inside just as the door to my mother's bedroom opened. We huddled in that darkened room, my heart pounding and my head woozy from shock, as my father looked up and down the hallway.

"Girls," he said in a voice so stern it turned my blood cold. "Were you eavesdropping?"

My sister kept her hand over my mouth as my father passed the open doorway, mere inches from us. I'd started to cry then, and my tears dripped over her fingers.

"Are you there, my dear and my darling?"

When he paused just past the door, I became certain he was about to leap inside, grab us both by our necks, and drag us out of the room. To my utter surprise, he moved on, down the hallway and to the Grand Stairs. When his footfalls faded to silence, my sister and I finally emerged and hurried to my bedroom. Inside, I threw myself onto the bed and began to weep, fully and openly.

My sister stood by the wall, her arms folded, in no mood to comfort me. I'm sure it never even crossed her mind.

"Do you think it's true?" she said. "That we could lose Hope's End?"

"That's what you're concerned about? Even after what Father said?"

"Oh, that." My sister shrugged. "Mother was in love with one of her parents' servants and got pregnant. He abandoned her and she had to marry Father to avoid a scandal. I thought you knew."

I shook my head. I had no idea.

Although, in hindsight, I think I should have. My sister and I bore only a slight resemblance to each other. Our noses were different. As were our hair and eyes. We looked less like siblings and more like cousins, which strangers had mistaken us for on more than one occasion.

"Well, now you do." My sister paused as a cruel smirk formed across her lips. "Honestly, you should be relieved. Now you know where you get it from. And that you're not the only slut in the family."

She then swanned out of the room, leaving me alone and with a hollow feeling in my gut that she knew about me and Ricky.

And it was only a matter of time before she told everyone else.

The only choice I had was to beat her to the punch and tell at least someone other than Archie. In my mind, the best person was my mother. She'd take the news far better than my father, for one thing. Also, I hoped she'd understand, having gone through the same predicament herself.

My mind made up, I walked to the end of the hall and crept into her room. My mother was barely awake, even though it was only late afternoon. Sunlight peeked between the drawn curtains at the windows, trying to trickle in the same way water did through a crack.

"Is that you, my darling?" she murmured from the bed.

I stood at the foot of it, trying to come up with the right words to say. But there was so much to be said--and so many questions to be asked--that I simply blurted out, "Is it true? What Father said?"

A sigh rose from the covers my mother had buried herself under.

"Yes, my darling."

"So you don't love him?"

"No," my mother said.

"Did you ever?"

"Never." My mother sounded dreamy and distant. Like someone talking in her sleep. "Never, ever. He knew it, too. He knew it and paid the man I did love to run away and never see me again. When that happened, I was trapped. I had no choice but to marry him."

My mother's voice drifted into a slur.

"No choice at all."

The slur became a whisper.

"Sorry, my darling."

The whisper faded to a gasp.

And then . . . nothing.

"Mother?" I rushed to her side, grabbing her shoulders and giving her a good shake. Jostled by the movement, her right hand flopped against the mattress, releasing the laudanum bottle she'd been holding.

It was completely empty.

She'd swallowed it all, likely right before I'd entered her room.

"Mother?" I cried, shaking her even harder, trying to jolt her back into consciousness. But it was no use. As my mother lay there, motionless, the empty bottle of laudanum rolled across the mattress and hit the floor with a crash.

# TWENTY-NINE

Lenora is giving me her version of the silent treatment, which involves refusing to tap out a response to even the most basic questions. Still, I try, continuing to ask her what she'd like to do this evening.

"Would you like to try typing?"

Lenora's left hand doesn't rise from the bed.

"You can listen to more of the book Jessie recorded for you. Would you like that?"

Again, nothing.

"Or I could read to you instead," I say. "That might be fun for neither of us."

This at least gets a reaction. The corners of Lenora's mouth perk up into a half smile. But it fades as quickly as it formed, and her face returns to stony expressionlessness.

"I'm sorry," I say for at least the fifth time that day. "I mean it. And I'll replace the snow globe. I swear."

We both know I can't. Lenora's murdered parents gave it to her more than fifty years ago. And I'm the suspicious bitch who broke it. No wonder she's furious at me. I'm mad at myself.

For thinking she could possibly be faking her condition. And for being so paranoid that I thought a mostly paralyzed woman could have killed Mary. And for letting that paranoia destroy what's likely the last treasured possession she had. Now all I can do is continue to beg for her forgiveness. I even get down on my knees, kneeling in the flecks of gold glitter that remain on the floor. I can't rid my brain of the heart-broken way Lenora looked as I tried to salvage what was left of the snow globe. It was impossible. The globe itself was nothing but shards, and very little of the Parisian scene inside survived. Even the Eiffel Tower was ruined, having been snapped in two. All that remained was the base. A stump of gold. I had no choice but to sweep up the shattered pieces and drop them into the trash as a single tear leaked from Lenora's eyes.

"Please, please forgive me," I said then and say again now.

Finally, Lenora responds.

A single tap against the mattress.

No.

"What can I do to make it up to you? Anything you want, I'll do it."

Lenora shifts her gaze to the typewriter on the other side of the room. Now she wants to type. Quickly, I get up and wind a fresh page into the carriage. I bring the typewriter to the bed and place Lenora's left hand atop the keys.

She presses seven of them.

outside

I stare at the word, surprised. "You want to go outside?"

Lenora raps twice against the typewriter.

"But that's against the rules."

Lenora bangs out another word.

so

Even without punctuation, I can tell she means it as a question.

"But you don't want to go outside."

i do, Lenora types. Adding, i miss it.

"So you never told Mrs. Baker not to take you outside?"

Lenora balls her hand into a fist before smashing her knuckles against the typewriter, sending up a spray of keys that clatter together, none of them striking the page. Not that they need to. I understand her perfectly.

No.

But there must be a good reason why Mrs. Baker doesn't want her to go outside. I can think of three off the top of my head: The weather. Lenora's fragile condition. The sheer hassle of getting a wheelchair-bound woman down the steps.

"Are you sure that's a good idea?" I say.

Lenora taps yes. No surprise there.

"Mrs. Baker won't be happy when she sees me trying to do it."

**she cant know**

It's official—this is definitely a bad idea. I'll get in trouble if Mrs. Baker catches us. Which she will. There's no way I can bring Lenora down to the first floor and outside without someone noticing. I'm not sure I can even do it at all. Not by myself. And when I get caught, I'll surely be sent packing, which will lead to being fired by Mr. Gurlain. I pace the room, my stomach clenching at the thought of being forced to return to my father's house, trapped in that endless cycle of loneliness and silence.

"I can't," I tell Lenora. "I'm sorry. It's too risky."

She types as I continue to pace. A full sentence banged out as quickly as her one good hand will allow.

**ill tell you what happened to the baby**

Lenora gives me a pleased-with-herself look. She knows it's an offer I can't resist. One that makes me wonder if this was her plan all along. Not for me to break the snow globe and feel so guilty I'd promise her anything. No one could have planned that. But giving me just enough details about the night of the murders to make me want more? Refusing to type the moment I mentioned the baby? It's entirely possible Lenora did all that on purpose, waiting for the perfect moment to manipulate me into giving her what she wants.

Two can play that game.

"You'll also need to give me the rest of your story," I say. "If we do this, you'll have to tell me everything you told Mary. Just like you promised."

Lenora doesn't type or tap a response, probably because she doesn't know what it'll be yet. Filling her silence is a swift knock on the door, followed by a voice saying, "Kit? Are you in there?"

Mrs. Baker.

Speak of the devil.

"Just a second," I call before lugging the typewriter back to the desk. On my way to the door, I try to kick some of the remaining gold flakes under Lenora's bed. A fruitless attempt to cover up what I did. One glance at the shattered snow globe in the room's trash can will tell Mrs. Baker everything.

I open the door, prepared for a lecture about how it's past Lenora's bedtime, which must be strictly observed. Instead, Mrs. Baker simply says, "There's someone here to see you."

My body jolts in surprise. "Who?"

"He didn't say," Mrs. Baker replies, which I interpret to mean she didn't ask because she doesn't care. "He's waiting outside the front gate."

"I'll go out to see him," I say, adding, "As soon as I put Miss Hope to bed. We're running behind this evening."

Mrs. Baker surveys the room, practically sniffing like a bloodhound for signs something is amiss. If she sees the glitter on the floor or the broken glass in the trash, she doesn't show it. "Please tell your guest to call at a decent hour next time," she says, waiting until she's out the door to add the kicker. "Or not at all."

Quickly, I change Lenora into her bedclothes and arrange her beneath the covers. As I place the call button in her left hand, I whisper, "We'll talk more when I get back." Then I turn out the lights, grab a sweater from my room, and rush downstairs.

Outside, the night is cold but clear, with stars twinkling brightly against a black velvet sky. I walk down the center of the driveway, wondering not just who awaits me at the end of it but why they're here. My hope is that it's Detective Vick, pulling me away from the others in the house to finally admit he believes me. My fear is that it's Kenny, angling for a peek of Lenora Hope for the second night in a row.

I'm wrong on both counts.

It ends up being my father standing on the other side of the gate, gripping the bars like an inmate in a jail cell. He does a double take as I approach, as if I'm the one making a surprise visit.

"What's with the uniform?" he says.

I ignore the question. "What are you doing here?"

"I came to take you home."

His calling it that makes me roll my eyes. That house hasn't felt like home in six months.

"Who told you I was here?"

"Kenny," my father says. "And Rich Vick. And half the damn town. You didn't think I'd find out you were taking care of Lenora Hope?"

I knew he would. Eventually. But judging by his reaction now, I was right not to tell him when I left. Giving him a cold stare through the gate's bars, I say, "Why do you care?"

"Because every person who knows you're working for that woman will think what the police have said is true. Soon everyone will think you're guilty."

"And what do *you* think, Dad?" I say, pain slicing through my voice like a switchblade.

"What happened to your mother was an accident." He says it quickly. The way people do when they don't want you to notice they're lying. But my father's bad at it. He doesn't even look at me while he's doing it.

"I wish you really believed that."

My chest tightens as grief and disappointment well up inside it, spilling out of my heart, pouring over my ribs. My eyes will be next if I don't leave immediately. I back away from the gate and start moving up the driveway. I refuse to let my father see me cry over him.

"Goodbye, Dad," I say. "I'll see you when I see you."

"I'm worried about you being here. Rich Vick told me you're the one who found that dead girl."

"I was," I say, leaving out how Mary now haunts my every waking hour. I'm sure she'd haunt my dreams, too, if my mother left room for her.

"He also told me you think she was murdered," my father adds.

"According to Kenny, so does everyone else. Everyone except your detective friend."

"So it's true? That's what you really think?"

My father's back to gripping the gate, staring at me through the bars with an expression that's one part concern, two parts disbelief. He wants me to say no. Probably to spare him from looking like a fool when word of it inevitably spreads through town like the flu. Unlike him, I don't have the energy to lie.

"Yeah. That's what I think."

"That's all the more reason to get you away from this place."

It gives me an even greater reason to stay. Since the town's only police detective doesn't believe Mary was murdered, it's up to me to prove that she was. And to find out who did it. Because it all seems to hinge on Lenora's past—and how much of it Mary knew—I can't leave until I learn the truth.

I turn back toward Hope's End and say, "Dad, go home."

"Kit, wait."

I don't. I continue up the drive, fully aware my father's still watching, hoping I'll turn around, open the gate, follow him back to a house I no longer recognize. I keep my eyes fixed on the lights of Hope's End. It's not home, either. But I can't shake the feeling that my future rests inside this place where tragedy struck twice.

Two separate nights.

Decades apart.

Yet linked to one person who I'm pretty sure has all the answers but won't reveal them until she gets what she wants.

Back in the house, I head straight for Lenora's room. She's still awake, her bright eyes aimed at the ceiling.

"Do we have a deal?" I say.

She taps twice against the call button.

The matter's settled.

Lenora's going outside.

And the price for taking her there is the truth.

# THIRTY

An opportunity to sneak Lenora outside presents itself two days later, when everyone else at Hope's End leaves to attend the funeral of Mary Milton.

Although the mood is solemn, the weather is anything but. It's a gorgeous autumn day—perhaps the last one of the season. Sun floods the sky, throwing off rays that take the sting out of the October chill. The cloudless sky is so blue it reminds me of sapphires. The Atlantic is calm, and for once the wind decides to take the day off.

Not that the weather matters. Even if a hurricane was blowing through, I'd take Lenora outside when given the chance. For the past two days, she continued to be mostly unresponsive, tapping out answers only when necessary. The result was long days of tense silence and uninterrupted boredom. The two of us simply sat, doing nothing. After that, even I'm eager to get outdoors.

I haven't told anyone else about my plan. Not even Lenora. I was tempted to tell Carter, but I opted not to just to be on the safe side. The last thing I want to do is run the risk of Mrs. Baker finding out and putting a stop to it.

I watch from the top of the Grand Stairs as the others gather to leave, Archie and Carter in dark suits, Jessie going against the grain in a white wrap dress, and Mrs. Baker wearing what she normally does, with the addition of a wide-brimmed hat and cat's-eye sunglasses. As soon as they're gone, I rush to Lenora's room.

It startles her when I begin to push her wheelchair toward the door. Her left hand flies off the armrest, flapping like the wing of a frightened bird. She looks up at me, her face a giant question mark.

"You're getting your wish," I say before wheeling her out of her room. "But then you need to hold up your end of the bargain, okay?"

She happily taps twice on the armrest.

"Good," I say. "Let's go."

I back the wheelchair out of the room. When we pass into the hall, Lenora lets out a huff of awe. It sounds like the relieved exhalation of someone who's been holding her breath a long, long time. Her eyes widen as we move backward down the hallway, trying to take in everything all at once. The carpet, the wallpaper, every door we pass. It makes me wonder how long it's been since she last left her room. Months? Years? Decades?

Because the service stairs are too narrow for her wheelchair, I have no choice but to use the Grand Stairs. My first thought is to try to hoist Lenora over one shoulder and carry her down the steps and out the door. Good in theory, perhaps, but difficult in practice. I know my limits. Even if I can somehow manage to carry her all the way down the Grand Stairs, getting her back up will be twice as hard. My only choice is to slowly back the wheelchair down each step and hope for the best.

"Hold on," I warn. "It's about to get bumpy."

I tilt the wheelchair, say a little prayer, and slowly pull it down the first step. The impact jostles Lenora so hard I worry she's about to fall out.

"Keep going?"

Lenora unclenches her left hand from the armrest and responds with a hearty double tap.

The next few steps are just as rough, but I soon find my groove. Going fast, ironically, is better than going slow. Rather than stopping and starting step by jarring step, I lower the wheelchair to the landing in one continuous pull. Lenora shimmies like a bowl of Jell-O the whole time, but at least she's not almost knocked out of the chair. I do it again on the way to the ground floor, the chair settling onto the tile in a shuddering thud.

"You okay?" I ask Lenora.

She looks back at me with unabashed glee. Her green eyes dance, and a blush of joy paints her cheeks. If she could laugh, I suspect she'd be cackling right now.

We head toward the dining room, doing a quick spin around the massive table there and passing the equally large fireplace before heading to the French doors. I fling them open and make sure there's a clear path for the wheelchair.

More slate shingles have fallen from the roof in the past two days. A veritable rainfall of them. Each day, Jessie and Carter have swept them up, only to have more appear in the morning. Today, the terrace is clean of them, allowing me to see fresh cracks crisscrossing its marble surface. Not a good sign. But also not enough to keep me from granting Lenora's single wish.

I return to the wheelchair. Before emerging onto the terrace, Lenora reaches out to me with her left hand. I take it, feeling the rush of her pulse beneath the skin.

Then I lead her outside.

The wind, sunshine, and sea air hit us all at once. Lenora gasps, delighted. I bring her to the edge of the terrace, stopping only when her knees touch the railing. Closing her eyes, she tilts her face to the sky and basks in the sun. Her hair catches the wind, the gray tendrils streaming in the breeze. Seeing her so ecstatic about something as simple as being outside makes me both sad that she can't enjoy this on a regular basis and furious at Mrs. Baker for confining her indoors.

I stand beside Lenora, leaning on the railing, watching the waves far below. While certainly lovely, it's not much different than the view she gets from her bedroom windows. Because there's so much risk involved—and because it might never happen again—I want her to experience something different. Something special.

"Lenora," I say, "when was the last time you got to lie down in the grass and look up at the clouds?"

I know the answer, even if Lenora can't provide it. Decades.

I guide the wheelchair to the end of the terrace, pull it down the steps to the lawn, and, careful to stay far away from the new, unimproved cliff's edge, park it in the grass. I then lift Lenora out of her chair and lower her until she's on her back, facing the sky. I lie down next to her, and together we stare at the endless blue overhead.

We stay like that for a long time. Maybe an hour. Maybe more. I'm not sure because I doze off, lulled to sleep by the wind, waves, and sunshine. Nights at Hope's End haven't gotten any easier. I'm still having nightmares of my mother and still hearing sounds from Lenora's room that, when I inevitably get out of bed to check, end up being nothing. I wake each morning exhausted, blinking in the harsh light of sunrise and finding a mattress slid slightly lower than the morning before it.

Now, though, I awake to the sun higher in the sky and Lenora next to me, taking deep, contented breaths.

"It's time to talk about the baby," I say.

Lenora's breathing stops. A sign she doesn't want to. But she must. Even though I don't want to ruin her special outing, she needs to hold up her end of the bargain. When she exhales, I say, "Was the baby born?"

I sit up, watching her left hand as it taps twice against the ground.

"A boy or a girl?" I say, even though I know Lenora can't answer by tapping. I rephrase the question. "Was it a girl?"

One tap.

"So it was a boy."

Lenora nods this time, a flicker of a smile crossing her face. It quickly fades when I say, "What happened to him? Did he die?"

One tap.

"Did you give him away?"

One tap.

My heart sinks. I don't want to ask the next question. After a pause, I say, "Was he taken away?"

Lenora pauses as well, waiting a good thirty seconds before she taps the ground once, twice.

"Do you know what happened to him after that?"

After another long pause, I receive only a single tap from Lenora.

"I'm so sorry," I say, closing my eyes to hold back tears that have suddenly formed. I can't imagine being that young, getting pregnant, giving birth, and then having the baby taken from me. It's beyond cruel. It's horrific.

I open my eyes to see that Lenora's expression hasn't changed. It's a blank mask facing the sky, hiding the deep pain that's surely present all these years later. If it turns out Carter really is her grandson, maybe some of that pain will ease. I hope so.

"Before she died, did Mary draw blood from your arm?"

Lenora taps twice, confirming my suspicion about the cause of the bruise on her left arm.

"Did she tell you why?"

One tap.

"But she knew about the baby, right? You told her?"

Two taps.

"Just like you also told her who killed your parents and sister."

Another two taps, slower this time.

"There's a reason you haven't told me yet," I say, because there must be. She's typed nothing for almost three days. In that time, she could have revealed all. Hell, she could have done it my first night here. One sentence is all it would take.

"Are you ever going to tell me?"

Lenora hesitates, her left hand hovering over the ground, as if she's not sure of the answer. I feel the same way. Also hovering. Also uncertain. As much as I need to know the truth, I'm also cognizant of the danger it might put me in. If Lenora finally tells me and someone else finds out, I could end up just like Mary.

I stare across the grass to the edge of the cliff. No railing there. Just a straight, screaming drop into the ocean. Lenora's aware of it, too, even though she can't see it from where she lies. There's no way to miss its presence. It pulls at us, daring us to come closer, peer over the edge, tempt fate.

It dawns on me that's what I've been doing since the moment I arrived at Hope's End. Edging toward the forbidden. Looking at things I shouldn't see, poking at things that shouldn't be poked. All because of a misguided hope that proving Lenora's innocence might somehow make me look innocent as well.

Her left hand finally taps the ground.

Just once.

No.

Seeing it sends anger sparking through my body. "But you promised."

Lenora winces, as if she regrets that. I don't care. We had a deal. I take her outside—not an easy task—and she finally tells me everything. I'm damn well going to hold her to it.

"You need to uphold your end of the bargain."

Lenora gives the ground an adamant single tap.

"Yes," I say. "Right now."

I stand as Lenora steadily raps her fist against the grass, making her stance crystal clear. No, no, no. I ignore it, even as I understand all the obvious reasons she doesn't want to tell me.

Mary.

Her missing suitcase.

Her corpse buried in the sand.

The big difference between Mary's situation and mine is that she left with Lenora's story when others were here, mistakenly believing the cover of night would keep her safe. But right now, in broad daylight, there's no one else at Hope's End. It's just me and Lenora and an opportunity to finish what we started.

I'm ready to tempt fate one last time.

And Lenora's going to be along for the ride whether she wants to or not.

I run back into the house, take the service stairs two at a time, and burst into Lenora's room. At the desk, I grab a fresh sheet of paper and roll it into the typewriter carriage. Because Lenora might use more than one piece, I take a whole stack, setting the paper on top of the typewriter before hoisting it off the desk.

Carrying the typewriter down the stairs is harder than moving it to Lenora's bed. The greater distance puts more strain on my arms, and the typewriter feels heavier with each passing step. To keep the blank pages on top from slipping, I bend forward and use my chin as a paperweight. At the service stairs, I realize I can't see where I'm going. I take each step slowly, dropping blindly from one to the next. At one point I misstep and knock into the cracked wall, jostling loose a chunk of plaster that falls onto the staircase. I crunch over it on my way to the bottom.

After clearing the stairs, I shuffle through the kitchen, the typewriter getting heavier and heavier. My arms feel like jelly. My legs do, too. In the dining room, I huff a sigh of relief when I realize I never closed the French doors on my way inside. That's at least one thing I won't need to deal with. Tired and heaving, I carry the typewriter onto the terrace.

Lenora's there.

Not on the grass, where I'd left her, but right there on the terrace, sitting in her wheelchair and staring at the sea.

"How did you—"

My voice leaves me when I see them.

Mrs. Baker and Archie, Carter and Jessie. They all stand off to the side of the terrace, their expressions as varied as their personalities. Carter's is concerned. Jessie looks mildly surprised. Archie's face is blank. And Mrs. Baker? She's pissed.

Clearly busted, I lower the typewriter. The blank pages come loose and catch the breeze. I watch them swirl and skid across the terrace before taking flight.

Over the railing.

Off the cliff.

Into the churning water far below.

My mother would have died if I hadn't entered her room, a fact made clear by Dr. Walden, the family physician. What wasn't clear was if she drank all the laudanum by accident or did it on purpose. Everyone else swore it had to have been accidental. I, on the other hand, assumed my mother intended to take her own life. She remained silent on the matter, making it more uncertain.

Dr. Walden, either through stupidity or greed, continued to keep the laudanum flowing, using the excuse that cutting my mother off all at once would cause more harm than good. He recommended weaning her off the substance slowly.

As a result, nothing changed. Life at Hope's End quickly returned to the way it had always been. My mother remained wasting away in her room, my father was frequently gone on business, and my sister pretended nothing was wrong by filling her social calendar.

The only thing that changed was me. By the end of September, my pregnancy was showing more and more. That I had managed to hide it for so long was a small miracle accomplished only through craftiness on my part and inattentiveness on the part of everyone else.

But time was running out. I knew that soon it would be

impossible to hide. Until that day came, however, I was determined to keep it a secret from my family.

Yet there was only so much I could do on my own. Food, for example, became a problem. I was ravenous all day and night, prompting a weight gain too noticeable to escape even my father's lax attention. He put me on a diet so strict it wasn't fit for a woman of any condition, let alone one who was eating for two. I needed someone besides Archie to sneak proper meals to me.

It was the same with clothing. My mother's maid continued to let out my dresses, tsking at each request to alter yet another garment. I needed new clothes designed to better hide my pregnancy, which I couldn't just sneak out and buy for myself. Someone else had to do it for me.

Then there was the matter of my health. I hadn't seen a doctor since becoming pregnant. I spent nights lying awake worrying about how I didn't know if something was wrong with the baby. But I didn't dare approach Dr. Walden about an examination. I needed to see a new doctor. A stranger. One who would remain silent about my condition.

If the two of us had shared a typical bond, I would have turned to my sister for help. I'd always hated that we weren't close, always assuming it was my fault instead of hers. In truth, it was no one's fault. We were simply different. There was a gulf in our personalities that was too wide to overcome. I was like my mother, always feeling too much, wanting too much, needing too much. Like my father, my sister had wants and needs, too, but they were surface pleasures. Cars and clothes and societal approval from snobs just like them. They held no emotion other than ambition.

Without my sister to depend on, I required help from a member of the household staff. Someone discreet. Someone who knew how to keep a secret.

The only person I could think of was the one you'd least expect. My father's mistress.

That's how I found myself standing in the southern hall on the last day of September. My father had returned from Boston the day before, looking more tired than I'd ever seen him. His mood was foul at dinner as he and my sister enjoyed a full meal while I picked at a salad designed to, in his words, "restore my girlish figure."

After dinner, he retreated to the sunroom. A few minutes later, I followed, creeping toward the end of the hall. Noises rose from behind the sunroom's closed doors. My father's low chuckle and the high-pitched peal of a woman's laugh. A laugh that wasn't my mother's. Even if it sounded the same, which it didn't, I knew it wasn't her because she was currently upstairs in her room, likely taking yet another swig from her bottle of laudanum.

I snuck down the hall, which had turned gloomy in the evening dusk. I could barely make out the portraits as I passed. That was for the best. I had zero desire to look at them.

Father. Mother. Two dutiful daughters.

All of it was a lie.

Upon reaching the sunroom, I held my breath, fearful one small exhalation would expose my presence. I stood outside the door, listening to my father's groaning and panting, disgusted by his animalistic needs. It didn't occur to me then that they were the same sounds Ricky made when we were together. Only later did I realize all men were alike. It didn't matter if they were rich or poor, fat or thin, old or young. Their needs were so basic it was laughable.

Once the passionate moaning had ended, I hurried away to the library, pretending to read a book in case my father looked in as he passed. He didn't, of course. He simply strode by, sated, on his way to another part of the house.

It wasn't until I heard his mistress leave the sunroom that I sprang from my chair and ran to the doorway, ready to intercept her.

I expected to see someone like Sally, the voluptuous new maid, or even brittle, bitter Berniece Mayhew. Instead, the woman who emerged from the sunroom smoothing her skirts was the person I least expected to be engaged in an affair with my father.

Frozen in shock, I could only stand in the middle of the hallway and stare at her. She stared back, also surprised.

"You?" I said.

"Yes," Miss Baker replied with a weary huff. "Me."

# THIRTY-ONE

The typewriter is gone.

Mrs. Baker removed it from my arms once the last loose sheet of paper had taken flight. At first, I stupidly thought she was trying to help me. Or at least get the typewriter out of my hands while she berated me for bringing Lenora outside. Instead, she said nothing as she lugged it across the terrace, the lone page in the carriage flapping in the breeze.

Then, with a grunt and a heave, she hoisted the typewriter over the railing and let it drop.

I gasped when it fell from view. Jessie let out a horrified yelp. Even Lenora reacted, her left hand reaching out as far as she could muster, as if that alone might reverse the typewriter's fall.

Pleased with herself, Mrs. Baker wiped her hands together and strode to the French doors. All she said as she passed me was, "Take Miss Hope back upstairs where she belongs."

Carter helped me with that, scooping Lenora in his arms and carrying her up the Grand Stairs as I pulled the wheelchair up step by rattling step. In Lenora's room, he gently placed her in the wheelchair before turning to me.

"What do you think's going to happen?"

"I think I'm going to be fired," I said. It was the only logical outcome. But it wouldn't be Mrs. Baker doing the firing. She'd leave that to Mr. Gurlain, who I was certain would be all too happy to banish me from the agency.

"Shit," Carter said. "I'm so sorry, Kit. This is all my fault."

In truth, it was mine. I knew the rules. I broke them anyway, simply because I wanted answers that I'll never get now that the typewriter is gone. All I received in exchange for my transgression was a tidbit of information that might help Carter. The only silver lining in this dark cloud of a day.

"Lenora had the baby," I said after pulling him into my room and closing the adjoining door so Lenora couldn't hear us from hers. "A boy. She confirmed it."

"What happened to him?"

"She doesn't know. All Lenora could tell me is that they took the baby away from her."

Carter dropped onto my bed, trying to process it all. Not just the suffering Lenora went through or the cruelty behind it, but also how it seemed to support his theory about being her grandson.

"So I might be right," he said. "Lenora and I might really be related."

"It's a definite possibility."

I joined him on the bed, our shoulders touching. "I'm sorry I couldn't find out more."

Carter flashed that crooked smile I'd become slightly enamored of over the past few days. "Don't be ridiculous. I wouldn't have learned any of this without you."

"But now that you know it, be careful. Whoever killed Mary is still here."

"Or out there," Carter said.

Maybe, but I doubted it. I thought more than ever that Mary's killer was someone at Hope's End.

Specifically the woman who would be sending me packing at any minute.

But those minutes turned to hours, bleeding from afternoon into evening. In that time, I heard nothing about being let go. Not when Archie brought up dinner for me and Lenora. Not when I mixed her crushed pills into her food or did her circulation exercises or gave her a bath. Now I'm putting Lenora to bed, noticing the way in which her gaze flits to the desk. It seems so big without the typewriter on it, so empty.

The same can be said of the sideboard, on which used to rest her snow globe. Now there's just the Walkman. Likely the next thing Lenora will lose. And she's already lost so much.

"I'm sorry, Lenora," I say as I place the call button in her left hand. "I know how much you liked using it. I wish I could have heard the rest of your story."

Even though it's not an official goodbye, it feels like one. Because surely I'll be gone by morning—if not sooner. I suspect the only reason I'm still here is because Mrs. Baker is trying to cajole Mr. Gurlain into assigning another caregiver to Lenora. One who, unlike me, has the power to decline the job.

Assuming I'll never see her again after this, I pat Lenora's hand and say, "It was a pleasure caring for you. I hope whoever takes my place will make you happy."

I leave her after that, sweeping into my room and closing the adjoining door behind me. Now all I need to do is pack up my things and wait for the axe to inevitably fall. Not that there's much packing to be done. I never did get around to replacing Mary's belongings with my own. The books are still in their box. My suitcase full of clothes sits atop the dresser. All that's left to be done is take the lockbox out from under the bed, collect grooming products from the bathroom, and change out of my uniform and into the clothes I wore when I arrived.

I start with the lockbox. Opening the nightstand, I take out the key. I then drop to my knees and slide the box from beneath the bed. I unlock it and open the lid. Inside are Lenora's pills—and nothing else.

The pages we'd typed—all of them—are gone.

I hop to my feet, push out the door, and stomp down the hallway. The service stairs shake as I angrily descend to the kitchen, in search of Mrs. Baker.

I find her in the dining room, sitting alone at the massive table, a recently opened bottle of wine in front of her. The room is dim—lit only by a small blaze in the fireplace. Its flickering glow reflects off Mrs. Baker's glasses, masking her eyes as she lifts a wineglass to her lips and takes a sip.

"Where are they?" I say.

"You'll have to be more specific than that, dear."

"The pages Lenora and I typed," I say, forcing the words through clenched teeth. "I know you have them."

"Had, dear," Mrs. Baker says. "I *had* them."

She gestures to the fireplace, where a few bits of scorched paper surround the single log burning inside. On one of them, I spot a typed word halfway eaten by flame. Seeing it sends me stumbling backward into one of the dining room chairs, which hits the floor with a clatter.

"You had no right to do that," I say. "Those pages belonged to me."

"And what was on them belonged to Miss Hope. Which means they fell under my authority." Mrs. Baker takes another satisfied sip of wine. "Just like the typewriter."

"You didn't need to destroy them!" I yell, the words bursting out of me. Since I'm about to be sent packing, I see no need to control my anger.

Mrs. Baker, far calmer than I, nods toward the toppled chair and says, "Sit with me a minute, Kit. I think it's time for a nice chat."

I remain standing, disobeying her yet again.

"Suit yourself," she says with a shrug. "I assume you expect to be fired."

"Yes," I say. Why lie at this point?

"You're free to go, if you're so inclined. No one is forcing you to stay here."

"But you're not forcing me to leave?"

"No, dear," Mrs. Baker says. "But I would like to know whose idea it was to take Miss Hope outside."

"Hers."

"I thought so. Honestly, it doesn't surprise me. Miss Hope can be very . . . persuasive. It makes sense she'd convince you to disobey my clear wishes."

"*Your* wishes," I say. "What about Lenora's?"

"They are one and the same." Mrs. Baker sets down her glass and runs the pad of her finger around the rim. "Although it's obvious you don't approve of my methods."

"I don't."

"Even if it's for Miss Hope's own good?"

"Is it?" I say. "You keep her a prisoner in her own house. She has no friends. No visitors. She only sees people who are paid to take care of her. You won't even let her go outside, for God's sake. Even inmates— literal prison inmates—are allowed to do that."

"What if I did? What do you think she'd encounter? Hatred, that's what. Judgment. Constant suspicion. The world is not a kind place for women accused of violence. You, of all people, should understand that. Don't people judge you for what happened to your mother?"

Too stunned to stand, I finally sit. Not on the chair, but on the floor beside it. I land next to the fireplace. Heat from the crackling blaze inside it stings my skin. But nothing's as hot as the shame that burns through me.

"How long have you known?" I say.

"Since before you arrived. Mr. Gurlain felt it was his duty to no-tify me."

Of course he did. I have no doubt he also assumed it would kill my chances of working here—or anywhere, for that matter. What I don't understand is why it didn't work.

"If you knew, why did you let me come here?"

"Because I thought you and Miss Hope would be a good fit," Mrs. Baker says. "And I was right. You understand her. In fact, you even like her."

The comment throws me, mostly because I'm not certain I do. I like Lenora some of the time. Other times, she scares me. Or leaves me frustrated. Or fills me with pity, which then brings me back full circle into wanting to like her.

"It's okay to admit it," Mrs. Baker says. "Miss Hope can be very charming when it suits her needs. But let me make one thing clear— you're nothing to her. I know you think you are. That you share a bond unique to her nurses. It's not. She's done this kind of thing before, go- ing back decades. She's smarter than she appears, as I'm sure you know. Some would even call her wily."

I nod, for the description fits. Lenora uses silence and stillness to her advantage, concealing much, revealing little. As a result, every small detail you learn about her leaves you only wanting more.

i want to tell you everything

That's what Lenora typed my first night here. And I've been starved for that information ever since, willing to break every rule. It doesn't matter that a week has passed and I still know next to nothing.

"What would you call her?" I say.

"Manipulative."

Although Mrs. Baker smacks her lips together, as if savoring the word like it's the wine in her glass, her tone reveals a different emotion.

Distaste.

"I wouldn't be surprised if that's what caused poor Mary to do what she did," Mrs. Baker continues. "Miss Hope made her feel needed. Made her feel special. When Mary realized that wasn't the case, it drove her to do the unthinkable."

Detective Vick's voice echoes through my thoughts, reciting Mary's alleged suicide note.

*"I'm sorry. I'm not the person you thought I was."*

Did he also tell Mrs. Baker what it said? And does she genuinely believe Mary killed herself? I try to study her face, looking for signs she does. It's unreadable, especially with the flames from the fireplace still dancing in the reflection of her glasses.

"Why do you stay here?" I say.

"That's a rather bold question."

"One I'd like you to answer. If you hate Lenora so much, why are you still here?"

"If I hated her, I would have left years ago. And this place would have fallen apart without me."

I think of the tiles raining from the roof, the cracks in the walls of the service stairs, the swath of lawn that now rests at the bottom of the ocean. "In case you haven't noticed, it is."

Mrs. Baker tilts her wineglass back and empties it. "It would already be rubble if not for me. The things I've had to do to keep this place standing. Selling it off bit by bit to pay for one repair or another. Trust me, it would be all too easy to leave. But Miss Hope needs me. I stay here out of a sense of devotion."

"But devotion only goes so far," I say. "You still get something out of being here, don't you?"

"I knew you were bright," Mrs. Baker says, making it sound like a liability. "Yes, our arrangement provides me with certain benefits. Miss Hope and I came to an agreement years ago. If I somehow keep this place standing, she'll pass it on to me when she dies."

"All of it?" I say.

"The land. The house. Everything in it."

The fire next to me is quickly dying, its glow finally fading from Mrs. Baker's glasses. Behind the lenses, her blue eyes seem to catch what little light remains and take on a vibrant shine. I stare at them, unsettled, wondering if she's aware of just how close she is to having that plan fall apart. All it would take is for someone to come along and contest the agreement. Lenora's grandson, for example.

I consider mentioning that I know Lenora had a baby. I don't because, just like Archie, I doubt Mrs. Baker will be honest about it. Also, I see no reason to make myself a target.

If I'm not one already.

Because her revelation that she'll inherit Hope's End makes me suspect there are secrets Mrs. Baker would do anything to keep.

And that she had every reason in the world to kill Mary.

Miss Baker made us tea and took me back to the sunroom for what she called "a nice chat." As if nothing about our respective roles had changed. I was still the pupil and she the proper lady tasked with teaching me how to become the same. Only I seemed to see the ridiculousness of that. After all, I knew what she'd been doing with my father in that same sunroom minutes earlier.

"What do we do now?" she said, addressing the situation as if we both had a say in the matter. She didn't.

"You can start by telling me why," I said. "Why my father? Do you love him?"

Miss Baker could barely hold back her laughter. "No, child. What we have is strictly transactional. I give him what he wants, and he rewards me with small tokens of appreciation."

Money, in other words. For all her talk of manners and propriety, Miss Baker was nothing but a high-class whore. My disgust with her must have shown in my expression, because she snapped, "Don't you dare judge me, young lady. Someone like you, born into enormous wealth, has no idea what it's like for the rest of us. The things we need to do to survive. Especially unmarried women like me. I'm simply looking out for my future."

"At what price?" I said.

"The highest one I can get." Miss Baker leaned back in her seat, daring me to say another critical word. "Is that what all this is about? You wanted to confront me? Try to shame me?"

"No," I said. "I wanted to show you this."

I stood, pulled the fabric of my dress tight against me, and turned so Miss Baker could see my growing stomach in profile.

"Dear me," she said as she set her teacup on its saucer. Her hands shook so much the teacup rattled the whole way to the table at her side. "How far along are you?"

"Six months."

"And the father?"

"I'm not going to tell you," I said, unwilling to risk bringing Ricky into this. If Miss Baker knew, she might tell my father, who would surely fire him. Then there'd be no hope of Ricky and me scraping together enough money for the one thing I most desperately wanted to do--escape.

"Did he force himself on you?" Miss Baker said.

My face turned red as I shook my head and looked at the floor, too ashamed to face her.

"I see." Miss Baker paused to clear her throat. "Does he know about your . . . predicament?"

"Yes."

"And what does he intend to do?"

"Make an honest woman out of me," I said, which prompted a rueful laugh from Miss Baker. Hearing it made me flinch.

"You're still practically a child," she said. "And a good man would have restrained himself. Or at least taken precautions."

Still stinging from the way her laughter echoed through the sunroom, I gave her a hard stare and said, "Does my father?"

Miss Baker stiffened in her seat. "What exactly do you want from me?"

"Your help."

I listed all the ways in which I needed assistance, from procuring maternity clothes to accessing the proper amount of food. This needed to occur long enough for Ricky and me to plan our escape. I finished by telling her that it all had to be done in secret.

"That's a tall order," Miss Baker said. "What makes you think I'll be willing to help?"

"Because if you don't, I'll tell my mother everything."

The corners of Miss Baker's mouth lifted in a cruel smile. "Your mother already knows."

"Then I'll tell Berniece Mayhew," I said, knowing full well she was the biggest gossip among the household staff. "About you and my father and what the two of you have been doing when you think no one is watching. Once that gets out, good luck finding another job teaching etiquette. Everyone will know exactly what kind of lady you are."

Miss Baker stood in a huff, looking like she wanted to slap me across the face, storm out of the room, or both. I suspected the only reason she didn't was because she knew she was trapped.

"I'll help you," she finally said.

We shook hands. She promised to see about buying me some new clothes in the morning, followed by arranging a visit from a doctor whose discretion was assured. I told her that Archie had agreed to set aside an extra plate of food at every meal and give it to her to bring up to my room.

"Who else knows about this?" Miss Baker said.

"Just Archie," I said. "And now you."

To her credit, Miss Baker refrained from mentioning my sister or my mother. She had been at Hope's End long enough to observe that neither of them would have been of any help to me.

When we parted ways, I felt a newfound sense of optimism that my plan could actually work. It would require caution, of course, and perhaps a little bit of luck. But for the first time in weeks I saw a path that led me away from Hope's End, away from my family, and into a bright, happy future with Ricky and our child.

The only thing I didn't count on was that, no matter how cautious I was, luck failed to be on my side.

And that when I shook hands with Miss Baker, I was in fact making a deal with the devil.

# THIRTY-TWO

I leave the dining room as Mrs. Baker pours another drink. The sound of wine spilling into her glass follows me across the kitchen, replaced by a loud, sloppy sip as I reach the service stairs. As I climb to the second floor, I try to piece together how she could have killed Mary.

First, Mrs. Baker got wind of the fact that Lenora was telling Mary her story. Most likely she was passing by, heard the typewriter, and realized what was happening. She could have even crept in at night and read what Lenora had written.

Maybe Mrs. Baker also knew about Carter's quest to prove he's Lenora's grandson. It's obvious she keeps a close eye on what's happening inside Hope's End. She likely spends more time observing than anything else. Which makes it equally as likely that she found out Mary and Carter's plan.

Then, on the night Mary left the house with the suitcase, Mrs. Baker struck.

I can even picture it as I continue up the stairs.

Mary rushing across the terrace with a suitcase that contained dozens of typewritten pages and a sample of Lenora's blood.

Mrs. Baker emerging from the shadow of the house.

Fast.

Grabbing the suitcase.

Breaking the handle.

Giving Mary a shove.

It's possible Mrs. Baker had no intention of killing her. Maybe she just wanted to throw Mary off-balance long enough to get the suitcase away from her. But death was the end result. Mary slipped over the railing, fell to her death, remained there for days. And Mrs. Baker had no choice but to tell everyone that Mary left in the middle of the night.

I know a lot of that is conjecture. Just like I know that the truth could be far different from what my wild imagination came up with. I even know it's possible Mrs. Baker had nothing to do with Mary's death.

The only things I'm sure of, really, are that Mary left Hope's End with a suitcase in her hand.

That whoever has it now is very likely the person who killed her.

And that Mrs. Baker is the most obvious culprit.

At the top of the stairs, I impulsively hurry past both my room and Lenora's, stopping only when I reach Mrs. Baker's door. I try the doorknob, which twists in my hand. When I let go, the door gently creaks wide open. Even though I know it's merely a trick of the house's tilt, I can't help but think of it as an invitation to enter.

I check the hall in both directions until I'm certain no one is around.

Then, with a breath and a prayer, I slip inside.

Closing the door behind me, I stop and gaze around the room. It's the same shape and size as Lenora's quarters, with the only differences being the lack of a door leading into another room and the location of the en suite bath. That's on the other side of the room in a mirror image of Lenora's.

Two lights are already on inside. A relief. It saves me from having to turn them on and then remember to flick them off before I leave. One is a lamp on the nightstand, which casts a glow over Mrs. Baker's immaculately made bed. The second is a floor lamp in the corner, which sheds enough light over the other half of the room. I see a dresser, an antique dressing table with an oval mirror, and a sideboard similar to the one in Lenora's room. Instead of a Walkman on top, this one holds a gramophone, complete with a lily-shaped horn to amplify the music.

Quickly and quietly, I slide open dresser drawers and peek into the sideboard, finding nothing of interest. They're too small to hold a suitcase, and if Mrs. Baker had the pages that were in it, I suspect they suffered the same fate as the ones Lenora and I typed. As for the sample of Lenora's blood Mary took, that was likely also destroyed.

Just in case, I sit at the dressing table and root through the drawers, which contain nothing but rattling jewelry and rolling lipstick tubes. Atop the table is a framed photograph of a young couple in front of the Eiffel Tower. Snow falls around the pair as they huddle together beneath the man's overcoat. The woman in the photo I assume to be Mrs. Baker, albeit fifty years younger than the person currently gulping down wine in the dining room. They have the same eyes, same nose, same chin. That's where the resemblance ends. In the photograph, she sports marcelled hair and a wide, genuine smile, something I've never seen from Mrs. Baker.

The man in the picture is tall, handsome, and maybe ten years older than her. I assume he's the fiancé Mrs. Baker mentioned the day I arrived. The one whose death prompted her return to Hope's End. From the way they're looking at each other in the photo, the two of them definitely seem in love.

I move to the other side of the room, where the most likely hiding places reside. Under the bed. In the armoire. Beneath the large sink in the bathroom, which is where I continue my search, yielding nothing. I get the same result when I crack open the armoire doors. Hanging inside is an array of black dresses, with a few pairs of sensible black shoes sitting in a row beneath them.

My last stop is to check the area around the bed. On the nightstand is another framed photograph of the same man as the one on the dressing table. He's alone in this one, looking dashing in an army uniform.

I drop to my hands and knees to check under the bed. Instead of a suitcase, I find several shoeboxes. I pull one out and open it, taking care not to leave clean marks on the dusty lid. Inside are more photographs. I sort through them, seeing a young Mrs. Baker in a variety of situations. Wearing a satin gown and lifting a glass of champagne in a toast. Walking down the street with two other women, their arms linked, mouths open in mid-laugh. Reclining naked on a chaise in what appears to be an artist's studio, her modesty preserved by only two well-placed feathered fans.

They're a potent reminder that Mrs. Baker once had a life outside the tilted walls of Hope's End. A happy one, from the looks of it. I wonder how much she misses it, how much she wants it again, and how far she'd go to make that happen.

I put the photos back in the box, replace the lid, and slide it back under the bed. Instead of photographs, the next box I grab is full of receipts and copies of cleared checks. All of them bear Lenora's signature, although it's clearly the work of Mrs. Baker.

I grab a handful and thumb through them.

Electric bill. Paid monthly, although there've been a few late payments and, once earlier this year, a warning that service was about to be terminated.

Grocery bill. Paid like clockwork every Tuesday when the delivery from the market in town arrives.

At the bottom of the box is a stack of checks all made out to Ocean View Retirement Home. One thousand dollars a month, going back at least a dozen years.

I've heard of Ocean View, of course. It's the only nursing home in town. I even applied to be an aide there after Mr. Gurlain suspended me. I was told I was overqualified for the job, which somehow felt more insulting than if they had told me the truth—that, given my reputation, they thought hiring me would be like inviting a wolf to watch over a flock of sheep. What I don't understand is why Mrs. Baker is paying all that money for a nursing home when Lenora's right here, being cared for by me, Mary, a long line of other nurses.

I'm still looking at the cleared checks when my attention is caught by a sound in the hallway.

Footsteps.

Coming down the hall.

Almost at the door.

I slap the lid atop the shoebox and shove it back under the bed. Then I leap to my feet and hurry . . . nowhere.

There's no place for me to go. I can't sprint out the door if Mrs. Baker's coming in, and the only hiding place I can think of is in the bathroom, which is likely where she'll head first. Resigned to being caught—which this time will surely get me fired—I start to raise my hands in surrender.

That's when I spot the armoire.

Without thinking, I bolt toward it, throw open the doors, and back myself inside. Crouched behind identical black sheaths, I pull the armoire doors shut just as the bedroom door is pushed open.

Through the thin crack between the armoire doors, I see Mrs. Baker enter the room. From the way she sways, I assume she quickly polished off the entire bottle of wine herself. She drifts to the gramophone on the sideboard and turns it on. One dropped needle later, music starts blasting through the room.

"Let's Misbehave."

Mrs. Baker drunkenly sings along, croaking out every other word.

"Alone . . . chaperone."

Her head bobs in time to the music, her hands undulate in the air, and her singing gets louder.

"Can get . . . number."

She plops down at the dressing table and yanks the same drawer I'd opened minutes earlier, pulling out a tube of lipstick.

"World's . . . slumber . . . misbehave!"

Eyeing her reflection in the mirror, Mrs. Baker swipes the tube across her bottom lip, her unsteady hand smearing it outside the lip line. She wipes it with her thumb, making it worse. A crimson streak now runs halfway to her cheek. Mrs. Baker chuckles softly to herself, leans forward, stares at her drunken reflection.

Something in the mirror suddenly catches her attention. I can tell by the way her gaze darts from her reflection to just over her right shoulder.

The armoire.

Mrs. Baker turns away from the mirror and faces it. From my point of view, it appears as if she's looking right at me. I hold my breath, unable to do anything but watch.

As Mrs. Baker sets the lipstick atop the dressing table.

As she stands.

As she takes an uneven step toward the armoire.

Her second step is steadier. The third even more so. Like she's sobering up with each consecutive stride. By the time she's in front of the armoire, all traces of drunkenness are gone. It's now the usual stern, stone-cold-sober version of Mrs. Baker who reaches out.

Touches the armoire doors.

Prepares to throw them open.

I shrink against the interior wall, knowing that in one second I'll be caught, fired, sent back to a house where my father thinks I killed my mother. But just before Mrs. Baker can pull the armoire doors open, the record player suddenly skips.

The music is replaced by a loud, low groan. It sounds through the entire house, starting at the first floor and moving upward, gaining volume as it goes.

I know what it is.

Mrs. Baker does, too, for her face darkens with concern.

The groan is followed by a crack, a clatter, and several sudden, sharp jerks. It sounds like something's smashing into the house. Inside the armoire, I'm jostled like a body in a coffin that's just been dropped. One of the doors flies open, exposing me being knocked back and forth behind Mrs. Baker's long black dresses.

But she's no longer there to see me. Instead, she's throwing open the bedroom door and peering into the hall, one withered hand gripping the wall for support as all of Hope's End bucks and heaves.

As quickly as it started, everything stops.

The noise.

The movement.

All is silent and still.

Mrs. Baker disappears into the hallway, off to investigate what just happened and where. Others in the house are doing the same. I hear footfalls overhead and the sound of someone thundering down the service stairs.

I stay huddled in a corner of the armoire, my heart beating a hundred times per minute. Above me, Mrs. Baker's dresses still sway on the rack. I wait until they've settled before crawling out of the armoire and hurrying to Lenora's room. She's awake, of course, her expression alarmed and her good hand clenched around the call button. Through our adjoining door, I hear the buzz of the alarm and see the red light filling my room.

"I'm here," I say. "Are you okay?"

Lenora drops the call button and taps twice on the bedspread. Her gaze then flicks to the far corner of the room, where someone stands, unnoticed by me until just now.

Archie.

He has the curtains pulled back and is looking out the window toward the terrace. "Looks like it's down there," he says.

"What is?"

Archie finally turns to face me. "The damage. We should go see what happened."

I already know what happened. Hope's End just got a bit closer to tumbling into the ocean.

"What are you doing in Lenora's room?" I say.

Archie and I look at each other with wary suspicion. It reminds me of a movie I watched with my mother when she was sick. Two cat burglars who interrupted each other while trying to rob the same mansion are forced to choose if they should work together or alone. They ultimately decide to trust each other. Archie makes a similar decision.

"I was saying goodnight."

"Since when do you say goodnight to Lenora?"

"Ever since Miss Hope first took ill," Archie says. "Every night, I make sure to stop by and see how she's doing."

"Let's walk," I say.

What I really mean is that I want to talk where Lenora can't hear us. Archie nods and follows me into the hallway, where the tilt of the house is noticeably more pronounced. Just when I had gotten used to it, too.

"*Every* night?" I say. "You told me you and Lenora were no longer close."

"I said it wasn't like it used to be," Archie says. "And that's the truth. It's evolved over the years. Just because I don't make a show of it doesn't mean I don't care about Miss Hope. We're both on the same side, Kit. We're both here to watch over her. We just go about it in different ways."

"Why haven't I seen you visit her before?"

"Because it's kind of our little secret. Something kept just between me and Miss Hope. I'm sure you understand."

Archie pauses, as if he now wants me to share one of my secrets. I decline. Because that movie about the cat burglars who decided to trust each other? It ends with one betraying the other. I'm not about to let the same thing happen to me.

"How late do you visit?"

"Usually a little after Miss Hope goes to bed and a little before I do the same."

We descend the service stairs slowly, our shoes crunching over bits of plaster that have fallen from the walls.

"Ever visit her in the middle of the night?"

"No," Archie says. "An early riser like me can't afford to stay up that late."

He sounds honest enough that I almost believe him. Then again, Archie also sounded honest when he lied about knowing Lenora had a baby. Right now, I suspect there's a seventy-five percent chance he's telling the truth. Using that math, I conclude that Archie was the gray blur I saw at Lenora's window my first night here.

I'm less sure about him causing the middle-of-the-night noises in Lenora's room.

Or the shadow I watched pass the adjoining door.

Or the typewritten message Lenora blamed on Virginia.

"Do you know if anyone else sneaks into Lenora's room at night on a regular basis?"

"I doubt it," Archie says with a vagueness that drops the truth-o-meter to fifty percent. "I'm sure it's nothing."

"And I'm certain it's something." I stop halfway down the steps. "What aren't you telling me? When I told all of you Lenora said her sister—her *dead* sister—was in her room typing, you didn't seem surprised. Why is that?"

"Because it was outlandish," Archie says.

"Or maybe because something like that has happened before over the years."

Archie attempts to descend another step, but I block his way, standing with my arms outstretched and both palms against the stairwell's cracked walls.

"Was Lenora telling the truth?"

I should feel ridiculous for even thinking it, let alone saying it aloud. But Archie's reaction—a flinch, followed by a deliberate masking of his features—tells me I'm on to something.

"There's a lot you don't know about this place," he says as he gently removes one of my hands from the wall and sidesteps past me. "Things you're better off not knowing."

"So it's true?" I say. "Virginia's ghost is really haunting Hope's End?"

Archie makes a point of not looking at me as he continues down the steps. "Haunting's not the right word. But, yes, her presence can be felt here. At Hope's End, the past is always present."

I follow him to the bottom of the stairwell and into the kitchen, which appears mostly unharmed. Just a few fallen pots and pans and a broken jar on the floor. In the dining room, a large fissure has appeared above the fireplace mantel, zigging toward the ceiling. Both sets of French doors are open, letting in brisk night air and the hushed voices of everyone else already outside.

Archie and I step onto the terrace, where Mrs. Baker, Carter, and Jessie all press against the side of the house. At first, I don't understand why.

Then I see it.

Littering the terrace are more tiles from the roof plus a pile of bricks that I assume is the remains of a toppled chimney. Running through it all, about five feet from the house, is a fault line that stretches from one side of the terrace to the other.

One step over that line could send the cliff, the terrace, and, perhaps, all of Hope's End tumbling into the sea.

# THIRTY-THREE

The full extent of the damage can't be assessed until morning, when all of us gather on the terrace not long after dawn. If anyone else paid a visit to Lenora's room during the night, I didn't hear it. I was too focused on the sound of the waves pounding the base of the cliff, eating away at it inch by inch. Lying in the darkness, listening to that steady churn, I wondered how long we had left until the whole thing fell. To judge from the state of the terrace, not very long at all.

The damage appears even worse in daylight, with the rising sun shedding full light upon the fissure slicing across the terrace. About two inches wide and unfathomably deep, it runs down the steps on the left all the way into the empty swimming pool. Following its path is a line of broken marble tiles, many of which now jut from the terrace at jagged angles.

Mrs. Baker peers at it all through her glasses, her eyes weary and sad. "Is there someone we could call?" she says.

Carter, who'd been on his stomach studying the crevasse, climbs to his feet and brushes dirt from his jeans. "To do what?"

"Fix it. Or support it. Or something."

"There's no fixing this," Carter says. "This cliff is going to go eventually. And when it does, Hope's End is going to go with it."

"I won't let that happen," Mrs. Baker says, as if she has any say in the matter. "I'll go make some calls."

She hurries back into the house, leaving the rest of us to stare anxiously at the cracked terrace.

"She's delusional," Carter says.

"Totally," Jessie echoes.

I turn to Archie, hoping our trust pact is still intact. "Do you think there's a way to convince her to abandon this place?"

"Leave Hope's End?" he says. "She'll never do it."

"I'm more concerned about Lenora. If something like this happens again—"

"When it happens again," Jessie says. "Come on, guys, you know it will. And next time it'll probably be worse."

I sigh, because I agree with her. "*When* it happens, the rest of us can escape if we need to. But Lenora can't."

Archie promises me he'll talk to Mrs. Baker about it before going back inside to start breakfast. Jessie quickly follows, saying nothing as she takes a long, disbelieving look at what's left of the terrace.

Carter and I remain, our backs against the mansion and the brisk sea breeze in our faces.

"I didn't think I'd ever see you again," Carter says with a shyness I haven't seen from him before. "I'm glad you're still here."

The wind picks up, bringing with it a biting chill that warns winter is on its way. I pull my cardigan tight around me and wonder if Hope's End will still be here when winter does arrive.

"I'm not sure I am. Honestly, how long do you think this place will remain standing?"

"I have no clue. It could be years. Or months."

"Or hours?" I say.

"Yeah, that, too."

"I long for the days when I thought the scariest thing about this place was the three murders that happened here."

"Four murders," Carter says.

"Right." I lower my head, ashamed to have momentarily forgotten about Mary and what befell her on this same terrace.

"Anything new about that?" Carter says. "Or about anything?"

I fill him in on both my conversation with Mrs. Baker and my clandestine search of her room. "No suitcase. But I did find something interesting. Do you know anyone who might be staying at Ocean View?"

"That nursing home in town?"

"Yes. I found a bunch of cleared checks, going back years. Mrs. Baker's been giving them a thousand dollars a month."

Carter lets out a low whistle. "Charitable donation?"

"I doubt Mrs. Baker would be giving away thousands of dollars a year when Hope's End looks like this." I survey the broken terrace and the rubble scattered across it. It resembles a war zone. I'm all for philanthropy, but in the case of Hope's End, charity really does begin at home. "She wouldn't be wasting that kind of money unless she had to. She's paying for someone to stay at Ocean View."

Carter goes rigid beside me. Clutching my arm, he says, "I think I know who it is. I remember Tony mentioning once or twice when I worked at the bar that a couple people who used to work here are still around. And one of them is at Ocean View."

"Who?"

"Berniece Mayhew."

A look passes between us. One borne of surprise and confusion. For some reason—and for many, many years—Mrs. Baker has been paying the living costs of Ricardo Mayhew's wife.

"Why would she do that?" Carter says.

"I don't know," I say. "But I have a feeling Lenora might."

Carter scratches the back of his neck, thinking. "Good luck getting her to tell you anything now that the typewriter's gone."

I thought the same thing this morning after waking on a mattress slid halfway down the bed frame. I hauled it back into place, showered in an alarmingly uneven tub, and put on another of Mary's uniforms before checking in on Lenora. The moment I entered her room, I instinctively looked for the typewriter I'd forgotten was no longer there. Staring at the empty desk, I realized communication between the two of us had just gotten a lot harder. Some answers require more than just tapping yes or no.

"Maybe she can write with her left hand," I say, wishful-thinking aloud. Even if Lenora was left-handed before her series of strokes, I don't think she has the strength to hold a pen and scrawl something on paper for any extended period of time. The only thing I can think to do is write out the alphabet and have her point to the letters.

Which, truth be told, isn't a bad idea.

In fact, I don't even need to go that far.

Someone's already done it for me.

"I just thought of a way," I say, moving to the French doors. "It's not typing, but it'll do in a pinch."

I leave Carter on the terrace and hurry through the dining room into the kitchen. I climb the service stairs quickly, passing the second-floor landing and going straight to the third, which feels like walking through a fun house. Staggering like a drunkard, I make my way to Jessie's room. Her door is open, so I peek inside and try to casually say, "Hi. I was wondering if I could borrow your Ouija board."

Jessie, standing at the foot of her bed, gestures to the top of her dresser, where the Ouija board and planchette sit. "You can have it. It'll just be one less thing I need to pack."

Every drawer in the dresser, I notice, is open, and a suitcase sits on the bed in front of Jessie.

"You're leaving?" I say.

"Yep."

"Where are you going?"

"I don't know, and I don't care." For emphasis, Jessie balls up a sweater and stuffs it into the suitcase. "Just as long as it's anywhere but here. You heard Carter. This whole place is falling apart. Literally. I'm not going to be here when it does. You shouldn't, either. Honestly, we both should have left right after you found Mary."

There's no arguing with that. Watching Jessie toss more clothes into the suitcase, I can't help but imagine what my life would be like right now if I'd walked away that day and never looked back.

But I stayed as Mary's death and the Hope family murders filled my waking hours. And I'll continue to stay, even though the smart thing would be to follow Jessie's lead.

"I can't abandon Lenora," I say, which is both the truth and an excuse.

I'm also staying because I can't shake the feeling that the full story is right at my fingertips, just out of reach. That same feeling is what draws me to the dresser, where I grab Jessie's Ouija board and planchette.

"I'm only borrowing it," I tell her, pretending we'll see each other again when in all likelihood we won't. "I plan on giving it back."

Jessie gives me a surprise hug, which she finishes off with a girlish squeeze. "Take care of yourself, Kit. And take care of Lenora, too. And please promise me you'll get her away from this place as soon as possible."

"I will."

"I'm serious," Jessie says. "I'm worried about her. And you."

"I promise," I say. "I swear."

I'm about to leave the room when Jessie says, "Wait! I forgot something." She hurries to the dresser and hands me a cassette tape. "The end of the book I was reading for Lenora. I hope she likes it."

"Thanks," I say. "I'm sure she will."

I pocket the cassette and let Jessie resume packing, knowing I should be doing the same thing. Instead, I'm carrying a Ouija board down a hallway no one should be allowed to walk through, on my way to get a mute woman to speak not with the dead, but like them.

Five minutes later, the meal tray is attached to Lenora's wheelchair. On top of it sits the Ouija board, with the planchette placed in the center beneath Lenora's left hand.

"You ever use one of these things?" I say.

Lenora lifts the planchette to give a single tap against the board.

"It's easy." I place my hand over hers and glide the planchette around the board. "Just slide this to whatever letters you need to spell out your answer. Got it?"

Biting her bottom lip in concentration, Lenora pushes the planchette to the YES located in the upper-left corner of the board.

"Perfect," I say. "You ready to answer a question?"

The planchette stays where it is, which I assume is another yes.

"How well did you know Berniece Mayhew?"

Lenora slides the planchette to the double row of letters arcing over the center of the board. Slowly, she brings it to the L.

Then the I.

Then the T.

Then the T a second time.

Then the L again.

Then the E.

"A little?" I say, making sure it's what she meant.

Rather than return the planchette to the YES, Lenora taps it twice against the board.

"What was she like?"

Lenora slides the planchette again, spelling out a word with a meaning that needs no confirmation.

NASTY

"Then why is Mrs. Baker giving her money every month?" I look to the Ouija board, where the planchette remains still beneath Lenora's hand. "Did you know she was doing that?"

This time, Lenora spells out her answer.

YES

"How long has it been going on?"

Beneath the letters, a row of numbers is centered on the Ouija board, going from zero to nine. Lenora jerks the planchette to four of them, forming a telltale year.

1929

Because I was never good at math, it takes me a minute to add it all up in my head. The figure I come up with boggles my mind. Since 1929, Berniece Mayhew has been paid more than six hundred thousand dollars.

"Why?" I say, too stunned to phrase it any better than that.

Lenora returns the planchette to the letters, falling into the same kind of rhythm as when she used the typewriter. In roughly the same time it would have taken her to type it, she's spelled out her answer.

BECAUSE SHE KNOWS

I still don't understand. "Knows what?"

Lenora keeps the planchette sliding.

ABOUT THAT NIGHT

I nod. There's only one night she could be referring to.

"What about that night?"

Lenora keeps the planchette moving, skipping from one letter to another to another.

SHE

The planchette continues to slide. Down to one of the last letters on the second row, then up to the first one in the first row, then back down to the second.

WAS

I keep my gaze fixed on the Ouija board, too afraid of missing a letter that I don't even blink.

HERE

My heart thuds once against my rib cage.

Berniece Mayhew was at Hope's End that night.

Not just before and after the murders, but during them.

By the start of October, I had reached the point where I could no longer hide my condition, even with the help of Archie and Miss Baker. My body had changed too much to merely blame on weight gain. Soon anyone who looked at me would know I was pregnant.

Without another way to keep it a secret, Miss Baker suggested I take a cue from my mother and stay in bed. Reluctantly, that's what I did. Anyone who came into my room and saw me propped up on pillows and covered by ample blankets wouldn't know I was pregnant.

My excuse for taking to my bed--exhaustion brought about by extreme nervousness--was also inspired by my mother. Everyone believed it. Like mother, like daughter. Even clueless Dr. Walden had no trouble thinking it was the truth. Rather than examine me, he simply provided a bottle of laudanum and told me to sip it regularly to ease my delicate condition. I poured the foul liquid down the sink as soon as I was alone. I might have been acting like my mother, but I certainly had no plan to become her.

For a restless girl like me who lost every time my father forced us to play the game in which he locked us in our rooms, I shockingly had no trouble spending most of my time in bed. Very quickly, I learned how to lay very still, sometimes for hours, while my mind roamed the world, going wherever I wanted, whenever I wanted.

Often, I'd put my hands on my stomach and whisper to the child growing inside it about all the things I had planned for us and all the places we would go. Paris, of course, but other, more adventurous locales. Jungles and mountains and tropical islands with water that shimmered like sapphires.

I thought of it as nothing more than daydreaming, but Archie, whose curious nature compelled him to read about such things, said I was practicing meditation.

"What's that?" I asked him on one of the rare times he could sneak into my room.

"Disassociating the mind from the body," he replied, which didn't clear up much.

Still, I had ample time to let my mind wander. Few people came to see me. My mother was bedridden herself, and my father, overwhelmed by business woes I knew very little about, had taken to spending more time in Boston. Even Archie's visits grew scarce as the weeks passed.

The only two people I saw on a regular basis were Miss Baker, who brought me meals and made sure I ate every bite, and my sister, who seemed to revel in discussing her social life, including all the things she was doing, people she was seeing, and places she was going.

"Peter and I are going on a picnic," she said the day before everything changed, even though none of us knew it yet. "I do wish you could join us."

She didn't mean it, of course. It was simply her way of making sure I knew she had the carefree existence I could only long for. Little did she know that I was doing fine. I had someone who loved me, his child growing inside me, and a happy family in my future.

Or so I told myself.

But doubt had crept in, and no amount of daydreaming--or meditation--could keep it at bay.

The truth was that Ricky hadn't once checked in on me in the three weeks since I had been forced to fake being an invalid. He knew it was a ruse to hide the pregnancy, for I made sure to tell him.

Day after day, week after week, I asked Miss Baker, who by then knew Ricky's identity, if he had come around trying to see me. And day after day, week after week, I was told no.

"I'm sure it's very difficult for him to sneak away," Miss Baker said each time I asked.

Of that, I had no doubt. What bothered me was that he didn't even seem to be attempting to check on me. My patience eventually wore thin, as did my certainty that Ricky truly loved me and wanted this child as much as I did.

Fueled in part by my sister's flaunting of her robust social life, I chose that night to sneak out and see him. The doubt had become too much to bear.

When Miss Baker arrived with dinner that evening, I pleaded with her to locate Ricky and tell him I would meet him on the terrace at midnight. It was the only time I could leave my room without being seen. Reluctantly, she agreed.

At the stroke of midnight, after I was certain everyone else had gone to bed, I crept downstairs into the kitchen, on my way to the terrace. I was halfway across the kitchen when I realized I wasn't alone.

Berniece was also there. Although she pretended to busy herself with late-night work, it was clear she had been waiting for me.

"I knew it," she said when she saw my rounded stomach. "Well, you're one apple that didn't fall far from the tree."

"What is that supposed to mean?" I replied, trying to muster anger when all I felt was pure fear.

Berniece sneered. "That you're a whore. Just like every other member of your family."

I was so stunned I couldn't speak. I knew what the servants said about us behind our backs, of course. I just thought they valued their jobs too much to say it to my face. Not Berniece, apparently.

"You honestly think I don't know what's going on?" she said. "My husband sneaking out at odd hours, hardly paying any attention to me, looking like he'd rather die than touch me. I've known for months. It's not the first time it's happened."

She glared at me, as if everything about me repulsed her.

"What do you intend to do about it?" I said, which I'm sure sounded like a challenge to Berniece even though it wasn't. I was intensely curious--not to mention frightened--of her next move.

"I intend to get rich," she said. "I'll stay silent and look the other way if you and your family pay up."

I stayed completely still, stunned. "How much?"

"Fifty thousand dollars should be enough," she said before tacking on a threat I was certain she'd carry out. "For now. You have until tomorrow night to think it over."

Immediately, I began to panic.

Tomorrow.

That wasn't much time. Not nearly enough to plan our escape. But escape was the only option. Of that, I had no doubt.

I burst from the kitchen, running outside to the terrace, where Ricky waited in the shadows. I hushed him before he could say a word, worried that Berniece had followed me out.

"Not here," I whispered before whisking him away to the first floor of the garage, where the gleaming Packards my father owned but never drove were kept. We climbed into the back seat of one of them, hiding from the rest of the world.

"Will you tell me what's going on?" Ricky said.

"She knows," I blurted out. "Berniece knows. And she wants money or she's going to tell my father. But telling my father is the only way to get the money."

"How much does she want?" Ricky said, his voice more curious than angry.

"Fifty thousand dollars." I wanted to sob. The situation was so dire that I had no idea what to do. No matter what we chose, the decision would irrevocably change my life. "What are we going to do?"

Ricky had the only answer.

"Run away," he said. "Tomorrow night."

# THIRTY-FOUR

I 'll give whoever named Ocean View Retirement Home credit where it's due. The place does have what its name promises. From a distance. And only if you look between the buildings on the other side of the street, the backs of which really do have an ocean view.

Inside is a large, tasteful lobby that makes the place look more like a hotel than a nursing home. There are potted palms, plush chairs, and paintings of seashells in pastel shades on the walls. A registration desk stretches along one end of the lobby, behind which sits a woman who appears old enough to be a resident. Gray hair. Mint green pantsuit. Lit cigarette jammed between her lips. She squints through the smoke, watching my approach.

"Welcome to Ocean View," she says. "How may I be of assistance?"

I look to the doors on either side of the desk. One is closed and marked as being for employees only. The other is propped open, revealing a glimpse of a man pushing a walker down a hallway lined with burgundy carpet. The way into Ocean View.

"I'm here to see Bernice Mayhew," I say.

The receptionist looks me up and down, assessing my uniform. "You're not one of our nurses."

"No. I'm with the insurance company." I lift the medical bag I brought with me as part of the ruse. "They ordered me to check her vitals."

"Why?"

"They didn't tell me. You know how insurance companies can be."

The receptionist nods, silently acknowledging that yes, insurance companies are terrible and yes, the two of us are just cogs in a vast healthcare industrial complex that puts profits over people every damn time. Still, she hesitates. "We have our own medical staff that evaluates the patients."

"I'm just doing what I was told," I say.

"I understand that. But them sending you here at this hour is very unusual."

"I totally agree," I say. "You can call the main office, if you want. But you'll be on hold for an hour and what I need to do only takes five minutes. Check blood pressure, heart rate, temperature. Then I'm gone."

I take a breath, proud of myself—not to mention a little alarmed—for being able to lie so effortlessly. The receptionist exhales a line of smoke and eyes the phone by her elbow, no doubt debating how much time she wants to waste on this. Not a lot, apparently, because she says, "Five minutes? That's it?"

It's all I can spare. I couldn't get away until Archie brought dinner up to Lenora's room. I asked him to stay with her while I ran into town to run an important errand. I told him I'd be gone for thirty minutes. Since the drive here took fifteen minutes and the drive back will take the same, I figure I can spend only five minutes with Berniece Mayhew before he starts to get suspicious.

I smile at the receptionist. "Depending on Mrs. Mayhew, it might only take four."

"She's in the Dunes wing," the receptionist says as she takes a drag on her cigarette. "Room 113."

I follow the burgundy carpet deeper into Ocean View. A directory just inside the door helps me get my bearings. Waves wing on the left, Dunes wing on the right, common area straight ahead. I go right, moving down a hallway that smells like bleach, lemon air freshener, and just a hint of urine.

At Room 111, I slow my pace. At Room 112, I adjust my nurse's cap and smooth the skirt of my uniform. I then plaster a smile on my face and step into Room 113.

The room is small but tidy. Decent enough to visit, but not a place you want to spend much time in. Berniece Mayhew, though, has spent years here. And it shows. Propped up by pillows and wearing a terry-cloth robe, she has the look of someone who doesn't get out much. Her hair is a shock of white, which stands in contrast to a face darkened by age spots. She's got a flat nose, chubby cheeks, and a chin that's non-existent. In its place is a flap of loose skin that droops like a wet rag on a hook. It sways when she turns to glare at me.

"Who are you?"

"My name's Kit." The time for lying ended in the hallway. Now I have no choice but to tell her the truth. "I work for Lenora Hope."

"Are you her nurse?"

"Something like that, yes."

Berniece turns back to the small TV sitting opposite the bed. *Wheel of Fortune* is on. My mother loved that show. "How's Lenora doing?" she says.

"Fine, all things considered."

She huffs with disappointment. "That's a damn shame."

"Would it make you happy to know her whole body's paralyzed except for her left hand?"

Berniece Mayhew looks my way again, delight dancing in her eyes. "Is she suffering?"

"I don't think so," I say.

"I'd be happier if she was."

A wooden chair sits just inside the door. I drop onto it and place my medical bag on the floor. "That's an interesting thing to say about the woman whose generosity keeps you here."

"Is that what you think it is?" Berniece says bitterly. "Generosity?"

"The only other thing I can think of is hush money. My best guess is it's so you wouldn't tell anyone Lenora Hope was having an affair with your husband. Or is it because you saw something you weren't supposed to see the night most of the Hope family was murdered?"

Berniece Mayhew gives me a squinty-eyed look, as if seeing me for the very first time. "You're a shrewd one, I'll give you that. Bold, too. Just waltzing in here and saying something like that."

"It's true, isn't it?"

"I didn't say it wasn't," Berniece snaps.

"Which one do you want to tell me about first?"

"I've stayed silent since 1929. What makes you think I'm going to start blabbing now?"

"Because someone else is dead."

Berniece's eyes narrow. "Who?"

"Lenora's previous nurse," I say. "A worker. Just like me. Just like you. I think she was murdered. And I think it has something to do with what happened that night in 1929."

I pause, waiting to see what kind of response I get. My hope is that the mention of Mary will play to her sympathies. If she has any. I'm about to see if Berniece Mayhew is as nasty as Lenora says she is.

The old woman turns back to the television, where Vanna White, pert and perky in a sparkly dress, turns letters. But Berniece doesn't seem to be looking at the TV at all. Her gaze is fixed somewhere else, somewhere distant. A moment in the past only she can see.

"Ricardo wasn't perfect." Berniece sighs, and contained in that single sound is a lifetime of disappointment. "I knew that when I married him. He had, shall we say, a wandering eye. But he wasn't mean, even when he drank, which is more than I can say about my father. So I wasn't surprised when that rich bitch got her hooks into him. She could have had the pick of all those young men working the place. Some were full-time. Some were townies. Some of them fine-looking, too. But none as handsome as my Ricardo. I guess that's why she set her sights on him. All she needed to do was bat those big, blue eyes at him and he was a goner."

"Did you confront him about it?"

"Of course. Do I look like some shrinking violet to you?"

I have to concede that no, she does not. "What did he say?"

"He denied it, of course. He was a smooth talker, my Ricardo. Could talk his way out of anything. He tried to convince me nothing was going on between them, and I pretended to believe him. But I had a plan, you see."

The chair creaks as I lean forward, elbows on my knees. "The hush money."

"It only seemed fair," Berniece says. "My husband was carrying on with one of the High and Mighty Hopes. I deserved something for my pain and suffering. So I gave them an ultimatum—pay up or I'd tell everyone exactly what kind of people they were."

"And they had to decide—"

"The night all hell broke loose."

Berniece tells me how all the Hope's End staff was given the night off. That was apparently common every other Tuesday in the off-season. There wasn't a whole lot to do there once October rolled around. Berniece told her husband she was going into town to see a movie.

"I asked if he wanted to come along, knowing he wouldn't," she says. "So I grabbed my coat, hat, and purse and left the cottage."

"But you didn't leave Hope's End," I say.

Berniece touches the tip of her nose, signaling I'm right. "I waited around outside, hoping to see Ricardo sneaking off to meet her. Sure enough, he left the cottage about fifteen minutes later, sauntering across the terrace and past the swimming pool to the garage. At first, I was surprised. Imagine a place that big, with all those rooms, and choosing to fuck in the garage."

I jolt in shock. No, Berniece Mayhew is definitely not a shrinking violet. She smiles, pleased to have scandalized me.

"But then I realized what he was doing," she continues. "Ricardo wasn't a stupid man, despite doing many stupid things. He knew I was on to him. And I realized he knew I hadn't gone to the movies. Heading to the garage was just a way of throwing me off his trail."

I get her gist. Instead of entering through the back, he went to the garage before going around to the front of the house and using the main door.

"I marched right into that house, ready to catch the two of them in the act and then tell Winston Hope exactly what his daughter was doing with my husband. I was certain he'd pay up. After firing Ricardo, of course. And probably me, as well. Which was even more reason to try to get as much money as I could."

"But it didn't work out that way."

"No," Berniece says quietly. "It didn't."

I glance at my watch. My five minutes are up. But I can't leave. Not until I hear the full story. Trying to move her along, I say, "What happened when you went inside?"

"I got as far as the kitchen before that bitch ran in."

I can only assume the bitch in question is Lenora.

"She looked scared," Berniece says. "At first I thought it was because of me. That she knew they'd been found out. But then I noticed her hands."

My chair starts to vibrate. I look down and notice I'm tapping my right foot, set into motion by both impatience and suspense. "What about them?"

"They were bloody."

My foot stills instantly, as does the rest of my body as I picture young Lenora standing in the kitchen, blood dripping from her hands. A horrible image for many reasons.

"Did she say anything?"

"Not at first," Berniece says. "She just stared at me, shocked to see me there. And then we both heard a scream. It came from upstairs, echoing down the service stairs."

"Do you know who it was?" I say.

"Either Mrs. Hope or the younger daughter," Berniece says. "It was definitely a woman. As she kept on screaming, Lenora grabbed a knife from the kitchen counter. Then she glared at me and said, 'Get out right now.'"

"What did you say?"

"Nothing. I just nodded and left. I was too scared to do anything else. But I knew something awful was happening inside that house. It wasn't until the police came that I realized just how awful it really was." Berniece looks down at her lap, ashamed. "I think about that moment a lot. If I'd refused to go, maybe Lenora would have killed me on the spot. Or maybe the other killings wouldn't have happened. Maybe some of them could have been saved. Especially the younger daughter. Virginia. The poor thing. In such a state, too."

"Why didn't you tell the police any of this?"

"Because I wanted to protect Ricardo," Berniece says, a catch in her throat. "I knew it wasn't just Lenora responsible for those murders. Ricardo was part of it, too. He had to be. Because he never came back to the cottage. Not that night. Not ever. Once he disappeared, I knew deep down what had happened. That he had helped her kill that family."

"Why would he do that?" I say. "You said yourself he wasn't mean."

"But he was easily swayed. My assumption is she tricked him. I'd seen how manipulative she could be."

There's that word again. The same one Mrs. Baker had used to describe Lenora.

Manipulative.

"I bet she gave him some sob story about her cruel parents and her awful life and how she was a prisoner in that big old mansion. And I bet Ricardo believed it. After a few months of hearing bullshit like that, he was probably brainwashed into thinking the only way they could be together is if the rest of her family was dead. So he helped her kill them."

"Then he ran away," I say.

"No, sweetie," Berniece says, her voice so vicious it's practically a snarl. "Lenora killed him, too."

I remain completely still in the chair, incapable of movement. I try to imagine Lenora doing any of this. Killing not just her father, mother, and sister, but her lover as well. Only a monster would do that. And the Lenora Hope I know isn't a monster.

Not that I thought she was completely innocent. She told me so herself.

*I wasn't a good girl.*

*Not in the least.*

*You'll see for yourself very soon.*

I also knew she had gotten rid of the knife used to kill her parents. Lenora made no attempt to hide that from me. Even so, I'd started to think she was innocent of the actual killings. In my mind, the only thing she was guilty of was covering for the man who really committed them, out of a misguided sense of love and loyalty.

But what Berniece is telling me shatters all my assumptions. If what she's saying is true, then Lenora is just as guilty as Ricardo Mayhew. Probably more so, since she's still alive and he's . . . gone.

Unless Berniece is lying.

Not an impossibility, seeing how she just admitted to taking money for decades from the woman she says killed her husband.

"If Lenora murdered Ricardo," I say, "why wasn't his body found with the others?"

Berniece has a simple answer for that. "She shoved him off that terrace. You've seen it. That's a long drop to the ocean."

Yet that still doesn't make any sense. Why would Lenora make her accomplice disappear? Especially when it meant all suspicion was directed at her? Either Berniece is making all of this up—or she misunderstood what she saw. And judging by her silence all these years, she doesn't care about that as long as she's getting paid.

"I don't think this is about protecting your husband," I say. "After the murders, you realized you had a new way to get your hush money."

"And good thing I did, too," Berniece says. "Because sure enough, we were all fired within the week. Those of us who were left, anyway.

Half the staff quit as soon as they found out what happened. Lenora was too busy being questioned by the police to do it herself. She sent the kitchen boy to do it."

"Archie?"

"That's his name," Berniece says with a nod. "I never could remember it. Poor kid, though. Barely eighteen and being told to fire everyone he worked with. When he got to the cottage, he could barely look me in the eye. He just handed me a check for a thousand dollars, written out by Lenora Hope herself."

I check my watch again. Five minutes has turned to ten. And the man waiting for my return is the same person who first paid off Berniece.

"Did he tell you it was hush money?"

"He didn't need to, hon," Berniece says. "Paying off people was the Hope family way. They did it to get what they wanted, whether it was that concoction Mrs. Hope was always drinking or the pretty young maids Mr. Hope was always screwing. And it was how they kept people quiet, like whenever one of those pretty maids found themselves in trouble."

"So you just took the check and left."

A cold glint appears in Berniece's eyes. "Not quite. I told him to inform Miss Hope that there needed to be a similar check every month or I'd tell the police I saw her with a knife the same night her parents were stabbed to death. Sure enough, one came for the same amount the next month. And the one after that. The money faucet's been running ever since."

I stand, feeling dirty in her presence. Yet I'm also reluctant to get back to Hope's End, because I know at least some of what she's said is true. About Mrs. Hope's addiction and Mr. Hope's sexual proclivities and how the family threw money at whatever problem they encountered. I know because I helped Lenora type it.

Which means everyone in that house other than Carter is corrupt.

Including Lenora.

"It's about to be turned off," I say. "Because either you go to the police or I will."

Berniece glances over my shoulder to the doorway behind me, her features brightening. "Looks like they're already here."

A hand clamps down on my shoulder as the familiar voice of Detective Vick says, "Come with me, Kit. You know you shouldn't be here."

"We're just talking," I protest.

"You're trespassing." Detective Vick grips my arm and tugs. "And lying about it in the process."

I unwillingly turn to the doorway. Behind the detective stands the woman I talked to at the reception desk. She glares at me and says, "Guess who called the insurance company after all? They have no idea who you are."

"But I do," Detective Vick says. "I'll take it from here. Unless you want to press charges."

The woman considers it, taking an uncomfortably long time to make up her mind. She looks to Berniece and says, "Did she hurt you in any way, Mrs. Mayhew?"

"It's fine. She just asked me a few questions."

"And now you need to tell them what you just told me," I say.

Detective Vick won't hear of it. "You've bothered her enough, Kit. Let's go."

He gives me just enough time to grab my medical bag before pulling me out of the room. As we leave, Berniece flashes me a gap-toothed grin.

"Tell Lenora I said hello," she says. "And that I'll see her in hell."

# THIRTY-FIVE

Detective Vick keeps a firm grip around my wrist as he walks me to my car. I should be flattered he thinks I'm that much of a threat.

"You can let go now," I say, twisting my arm. "I'm not going to run back inside and bother Berniece some more. Although I highly recommend *you* do. You'll want to hear what she has to say."

"The police talked to Berniece Mayhew fifty-four years ago."

"So you looked at the case file from back then?"

"I did. Berniece didn't have anything to say other than that her husband hadn't come home."

"She was lying," I say. "And you'd know that if you went back there and did your goddamn job."

Detective Vick finally releases my wrist when we reach my car. From the pissed-off look on his face, I expect him to up the stakes and put me in handcuffs. Instead, he says, "Go back and do *your* goddamn job. Leave the investigating to me. Better yet, quit that place and go home. Your dad misses you."

I blink, surprised. "He said that?"

"No," Detective Vick says. "But I assume it's lonely for him now."

"Trust me," I say. "It's not."

"So you decided to bother an innocent old lady instead?"

I stifle a harsh laugh. *Innocent* is the last word I'd use to describe a woman who's collected money for decades to stay silent about what she thinks was a quadruple homicide. Then again, that's nothing compared with the crimes Berniece says her husband and Lenora committed.

"I was here asking about Ricardo Mayhew," I say. "His wife thinks he did it, by the way. With Lenora's help. And then she killed him."

"And what do you think?"

I lean against my car, mulling over the question. "I think something happened that night beyond the murders of three people and the disappearance of another. Something that either instigated the violence or was the result of it."

That Lenora was part of it is a given. What I struggle with is deciding how big of a role she played. Is it all her fault, as both Berniece and the mystery typist who came into Lenora's room claim? Or was she swept up in events beyond her control? Did she toss the murder weapon to try to mitigate the damage but ended up being blamed for everything?

I hope it's the latter. I fear it's the former.

"What else did the police reports say?"

"They got a call a little after eleven p.m. on Tuesday, October 29," Detective Vick says. "The caller told them two people were dead at Hope's End."

I cock my head. "Two?"

"That's what the report says."

But three people were murdered that night. The only way that can possibly be right is if the person who called the police did so after finding only two of the bodies.

"Who was the caller?"

"Lenora Hope."

It makes sense she'd be the one to call the police. It's naturally the first thing Lenora would do if she was innocent—or trying to make herself *look* innocent. But in both cases, she'd surely know the number of victims. Either Lenora lied to the police—or someone else was still alive while she was on the phone.

I reach into my memory, summoning the first few pages Lenora had typed. They're easy to recall because she stressed how it was the moment she remembered most. The thing she still had nightmares about.

Her on the terrace.

Bloody knife washed clean by the rain before she tossed it into the ocean below.

Her sister screaming inside the house.

Virginia.

That's who was still alive. And then Lenora went to the garage to fetch some rope.

I'm hit with a headache as I consider what that means. And it doesn't look too good for Lenora. In fact, it looks like Virginia was collateral damage, stumbling into the wrong place at the wrong time. And someone decided she had to die, too.

That someone was most likely Lenora, who no longer had the knife that killed her parents and needed a new weapon. As for who did the hanging, maybe that was Ricardo, who either fled afterward or, if Berniece is right, was then shoved off the terrace by Lenora.

The same terrace Mary was pushed from.

"Police responding to the scene found the front gate open," Detective Vick says. "When they entered the house, they discovered Evangeline Hope on the staircase landing. The officers then fanned out through the rest of the house, finding Winston Hope in the billiard room and Virginia Hope hanging from a chandelier in the ballroom."

"Where was Lenora?"

"On the terrace."

So she went back out there after Virginia was killed. My headache gets worse. Because the more I hear, the more I think that Berniece is right.

And that Lenora is guilty.

"Mr. and Mrs. Hope were declared dead at the scene. Virginia was taken upstairs."

"Also dead," I say.

Detective Vick shakes his head. "Not for another six months."

A shock.

I'd assumed Virginia died the same night her parents did. Instead, she clung to life for six more months. I'm not sure which is worse—going instantly like her mother and father or lingering at death's door that long before finally slipping through.

"Why did no one suspect Ricardo Mayhew?"

"They did," Detective Vick says. "Once everyone realized he was gone and not coming back, he was the prime suspect. Especially when it was discovered that one of Winston Hope's Packards was missing from the garage. It was possible he killed them, stole the car, and drove as far away as he could. But there was nothing to prove that's what happened—or that he was even in the house at all."

"Did someone at least ask Lenora about Ricardo?"

A car pulls into the parking lot, its headlights skimming the Ocean View's façade before landing on the weathered face of Detective Vick. Usually, he looks flinty. Tonight, he just looks tired.

"As a matter of fact they did," he says. "She claimed she didn't know who he was. One of the cops had to clarify that he was the head groundskeeper at Hope's End. The cop made a note that she genuinely seemed to not know the man's name."

"How many times did they talk to her?"

"Multiple times over several weeks," Detective Vick says. "Her story was always the same. She didn't see anything, didn't hear anything, never saw a soul inside that house other than her family."

That's at least one lie on Lenora's part. She saw Berniece, who caught her in the kitchen with blood on her hands as she grabbed a knife.

Yet that doesn't make sense. If Lenora was indeed guilty, how could there be blood on her hands *before* she fetched the knife? That's only possible if more than one knife had been used.

"What about the weapon?" I say. "They never found it, right?"

"Correct."

"Were the police certain only one knife was used?"

"As certain as they could be," Detective Vick says. "No other knife seemed to be missing from the kitchen, and the stab wounds on both Winston and Evangeline Hope were roughly the same width, suggesting only one weapon was used."

"Did they notice anything out of the ordinary about the place? Anything at all?"

"Just that Virginia Hope's room had recently been cleaned. One of the cops smelled floor polish when they brought her upstairs."

I touch my temples, the headache growing. It's so bad I'm surprised my skull hasn't fractured yet, forming a crack as big as the one now running across the terrace at Hope's End. "Since they couldn't prove—or disprove—that Ricardo did it, and since they couldn't do the same with Lenora, the case just stalled?"

"Correct," Detective Vick says. "Sound familiar?"

Anger flashes through me like lightning. Electric. Searing.

"Fuck you," I tell Detective Vick, which might be illegal. I'm not up to date on laws against swearing at police detectives. If it is a crime, Detective Vick makes no move to do anything about it as I yank open the door to my Escort and slide behind the wheel.

"I don't blame you, you know," he says before I can slam the door shut. "Your mother was suffering. I understand that. My own parents suffered when their time came. But I didn't break the law to try to end it."

"Neither did I."

I'm on the verge of tears, and I don't know if it's from rage or grief or the fact that everything about the past six months has been too damn much. When I got to Hope's End, I threw myself into learning Lenora's story because I was desperate to change my own pathetic existence by focusing on someone else's. But then I found Mary dead, and things have only spiraled since then.

"I didn't make my mother take those pills," I say, swiping at a tear before it can fall because I'll be damned if I cry in front of Detective

Vick. "She killed herself. Mary didn't. And someone smarter than you would understand that."

The detective's nostrils flare. The only sign I've gotten to him. Unlike me, he knows how to keep his emotions in check.

"Kit, for the last time, Mary Milton wasn't murdered."

"How can you be so sure of that?"

Detective Vick removes a piece of paper from inside his jacket. A photocopy of a page made ragged and faint from water damage. Thrusting it at me, he says, "Because of this."

My hands go numb as I read the single sentence typed across the page. "What is this?"

"A copy of Mary Milton's suicide note," Detective Vick says. "I told you we found it with her body."

I scan the page a second, third, fourth time, hoping each pass will produce a different meaning. But it all reads the same every damn time.

im sorry im not the person you thought i was

"Mary—" I stop, unnerved by the way my voice sounds. Like I'm underwater. Like I'm a thousand miles away. "Mary didn't write this."

"Of course she did," Detective Vick says. "Who else could it be?"

Rather than answer, I struggle to jam the key into the ignition and struggle even more to pull out of the parking spot. Then I drive off, leaving Detective Vick standing in exhaust fumes, still ignorant to the fact that what he found with Mary's body wasn't a suicide note.

It's something else.

Typed by someone else.

And I think I know exactly what it means.

# THIRTY-SIX

ecause I didn't want to use the intercom to be let in upon my return, I never closed the front gate to Hope's End behind me when I left. It's still open, thank God, letting me steer the car right past it. I stop long enough to smack the button embedded in the interior wall to finally close the gate behind me. Then it's back to the car, where I speed to the front door, cut the engine, and hurry inside. The house is unnervingly quiet as I sweep down the hallway, coming to a stop at the family portraits on the wall.

Pausing a moment at the painting of Lenora, I take in her pert nose, ripe lips, green eyes. Despite the many years between them, the girl in the portrait is unmistakably the woman I've been caring for.

I head to the first portrait in the row and use my car key to jab the silk crepe covering it. Once I've made a hole big enough to poke a finger through, I start clawing at the fabric. The silk crepe makes a tearing sound—slick, almost wet. I wonder if the knife blade sliding across Winston Hope's throat made a similar noise.

That's who's underneath the fabric. Winston Hope himself, looking like every other captain of industry from that period. Ruddy and smug and pudgy from too much food, too much wine, too much everything. Men like him gobbled up all they could, leaving nothing for everyone else.

Staring at the greedy visage of Winston Hope, I can tell he had no idea what fate had in store for him. He probably thought he'd live forever. Instead, he ended up dead in the room just across the hall, slumped over a pool table, his blood seeping into the green felt.

I move on to the next portrait, repeating my steps. Jab, poke, claw, tear. The black fabric pulls away to reveal Evangeline Hope. She truly was beautiful. Lenora hadn't lied about that. Alabaster skin. Golden hair. Slim, elegant frame draped in an equally slim and elegant gown. But for all the ethereal beauty on display, there's something not right about Mrs. Hope's appearance. She's disconcertingly pale, making her seem delicate and fragile. I look at her and am reminded of a daylily on the cusp of wilting.

Unlike her husband, Evangeline Hope looks very much like she knew what was coming.

There's only one portrait left.

Virginia.

I jab and poke. I claw and tear. I keep ripping until I see a young woman who bears some of the features of her mother and absolutely none of her father. She's beautiful, too, in a slightly haughty way. In the painting, her smile comes off as forced, almost cruel. Then there are her eyes, which are colored an icy blue. Staring at them makes me recall what Berniece Mayhew said about Ricardo being a goner once Lenora batted her big eyes at him.

Her big, *blue* eyes.

Both my heart and mind race as I rush into the library, zeroing in on the fireplace mantel, where those three unsettling urns sit.

Father, mother, daughter.

With trembling hands, I reach out and lift the lid from the urn on the left.

Inside is a pile of dull gray powder that brings to mind something the priest said during my mother's funeral.

*Ashes to ashes, dust to dust.*

Both are present and accounted for inside the urn, shifting like sand as I set it back on the mantel and replace the lid.

I grab the second urn, lift the lid, take a peek at more ashes.

Then it's on to the third urn, where my movements seem to slow like a bad memory. Seconds stretch to minutes as my fingers touch the lid, lift it, set it aside on the mantel. My senses work overtime when I grasp the urn.

I feel the porcelain cold against my palm.

I see the dust motes drifting through the stale air.

I smell the yellowed pages of books that haven't been opened for decades.

I taste something metallic on my tongue. Fear, I realize, of what will happen when I look inside the urn.

Then I do look, and my gasp is loud enough to echo off the library bookshelves.

Because what I see is . . . nothing.

No ashes. No dust.

The urn is completely empty.

I should have known the night would end in disaster. I should have sensed it in the stormy air. All day, while pretending to be bedridden, I'd heard the thunder rumbling over the ocean like the cannon fire of an approaching horde.

A battle was coming.

And there would be casualties.

But I ignored the signs, too preoccupied with getting away to notice them. Our plan, such as it was, involved me gathering as much of my things as possible after everyone in the house had gone to bed. While I did that, Ricky would sneak into the garage and steal the keys to one of my father's Packards. At ten p.m., if all went well, he'd be pulling up to the front door just as I slipped out with my suitcase. Then we'd drive away and never look back.

At the time, I thought it would work.

All the servants had been given their biweekly night off, which is what made Ricky think the plan was possible. Because my mother remained in a round-the-clock laudanum haze, there'd be no one else but my sister and father around to catch us.

I never expected one of them would.

At quarter to nine, I slid out of bed and quickly changed clothes. I had no idea what the rest of the night had in store, but I secretly hoped it involved a trip to a justice of the peace. I loved the idea of Ricky and me getting married before the baby was born. The last thing I wanted was for our child to be considered a bastard. If marriage was in store for me that night, I needed to wear the prettiest thing I owned--the pink satin dress I'd worn for my birthday portrait. It barely fit, even though it'd been let out multiple times since then, and did nothing to disguise my pregnant state.

After squeezing into the dress, I tossed my suitcase onto the bed and flung it open. I then went to the armoire, grabbing as many dresses as my arms could hold. When I turned back to the suitcase, I found my sister in the doorway. She stood with her hands behind her back, holding something she didn't want me to see.

"What are you doing?" she said, looking delighted to have caught me up and about.

"Leaving."

"Where?"

"I don't know. Anywhere but here."

My sister's eyes gleamed. "You're running away with him, aren't you?"

"Yes," I said as I dropped the dresses I'd been holding into my suitcase. Without them to cover me, my sister could now see what I'd been hiding for months. The gleam in her eyes was quickly replaced by shock.

"Dear God," she said, her mouth agape. "What have you done?"

I returned to the armoire and grabbed another armful of dresses. "Now do you understand why I'm leaving?"

What I needed from my sister at that moment was for her to help me, comfort me, support me. That's what sisters are supposed to do for each other. Instead, mine simply said, "Father will never allow it."

The mention of my father stopped me dead.

"Please don't tell him," I said. "Please just let me leave. You hate me, after all. Won't that make your life easier, being the only child?"

"Not when the family's name is ruined." My sister stood perfectly erect, her chin raised, smug in her superiority. She thought herself better than me in every way, and no longer made any attempt to hide it. "It's not just you who'll be affected. All of us will pay a price. Think of your reputation. Think of mine!"

"You expect me to stay here, loveless and miserable, for the rest of my life, just to preserve your precious reputation?"

"No," my sister said. "Yours should be concern enough. If you leave, you'll be throwing your life away."

"Or gaining a new one," I was quick to reply.

"Either way, I can't let you do it."

"Go ahead then," I said. "Tell him. It won't keep me from leaving."

"Then I think it's time for one of our old games," my sister said. "You remember how to play it, don't you?"

My sister removed her hand from behind her back, revealing what she'd been holding all this time.

A key.

To my bedroom door.

Which could only be locked from the outside.

"No! Please!" I said, unable to get the words out before my sister left the room. I rushed to the door, feeling the brush of swift air on my face as she slammed it shut behind her. By the time I reached for the doorknob, it was too late. The key clicked in the lock just before I could grab it. I twisted the knob anyway. It didn't budge.

The door was firmly locked.

I caught sight of the door on the other side of the room, the one that led to Miss Baker's room. Unfortunately, my sister had also thought of it. I heard the key turning in that lock as I burst into the room.

I was completely trapped.

Still, I threw myself against the door and began pounding on it. On the other side, my sister's evil laughter echoed down the hall as she ran to tell my father what I was about to do.

"Let me out!" I screamed after her. "Please let me out."

I slammed into the door again and felt something inside me give way.

Liquid.

Gushing from between my legs onto the floor.

Panic flooded my body, for I knew it meant the baby was coming.

Early.

And fast.

Terrified, I pounded on the door, calling for my sister.

"Please!" I screamed. "Please, Lenora!"

# THIRTY-SEVEN

I find Mrs. Baker in the kitchen, corkscrew in hand, opening a bottle of Cabernet on the counter. She looks up, surprised to see me enter from the hallway and not the service stairs.

"Is everything all right with Miss Hope?"

"Yes, Lenora," I say. "Virginia is fine."

The corkscrew goes still. Just for a moment. Then she yanks, uncorking the bottle with a whisper-like pop.

"I have no idea what you're talking about."

Her denial, ironically, confirms my suspicion. The rigid way she stands, her forced smile and her steely blue eyes are an exact re-creation of the uncovered portrait in the hall.

"Maybe this will help," I say, removing Mary's alleged suicide note from my pocket and slapping it onto the table.

The woman pretending to be Mrs. Baker scans it, cool as a cucumber, before filling a glass with wine. As she does, I swipe the corkscrew from the counter. Considering the conversation we're about to have, I don't want a sharp object within her reach.

But I do want one in mine.

The corkscrew goes into my pocket as Lenora Hope—the real one—takes a sip of wine and says, "Am I supposed to know what this is?"

"Mary Milton had it in her pocket the night she died. Detective Vick thought it was a suicide note. But no one types that way. No one but your sister. Who typed it after she revealed to Mary who she really was, apologizing for pretending to be someone else for so long."

Whether Virginia—the real one, the *living* one—planned on officially revealing it to me is unclear. I think she wanted to. After what happened to Mary, I suspect she feared doing it. But she never lied to me. Nothing she typed was untrue. When I asked who'd been in her room at night, she provided an honest answer.

Virginia.

Her real name.

When I asked who'd used the typewriter during the night, she gave the same truthful response as when I asked her who Mary was afraid of.

Her sister.

The woman standing directly across the counter from me.

"But you already know this," I tell her. "You knew it when you shoved Mary off the terrace."

Lenora grips her wineglass so tightly I fear it might shatter. "I did no such thing! She killed herself."

I pat my pocket, feeling the corkscrew's curved ridge and the knife-point sharpness of its tip. "We both know that's not true."

"Whatever happened to that poor girl has nothing to do with me."

"But it does," I say. "Because she knew you've been hiding the fact that your sister is alive and that you're really Lenora. How long has it been going on?"

"A long time," she says, admitting at least one thing—Mrs. Baker, she of the unknown first name, is indeed the infamous Lenora Hope. "Almost all the way back to the murders."

Fifty-four years. A staggering amount of time.

"Why did you do it?" I say. "And how?"

"Which part?" Lenora says between giant swallows from her glass. Already, the wine is doing its job. She's looser now, and far more forthcoming. "Faking my sister's death or forcing her to assume my identity?"

"Both," I say, my head now spinning from literally all of it. "What really happened that night?"

"I can only tell you what *I* experienced." Lenora climbs onto a stool and sits across from me, elbows on the counter. As if we're best friends out for a drink. As if any of this is normal. "I was upstairs in my room, sitting at my dressing table and listening to my record player while pretending I wasn't hiding from everything going wrong in this house."

It's easy to picture because I spied on her doing exactly that last night.

"It had already been a long, terrible night," she says. "Things happened. Awful things. And then it escalated. And then everything went quiet. Eventually, I decided to go downstairs and see if everything was okay."

"It wasn't," I say.

When Lenora shakes her head, I spot a glint of moisture in her telltale blue eyes. Tears that she refuses to let fall.

"I found my mother on the Grand Stairs. Dead, of course. I knew that right away. There was blood . . . everywhere." Lenora pauses, shuddering at the memory. "I started screaming and running through the house like a chicken with its head cut off. My God, that's a terrible saying. Still, it fits my reaction that night. Running and screaming. Screaming and running. Right into the billiard room, where I saw my father."

As she takes another sip of wine to fortify herself, I think about how it must have felt to walk into that room, to see her father slumped over the pool table, to notice the blood trickling into the table pockets.

"I ran to the kitchen, phoned the police, and told them my parents had been murdered."

I nod, because it tracks with what Detective Vick told me about the police getting the call shortly after eleven.

"I then went looking for Virginia. I found her hanging in there." Lenora nods toward the kitchen doorway and the ballroom down the hall just beyond it. "She was hanging from one of the chandeliers. I should have tried to take her down. I realize that now. But I thought she was dead, just like my parents. Faced with such an irrational situation, I could only behave in an irrational manner—I went out to the terrace and screamed. Out of fear and grief and confusion. I screamed until my throat seized up and I couldn't scream anymore. That's when the police arrived."

Lenora traces the rim of the wineglass with her index finger as she tells me about the cops finding her family presumably dead and no one else in the house but her.

"They looked at me like I was a maniac," she says. "Even though I'd done nothing wrong. The first words I told them were 'It wasn't me.' Which only made them suspect me more. The complete opposite of what I intended. They sat me down in the dining room and asked me all sorts of awful questions. Who else was here? Did I have a reason to want my family dead? And I just kept giving them the same answer: 'It wasn't me. It wasn't me.'"

I get déjà vu listening to her, thinking about me in a featureless interrogation room, Detective Vick's accusatory stare, the reels of the tape recorder going round and round.

"Then a miracle happened," Lenora says. "One of the cops yelled from the ballroom that Virginia was still alive. It turns out the noose around her neck wasn't much of a noose at all. That haphazard tangle of rope is likely what saved her life. It allowed just enough oxygen in to keep her alive. Barely. No one expected her to live through the night, which was why she was taken upstairs to her room instead of to the hospital."

She tips back her glass and empties it before filling it again and taking another sip. Steeling herself for the rest of the story. Because despite being horrible already, I know much worse is about to come.

"Dr. Walden, the family physician, was summoned," she says. "He said Virginia was brain dead and that the rest of her body would soon follow suit. Only it didn't. She hung on for days, weeks, months. It turned out Dr. Walden was wrong in every way. Virginia's mind was very much alive. She seemed to comprehend whatever was said to her. It was her body that had died. She was paralyzed, motionless, unable to talk, unable to do anything."

"So what you told me about the strokes and the polio were—"

"All lies," Lenora says. "To cover the fact that the hanging had damaged her larynx, leaving her unable to speak, and snapped her spinal cord, leaving her mostly paralyzed."

"Why lie about that?" I say. "Why go to all that effort to cover up everything?"

"You don't understand what it was like for me. I was only seventeen, scared and alone. I had no other family and no one to guide me. My parents were dead. My sister was basically comatose. And suddenly I was in charge of Hope's End, my father's business, everything. My father's attorney came to tell me the market crash had reduced the family business to ruins. My mother's attorney then came to tell me I'd inherit millions from my grandparents when I turned eighteen and that Virginia would, too, if she managed to live that long."

Lenora stares into her glass like it's a crystal ball. But instead of the future, all she can see is the past.

"Meanwhile, the police kept coming around with their suspicions and insinuations," she says. "The servants quit in droves. I had the others fired, worried they thought the same way as the police and might take matters into their own hands. My friends dropped me immediately. As did Peter."

"Peter Ward?" I say, picturing the portraits in the hall, black silk crepe now hanging from three of them like party streamers. "The painter?"

"We were in love," Lenora says. "At least, I was. After the murders, he wanted nothing to do with me. I never saw him again. Then there was my sister to care for and an estate to run and no one to help me but Archie, who did it solely out of devotion to Virginia. I knew he didn't give a damn about me. And all I wanted was to be somewhere else— and someone else."

Lenora looks up from her glass, seeking sympathy.

"Certainly you can understand that. You know what it's like to be accused of something you didn't do. To have everyone leave, to grapple with fear and grief alone. In the past six months, haven't you wanted to change everything about your situation?"

I have. And I did. I came to Hope's End.

"Yes," I say. "But my options were limited."

Lenora flinches, as if this is the first time someone has pointed out that people like her have advantages people like me can only dream about.

"Mine weren't," she says. "When six months passed and it became clear the police had no proof to charge me of any wrongdoing, I realized how I could escape."

"You had Virginia declared dead," I say.

"It was easy," Lenora says with a nod. "Especially with someone as corruptible as Dr. Walden. I took him to the garage, showed him my father's remaining Packards, and said he could take his pick if he declared Virginia legally dead. I threw in another car for his wife if he also claimed that my health depended on getting rest and relaxation far away from Hope's End. That settled it. Virginia was dead, I turned eighteen and inherited not just my share of my grandparents' inheritance but hers as well. Then I departed for Europe on my doctor's orders. Right before I left, though, I made sure to become Mrs. Baker. And Virginia—"

I exhale, astonished not just by the craftiness of her plan but by its cruelty.

"Became Lenora Hope," I say.

I see you nodding, Mary.

You knew, didn't you?

Good girl.

I had a feeling you at least suspected it.

Yes, my real name is Virginia Hope, although she's officially been dead for decades. In that time, through my sister's sheer force of will, I became Lenora.

How this happened requires skipping ahead, I'm afraid. Don't worry. You'll get the full story about the murders soon. But for now, I must jump to six months after that night.

I'd been confined to my bed that whole time, unable to speak, incapable of moving anything but my left hand. Useless Dr. Walden had declared me brain dead, when the truth was my brain was one of the few things about me that actually worked. I knew from Archie, by my side more often than not, that my parents were dead and that my sister had them cremated the moment the law allowed it. I also knew that she was the one everyone blamed for their deaths, although there was scant evidence to prove it.

And I knew that my name had been changed.

Not legally, of course. That would have left a paper trail, which is the last thing my sister wanted. This was a more informal change, slipped into my life as quickly as a knife to the ribs.

One day, she strode into my room without warning and said, "Your name is Lenora Hope. Mine is Mrs. Baker. Never forget that."

At first, I was confused. Even though I was at my weakest and most addled, I knew I was Virginia. Yet my sister kept calling me Lenora, as if I'd been mistaken. As if all my life I'd been wrong about something so defining as my own name.

"How are you, Lenora?" she said every time she peeked into my room to check in on me.

At night, she told me, "Time for sleep, Lenora."

At meals, she announced, "Time to eat, Lenora."

One morning, I awoke to her sitting beside the bed, my hand in hers. She stroked the back of it gently, the way our mother had done. Without looking at me, she said, "I'm leaving for a while. I don't know how long I'll be gone. Archie will take care of you until I return. Goodbye, Lenora."

Then she was gone.

For years.

How many, I'm no longer sure. Time passes differently when you don't speak, barely move, spend most of your time watching the seasons gradually change outside your window.

She returned as suddenly as she had departed. Marching into my room one day, she said, "I'm back, Lenora. Did you miss your beloved Mrs. Baker?"

Again, I was confused. The whole time she was away, Archie had called me Virginia. Yet here was my sister, back to addressing me as Lenora. It went on like this for months.

"How are you, Lenora?"

"Time for sleep, Lenora."

"Time to eat, Lenora."

I surrendered eventually. I had no choice.

I was Lenora.

The physician who replaced Dr. Walden called me that, as did every nurse I had. I got so used to it that sometimes even I forgot who I really was.

And what of the real Lenora?

She was fully Mrs. Baker, of course, taking the place of the real Miss Baker, who'd fled Hope's End just before the murders. The only time she ever acknowledged what she'd done was one night a few months after her return. She crept into my room and gathered me into her arms. A sure sign she was drunk. My sister never touched me when she was sober.

"I'm sorry," she whispered. "I had to do it. I had to have a life of my own. Just for a little bit."

Since then, it's been a game of pretend. That I'm Lenora. That she's Mrs. Baker. That we're not sisters but just an incapacitated boss and her devoted servant. And it's how things will remain until one of us Hope girls dies.

I know she thinks it's me who will go first.

Now my only goal in a life that had once been filled with many dreams and desires is to make sure that doesn't happen.

# THIRTY-EIGHT

Y ou must think me a terrible person," Lenora says after detailing her
life away from Hope's End. Spending two years in France. Drinking in music halls. Mingling with artists. Kissing strangers on the
streets of Paris. She met an American serviceman, fell in love, got engaged, was crushed when he died. All those photographs I found in her
bedroom were snapshots of that other life.

The one Virginia had dreamed about.

And the one Lenora stole from her.

"Yes." Even if I lie, she'll know from the look of repulsion I'm certain is on my face. "You are."

Terrible. And selfish. And heartless.

Because Lenora didn't just take the life her sister longed for. She
took away the chance for Virginia to have any kind of life at all.

"How could you?" I say. "She was your sister. I know you didn't like
each other. But she was the only family you had left."

"What else could I have done?"

"Told the truth."

Lenora slams the glass down, sloshing wine. It spatters the counter
like blood. "I tried! No one believed me! In everyone's mind, Lenora
Hope had slaughtered her family. I couldn't continue to be her. I would
have been as much a captive in this house as my sister. And what good

would that have done? Virginia couldn't talk, couldn't walk, couldn't do anything. By pushing my identity onto her—"

"Against her will," I interject.

"Yes, against her will. But by doing that, at least one of us got to enjoy a little freedom. At least one of us got to have a life outside of Hope's End."

"Why did you come back?"

"Europe was changing," Lenora says as she blots at the spilled wine with the cuff of her sleeve, the black fabric sucking up the red liquid. "The storm was gathering, and everyone knew it was only a matter of time before it swept across the continent. I got out and came back here, pretending to be Miss Baker, the prodigal tutor returning to an estate in dire need of her assistance. My sister was Lenora Hope, unfortunate victim of polio and multiple strokes. Because we kept a low profile, no one knew it was all a lie. No one but Archie, who understood the benefit of keeping silent."

"Why didn't you leave again after the war?"

"I no longer had the desire," Lenora says with a shrug. "Or, frankly, the money. What I inherited wasn't infinite. It's expensive keeping this place going. And keeping our secrets required additional but necessary costs."

"Like paying off Berniece Mayhew," I say.

Lenora nods, grudgingly impressed I know about that. "The night of the murders, she saw me in the kitchen fetching a knife. And no, I did *not* use it to kill my parents."

"Then why did you spend so much money making sure Berniece kept quiet?"

"Because even though I'm innocent, her testimony would have been the proof the police needed to charge me with multiple homicides. I knew it, and Berniece knew it, too, so I paid her off. But now the money's running out. There's no third act for me. I got away. Not for long. But it was enough."

"For you, maybe," I say bitterly. "But Virginia didn't even get that."

Lenora crosses her arms and fixes me with one of her frigid stares. "If my sister had wanted—truly wanted—a life like mine, then she wouldn't have tried to take her own."

"What do you mean?"

"My dear, how else do you think Virginia ended up dangling from that chandelier?"

Shock rolls through me like thunder. "*She* hanged herself? How do you know that?"

"There was a chair placed under the chandelier," Lenora says. "I assume she stood on it to loop the rope around one of the arms of the chandelier. She then tied the rope around her neck and stepped off the chair. The chandelier barely held her."

I think back to Jessie's murder tour and how I noticed the slanted chandelier that looked as if it had been jarred out of the ceiling.

"Wasn't she pregnant?"

"No," Lenora says, her voice clipped. "Not then."

I wait for her to elaborate. She doesn't.

"Why didn't the police suspect Virginia tried to kill herself if there was a chair there?"

Lenora stares at me, unblinking.

"It wasn't there when they arrived."

This time, no elaboration is necessary. I understand exactly what she means—rather than try to help her sister, Lenora moved the chair so the police wouldn't know Virginia killed herself.

That realization causes me to recoil. I take several backward steps, wanting to put as much distance between us as possible. Until now, I could almost summon some grudging sympathy for Lenora. But this? This was monstrous.

"I did it to protect her," she says, no doubt knowing what I'm thinking because I make no attempt to hide it.

"How was that protecting her?" I say. "She tried to kill herself and you did nothing but cover it up."

"If I hadn't, then the police would have known the truth," Lenora says, her voice ice cold. "They, like me, would have realized the reason Virginia tried to commit suicide."

I take another backward step, this one driven purely by shock. "You think Virginia murdered your parents."

"I *know* she murdered them." Lenora's tone shifts from steely to tremulous, as if it's being chipped away with a chisel. "Honestly, I'm not surprised, considering what we did to her."

"Who's 'we'?"

"Me," Lenora says, punctuating the word with a sip of wine and a hard swallow. "My father. The real Miss Baker. After what we did, the only surprise is that she didn't kill us all."

I gave birth on the floor of my bedroom.

It's one of the few things I remember.

The baby coming so quickly that there wasn't time to get onto the bed. So I was forced to lay in the puddle I'd created on the floor, my head knocking against the wall as I writhed in pain.

Another thing I'll never forget--the sweaty agony of it all. Like I was splitting in half, shedding my skin, being reborn through the fire of pure pain.

I had only my sister and Miss Baker, who rushed in to help after hearing my cries. Neither of them knew what they were doing. So I pushed. I screamed. I hurt.

At some point, exhausted and delirious from pain, I blacked out. My body was still pushing, crying, screaming, and hurting, but my mind was elsewhere. I pictured me and Ricky on a hillside studded with wildflowers and white-capped mountains in the distance. We stood in the sunlight, our child in my arms, as birds in the surrounding pines sang a song meant just for us.

Only when the birdsong turned to crying did I snap back to reality. Mother's instinct. I knew my child had been born.

And that it needed me.

He needed me.

I saw my child was a boy when my sister returned from the kitchen with a butcher knife she used to cut the umbilical cord. He was so tiny. So fragile. But when I looked at him, I felt a love so fierce it startled me. Nothing else in the world mattered but him. I was his mother, and I knew I would do anything to protect him.

At last, my life had a purpose, which was to love my child more than anything else. That realization was the happiest moment of my life.

That happiness left me the second I saw that my father was also in the room. He'd spent the labor pacing Miss Baker's room next door, not emerging until he heard my baby crying. As my sister was about to put my son into my arms, he said, "Lenora, take the baby into the other room."

My sister froze. My child in her arms did not. He wriggled, kicked, and cried. One of his tiny hands reached out for me, as if he already knew I was his mother and that he belonged in my empty arms. I reached out, too, stretching my hand until our fingers touched.

A single second of contact.

That's all I was allowed.

"Lenora," my father said, more sternly this time. "Take the child."

"Can't she at least hold him?"

My father shook his head. "It'll only make it worse."

"But she's his mother," my sister said.

"She's not," my father replied. "She never had a child. And that baby is not a Hope. None of this happened. Now you'll either take that bastard into the other room or I'll take it from you and throw it off the terrace. Then I'll disown both you and your sister."

Lenora couldn't bring herself to look at me as she stood and carried my son out of the room, even as I begged her to stay.

"No, Lenora! Please, please don't go! Please give him to me!"

I wanted to chase after her, but I couldn't. My body was too weak. The effort of bringing a new life into the world had sapped all life from me. Still, I tried, continuing to scream.

"Please, Lenora! Let me have my baby!"

But she was already gone, shutting the door between the rooms and blocking out the sound of my child's cries. Miss Baker grabbed my father by the shoulders and shook him.

"Winston, you can't do this," she hissed. "It's barbaric."

"It's for the best," my father said. "This family can't afford another scandal."

"But Virginia is your daughter. Your only legitimate daughter. And if you take that child away from her, you'll lose her forever."

"I refuse to have another bastard in this family," my father said.

"Says a man who's likely fathered several," Miss Baker shot back.

Ignoring the remark, my father knelt before me, untouched by my despair. Even as I wept, he said, "I'm sorry, my darling. You brought this on yourself."

"Please," I said, my voice weakening as quickly as my body. "Please let me keep him. I'll be a good girl if you do. I'll never do anything wrong again."

My father chucked my chin. "My darling, you've done enough wrong to last a lifetime."

Exhaustion lapped over me in waves so strong I suspected I was dying of heartbreak. I hoped so. Death seemed a better option than this unfathomable grief. Yet I remained alive as Miss Baker dressed me in a fresh nightgown and put me to bed. As she mopped up the mess I'd made on the floor, I listened for the sound of my son in the other room.

All was quiet.

The only one still crying was me.

Miss Baker, done with cleaning, clasped my hand. "Don't worry, Virginia. I'll think of something to make him change his mind."

I was too tired--and too utterly despondent--to reply. Grief and exhaustion had me in their grip, and I felt like I was being pulled into a dark pit from which I'd never emerge. The last thing I heard was Miss Baker saying, "I swear to you, he won't take that child from you forever."

She was lying.

I never saw her--or my child--again.

# THIRTY-NINE

I didn't think it could get any worse. That Virginia had endured enough.

I was wrong.

Because Lenora keeps talking, revealing all the ways in which her sister had suffered. Forced to give birth on the floor. The baby taken from her before she could even hold him. Her father's casual disdain in the face of her heartbreak. It's all so tragic it takes my breath away.

"You should have stopped him," I say, speaking despite the sudden tightness in my chest. "You should have defied his orders."

"I wanted to," Lenora says, her voice cracking. "Truly, I did. But you didn't know my father. He was capable of great cruelty. I worried he really would murder that child if given the chance. And I was certain he'd go through with his threat to disown me. I wasn't his daughter. Not really."

"But she *was* your sister!"

"In name only. We were never close. Virginia and I were as opposite as summer and winter."

The comparison is apt. Looking at Lenora Hope, all I see is frigid coldness. Upstairs lies Virginia, as warm and restless as a July afternoon. Two sisters who, like the seasons they represent, never connected. Something always stood between them.

So Lenora took the baby into what was Miss Baker's room but is now mine. She cradled him and shushed his cries by letting him suckle her pinkie finger. She waited for her father to return and tell her what to do.

According to Lenora, he never did.

"Miss Baker eventually came into the room and began packing up her things," she says. "When I asked what she was doing, she said, 'Leaving, of course. With the child.'"

Lenora registers my surprise and shakes her head.

"It's not what you think. For all her faults, Miss Baker was a good woman. She convinced my father to do what he always did—use money to make the problem go away. In exchange for some money and one of his Packards, she'd take custody of the baby. Her plan was to be a temporary mother to him until he and Virginia could be reunited. I agreed to help as long as my father never learned of my involvement. Then she drove off in the night, taking the baby with her."

"Do you know where she went?"

Lenora nods. "Canada."

I spare a thought for Carter, who was mistaken about his true heritage. There's no way Virginia's baby is the same one left on that church doorstep on Christmas morning. He's no more related to the Hope family than I am.

At the same time, it appears to exonerate Lenora, the person I thought was responsible. Since Carter isn't related to Virginia, he'll inherit nothing. There was no reason for Lenora to keep him and Mary from finding that out.

"Miss Baker wrote to me a few weeks after the murders," Lenora says. "She'd heard what happened and said that, under the circumstances, it would be best if she continued to raise the child as her own. I didn't protest."

I stare at her, shocked. "But he was your nephew."

"What do you think I should have done?"

"Kept him!" I cry. "Raised him. Loved him. And you damn well should have let Virginia love him."

"And what kind of life would that have been? For both Virginia and the child? She couldn't hold him, let alone feed him. She couldn't talk to him or play with him or do anything for him."

"You would have figured out a way."

"How?" Lenora says. "I was seventeen. I knew nothing about taking care of a baby."

"That's still no reason to keep your sister and her child apart!" Anger churns in my chest, crashing inside me like the waves smashing against the cliff directly below us. "How could you be so cruel?"

"Cruel?" Lenora says. "It's quite the opposite, I assure you. Keeping that child away from this family was the ultimate act of kindness. Because of me and Miss Baker, that child grew up never knowing that his real mother was a murderer."

"And you're punishing Virginia because of that fact."

"She deserves punishment! After what she did, a price needed to be paid. But I'm protecting her, too. I always have. Think about what would happen to a woman in her condition if the police learned what she'd done."

I shake my head. That's not a good enough reason. Especially when, other than trying to hang herself, there's nothing to suggest Virginia killed her parents.

"Why are you so certain she did it? What about Ricardo Mayhew?"

"What about him?"

"He and Virginia were having an affair," I say. "He was the baby's father. And Berniece Mayhew followed him here that night."

Lenora laughs. The last reaction I'd expected. There's nothing remotely funny about the fact that she's blamed her sister for murders she might not have committed. Yet Lenora keeps laughing, a low chuckle that's more disbelieving than amused.

"That's impossible," she says.

"Why?"

I hear footsteps on the service stairs. A second later, Archie emerges into the kitchen. I have no idea how long he's been there or how much he's heard. All I know is it was long enough for him to answer my question.

"Because Ricardo was with me that night."

It takes me a second to understand what he's getting at. When I do, all I can say is, "Oh. The two of you were—"

"Lovers," Archie says, sparing me from having to say it.

In the span of seconds, I think of a dozen follow-up questions. Archie doesn't give me time to ask a single one.

"I was as surprised as you are now," he says. "For one, he was married, although in those days and in my limited experience, that was usually the case. It's not like today, which allows for slightly more freedom. Back then, it had to be kept secret. Especially for someone like me. I was barely eighteen. One wrong move and my whole life could have been ruined."

Archie tells me how he and Ricardo met in secret, sneaking away whenever they could. It wasn't easy. Ricardo shared the cottage with his wife. Archie lived in one of the rooms over the garage, which is where they usually met.

"We called it our love nest." Archie allows himself a brief smile of fondness before it fades into a frown. "It's where we were the night of the murders."

It turns out Berniece had been wrong about her husband trying to throw her off his trail by going to the garage first before sneaking into the mansion through the front door. Then again, Berniece had been wrong about many things, including who her husband was really having an affair with.

"Since everyone had been given the night off and Berniece had gone to the movies, we knew we had a few hours just to ourselves," Archie says. "But Ricardo was upset. He said Berniece confronted him about having an affair with Lenora."

Lenora chimes in. "Which was utterly ridiculous. I didn't even know who he was."

"She told him he had to end it," Archie adds. *"After* they blackmailed Winston Hope. Ricardo wanted nothing to do with the plan. It was wrong, both morally and factually, and he feared it would eventually lead to the truth about the two of us getting out. A disaster for both of us. But he had a plan of his own. He asked me to run away with him."

"That night?"

"Immediately. He wanted to head west. Maybe to California. He said he heard people there were more tolerant. He said there was a chance we could be happy there. But I knew better." Archie shuffles to a stool. He sits, slumped, as if the sad memories he's recalling are literally weighing him down. "Running away is never as easy as it seems. I know because I'd already done it, fleeing a family who hated me because I was different, because I wasn't like most other boys. But I found my way here—and to Virginia."

"Did she know?" I say.

Archie responds with a nod. "It's one of the reasons I loved her so much. She didn't judge me. Or shame me. Or, thank goodness, try to change who I am. She simply accepted me. And I couldn't leave her. Not when she was pregnant. Not when she needed me. Because that's another thing Ricardo told me—that Berniece had spotted her the night before and knew of her condition. That meant everyone would soon know. When that happened, Virginia would need me more than ever."

"So you stayed," I say, meaning not just that night but all the ones after it. Decades of nights in which he'd sneak into Virginia's room to check on her and wish her pleasant dreams.

"I stayed," Archie says. "Ricardo left. I never heard from him again."

The sadness of his story leaves me convinced that Hope's End is cursed in some way. Maybe it was merely bad luck. Or perhaps because of Winston Hope's hubris in building a mansion at the edge of a cliff despite knowing it was only a matter of time before it crumbled into the ocean. Whatever the cause, no one here got the life they wanted. No one was granted a happy ending.

Not Archie. Not Lenora. And certainly not Virginia. Yet despite now knowing all their tragic tales, one question remains unanswered.

"Then who was Ricky?"

"One of the local boys hired for seasonal help," Archie says. "A bunch of them came and went all the time. Virginia never told me his last name. Or his first. She just used the nickname, making it impossible to track him down after the murders. I suspect by that point, he didn't want to be found."

A strange mix of emotions swirls through me. There's disappointment from the reality that Ricky wasn't the person I assumed he was. In fact, he wasn't anyone important at all. Just a boy who took advantage of a girl so desperately lonely she gave away her innocence and, ultimately, her freedom.

But Virginia isn't blameless. I'm angry at her. Not for being naïve. She was just a child when Ricky came along. She didn't know any better. But what she did to her parents was so unimaginably terrible that I simultaneously hate her, feel sorry for her, and, despite everything I've learned tonight, still hold out hope that Archie and Lenora are wrong.

I suppose that makes me the naïve one.

"The murders still could have been committed by someone other than Virginia, right?"

"There was no one else it could have been, Kit," Archie says with a sigh. "And I know it changes your perception of her. I've spent a lot of time wondering why she did it. But I made peace with the fact that I'll never know. I might not approve of what Virginia did, but it doesn't make me hate her. It's possible to love someone while hating something they've done."

"I'm still trying to come to terms with it," Lenora says as a look passes between us. I take it to mean she knows I know it was her who used the typewriter in the middle of the night, filling a page with the same accusation.

**It's all your fault**

I'm stuck somewhere in between, resigned to the fact that Virginia murdered her parents yet still clinging to one last bit of hope.

"But why are you absolutely certain it was her?" I say.

"Because I saw her," Lenora says. "Later that night, after Miss Baker departed with the baby, I heard Virginia leave her room. I went to see where she was going and saw her descending the Grand Stairs."

"That doesn't mean she's guilty."

Lenora picks up her wineglass. Before emptying it, she says, "It does when Virginia was carrying a knife."

To this day, I'm still not sure where I found the strength to get out of bed and leave my room. Sheer force of will, I suppose, brought on by a mother's fierce determination. Yet pain still tore through my body as I slid out of bed. My legs buckled, and for a moment I thought I'd collapse onto the floor. But I remained steady, pushing through the agony, needing to find my child.

Before leaving the room, I spotted something sitting on the nightstand.

A knife.

The same one used to sever the cord connecting me and my baby, now forgotten during the commotion following the birth. I picked it up, telling myself I needed something to use as protection. Against what, I didn't know. Perhaps my father. Or my sister and Miss Baker. Deep down, though, I knew the opposite to be true.

I was seeking a weapon.

And if anyone needed protection, it was my father.

Knife in hand, I left my room, pushed through pain on my way down the hallway, and began to hobble down the Grand Stairs. At the landing, I stopped and listened. There were voices coming from the billiard room. One was my father. The other belonged to

Ricky. And although I couldn't make out what they were saying, both of them sounded angry.

I descended the remaining steps slowly, careful not to make a sound. I needed to know what they were saying before deciding if I should make my presence known. If their voices calmed, then perhaps it meant Ricky was successful in persuading my father to let us wed, let us keep the baby, let us live happily ever after.

I should have realized that those things only exist in fairy tales. For there was no happily ever after. Not for me.

As I reached the ground floor, I glimpsed Lenora near the top of the Grand Stairs. "Virginia," she whispered as she nervously clung to the banister. "What are you doing?"

I refused to answer.

She'd find out soon enough.

As I continued moving to the billiard room, I heard her footfalls on the second-floor hallway. Running away, of course. Too cowardly to face the damage she'd helped create. If only she had let me run away instead, none of this would have happened.

There was noise up ahead as well, making it clear nothing about the situation had calmed. My father's voice had only gotten louder, booming out of the billiard room and echoing down the hall.

Before I reached them, I paused for a moment at the four portraits in the hall. My father intended the paintings to make us appear like one big, happy family, secure in our status, content with our lives.

To achieve that effect, he should have had Peter Ward picture us together. A vast canvas depicting the four of us in our regal best, posed oh so carefully in one of Hope's End's many well-appointed rooms.

Instead, Peter had painted us separately. In the process, he accidentally depicted the family as we really were--four strangers, utterly alone, each one of us boxed in by a gilded frame, unable or unwilling to escape.

Not me, I decided.

I was determined to leave this place forever.

And I would take my baby with me.

Even if I had to kill to do it.

Tightening my grip on the knife, I then turned and entered the billiard room.

# FORTY

Upstairs, the woman I'd thought was Lenora Hope is in bed but wide awake, as if she knew I'd be coming.

No surprise there.

I always had the feeling she was more aware than she let on. Virginia likely had known this moment would arrive since my first night here, when she typed those tantalizing words.

**i want to tell you everything**

She didn't, yet I learned it all anyway. Right up to the moment she went searching for her father, a knife gripped in her hand.

"I ran to alert my mother, who was in her usual daze," Lenora told me. "No one had bothered to tell her about Virginia, the urgent labor, my father's orders to take the baby. She had no idea. But her mind seemed to sharpen as I told her what had happened—and what I worried was about to happen. She patted my cheek and said, 'Don't worry, my dear. I'll handle this.' It was the last thing she ever said to me."

Silence fell over the kitchen then. Even though we didn't acknowledge it, I knew both Lenora and I were recalling our mothers' final words.

*Please, Kit-Kat. Please. I'll only take one. I promise.*

"I don't think Virginia intended to kill her," Lenora eventually said.

"I think my father was her sole target and that my mother got caught up in it somehow. Collateral damage. And I suspect my sister felt so guilty about it that she then tried to hang herself."

"That's why I've gone along with everything for so many years," Archie said. "Here, Virginia is safe. Here, no one knows what she's done. It's for her own good. I believe that to my very soul."

"That's why I don't let her go outside," Lenora added. "And why we always refer to her as Miss Hope. If others found out who she is and what she did—what we continue to do—it could destroy Virginia. Imagine her in some state facility, wasting away. At least here she's home."

But Hope's End isn't a home. It's a cage built of secrets. And Virginia's not the only person trapped in it. Lenora and Archie are, too.

I refuse to join them. That's why I now stand at the foot of Virginia's bed. It's time to say goodbye.

"I know who you are," I tell her.

She gazes at me, unsurprised. In fact, I detect a hint of satisfaction in her eyes, as if she's proud of me for sussing everything out.

"I also know you murdered your parents."

Virginia lifts her left hand, ready to tap a response.

"Don't," I say, in no mood for a denial. But I also don't want confirmation. In a sense, nothing has changed since my first night here. Despite assuming she was guilty, I was also hesitant to find out if I was right. Once the typing started, the opposite ended up happening. I began to assume she was innocent and became hell-bent on being proven correct. It turns out I was only fooling myself into believing what I *wanted* to be the truth, even though deep down I knew it wasn't.

It's likely how my father felt right before he stopped speaking to me. The newspaper in his hand, the disbelief in his eyes, the telling himself the complete opposite of what he assumed deep down in his bones.

*What they're saying's not true, Kit-Kat.*

"I understand why you felt the need to do it," I tell Virginia. "You had your reasons. And I hope you regret it now. You've had plenty of time to think about your actions. And I just wish—"

I stop, unable to articulate exactly how I feel. If there's a word for feeling betrayed, foolish, and disappointed all at once, I've yet to learn it. Because the truth is, I *liked* Virginia. I *still* like her, despite everything. That's what makes this so hard.

It's likely Mary reacted the same way when she found out, necessitating that typed apology from Virginia.

im sorry im not the person you thought i was

"I wish you'd been able to tell me everything yourself," I say.

Instead, I got only hints and half-truths. Although she never outright lied to me, she never told me the whole story, either. It would have been so easy, too. A simple sentence, typed with her left hand, telling me that she was Virginia Hope, that everything I thought I knew was a lie, that she was guilty.

If she had done that, I might have been able to stay. The job was to take care of a killer. I knew that from the start. And I think I could have done that for as long as necessary. But now? Now I don't think I'll ever trust or believe Virginia again.

Which means my only option is to leave.

"Goodbye, Virginia," I say. "I hope whoever's assigned to care for you next never tries to learn the truth."

Giving her a sad little wave, I move into my own room, forcing myself not to look at Virginia on the way out. I feel her stare anyway, the heat of her green eyes following me as I go. Then, as promised, I leave without packing.

No suitcase of clothes.

No box of books.

No medical bag.

I decide to arrange for Carter to bring them to me later. Or maybe I'll just leave them here, joining Mary's belongings. A growing collection of things abandoned by previous caregivers for the next unfortunate one to discover.

The only thing I take is my car keys, which I clutch in my hands as I hurry down the service stairs. The kitchen is empty, thank God. I don't know where Lenora or Archie went, and I don't care. I'm in no mood to see them again, either. Before leaving, I go to the phone hanging on the wall and dial quickly, knowing either of them could enter as the phone rings and rings.

When my father finally answers, he sounds groggy and confused. I check the kitchen clock. It's almost midnight. I woke him up.

"Daddy," I say.

"Kit-Kat?"

My heart, thudding so heavily for so long, skips a joyous beat. I had no idea how much I needed to hear that.

"Can I come home? Right now?"

"Of course. What's going on? You sound scared."

"I can't stay here any longer," I say. "I need to get away from this place. And them."

"Them?"

"Lenora and Virginia. They've been lying all this time. And I can't be a part of it."

But it's not just that. There's something else as well.

I need to confess.

"When I get home, I have things to tell you. About what happened to Mom."

I hang up to keep myself from saying the rest. That can't be spoken on the phone. It needs to be said in person, face-to-face, which is what I should have done six months ago.

*What they're saying's not true, Kit-Kat.*

But it is.

All of it.

Memories of that night wash over me as I leave the kitchen, trot down the hallway, whisk my way toward the front door.

My mother, in pain so severe that few words exist to describe it. She wasn't wracked with pain. She was aflame with it. She was *possessed* by it.

Me, literally creaking from exhaustion and worry and aching empathy, waiting for the painkiller to kick in, desperate to provide her with some small amount of relief. I stroked her hair. I whispered soothing words into her ears. I prayed to a God I wasn't sure I believed in to do *something* to put her out of her misery.

Eventually, the pain broke. It was still there, of course, but just a simmer instead of a full boil. The fentanyl had leashed it enough to allow my mother to rest, which was all I could reasonably hope for at that moment.

As she fell asleep, I reached for the fentanyl bottle, ready to take it back to the lockbox under my bed. I'd barely wrapped my fingers around it when I felt my mother's hand on mine, stilling it.

"Leave them," she whispered.

"You know I'm not allowed to do that."

"Just for tonight." Her voice was raspy, labored, slowly but surely filling with renewed pain. "Just in case I need one."

"Mom, I can't."

She tightened her grip atop my hand, shockingly strong for someone so utterly depleted. In hindsight, I don't think it was her doing it.

It was the pain, taking over and moving her like a marionette.

"Please, Kit-Kat," my mother whispered. "*Please.*"

What followed was an internal tug-of-war that felt like hours but in reality lasted mere seconds. Part of me was compelled to follow protocol, do the right thing, care for her in the responsible way I'd been trained to do. But another part of me knew that my mother was suffering—and that I could help alleviate it.

"I'll only take one," she said. "I promise."

One more pill.

That wasn't so bad.

It was more than recommended, but sometimes rules had to be broken.

This, I concluded, was one of those times.

"Just one," I said.

Then I placed the pill bottle back on the nightstand. Even though

I'm sure it barely made a sound then, in my memory it's as loud as the front door to Hope's End slamming shut behind me.

When I went to bed that night, I had a sickening feeling my mother intended to take every pill in that bottle. Call it a sixth sense. Or a premonition. Yet I convinced myself that she knew better, ignoring how extreme suffering could cloud someone's judgment. I wanted to think she wouldn't purposefully overdose, so that was what I believed.

As a result, my mother is dead.

All because of my actions.

I hop into my car and drive off, the steering wheel unsteady beneath my shaking hands. I refuse to treat my father the way Virginia treated me. Pretending to be innocent. Forcing him to live with nagging doubt for the rest of his days. Driving a wedge between us until we've become exactly like the Hope sisters—stuck with each other in a cycle of suspicion and guilt.

The truth will set me free—even if it might also send me to prison.

I bring the car to a stop at the gate, which blocks the driveway like the bars of a jail cell. I get out of the car and hit the button embedded into the wall. As I walk back to the car, the gate shimmies open.

Then it rattles.

Then it stops.

I pound the roof of the Escort in frustration. Not this. Not *now*.

As I march back to the gate, determined to push it all the way open, I hear footfalls fast and furious in the grass, followed by Carter's panting voice.

"Kit? Where are you going?" I spin around, squinting in the glare of the car's headlights as Carter emerges from the darkness. "I heard you driving away and ran to catch up. Are you leaving?"

"Yeah."

"Why?"

"Because I was wrong," I say. "*We* were wrong."

I pull on the gate, forgetting Carter's warning when I first arrived.

This place can bite.

He was at least right about that. Because when I give the gate another tug, I touch the wrong place at the wrong time. The story of my life. My hand's already wrapped around one of the bars before I feel it—a spot of rusted wrought iron, weathered by salt air into a razor-sharp point.

The metal pierces the skin of my left hand. Swearing, I jerk my hand back and examine the damage. Although small, the cut's bad enough to leave me bleeding. At least it wasn't for nothing. The gate is now open enough for my car to ease through it.

"Wrong about what?" Carter says.

"Lenora's not your grandmother. She's not even Lenora. She's Virginia, Lenora's sister."

Carter's face pales as he reels backward like a man who's just been shot.

"I—I don't understand."

I start walking toward the Escort. "Get in and I'll tell you."

Carter doesn't move as I slide behind the wheel and rev the engine. I understand his shock, just as clearly as I understand the need to leave this place before it can cause further damage.

Not just to me, but to Carter as well.

"Come with me," I tell him. "Just for tonight. Come with me and we'll—"

I have no idea what we'll do. Figure something out. I picture Ricardo Mayhew saying the same thing to Archie fifty-four years ago, urging the man he loved to escape Hope's End.

Archie stayed.

Carter doesn't.

Without a word, he opens the passenger door and hops in. I hit the gas pedal, and together we pass through the gate, leaving Hope's End behind.

# FORTY-ONE

et me get this straight," Carter says. "Mrs. Baker is actually Lenora
Hope. And Lenora is really Virginia Hope. And she's the one who
killed her parents?"

"Correct."

We've been on the road for ten minutes, during which time I managed to tell him all that I've learned during this long, surreal night. Still,
I get why he's confused. It's a lot to take in, especially when it means he
came to Hope's End for nothing.

"And I'm not related to any of them," Carter says with a sigh, resigned to the fact that his birth family remains a mystery.

"I'm sorry. I know how much you wanted to know."

"I thought I *did* know." Carter stares out the window, watching the
scrubby pines of the Cliffs zip past as we descend into town. "The
timeline seemed to fit perfectly."

What neither of us counted on was the possibility of a premature
birth, which I learned during my health aide training is more common
in teenage mothers. As a result, Virginia likely has a child living somewhere in Canada, oblivious to who her mother is or what she's done,
and Carter, who knows both of those things, still has no idea who his
real grandmother could be.

And Mary is dead because of it—a horrible truth temporarily forgotten in a night filled with them.

"I can't stop thinking about Mary," I say. "How she was killed for no reason whatsoever."

Carter looks away from the window long enough to say, "You still think she was pushed?"

"Don't you?"

"I don't know anymore." He sighs again. "I'm not Lenora's—sorry, Virginia's—grandson. So there'd be no reason for someone to kill her because of that."

"But she knew all the other secrets about that place," I say. "Lenora's true identity. Virginia's guilt. The fact that both have been lying about it for decades. Someone felt the need to stop her before she could reveal it all."

"So that leaves either Archie or Lenora."

"Maybe," I say. "But I don't think so."

Both Lenora and Archie laid bare all their secrets tonight. Yes, I'd forced Lenora's hand when I told her I knew she wasn't really Mrs. Baker. But both were forthcoming after that. They did what Virginia had promised to do my first night at Hope's End—tell me everything.

What they didn't do was swear me to secrecy or threaten me in any way. If one of them was so concerned about Mary knowing the truth that they felt the need to murder her, then why am I still alive?

Because I'm not a threat to them.

I doubt Mary was, either.

But she was to someone.

My left hand slips off the steering wheel, leaving a smear of blood, sticky and hot. Using my right hand to steer, I glance at the wound. It's still bleeding and probably infected, but I'll survive.

That gate, however, should be melted into scrap metal.

I wipe my hand on the skirt of my uniform, not caring about the stain it will leave. I'll never be wearing it again. In fact, I won't even be a caregiver again once Mr. Gurlain finds out I quit, fleeing Hope's End without even closing the damn gate behind me.

Another thought occurs to me, about another time the gate was left open.

"Hey, Carter," I say. "When did you say you found the gate open?"

"The day Mary died."

"I meant the day. What day of the week?"

"Monday."

"And what time?"

"Midmorning. Why?"

Because Carter said he assumed it was left open after the groceries were delivered. But Archie told me those arrive on Tuesdays. A fact confirmed by all those receipts I found under Lenora's bed.

That means the gate had been opened for a different reason.

Not to let someone enter and leave, but to let someone leave and come back undetected. I did it myself earlier tonight. Opening the gate when I left for Ocean View Retirement Home and leaving it like that so I wouldn't need to call the main house to be let back in.

Since the gate was open Monday morning, it's possible it had been like that since the night before.

"The lab already had your blood sample, right?" I say.

"Yeah. I got it drawn the week before. All they needed was Virginia's blood."

"Which Mary was supposed to get Monday night for you to bring to the lab the next day."

"Which never happened," Carter reminds me.

We've entered town, the streets I've known my entire life lit by the dull glow of streetlights. We pass Ocean View, where Berniece Mayhew is likely watching TV this very minute, and then Gurlain Home Health Aides. I make a right, heading to my father's house two blocks away. Even though I should be thinking about what I'm going to tell him when I get there, my mind is preoccupied with something else.

"How long does it take to get a blood sample analyzed?"

"About a day," Carter says.

"So if you took a sample to the lab on, say, a Sunday night, they'd have the results Monday night?"

"I guess so." Carter eyes me from the passenger seat. "Why are you so focused on that?"

Because it seems to be exactly what happened. Someone left Hope's End on Sunday night, leaving the gate open so they could return without anyone realizing they were gone. Carter noticed the open gate on Monday morning. He then left it open overnight because he intended to leave for the lab early Tuesday. During that time, someone could have left and returned once again.

Someone like Mary.

Coming back from the lab on Monday night.

With the results of a blood analysis performed on a sample she brought there the night before.

I slam the brakes, and the car comes to a screeching stop in the middle of the street. Carter looks at me, one hand braced against the dashboard and his body still thrust forward from the sudden stop. "What are you doing?"

"It was you," I say.

When she was pushed off the terrace, Mary wasn't leaving with a suitcase that contained a bunch of pages typed by Virginia and a sample of blood about to be tested.

She was coming back with the results.

"You knew Virginia wasn't your grandmother," I say. "Mary drew her blood and took it to the lab a day early. Because your bloodwork was already done, they could tell pretty quickly if it was a match. It wasn't. And when Mary told you the results, you—"

"Killed her?" Carter says. "Why would I do that?"

Because he wanted Hope's End. He changed where he worked, where he lived, his entire life. All because of the possibility he might be related to the infamous Lenora Hope and could one day inherit everything she owned. When Mary told him that wasn't the case, he did whatever he could to hide that fact.

"You did it," I say. "You killed Mary."

"Do I look like a killer to you?"

He doesn't. Then again, neither does Virginia. Yet he's as guilty as she is. The only difference between them is that she's now harmless.

Carter, however, isn't.

I shoot a glance up the street, weighing my options. My father's house sits on the next block. I can see the warm glow of the porch light, beckoning me home. I can make a run for it and hope Carter doesn't catch up, or I can force him out of the Escort and speed the rest of the way home. I pick plan B. Being inside the car seems like the safest bet.

I shove my right hand into my pocket, fumbling for the corkscrew. I pull it out and hold it up, its pointed tip aimed at Carter's side. He sees it and raises his hands.

"Jesus, Kit. There's no need for this."

"Get out of the car," I say.

Keeping his hands where I can see them, Carter unfastens his seat belt and pulls the handle of the passenger door. It clicks open, setting off a warning beep because the car's still running.

"You're making a mistake," he says. "I swear to you I didn't do it."

"I don't believe you!"

Anger courses through me, making my blood pump so hard I can feel the cut on my hand pulse. He lied to me. Just like Virginia lied to me. The pain of their twin betrayals stings like a third-degree burn. I jab the air with the corkscrew, forcing Carter closer to the open door.

"Kit, please!"

I jab the corkscrew again, this time lunging forward until its tip is a breath away from Carter's neck. He scrambles out of the car and stands in the street, calling to me as I speed away, the passenger door flapping like a broken wing.

Knowing Carter can still easily catch up to me, I aim not for the driveway but the yard, thumping over the sidewalk and skidding to a stop mere feet from the front door. I burst from the car, Carter's loud and fast footfalls echoing up the street behind me.

"Kit, wait!" he calls.

I do the opposite, running to the front door, flinging it open, slamming it shut behind me. Carter reaches it just as I turn the deadbolt. He pounds on the door, pleading with me.

"Kit, please! You've got it all wrong."

I back away from the door, unsure what to do next. I need a phone to call Detective Vick, peroxide and a Band-Aid for my hand, and to find my father, so I can finally reveal the truth about my mother's death.

I head to the living room, expecting to find my father in his La-Z-Boy, waiting up for me like he did when I was a teenager. Only his chair is empty. As is the living room. And, it seems, the whole house.

"Dad?"

I move down the hall, to the bedroom he once shared with my mother but now sleeps in alone. Peeking through the doorway, I spot a suitcase on the bed.

One that doesn't belong to him.

It's smaller than his battered suitcase, which I remember from so many family vacations. Nicer, too. Quality leather as dark as brandy. Its single flaw is a broken handle, which dangles from the suitcase, held on at only one end.

My vision narrows, darkness pushing in from all sides until it looks like I'm staring down a train tunnel. But there's no light at the end of it. Only confusion as I zero in on the suitcase's lid. My hand shakes so hard I can barely lift it open.

When I do, I see a test tube with blood inside it and a stack of typewritten pages. I scan the first line of the top one.

The thing I remember most--the thing I still have
nightmares about--is when it was all but over.

A sob croaks out of me. I can't hear it because my pounding heart is loud in my ears. A shock. I'm so heartbroken I'm surprised it can even beat at all.

Because I know what my father did to get this suitcase.

And I know why.

All my life I'd only heard him referred to as Pat.

But his real name is Patrick.

Patrick McDeere.

It didn't occur to me that the second half of his name could also be turned into a different nickname.

Ricky.

Ricky sat in one of the leather chairs next to the fireplace. My father stood beside the other one, his back toward the door. Neither one of them noticed me as I crept into the room, the glinting knife in my grip leading the way. They only became aware of my presence once I said, "Where's my baby?"

"It's gone, Virginia," my father said with his back still to me, as if I wasn't even worth the effort of turning around.

"Bring him back."

"It's too late for that, my darling."

"Don't call me that!" I snapped, my hand tightening around the knife. "Don't you dare call me that ever again! Now tell me what happened to my son."

"Miss Baker took him. She won't be returning."

"What do you mean?"

"That she's gone for good." My father said it like it was the most reasonable thing in the world. "She agreed to leave Hope's End with the child, find it a good home, and never speak of the incident again."

A hot and stinging jolt of pain went through me. It was, I realized, the pain of betrayal. I felt so stupid then. So utterly foolish that I had deemed Miss Baker worthy of trust when all she truly cared about was herself.

"For how much?" I said, for I knew there was a price.

"Not as much as Patrick here." My father looked at Ricky. "I did get the name right, didn't I? Patrick McDeere?"

Ricky swallowed hard and nodded.

"For fifty thousand dollars, Mr. McDeere will leave, never return, and never speak of his bastard child. Isn't that right, son?"

"Yes, sir," Ricky mumbled, refusing to look at me.

"You made him agree to this," I said to my father. To Ricky, I added, "Tell him no."

At last, my father turned around, his gaze bouncing from one part of me to another. My crestfallen face first, then to my hand, where the knife remained.

"Now, look here, Virginia," my father said as he continued to stare at the knife. "There's no need for that."

I kept my own gaze on Ricky. "Tell him! Tell him you love me and that we're going to run away and find our baby and have a happy family."

"But he doesn't want that," my father said. "Do you, son?"

"You're lying." I turned to Ricky. "Tell me he's lying!"

Ricky's gaze also skipped about. To the unlit fireplace, to his hands, to the zebra rug under his feet. Anywhere but at me.

"It's true, Ginny," he mumbled. "I'm sorry."

"See?" My father's tone was shockingly boastful. He was, I realized, enjoying the worst moment of my life. "I know you're hurt now, but it's for the best. You don't want trash like him dragging you down for the rest of your life."

"But--"

It was all I could muster. Shock and heartbreak had silenced me. But I knew I could still speak volumes with the knife in my hand.

I tried to rush at both of them, not caring which one I hurt just as long as I inflicted pain on someone. But before I could take a step, I was halted by a gentle grip on the arm that held the knife.

My mother.

No doubt summoned by my sister.

Although I was surprised to see her out of bed and walking around on her own, my mother barely seemed fazed by the sight of me holding a knife. Alert for the first time in weeks, she knew exactly what was transpiring in that billiard room.

"Don't, my darling," she said, her hands disconcertingly strong as she wrested the knife from my grip. "They're not worth destroying your young life over."

I let her take the knife from my hand and collapsed against her, weeping. With the knife in one hand and stroking my hair with the other, she addressed my father.

"Fifty thousand dollars, Winston? Your price has gone up. If I recall, you only offered twenty-five thousand to make the man I loved go away."

"That didn't stop him from taking it," my father said with not an ounce of softness in his voice. "You can judge me for it all you want--and you certainly have--but it was the best thing to happen to you. It allowed you to get married, pretend that Lenora was my child, and keep your precious reputation intact."

His words caused something inside my mother to break. I watched it happen. Her eyes went dark and her body still. Standing silent and motionless, she reminded me of a clock unnervingly stopped at midnight.

Yet one small part of her continued to tick. I saw that, too. Something coiled around the gears of her mind, ready to spring.

And spring she did.

Toward my father.

Knife in hand.

Not stopping until the blade was deep in his side.

My father didn't scream when the knife plunged into him. I did that for him, letting out a sharp cry that pinged around the room in an infernal echo. I could still hear it when my mother yanked the knife from my father's gut.

He clutched at the wound, blood seeping between his fingers as he stumbled against the pool table.

"Please take my daughter out of the room," my mother said to Ricky in a voice as calm as a spring morn. "Now."

Ricky leapt from the chair and took me by the hand, although the last thing I wanted was to feel his touch. Yet I was too stunned and horrified to do anything but let him pull me from the room, into the hallway, and toward the foyer.

"It's a dream, right?" I said, more to myself than to Ricky. "Just a terrible dream."

Yet the waking nightmare continued as a grunt and a gurgle sounded from the billiard room. My mother emerged a few moments later, still holding the now-crimson knife. Blood covered her nightgown and dripped from her hands in large dollops that fell across the foyer floor.

I pulled myself from Ricky's grasp and ran up the Grand Stairs, wanting nothing more than to be upstairs in bed, fast asleep, waking up to a new day in which none of this had happened. My mother took a few shuffling steps, moving as if in a daze. Perhaps she thought it was a dream as well. A horrible, terrible, blood-drenched dream.

But as my mother climbed the steps to join Ricky on the landing, I saw it was all too real--and that the blood covering her wasn't just my father's.

It was also her own.

A tear in the fabric of her nightgown revealed a gushing wound in her stomach. The moment I saw it, I knew my mother had also used the knife on herself.

"Mother!" I cried as I started to run back down the stairs.

Ricky, still on the landing, halted me with a gruff "Don't come any closer, Ginny!"

I stopped halfway to the landing, frozen by confusion and fear. I watched as Ricky approached my mother and took the blood-soaked knife from her hands.

"Please," my mother whispered to him. "Please put an end to my misery."

Ricky shook his head. "You don't mean that."

"Don't tell me what I mean," my mother snapped. "You don't know me. You don't know how much I've suffered. You wouldn't, of course. You're just a shiftless, worthless cad who will amount to nothing."

My mother's eyes contained a determined spark that worried me. I knew what she was trying to do--and that Ricky was falling for it.

"Don't talk about me like that," he said.

"Why?" my mother said. "It's true, isn't it? You come from nothing, you'll live with nothing, and you'll die with nothing. You're worthless."

Ricky stiffened, his body coiled with tension. "I'm not."

"Then prove it," my mother said. "Be a man for once and prove you're not a piece of--"

From the stairs, I screamed as I saw a flash of movement at Ricky's hand.

The knife.

The rest happened so quickly I can scarcely recall it. A small mercy. What I do remember--the sound of the knife entering my mother's torso, her collapsing on the landing--is horrible enough.

When it was over, I flew down the stairs to my mother's side. It was clear she was mortally wounded. Her face had become stark white, and there was blood everywhere. It soaked into my nightgown as I screamed at Ricky to call for help.

"Help us! Please!"

The knife remained in Ricky's grip. He stared at it in disbelief for a moment before looking directly at me and my dying mother.

"I-I'm sorry," he murmured. "I didn't mean to--"

"Get out," I said, my voice a ragged whisper.

"It's true, Ginny. You have to believe me."

"Get out!" I said again, this time in a roar borne of pain, anger, and fear.

Ricky dropped the knife and fled out the front door and into the dark night.

A minute after he left, so, too, did my mother. I was holding her hand when I felt the last flicker of her pulse. I kept holding it even as the skin grew cold, not knowing what else to do. My parents were dead. My child was gone. The man I had once loved but didn't any longer had fled. How is one supposed to carry on when they have nothing left?

The only thing that pulled me away from my mother's corpse was the knife that killed her. Still on the foyer floor, it caught the light in a way that felt like a taunt.

"Use me," it seemed to say. "That's what you need to do now. Here's your way out."

I went to it, picked it up, and considered driving it into my heart. I stopped myself before I could do so, worried that once the blade entered my chest, there'd be no heart left for it to pierce.

Instead, I walked out to the terrace, buffeted by the wind and driving rain, and threw the knife into the ocean. Something capable of such violence deserved to be in a place where no one could find it.

Yet I still wanted to end my life. No, that's not quite it. I felt like I had to end my life. To me, it already seemed over. All those hopes and dreams I'd held close to my heart had gone with everything else. In their place was a dark void from which I never thought I'd escape. My body might have been alive, but my soul was dead.

The quickest and easiest thing to do would have been throwing myself off the terrace. But then I'd be as lost as the knife I'd just tossed into the waves. I wanted to be found, so people would understand the depths of my despair.

I decided to go to the garage, where I knew rope was stored. I grabbed a long loop of it and carried it back inside, to the ballroom. I chose that room because it seemed the most like myself. Lovely, yes, but also empty and neglected.

In the kitchen, I heard Lenora on the phone, frantically calling the police. I should have considered how the night's events would affect her. They were her parents, too. At least my mother was. And I was her sister. Yet I selfishly never stopped to think if she would mourn them or me. The same went for Archie, who I knew would miss me deeply.

All thoughts were pushed out of my head as I stood on a chair and tossed the rope until it was looped several times around one of the chandelier's arms. I then knotted it around my neck the best I could.

After a tug to make sure the rope wouldn't unravel from the chandelier, I closed my eyes, took what I thought would be my last breath, and stepped off the chair.

And that's the full story, Mary.

Not what you expected, is it? It isn't for me, as well. Now that you have it, do with it what you'd like. Tell the world. Or tell no one.

It's in your hands now.

My hope, though, is that you'll share it with someone, that it will spread far and wide, and that word of it will somehow reach my son, wherever he is, and the two of us may be briefly reunited.

# FORTY-TWO

Tears fill my eyes, making it hard to see as I drive back to Hope's End. I tighten my grip on the steering wheel, as if that will make up for my blurry vision. I briefly consider not trying to see at all. That way maybe I'll veer off the road and go sailing over the cliff into the ocean, thereby having to avoid confronting my father. A tempting prospect, considering everything I now know.

But that would make me just like Virginia.

Attempting to kill myself over something my father has done.

She survived.

I intend to do the same.

I have no plan for what to do when I reach Hope's End. I'm not even certain that's where my father went, although in all likelihood it is. On the phone, I gave away that Virginia was alive, accidentally leading him right to her.

I wipe my eyes, grip the steering wheel tighter, and press down harder on the gas pedal, taking my rattling Escort ever higher into the Cliffs. As I drive, I continue to keep an eye out for Carter, just in case he decided to make the long trek back to Hope's End on foot. Once the initial shock of realizing my father had killed Mary passed, I ran to the front door, hoping to still find him there. But Carter was gone. The fact that I was wrong about him, going so far as to force him out of the car, is one of my more regrettable actions tonight.

Another thing I regret is speed-reading the typed pages I found in Mary's suitcase. So much more than what Virginia and I had managed to type. This was indeed the full story. One that I couldn't stop reading even as it made me dizzy with grief.

Now I understand why Virginia had been so reluctant to reveal all of it. She didn't want to be the one to tell me who my father was.

And what he'd done.

Getting Virginia pregnant. Accepting a payment to go away forever from Winston Hope. Stabbing Evangeline Hope out of a combination of anger and pity. Killing Mary because she knew all of this.

That's the hardest part to contend with—the fact that he's still capable of murder. I can't stop picturing him in the shadow of the mansion, waiting, striking the moment he saw Mary creeping across the terrace. I know she'd been on her way to see Carter, because of the vial of Virginia's blood I also found in the suitcase.

My father grabbed it, gave Mary a shove, and watched as she flipped over the railing and fell into the abyss beyond it.

I fear Virginia will be his next victim.

Especially after I reach Hope's End and see my father's pickup truck parked next to the still-open gate. Why he would choose to make the remainder of the journey on foot isn't lost on me. All the better to sneak up to the house undetected, which is likely what he did the night he killed Mary.

I, having no reason to arrive quietly, keep driving.

Past the gate.

Down the drive.

To the front door of Hope's End, where Archie stands caught in the car's headlights like an actor on a stage. Relief floods his features when he sees me climb out of the car.

"Someone's here," he says in an urgent whisper. "I saw him walking up the driveway."

"Do you know where he is now?"

Archie shakes his head.

"Well, I know where he's going," I say.

"Who is it?"

"Ricky." I pause, wary of giving him the same information overload I've experienced multiple times tonight. "Who's also my father."

Before Archie can react, I press my car keys into his hand.

"Drive into town. Go to the police and ask for Detective Vick. He'll know what to do."

"But what about you?"

I start walking up the steps to the front door. "I'll be fine."

I'm not afraid my father will do me harm. I don't think he'd go to such an extreme. Besides, other than killing me, he can't hurt me more than he already has. It's Virginia I'm worried about. She's utterly helpless—and the only loose end he needs to tie up.

My plan, formed on the spot, is to make sure Virginia's safe and then distract my father from hurting her long enough for Detective Vick to show up. As Archie drives away in my car, I push inside Hope's End, where Virginia's past and my present are about to collide.

Standing in the foyer, I search for signs of my father. He could be anywhere, including still outside. Nevertheless, I can feel his presence. A shadow version of himself, repeating his actions from fifty-four years ago.

Standing right where I'm standing.

Simmering with humiliation and shame and rage.

Plunging the knife into Evangeline Hope.

It's so vivid I can almost hear it, as if the horrible sound has been echoing through the foyer since 1929.

What I don't hear are any noises from the present day. No footsteps or floor creaks. That might be a good thing.

It could also mean I'm too late.

That thought propels me down the hall to the kitchen and the service stairs. I can't bear the thought of taking the Grand Stairs, with their bloodstains that my father caused. Not that the service stairs are any better. They groan under my feet as I ascend, sounding like they could collapse at any moment. A distinct possibility. At the top of the stairs, I instantly feel the extreme pitch of the house. In the short time I've been away, it's only gotten worse.

I creep down the hallway, leaning into the tilt. As I go, I reach into my pocket and pull out the corkscrew. An act that boggles my mind. This is my father. The man who raised me. I can't imagine needing to protect myself from him. Yet, under the circumstances, it feels necessary.

Rather than head into Virginia's room, I duck into mine, startled by how different it feels. The floor is noticeably more slanted, forcing me to think twice before each step. On my way to the adjoining door, I notice the mattress bunched at the foot of the bed. A couple of books have fallen from the shelf and the mirror hanging on the wall appears tilted when in reality it's the rest of the room that's askew.

The door to Virginia's room is shut. Whether it's the work of my father or the ever-shifting house remains to be seen. Gripping the corkscrew tight, I crack open the door and peek inside.

The room is dim, lit only by moonlight coming through windows leaning precariously closer to the sea. In that muted light, I see Virginia in her bed, awake and alert.

I rush to her side and whisper, "My father's on his way."

She knows I'm talking about Ricky.

She's known since our first meeting, when she barely registered my presence until I told her my full name. That's when she finally snapped to attention.

"I'm going to get you out of here."

I set the corkscrew on Virginia's nightstand and fetch her wheelchair from the corner. While it would be quicker to lift her out of bed and carry her down the stairs, I know my limitations. Wheeling her down the Grand Stairs the same way I did during our ill-fated trip outside is the only option.

Lifting her by the underarms, I manage to get her out of bed and halfway to the wheelchair before I hear a noise in the hallway. Virginia hears it, too, and flashes a startled, stricken look. We both recognize the sound.

Footsteps.

Coming up the service stairs.

Slowly.

Uncertainly.

The moment I hear them, I know they belong to my father.

For a second, I'm frozen. I don't know what to do. Even if I get Virginia into the wheelchair before my father enters the room, he'll surely spot us as I try to wheel her out. But staying where we are is also a bad idea. Holding Virginia upright, I can't do anything to protect her or me. Her life is literally in my hands.

Virginia nods toward the far corner of the room, in a pitch-black space between the wall and the divan. Although barely enough space for Virginia to fit, it might be enough to hide her if my father merely peeks into the room and moves on. Also, with his footsteps getting louder on the creaking service stairs, it's our only option.

I drag Virginia to the space by the wall and drop her into it. Then I sprint for my own hiding place—my bedroom. There I huddle in a shadow-filled corner, hoping it, too, is enough to keep me hidden. Through the open doorway, I can see Virginia on the floor next to the divan. Also in shadow, but not very hidden. Not very hidden at all.

I hear a noise from the hall, just beyond my bedroom door.

My father, passing on his way to Virginia's room.

Of course he knows where it's located.

He's been here before.

When he eventually does enter her room, I have to clamp a hand over my mouth to keep from crying out. All this time I'd secretly hoped I was wrong, that it wasn't him, that despite Mary's suitcase and those typed pages, it couldn't possibly be true.

But his presence erases all doubt.

My father finds Virginia immediately. It's not hard. Her legs, incapable of moving on their own, jut from the dark corner into which she'd been dropped.

"Hey, Ginny," he says. "It's been a long time."

His voice is calm, warm, flirting with amusement. The voice of a man seeing a long-lost love. Under different circumstances, it could almost be considered romantic. Right now, though, it's chilling.

"Let's get you off the floor," he says.

My father bends down, lifts Virginia into his arms, and carries her to the bed. He did the same thing for my mother in her waning days, gently moving her from the living room sofa to their bedroom. Watching him do it now with Virginia cracks my heart wide open. Making it worse is the knowledge that such tenderness comes from a man also capable of horrible deeds.

"You still know how to surprise a fella, Ginny," he says as he places her on the bed. "I'll give you that."

My father eases himself onto the edge of the bed and, to my surprise, takes Virginia's hand in his.

Her right.

I hold my breath, waiting for him to tell me he knows I'm here and that I should emerge from the dark. Instead, he talks only to Virginia.

"All those years I thought you were dead. Hung with a rope. Isn't that how it goes? Now, unlike everyone else, I knew Lenora didn't do it. I knew you'd done it to yourself. Either way, you were dead all the same. That's why I never left town. I never felt the need to hide. I certainly didn't think I had to worry about you telling anyone what really happened. So I stayed. Started my own business. Met a wonderful woman. Had a daughter."

My blood runs cold as he says it.

He knows I'm here.

Now he's reminding me whose side I'm supposed to be on.

"I felt bad about what happened," he tells Virginia. "For what it's worth, I did love you. At least, I thought I did. And I intended to do right by you. But we were so young, and I was so scared. When your father told me the baby was gone and offered me that money, all I felt was relief. At last, there was a way out of the situation, even though I knew it would hurt you. And I do think about him sometimes. Our son. I think about him and hope he's happy. I don't think that would have happened if we'd stayed together. It wouldn't have lasted, Ginny. We were too different."

My father gives Virginia's hand a gentle squeeze, as if to drive the point home.

"As for your mother, I didn't mean to hurt her, Ginny. I swear. But something in me just snapped and I couldn't control it. I've thought about that night a lot. Not a day goes by when I don't regret what I did. But I learned to live with it. And I knew that, as big of a mistake as it was, I wouldn't be punished for it. Then that nurse of yours came to the house asking if I'd agree to a blood test."

Somehow I manage to keep from gasping. It sits, bubble-like, at the back of my throat. I swallow it down as the realization that prompted it settles over me.

Mary had been to our house.

That's where she went that Sunday night. Not to the lab, but to see my father.

While I was there.

She was the woman I'd heard talking to my father. Not a girlfriend he didn't want to tell me about. But Mary, bearing an even bigger secret. When I heard him sneak out the next night, he was actually on his way here.

"She told me she knew that I'd worked at Hope's End when I was sixteen," my father continues. "She knew I'd had a relationship with Virginia Hope and that I was the father of her child, who was taken away but might have had a kid of his own who now wanted to know who his real grandparents were. That's when I realized you were still alive. The only person she could have learned all that from is you. God, you should have seen her. So smug. Acted like she was so smart. Yet she didn't know half of it."

"But I know all of it."

Unlike the gasp, I can't keep myself from saying it. I know too much to stay hidden and have heard too much to remain silent. Stepping from my room into Virginia's, I see my father's hands move to her neck and give a little squeeze.

"Stop right there, Kit-Kat," he says. "I'm not going to hurt you. And I think you know that. But I will hurt her if you come any closer."

The sight of his hands—so large and so strong—around Virginia's throat stops me cold. But I don't show fear. You can sense fear. He taught me that.

"No one else needs to get hurt, Dad," I say. "You can end this."

My father turns to me, revealing the same look I saw the morning that article about me appeared in the newspaper. Hurt and betrayal and shame. "I'm not sure I can, Kit-Kat. I'm in too deep now."

"Why did you kill Mary? If she didn't know everything, why kill her?"

"Because she knew enough. Not the part about the murders. If she did, she didn't mention it." My father turns back to Virginia. "You finished the rest of the story when she came back after asking me to take a blood test. I know because I read about it later. All those pages you typed? I read them all. You really are a good writer, Ginny. You had promise. But you shouldn't have told her everything. You shouldn't have told her my goddamn name. But even before that, I knew she was a liability. So I said I'd do her stupid little blood test. But not at the house. Not with my daughter around. I told her I'd come here, to Hope's End, late the next night and that she should leave the gate open. Then I waited in the same spot I first met you, Ginny. When I saw Mary hurrying across the terrace with that suitcase, I did what I had to do."

"And now?" I say. "What do you plan to do now?"

"I don't know," my father says, even as his hands tighten around Virginia's neck. "I honestly don't."

"Then stop, Dad. Please."

"I can't." My father begins to squeeze her throat. "I can't risk her telling anyone else."

"She won't," I say. "She can't."

My father ignores me.

"I'm sorry, Ginny," he whispers as Virginia's eyes bulge and wet, choking sounds push out of her throat. "I'm so sorry."

"Dad, stop!"

I throw myself at him, trying to get him to stop. Even at age seventy, he's strong enough to shove me away with one arm. I stagger backward into Virginia's wheelchair, both of us toppling. Sprawled on the floor, I see my father return both hands to Virginia's neck.

Tightening.

Squeezing.

Then I notice Virginia's hands.

The right one sits on the bed, immobile.

The left one holds the corkscrew, which she grabbed from the nightstand.

With as much strength as she can muster, Virginia swings it toward my father, the corkscrew slicing the air before jabbing directly into the side of his stomach.

My father yelps in pain as his hands drop from Virginia's throat. He looks down at his side, where the corkscrew juts from his torso. A dark spot surrounds it as blood seeps into his shirt.

Before he can grab it, I'm on my feet, reaching out, snagging the handle. I pull and the corkscrew slides out of his flesh with a squelch of blood. Brandishing it like a switchblade, I say, "Don't touch her again."

My father presses a hand to the wound. He's hurt, but not badly. He even lets out a rueful chuckle. "I guess I deserve this."

"Yeah," I say, shocked by how a single syllable can contain six months of bitterness and disappointment.

"If I'd been a better father, you wouldn't have come here. You wouldn't have met Ginny. You wouldn't know about any of this."

"You pushed me away." I try to keep my sorrow hidden, but it shows itself anyway, cracking my voice with emotion. "I needed you, Dad. When Mom died, I fucking *needed* you! Because what happened with Mom was awful. But—"

I stop myself, unsure if I can speak the words that need to be said.

Even now.

Even here.

"But you were right to doubt me. I left those pills out. Even though Mom swore she'd only take one, I knew there was a possibility she'd take them all."

"Don't," my father says. "Don't say that, Kit-Kat."

"But it's true."

"No. You shouldn't blame yourself. It's my fault that you do. I shouldn't have put that burden on you. I shouldn't have let it get that far. I should have come forward and stopped the whole thing as soon as that article about you hit the newspaper."

Suddenly, I'm no longer at Hope's End. The whole cursed place disappears from my vision as I flash back to home, my father at the kitchen table, newspaper in hand. He looks up at me with watery eyes and says, "What they're saying's not true, Kit-Kat."

He didn't say that because he wanted it to be the truth.

My father said it because it *was* true.

He knew I hadn't given my mother those pills.

Because he's the one who did it.

# FORTY-THREE

Shock and despair.

That's all I feel.

Not anger. Not grief. Just those two extremes of shock and despair, feeding off each other, turning into an emotion I can't describe because I've never felt it before and I pray that no one else is forced to experience it. It feels like every part of me—brain, heart, lungs—has been ripped from my body, leaving me hollow.

That I remain standing is a miracle.

I can't think.

I can't speak.

I can't move.

My father, still blessed with all those qualities, steps toward me, arms outstretched, as if he wants to embrace me but knows I'll shatter if he does.

"I'm sorry, Kit-Kat," he says. "I know you wanted more time with her. I did, too. But she was suffering so much. All that pain. I understood why you left those pills out for her. Because you couldn't take any more of her suffering. None of us could. So I decided to end it."

I don't want to listen. Yet despite all the functions currently failing me, hearing is the only one left. I have no choice but to take in every word he says.

"I didn't force the pills on your mother. She took them willingly.

We both knew it was better that way. What I didn't intend—what neither of us intended—was for you to be blamed for it. When that happened, I didn't know what to do. But believe me when I say I wasn't going to let Richard Vick arrest you, Kit-Kat. I vowed to turn myself in if it came to that. But it never did. So I stayed quiet, because I knew you'd hate me if you ever found out."

I do hate him.

Finally, a third emotion, one that eclipses my shock and despair. Those fade to background noise as the hatred takes over. But it's a wounded sort of hate. Raw and burning. Like I'm the one who's just been stabbed.

I can't tell what hurts more—that he and my mother decided to end her life without telling me, thereby denying me a chance to say good-bye, or the fact that he stayed silent when the police came for me, when I was investigated by the state, when I was suspended from my job.

"That's why I couldn't talk to you afterward," my father says. "It was too hard to look you in the eyes, knowing what I did, knowing I was the cause of your suffering."

Somehow, I find my voice. "Yet you refused to stop it. You just let everyone think I killed my mother. Worse, you let *me* think that."

"I shouldn't have," my father says. "I was wrong."

He takes another step toward me, wincing as he touches his side. At any other moment, my caregiving instincts would kick in. I'd check the wound, try to clean it, find something to stop the bleeding. But I remain stock-still. His wound is nothing compared to mine.

I might have remained like that forever if not for a sound coming from the hallway.

A sharp clack as Lenora Hope finishes loading her shotgun before stepping into the bedroom. Upon hearing it, my father raises his hands and turns to face her.

"Hello, Lenora," he says.

Lenora levels the shotgun barrel at his chest. "Who are you? Why are you here?"

"I'm Patrick."

Unlike me, Lenora easily matches my father's name with the boy her sister had loved all those years ago. It even dawns on her, decades too late, that he and not Virginia is responsible for at least some of the violence that claimed the lives of her parents.

"It was you," she says.

My father responds with a curt nod. "Mostly, yes."

"Give me one reason not to shoot you dead right now."

"Because my daughter shouldn't be here to see it," my father says as he jerks his head in my direction.

Lenora looks to me, astonished. "Did you know?"

I shake my head. As Lenora watches me do it, the barrel of the shotgun drifts away from my father to the floor. Sensing an opportunity, my father lunges forward and shoves Lenora into the hallway.

"No!" I scream, not knowing which of them I'm actually screaming at. I do it again, even though they ignore me, too intent on destroying each other. I can only run into the hallway while continuing to scream as it all unfolds like a slow-motion car crash in front of me.

My father rushing Lenora.

Smashing into her.

The barrel of the shotgun moving, tilting, firing.

There's a blast of heat and noise as the gun goes off. A chunk of the wall behind my father explodes, spraying plaster, wood, and wallpaper. He and Lenora continue to collide, edging closer to the top of the Grand Stairs.

My father stops.

Lenora doesn't.

She falls onto her back, the shotgun leaving her hands as she shudders down the steps and does a single flip onto the landing. I push past my father and start down the Grand Stairs, stopping after only a few steps because I notice something strange.

The entire staircase is trembling.

As is the entire house.

I look around, suddenly terrified. The light fixture in the foyer sways back and forth. From above come several thuds as furniture on the third floor topples over. From below, the earth lets out a low groan, like a beast about to wake. Hearing it, I know in my gut it'll only be a matter of time—minutes, maybe even seconds—before it does.

When that happens, all of Hope's End will come tumbling down.

"Get out of the house!" I call to Lenora. "I'm going to get Virginia."

I start back up the stairs. They're shaking so hard I can no longer stand and must crawl up them. I continue crawling when I reach the second floor, scrambling past my father.

"What are you doing?" he says, shouting to be heard over the steadily building groan of the earth and the thumping, shaking clatter it creates.

"Saving Virginia!"

"There's not enough time!"

My father grabs me by the shoulders. I writhe in his grasp. "There is if you help me!"

We lock eyes, a lifetime of guilt and regret passing between us, unspoken yet keenly felt.

"Please," I say. "You owe me. You owe *her*."

My father blinks, as if snapping from a trance.

Then he releases me and, without another word, rushes to Virginia's room.

I follow him inside, where the room rattles like a broken carnival ride. The tilt, often felt but rarely seen, is now a memory. In its place is a full-on slant that turns the room into an obstacle course. All around us, furniture has started to slide toward the windows, including the bed Virginia still lies upon.

My father grabs her shoulders. I take her legs. Together, we lift and carry her out of the room as the entire house pitches.

Behind me, I hear the empty bed skid across the floor and thunk into the wall.

In the hallway, vases on pedestals crash to the floor and paintings on the walls sway.

Outside there's a cacophony of bricks raining onto the roof and terrace as, one by one, the chimneys of Hope's End collapse.

My father and I hurry down the Grand Stairs, trying not to drop Virginia as the steps themselves buck and sway. On the landing, my father hoists her onto his shoulder, freeing my hands to help Lenora.

She refuses to move.

"We need to go!" I shout. "Now!"

Lenora shakes her head. "I'm not leaving."

Her reply is so nonsensical that at first I think it's a joke, even though there's nothing remotely funny about the fact that Hope's End is collapsing all around us. But when Lenora makes no effort to join me at the doorway, I realize she's dead serious.

"I can't leave this place," she says. "I won't."

"Lenora, listen to me," I say, gripping her shoulders and trying to shake some sense into her. "You'll die if you stay here."

A waste of time, words, and breath. She already knows this.

"I had my time away from this place. Now it's Virginia's turn." Lenora touches my hand and gives me a sad smile. "She's waited long enough. Take good care of her, Kit."

With a light shove, Lenora Hope sends me away before I can respond. There's no time for it. I only have enough time to run down the Grand Stairs, skip over the fissures zigzagging across the foyer floor, and join my father and Virginia outside.

He carries her until we reach a place where the ground no longer shakes under our feet. There, my father lowers Virginia onto the grass. I join her, checking for signs of injury. Shockingly, other than the wound on my father's side, all three of us have made it out unscathed.

I reach for his shirt and say, "How bad are you hurt?"

My father pushes my hand away, gently, slowly, as if savoring the touch.

"You're a good girl, Kit-Kat," he says before kissing me on the cheek. "You always have been. I should have told you that more. I regret that now. I regret a lot of things. But you? You've always been my pride and joy."

Then my father turns back to the house and enters without hesitation.

I lurch forward, ready to run in after him, but Virginia grasps my wrist, clinging to it, reminding me she's still in my care. All I can do is scream for my father to come back as, through the still-open doors, I watch him join Lenora on the Grand Stairs. They don't look at each other, nor do they reach out for comfort.

They merely sit.

As chunks of ceiling fall around them.

As the stained-glass window over the landing shatters from the strain.

As the entire house shudders through its final death rattle.

The last I see of them is my father and Lenora finally clasping hands as the front doors swing shut.

Then, amid a chorus of groans, creaks, and ear-splitting pops, Hope's End follows the collapsing cliff and slides into the ocean.

# FORTY-FOUR

**M**usic drifts out of Virginia's room.

The Go-Go's, which she likes more than I thought she would. Or maybe it's just the novelty she enjoys. Denied most modern technology for so long, she thrills at all the things I've had for years and therefore take for granted. My boom box being the chief one. Most days, it plays nonstop. But also television, which left Virginia awestruck the first time I turned it on. She spent the whole night delighted by whatever was being broadcast. She was the same way when I took her to see *Return of the Jedi*, even though neither of us understood what the hell was going on. We simply enjoyed the spectacle.

I pause in the doorway of Virginia's new bedroom. Once my room, it bears no resemblance to the place where I grew up. Archie and Kenny helped me remove the ugly floral wallpaper and paint the walls a soothing shade of lavender. All my old furniture is gone, replaced with things more appropriate for Virginia's needs. A new Hoyer lift. A modern wheelchair. A bed donated by the local hospital that Virginia can raise and lower with the left-handed press of a button.

I've moved into my parents' old bedroom. A change I wasn't quite prepared for. Those first few nights, it felt strange to be sleeping on the other side of the hallway, in a bed and room larger than what I was familiar with. But I'm getting used to it day by day. So far, I've only had nightmares about my mother twice.

There have been none about my father.

I'm hoping it stays that way.

After what happened at Hope's End, there wasn't any question that Virginia would stay with me. I was still her caregiver, after all. Also, she had nowhere else to go. It was either here or a place like Ocean View Retirement Home.

It was rough those first fraught days. Both of us were grieving. Virginia had lost her sister and the only home she'd ever known. I'd lost my father, my sole remaining parent, and the idea of the person I thought he was. Now that two months have passed, things have become slightly more bearable.

It helps that Archie's still around, as supportive as ever. He got a job cooking at a fancy hotel two towns away and stops by every night after his shift to check in on us. Which is more than can be said for the rest of the people who had once lived at Hope's End. Jessie's all but disappeared, not bothering to reach out to us even after what happened made headlines around the world.

As for Carter, well, he's been having trouble forgiving and forgetting. I can't blame him, really. I did, after all, accuse him of murder and leave him stranded with no way home. When he finally did get back to Hope's End, it was hours after the entire place was gone. What had once been his cottage was now part of a massive pile of rubble littering the Atlantic surf.

I tried apologizing that night, and again a few weeks later when I entered the bar where he'd started working part-time. He said he understood why I thought what I did. He even went so far as to say I was forgiven. But I could tell he didn't fully mean it. It was merely something he said because he wanted me to go away.

So I did. He did, too, leaving town not long after that to search for his birth family. I wish him well. I hope he gets whatever closure he needs.

I hope the same for me.

Like Carter, I'm having trouble with that whole forgiveness thing. Despite helping me save Virginia, I continue to hate my father for what he did, just as I hate myself for also still loving him. I now know Archie was right about being able to do both. I should ask him how he handled it when he stops by tonight.

But for now, there's Virginia to focus on. Among her new belongings is an electric typewriter that she uses only sparingly, mostly as another way for us to communicate. So far, she's shown no sign of wanting to write any more of her story. I think she doesn't see the need now that everyone knows it.

While the initial murders at Hope's End were upstaged by a historic market crash and the beginning of the Great Depression, the media made a point of not letting it happen a second time. Coverage of the mansion's collapse, my father's guilt, and how a still-alive Virginia Hope lived under her sister's name for decades was everywhere. I still get the occasional phone call from a journalist asking to speak to Virginia.

My standard reply is "Sorry, she can't talk right now."

Yet there are days when I wish she could. I think it would help Virginia to be able to articulate how she feels about what happened to her. I can't imagine enduring everything she went through, from having her baby taken from her to seeing her mother killed by her lover to being hidden away by her very own sister. It makes my own trauma look like child's play.

Right now, though, Virginia radiates nothing but happiness as she sits in her wheelchair, listening to the steady beat of the song that's playing.

"Our Lips Are Sealed."

One of her favorites.

"I'm going to take a quick shower," I tell her when she catches me watching. "Do you need anything?"

Virginia replies with a single tap and goes back to listening to the music. I head to the bathroom to start my shower, turning on the water and waiting until it gets warm. That's when I'm hit with the thought that always strikes while I'm alone with nothing to do.

Somewhere out there, I have a half brother.

Maybe.

There's no way of knowing if he's still alive. Or, if so, where he is. Or if he has a family of his own. Archie and I have started putting out feelers, trying to find out what happened to the real Miss Baker, hoping that information can lead us to Virginia's son and my half brother. We do it in secret, reluctant to tell Virginia out of fear it'll get her hopes up. So far, the secrecy's been justified. All we've managed to learn is that Miss Baker got married sometime in 1930 and moved. Where, we don't know. The name of her husband is also unknown. For now, all we can do is wait and hope that more information comes our way.

I think Virginia would like that.

I would, too.

Despite technically not being related, she's the only known family I have left.

The Go-Go's are still playing when I get out of the shower. I hear the music echoing across the hall as I dry off and put on my uniform for the day. Jeans, comfy blouse, cardigan. No more nurse's whites for me.

I cross the hall while using my fingers to comb my still-wet hair. "Hey, Virginia, what flavor oatmeal would you like for—"

I freeze in the doorway. Although the music is playing and the wheelchair is right where I left it, Virginia herself is gone. I scan the room, stupidly, as if she's merely been misplaced and not completely missing from the room.

By the front door is a table normally used for mail and car keys. On it sits a single sheet of paper bearing six typed lines.

Holding my breath, I pick it up and begin to read.

> At sixty-nine, Virginia Hope
> Wrote her nurse this little note
> Thank you, dear, for saving me
> Now it's time to let you be
> I take my leave, walking tall
> Knowing that I fooled them all

My dearest Kit,

I hope you're not surprised to receive this letter. I hope you knew, deep down in your heart, that I would contact you again. Leaving you the way I did was for the best, you see, even though I hated doing it. But I was afraid of how you'd react once you learned the truth.

Then again, you always suspected I was capable of more than I let on. To most people, my silence and stillness rendered me almost invisible.

But you, Kit, saw me.

And now you know the truth. I can walk, talk, and use my whole body. Right now, I bet you're wondering why I spent such a long time pretending I couldn't. The reasons are many, beginning with the simple fact that at first I had no desire to move.

I was as surprised as anyone when I survived my suicide attempt. And disappointed as well. Despite a miracle occurring, I still wished I were dead. I longed for it. I wanted the sweet relief of death so badly that I pretended I truly had died. I simply lay there, not moving, trying not to breathe.

Stupid as he was, Dr. Walden might not have been entirely off base with his diagnosis. For something was indeed wrong with me, although I'm still unsure if it was physical, mental, or emotional. Perhaps it was a combination of all three, which rendered me paralyzed even though I technically wasn't. All I know is that I felt lifeless, mute, and immobile. And so that's how I stayed.

I might have remained that way forever if it hadn't been for Archie, who refused to leave my side. "You'll get better one day, Ginny," he often whispered. "I'm sure of it. And when you do, we'll find your son."

That got me wondering if he was right and that it was possible to one day find my little boy. The more I thought about it, the more I felt a spark of the old me still burning inside.

Without letting Archie know, I began the drawn-out task of forcing my body to start working again. It began with a wiggle of the fingers on my left hand and ended many, many years later with me walking around my room in secret.

I suspect the first question you have is: Why didn't I leave Hope's End then?

I wanted to. I wanted so many things. To travel. To run and dance and sing. To raise the child who was so cruelly stolen from me.

But I was frightened of what was beyond Hope's End. I knew the world had changed greatly since my youth. I feared that if I were to leave, I wouldn't recognize it. But Hope's End was familiar, and I took solace in that familiarity. Even a prison becomes comforting if it's the only thing you know.

The second question I bet you're asking yourself right now is: Why didn't I tell at least Archie that I could move, walk, talk?

The answer to that is slightly more selfish. I didn't tell him because I feared my sister would find out if anyone else knew. And after she'd returned from Europe, where she lived the kind of life I had long dreamed of, I wanted to punish her. That's the brutal truth of the matter.

At first, I simply considered killing her. A murder for which I would have happily taken the blame.

But death is quick.

And I wanted her punishment to last a long, long time.

So I made myself the burden she thought me to be. She assumed she was punishing me by keeping us both here. In truth, she was only punishing herself, and I enjoyed watching it. Think of it as a variation on the game my father forced us to play. I finally won. And the amount of time I chose to keep Lenora in her room was more than fifty years.

But it wasn't just about animosity toward my sister. The main reason I stayed was because I wanted to be there in case my son ever decided to come looking for me. I feared that if I left, he'd never know where I was and therefore would never be able to find me.

The idea that we might one day be reunited was, to me, worth the wait.

So I chose to continue to appear hopeless, even though I was capable of so much. Shockingly, not a single person noticed, including the many nurses I had before you arrived. So many that I've forgotten most of their names and faces. I suspect I was just as forgettable to them, for very few ever paid me much mind. Yes, they performed the basic job of keeping me alive. But only a handful treated me like I was an actual human being. Someone with thoughts and feelings and curiosity. I suppose my silence played a small part in that. One can be easily ignored when one doesn't speak. And so I was.

Of course, nearly all of those nurses were terrified of me. I can't blame them, really. I'd be scared, too, based on all the rumors that have swirled around me. None of those previous nurses were interested in the truth. Even the ones who deemed me worthy of a little kindness or a bit of conversation.

That all changed when Mary came along. Poor, sweet Mary. She's another person who saw me. Like you, she was curious. So much so that she bought that typewriter in the hope I'd learn how to use it and eventually write my story.

I did, as you well know.

I only wish I'd been able to do the same with you, Kit. You deserved to know the truth. Yet I couldn't bring myself to disappoint you with the news about your father. So I stalled, evaded, and misled, knowing it was inevitable that you'd one day find out.

I truly regret the way you did eventually learn the truth--and all the events that came after it. You didn't deserve that. The fact that you've handled it so well speaks highly of your character.

Around the same time Mary was teaching me how to type, something else extraordinary occurred.

I was given an amazing device called a Walkman. With it was a cassette featuring a book read aloud by Jessie, the new maid at Hope's End. Although I did read in secret at night, it was nice to be able to enjoy a book out in the open, so to speak. I didn't care what the story was about. I just liked being told a good tale.

Imagine my surprise when, halfway through that first cassette, the book stopped. One minute, I was listening to North and South by John Jakes. The next, Jessie's narration ended and regular talking began.

"Listen, I know you're not Lenora Hope, but her sister, Virginia. I know a lot about you. More than anyone else, I think."

And so it continued, a one-sided conversation between me and Jessie, conducted via the messages she slipped in between chapters.

"I don't think you killed your parents. And even if you did, from what I've been told, they kind of had it coming. At least your father did."

"I haven't told Mary, but I'm pretty sure you can move and possibly talk. I'm curious to hear what your voice sounds like."

Finally, the most important message came.

"By the way, I'm your granddaughter."

Jessie told me all about her father, who was named Marcel. He grew up in a loving home with Miss Baker and her husband. He played hockey, loved to read, and excelled at painting. After university, he got a job as a commercial artist in Toronto. He didn't get married until his thirties, when he met and fell in love with a fellow artist. They had one child, Jessie, and lived a happy life together, savoring every moment until Marcel passed away from illness in 1982.

After his death, Jessie was told the truth about Marcel's parents by Miss Baker, a woman she had always known as Grandma. Undertaking a bit of detective work, Jessie found out Hope's End needed a maid and applied for the job. Her intention was to try to dig up information about who I was and if I'd really killed my parents like everyone said.

What she ended up finding was me.

While I'm sad to never have gotten the chance to meet my son, I know that life doesn't always grant you your greatest wish. But happiness can still sneak in, and now I am overjoyed to be able to know my granddaughter. The noises I'm certain you heard during the night were Jessie, who would come to my room in the wee hours so we could whisper the ways in which we planned to escape. Plans that were derailed by Mary's murder, your arrival, and the eventual collapse of Hope's End. (Good riddance to that place, by the way!)

Jessie also had to return to Canada when Miss Baker passed away. Another disappointment. I wish I had been able to thank Miss Baker for taking care of my son, even though he ended up being her child much more than he was ever mine.

The day I disappeared from your house was the day Jessie came to my window. I let her inside and she quickly told me the new plan--leave immediately.

So we left, hurrying to Jessie's car parked at the curb. Once we were inside, she handed me a forged passport with my real name on it.

"Where do you want to go, Grandma?" she said.

I looked through the windshield, gazing at this great big world I had never been able to experience until now.

"Everywhere," I said.

By the time we reached the airport, I had narrowed it down to Paris. That's where I now type this letter, from a top-floor apartment with a view of the Eiffel Tower.

Please don't be angry at me for leaving you the way I did. I beg you. The way life has treated us, you and I have enough to be angry about. Let's not be that way with each other.

I wanted to tell you, my dear. I didn't because I feared you wouldn't let me leave or be angry that I hid so much from you the whole time you were caring for me. And, yes, I selfishly wanted some time alone with my granddaughter.

Who, don't forget, also happens to be your niece.

You also deserve time with her.

Just as you deserve to finally live a life that belongs to you and no one else.

To that end, I've included two one-way plane tickets to Paris. One for you and another for Archie, with whom I'm certain you'll share this letter. Your flight departs on the first of February. It is my dearest hope that both of you will be on it.

Until we meet again!

Virginia

# VIRGINIA HOPE DEAD AT AGE 101

ROME (AP)—Virginia Hope, the key figure in one of the most sensational crimes of the 20th century, died Monday at her villa in Porto Vergogna on Italy's Amalfi Coast. She was 101.

Hope's alleged murder alongside her well-heeled parents, Winston and Evangeline Hope, caused a stir in 1929 and shocking headlines 54 years later when it was revealed she was still alive and had been forced to assume the identity of her older sister, Lenora. Thought to be mute and paralyzed, Hope gained even greater notoriety when she admitted she had faked her condition for decades.

"Did I enact the greatest hoax of the century?" she wrote in her bestselling memoir, *Still Life*. "I don't think so. But I like to believe it's at least in the top ten."

That blend of wit and braggadocio made her a beloved fixture on the talk show circuit, where viewers gobbled up the details of her tabloid-ready story. When asked by David Letterman why she was so eager to talk after pretending she couldn't for decades, Hope replied, "Just making up for lost time, darling."

When she wasn't enjoying her late-in-life celebrity, Hope spent her time traveling the globe, visiting all seven continents, including Antarctica, where for a time she held the record for being the oldest woman to do so.

Hope is survived by her granddaughter, Jessica Oxford, and her husband, Robert; her great-granddaughter, Mary Hope Oxford; and her devoted friend, caregiver, and traveling companion, Kittredge McDeere.

# Acknowledgments

Although my (pen)name is on the cover, this book wouldn't exist without the hard work and dedication of many others working behind the scenes. Thank you to Maya Ziv, my amazing editor, and the incredible folks at Dutton and Penguin Random House, including, but not limited to, Emily Canders, Stephanie Cooper, Caroline Payne, Lexy Cassola, Amanda Walker, Ben Lee, John Parsley, Christine Ball, and Ivan Held. Being part of the Dutton family is a publishing dream come true.

The same can be said of my agent, Michelle Brower, and everyone at Trellis Literary Management and Aevitas Creative Management.

Thank you to the many family members, friends, and other authors who help, support, and inspire me on a daily basis. Writing a book can be a long, lonely process, and your presence outside of my writing cave helps me more than you know. Special thanks goes to Michael Livio, who once again helped me navigate the stress, pressure, and, yes, joy of creating another book. I truly can't do it without you.

I'd also like to take a moment to salute the many caregivers out there working in hospitals, nursing homes, and in patients' houses. These often-unsung heroes heal the sick and comfort the suffering on a daily basis, going about their work with diligence, dignity, and pride. You *care*. Thank you.

# ABOUT THE AUTHOR

Riley Sager is the *New York Times* bestselling author of seven novels, most recently *Survive the Night* and *The House Across the Lake*. A native of Pennsylvania, he now lives in Princeton, New Jersey.

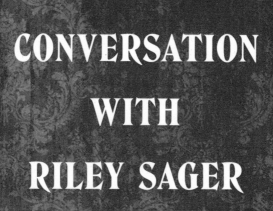

A
CONVERSATION
WITH
RILEY SAGER

*An exclusive Q&A between Riley Sager
and his longtime editor, Maya Ziv,
exploring his writing life, inspiration for the novel,
and further insight into the creative editing process*

*I have been describing* The Only One Left *as "Riley Sager goes Gothic." Why did you decide to go Gothic with this book? And did the process of coming up with this idea differ from previous books of yours?*

I didn't go into *The Only One Left* thinking it would be Gothic suspense. That's how it usually goes. When I start a book, I don't immediately put a label on it. I never think, "I need to write a haunted house book!" or "My next book will be Gothic!" For me, it always begins with a vague idea that, once it starts to grow, usually veers in a specific direction.

*The Only One Left* started, obviously, with Lizzie Borden. I am not a Lizzie Borden expert by any means. I know only the basics. But at some point—and I truly can't remember when, why, or how—I started thinking about Lizzie Borden in her old age, needing someone to care for her. (Again, I don't know if this happened in real life. Lizzie Borden's age when she died is one of the many things I haven't delved into about that case.) I became fascinated with the idea of a young nurse having to care for someone everyone thinks murdered the rest of her family. It made me think about this hypothetical nurse. What events brought her to this point? How does she feel about her patient? Is she suspicious? Scared? Curious? All that was the starting point of *The Only One Left*.

The Gothic aspect came about as I started plotting the book. Very early on, I had this mental image of a young woman wearing an old-fashioned nurse's uniform and standing in a dimly lit hallway. Since that screamed "Gothic" to me, I decided to really lean into it. So I came up with a creaky old mansion on a windswept cliff and filled the place with the kind of characters you'd find in a Gothic novel. The vaguely sinister housekeeper and handsome groundskeeper, not to mention the two main characters, the nurse and her patient, neither of whom is as innocent—or as guilty—as they seem.

**What was the most challenging aspect of writing The Only One Left?**

Definitely Lenora Hope herself. When I decided to make her unable to walk or talk or do anything but use her left hand, I didn't stop to consider the challenge I was creating for myself. She's one of the book's two main characters! How do you make someone who doesn't speak and doesn't really move engaging?

To solve that problem, I got the idea of her being able to type, which ended up becoming an integral aspect of the book. It felt like a very good way to give this silent and motionless character a personality and interior life while teasing out the truth of her situation.

That process of adding to Lenora's character extended all the way to the final edits. At every step of the way, I kept trying to make her as interesting as possible. The goal was to have Lenora Hope be simultaneously suspicious and sympathetic, menacing and oddly likable. Hopefully I succeeded.

*Your twists are always incredible, and this book had me gasping on many occasions! How do you weave in a twist (or multiple twists) without spoiling it?*

Twists and reveals are so hard to come up with, especially with so many great thriller writers working at the top of their game right now. I'm in awe of some of the twists I've read lately, and it stresses me out because I know I need to keep up with their brilliance. Take something like *Daisy Darker* by Alice Feeney, for instance. Such an amazing twist—and done so well! It's intimidating to try to match something like that.

When I do come up with what I think is a killer twist, it then becomes a tightrope walk between revealing too much and not revealing enough. Readers want to be surprised, yes, but also demand—quite rightly, I must add—that the author play fair. It's a tricky balance, but a necessary one. And it's impossible to know if I've pulled it off until the first draft is finished and someone else reads it.

The biggest thing I struggle with in regard to twists is knowledge. As the author, I know what's going on, so every clue I place seems like there's a bright neon arrow pointing to it. I tend to use multiple twists and reveals for that very reason. If I have one twist, I know some readers will figure it out ahead of time. But if I do two or more, then it lowers the odds of a reader figuring out the whole thing.

While I won't share any tricks of the trade regarding how I sprinkle in twists and hints, I will say that very often everything you need to know is hiding in plain sight. As Quincy says in *Final Girls*, "Details matter." I had her say that very early in the book so readers would know to pay careful attention. The devil is always in the details.

*Do you have any favorite books or authors in the Gothic space? Were there any favorite Gothic tropes you enjoyed playing with here?*

*Rebecca* by Daphne du Maurier was a big influence, even though the plot couldn't be more different from *The Only One Left*. For one, there would be no Mrs. Baker in my book if there hadn't been a Mrs. Danvers in *Rebecca*. I also wanted to create a place similar to Manderley—large, lavish, haunted, either by memories or an actual ghostly presence, and, ultimately, doomed.

Another influence was *The Fall of the House of Usher*. I loved the idea of having this Gilded Age mansion perched atop an unstable cliff that could literally fall apart at any minute. And fall apart it does! I thought it would be very cool to have the house crumble a little bit each time Kit learns something about the Hope family murders. By the time the full truth comes out, there's nothing left but for the house to fall into the sea.

Finally, one of the biggest tropes of Gothic novels is the young heroine who starts to doubt her sanity. I had a lot of fun playing with that notion of "Is some of this stuff all in Kit's head? Or is it really happening?" That extends to Lenora as well. Like Kit, I wanted the reader to change their opinion of Lenora several times, constantly veering between thinking she's completely innocent and guilty as sin.

*I am always so impressed by how clean and fully developed your books are when I see them for the first time! Do you outline your entire story before writing, or let the characters develop new plot lines as you go?*

This question made me chuckle, because you and I both remember a certain book of mine that was not even close to where it needed to be when I had to hand it in. Fixing it required so much work on such a tight deadline, not to mention you having to talk me down from a ledge or two. But that was an anomaly—and the book ended up turning out great! It's still the one people tell me they love the most.

For the most part, though, you're right. I always tell myself that it's part of my job to make *your* job easier. So I try to get the book into the best shape possible before letting you see it. How I get there depends on the book. With something like *Home Before Dark*, which had a very intricate book-within-a-book structure, I needed to outline the entire thing from start to finish.

Lately, though, I've been trying my hand at freestyling it. I've had a few books where I outlined everything and stubbornly stuck to that outline, even though I knew the book was moving away from it. And it didn't work. I finally had to give up and just follow wherever the book took me. Now I try to be more flexible. I always know what the big twists are going to be, but I've started to allow myself to experiment and just see what happens.

And it's still a learning process. With *The Only One Left*, I knew where I wanted to end up but didn't quite know how I'd get there. In hindsight that might not have been the best idea, considering how complex the narrative eventually became. I distinctly remember sending you and my agent an email basically saying, "I don't know where this is going and I'm worried it sucks and I need your help." Which I *never* do! But I was just lost there for a little bit, and it took me a while to get back on track. Once I did, writing the rest of the book was like riding a bullet train.

*And related, how does your process of self-editing work? When you are drafting edits, how do you make sure all the threads stay together? And for those readers interested in our back and forth during the editing process, what part do you enjoy the most about having others read the first draft—or the least?*

We've worked together long enough that I know what you're looking for—and what you'll be asking me to add later. So I always try to do a little bit of mind reading and include certain things in the first draft so you don't have to ask me to add them later. I suspect you do the same with me. Since you know my writing quirks and bad habits, you already have a mental list of areas that I always need to work on.

The strange thing about the editing process is that I eventually gain an encyclopedic knowledge of the text. By the time I'm editing and polishing the manuscript, I know exactly what's going on at all points in the book, sometimes to the very page. Like, "Oh, she says this on page 76, which sets up the twist on page 342." It's so bizarre, because the minute that book is finished, I forget almost everything.

The downside to having all that temporary knowledge is that when you suggest a change or ask me to add more, I'm so used to the structure of the manuscript as is that it's hard to even think about making it different. Whenever I get your first round of edit notes, I spend a day or two absolutely panicked and paralyzed. "I don't know how to do what she wants me to do!" That I always eventually manage to figure it out is part of the magic of the editing process.

As for my favorite part of having people read the first draft, it's always when my friend Sarah reads it. Because we've been friends since high school, I know she's not going to pull any punches. She *will* tell me if something doesn't work. What's most helpful about it, though, is that she'll text me her thoughts as she's reading, so I get real-time insight into the mind of a reader. That kind of input is invaluable, and helps so much when honing the finished product.

*You write a book every year, which is so incredible. And your books are always wonderfully different while being equally atmospheric and unputdownable. How do you do it?*

I honestly don't know. There's no magical secret to what I do, other than plain old hard work. I spent many years in the world of daily newspapers, which trained me to respect deadlines. If I didn't have a set time in which a book needed to be finished, I'd probably never get it done. But give me a deadline and I will do everything in my power to meet it, even if that means not sleeping or spending fifteen hours a day writing. (Both of which I have done to meet a deadline!)

What keeps me going when I'm feeling very tired and overwhelmed is knowing that it's truly a privilege to get to write stories for a living. That had been a dream of mine for as long as I can remember. To have it now be my reality because so many people out there want to read what I write is something I don't take for granted. I owe it to them to give it my all with each and every book. I try my best every time. And I'm always trying to get better, always striving to improve my craft. Readers deserve that.

*What does your writing space and routine look like? I wonder how you handle breaking up the day between finding time to write your novels and staying on top of emails and other author career-management tasks?*

I'm lucky enough to live in a house with a dedicated office space, which helps tremendously. I know from having written several books without one that it's a luxury to have, to paraphrase Virginia Woolf, a room of one's own. It shouldn't come as a surprise that it's filled with books. What does surprise people, though, is how bright and cheery it is. Since I spend a lot of time there, I didn't want it to feel like a cave. I write about some pretty dark things, so to counteract that, I decided that my office needed to be the opposite. There's a lot of light, a lot of color, a lot of art on the walls.

I try not to spend too much nonworking time there, so I mentally know that when I'm in that office, I should be writing. It helps that I follow a standard routine. Breakfast and exercise in the first half of the morning, email and business stuff in the second half of the morning, book work all afternoon until it's time to start dinner. Obviously, that changes depending on what I have to do. I usually spend more time writing as I near the end of a book. And sometimes the career aspects of being a full-time writer—promotion, meetings, book-ish events—means there'll be days when I don't write at all. It all tends to balance out in the end.

**How has your relationship to the pseudonym Riley Sager changed over the years as your brand has grown?**

I get asked about the pen name more than anything else, which is understandable. People are naturally curious about why I decided to use one. And I've been very forthright in my answer, which is that I needed to use a pseudonym to have any chance of success. At that point, years of poor sales had left my writing career in such dire shape that a pen name was absolutely necessary. I needed a clean slate, so to speak, in order to rebuild my career from the ground up. Now, never in my wildest dreams did I think it would result in this kind of success. All I wanted was to be a working author able to eke out a living through writing.

In hindsight, I'm glad I did need to use a pen name. I appreciate the slight barrier it creates between my professional life and my personal life. It's nice to have that separation. Now, that doesn't mean that Riley Sager is an act. It's not. Riley is 100 percent me. What I post on social media and how I act at book events totally reflect my interests and my personality. But I'm not 100 percent Riley, if that makes sense. There's more to my life than what I share with the public, which is as it should be.

*What is next for you? What can Riley Sager fans, and your editor(!), expect to show up in your next book?*

Oh, gosh. I never like this question because I always fear I'm going to say too much. Also, things change during the writing process, as you well know. What I send you in my annual "This is going to be my next book!" email always ends up being far different from the finished product. In this case, I guess it's okay to reveal that it's set in suburbia and involves a boy who went missing thirty years ago. If those two aspects change, then something in the writing process will have gone very, very wrong!